A DELIGHTFUL VISIT

"You haven't asked us what we came for," Allison said smiling.

"I thought you came for cookies," said Julia Cloud, with a mischievous twinkle in her gray eyes.

"Oh, yes!" said Allison, laughing. "But that wasn't all. You see, we've come East, Leslie and me, to go to college. But we're not going to college to live there in the usual way; we want a home. We're going to take a house, like real folks. We want a fireplace and a cookie-jar of our own; a place to bring our friend and have good times.

"But most of all," he said, looking at her in excitement, "we want a mother. And we've come all this way to coax you to come and live with us!"

Julia Cloud put her hand on her heart and lifted her bewildered eyes to the boy's eager face. What a wonderful gift God had granted her! Was it real? Would it last? Or was she only dreaming...?

Tyndale House books
by Grace Livingston Hill
Check with your area bookstore
for these bestsellers.

COLLECTOR'S CHOICE SERIES
1 The Christmas Bride
2 In Tune with Wedding Bells
3 Partners
4 The Strange Proposal

LIVING BOOKS®
1 Where Two Ways Met
2 Bright Arrows
3 A Girl to Come Home To
4 Amorelle
5 Kerry
6 All Through the Night
7 The Best Man
8 Ariel Custer
9 The Girl of the Woods
28 White Orchids
77 The Ransom
78 Found Treasure
79 The Big Blue Soldier
80 The Challengers
81 Duskin
82 The White Flower
83 Marcia Schuyler
84 Cloudy Jewel

CLASSIC SERIES
1 Crimson Roses
2 The Enchanted Barn
3 Happiness Hill
4 Patricia
5 Silver Wings

Grace Livingston Hill

CLOUDY JEWEL

LIVING BOOKS®
Tyndale House Publishers, Inc.
Wheaton, Illinois

This Tyndale House book
by Grace Livingston Hill
contains the complete text
of the original hardcover edition.
NOT ONE WORD
HAS BEEN OMITTED.

Printing History
J. B. Lippincott edition published 1920
Tyndale House edition/1989

Living Books is a registered trademark of Tyndale
House Publishers, Inc.

Library of Congress Catalog Card Number 89-50799
ISBN 0-8423-0474-6

1 2 3 4 5 6 7 8 93 92 91 90 89

"WELL, all I've got to say, then, is, you're a very foolish woman!"

Ellen Robinson buttoned her long cloak forcefully, and arose with a haughty air from the rocking-chair where she had pointed her remarks for the last half-hour by swaying noisily back and forth and touching the toes of her new high-heeled shoes with a click each time to the floor.

Julia Cloud said nothing. She stood at the front window, looking out across the sodden lawn to the road and the gray sky in the distance. She did not turn around to face her arrogant sister.

"What I'd like to know is what you do propose to do, then, if you don't accept our offer and come to live with us? Were you expecting to keep on living in this great barn of a house?" Ellen Robinson's voice was loud and strident with a crude kind of pain. She could not understand her sister, in fact, never had. She had thought her proposition that Julia come to live in her home and earn her board by looking after the four children and being useful about the house was most generous. She had admired the open-handedness of Herbert, her husband, for suggesting it. Some husbands wouldn't have wanted a poor relative about. Of course Julia always had been a hard worker; and it would relieve Ellen, and make it possible for her to go around with her husband more. It would save the wages of a servant, too, for Julia had always been a wonder at economy. It certainly was vexing to have Julia act in this way, calmly putting aside the proposition as if it were nothing and saying she hadn't decided what she was going to do yet, for all the world as if she were a millionaire!

"I don't know, Ellen. I haven't had time to think. There have been so many things to think about since the funeral I haven't got used yet to the idea that mother's really gone." Julia's voice was quiet and controlled, in sharp contrast with Ellen's high-pitched, nervous tones.

"That's it!" snapped Ellen. "When you do, you'll go all to pieces, staying here alone in this great barn. That's why I want you to decide now. I think you ought to lock up and come home with me to-night. I've spent just as much time away from home as I can spare the last three weeks, and I've got to get back to my house. I can't stay with you any more."

"Of course not, Ellen. I quite understand that," said Julia, turning around pleasantly. "I hadn't expected you to stay. It isn't in the least necessary. You know I'm not at all afraid."

"But it isn't decent to leave you here alone, when you've got folks that can take care of you. What will people think? It places us in an awfully awkward position."

"They will simply think that I have chosen to remain in my own house, Ellen. I don't see anything strange or indecent about that."

Julia Cloud had turned about, and was facing her sister calmly now. Her quiet voice seemed to irritate Ellen.

"What nonsense!" she said sharply. "How exceedingly childish, letting yourself be ruled by whims, when common sense must show you that you are wrong. I wonder if you aren't ever going to be a *woman*."

Ellen said this word "woman" as if her sister had already passed into the antique class and ought to realize it. It was one of the things that hurt Julia Cloud to realize that she was growing old apparently without the dignity that belonged to her years, for they all talked to her yet as if she were a little child and needed to be managed. She opened her lips to speak, but thought better of it, and shut them again, turning back to the window and the gray, sodden landscape.

"Well, as I said before, you're a very foolish woman; and you'll soon find it out. I shall have to go and leave you to the consequences of your folly. I'm sure I don't know what Herbert will say when he finds out how you've scorned his kindness. It isn't every brother-in-law would offer—yes, *offer*, Julia, for I never even suggested it—to take on extra expense in his family. But you won't see your ingratitude if I stand here and talk till doomsday; so I'm going back to my children. If you come to your senses, you can ride out with Boyce Bains to-morrow afternoon. Good-by, and I'm sure I hope you won't regret this all your life."

Julia walked to the door with her sister, and stood watching her sadly while she climbed into her smart little Ford and skillfully steered it out of the yard and down the road. The very set of her shoulders as she sailed away toward home was disapproving.

With a sigh of relief Julia Cloud shut the door and went back to her window and the dreary landscape. It was time for a sunset, but the sky was leaden. There would be nothing but grayness to look at, grayness in front of her, grayness behind in the dim, silent room. It was like her life, her long, gray life, behind and ahead.

All her life she had had to serve, and see others happy. First as a child, the oldest child. There had been the other children, three brothers and Ellen. She had brought them all up, as it were, for the mother had always been delicate and ailing. She had washed their faces, kissed their bruises, and taken them to school. She had watched their love-affairs and sent them out into the world one by one. Two of the brothers had come home to die, and she had nursed them through long months. The third brother married a wealthy girl in California, and never came home again except on flying visits. He was dead now, too, killed in action in France during the first year of the Great War. Then her father had been thrown from his horse and killed; and she had borne the burden for her mother, settled up the estate, and made both ends meet somehow, taking upon herself the burden of the mother, now a chronic invalid. From time to time her young nieces and nephews had been thrust upon her to care for in some home stress, and always she had done her duty by them all through long days of mischief and long nights of illness. She had done it cheerfully and patiently, and had never complained even to herself. Always there had been so much to be done that there had been no time to think how the years were going by, her youth passing from her forever without even a glimpse of the rose-color that she supposed was meant to come into every life for at least a little while.

She hadn't realized it fully, she had been so busy. But now, with the last service over, an empty house about her, an empty heart within her, she was looking with startled eyes into the future and facing facts.

It was Ellen's attempt to saddle her with a new responsibility and fit her out to drudge on to the end of her days that had suddenly brought the whole thing out in its true light. She was tired. Too tired to begin all over again and raise those children for Ellen. They were nice, healthy children and well behaved; but they were Ellen's children, and always would be. If she went out to live with the Robinsons, she would be Ellen's handmaid, at her beck and call, always feeling that she must do whatever she was asked, whether she was able or not, because she was a dependent. Never anything for love. Oh, Ellen loved her in a way, of course, and she loved Ellen; but they had never understood each other, and Ellen's children had been brought up to laugh and joke at her expense as if she were somehow mentally lacking.

"O Aunt *Julia!*" they would say in a tone of pity and scorn, as if she were too ignorant to understand even their sneers.

Perhaps it was pride, but Julia Cloud felt she would rather die than face a future like that. It was respectable, of course, and entirely reliable. She would be fed and clothed, and nursed when she was ill. She would be buried respectably when she died, and the neighbors would say the Robinsons had been kind and done the right thing by her; but Julia Cloud shuddered as she looked down the long, dull vista of that future which was offered her, and drew back for the first time in her life. Not that she had anything better in view, only that she shrank from taking the step that would bring inevitable and irrevocable grayness to the end of her days. She was not above cooking and nursing and toiling forever if there were independence to be had. She would have given her life if love beckoned her. She would have gone to France as a nurse in a moment if she had not been needed at her mother's bedside. Little children drew her powerfully, but to be a drudge for children who did not love her, in a home where love was the only condition that would make dependence possible, looked intolerable.

Julia Cloud had loved everybody that would let her, and had received very little love in return. Back in the years when she was twelve and went to school a boy of fifteen or sixteen had been her comrade and companion. They had played together whenever Julia had time to play, and had roamed the woods and waded the creeks in company. Then his people moved away, and he had kissed her good-by and told her that some day he was coming back to get her. It was a childish affection, but it was the only kiss of that kind she had to remember.

The boy had written to her for a whole year, when one day there came a letter from his grandmother telling how he was drowned in saving the life of a little child; and Julia Cloud had put the memory of that kiss away as the only bright thing in her life that belonged wholly to herself, and plodded patiently on. The tears that she shed in secret were never allowed to trouble her family, and gradually the pain had grown into a great calm. No one ever came her way to touch her heart again. Only little children brought the wistful look to her eyes, and a wonder whether people had it made up to them in heaven when they had failed of the natural things of this life.

Julia Cloud was not one to pity herself. She was sane, healthy, and not naturally morbid; but tonight, for some reason, the gray sky, and the gray, sodden earth, and the gray road of the future had got her in their clutches, and she could not get away from them. With straining eyes she searched the little bit of west between the orchard tree that always showed a sunset if there was one; but no streak of orange, rose, or gold broke the sullen clouds.

Well, what was she going to do, anyway? Ellen's question seemed to ring on stridently in her ears; she tried to face it looking down the gray road into the gray sky.

She had the house, but there were taxes to pay, and there would be repairs every little while to eat up the infinitesimal income which was left her, when all the expenses of her mother's long illness and death were paid. They had been spending their principal. It could not have been helped. In all, she knew, she had something like two hundred dollars a year remaining. Not enough to board her if she tried to board anywhere, to say nothing of clothing. All this had been fully and exhaustively commented upon by Ellen Robinson during the afternoon.

The house might be rented, of course—though it was too antiquated and shabby-looking to bring much—if Julia was not "so ridiculously sentimental about it." Julia had really very little sentiment connected with the house, but Ellen had chosen to think she had; so it amounted to the same thing as far as the argument went. Julia knew in her own heart that the only thing that held her to the dreary old house with its sad memories and its haunting emptiness was the fact that it was hers and that here she could be independent and do as she pleased. If she pleased to starve, no one else need know it. The big ache that was in her heart was the fact that there was nobody really to care if she did starve. Even Ellen's solicitations were largely from duty and a fear of what the neighbors would say if she did not look after her sister.

Julia was lonely and idle for the first time in her busy, dull life, and her heart had just discovered its love-hunger, and was crying out in desolation. She wanted something to love and be loved by. She missed even the peevish, childish invalid whose last five years had been little else than a living death, with a mind so vague and hazy as seldom to know the faithful daughter who cared for her night and day. She missed the heart and soul out of life, the bit of color that would glorify all living and make it beautiful.

Well, to come back to sordid things, what was there that she could do to eke out her pitiful little living? For live she must, since she was here in this bleak world and it seemed to be expected of her. Keep boarders? Yes, if there were any to keep; but in this town there were few who boarded. There was nothing to draw strangers, and the old inhabitants mostly owned their own houses.

She could sew, but there were already more sewing women in the community than could be supported by the work there was to be done, for most of the women in Sterling did their own sewing. There were two things which she knew she could do well, which everybody knew she could do, and for which she knew Ellen was anxious to have her services. She was the best nurse in town and a fine cook. But again the women of Sterling, most of them, did their own cooking, and there was comparatively little nursing where a trained nurse would not be hired. In short, the few things she could do were not in demand in this neighborhood.

Nevertheless, she knew in her heart that she intended trying to live by her own meagre efforts, going out for a few days nursing, or to care for some children while their mothers went out to dinner or to the city, to the theatre or shopping. There would be but little of that, but perhaps by and by she could manage to make it the fashion.

As she looked into the future, she saw herself trudging gloomily down the sunset way into a leaden sky, caring for the Brown twins all day while their mother was shopping; while they slept, mending stockings out of the big round basket that Mrs. Brown always kept by her sewing-chair; coming home at night to a cheerless house and a solitary meal for which she had no appetite; getting up in the night to go to Grandma Fergus taken down suddenly with one of her attacks; helping Mrs. Smith out with her sewing and spring cleaning. Menial, monotonous tasks many of them. Not that she minded that, if they only got somewhere and gave her something from life besides the mere fighting for existence.

She looked clear down to the end of her loveless life, and saw the neighbors coming virtuously to perform the last rites, and wondered why it all had to be. She was unaware of all her years of sacrifice, glorious patience, loving toil. Her life seemed to have been so without point, so useless heretofore; and all that could yet be, how useless and dreary it looked! Her spirit was at its lowest ebb. Her soul was weary unto death. She looked vainly for a break in that solid wall of cloud at the end of the road, and looked so hard that the tears came and fell plashing on the window-seat and on her thin, tired hands. It was because of the tears that she did not see the boy on a bicycle coming down the road, until he vaulted off at the front gate, left his wheel by the curb, and came whistling up the path, pulling a little book and pencil out of his pocket in a business-like way.

With a start she brushed the tears away, pushed back the gray hair from her forehead, and made ready to go to the door. It was Johnny Knox, the little boy from the telegraph office. He had made a mistake, of course. There would be no telegram for her. It would likely be for the Cramers next door. Johnny Knox had not been long in the village, and did not know.

But Johnny did know.

"Telegram for Miss Julia Cloud!" he announced smartly, flourishing the yellow envelope at her and putting the pencil in her hand. "Sign 'ere!" indicating a line in the book.

Julia Cloud looked hard at the envelope. Yes, there was her name, though it was against all reason. She could not think of a disaster in life of which it might possibly be the forerunner. Telegrams of course meant death or trouble. They had never brought anything else to her.

She signed her name with a vague wonder that there

was nothing to pay. There had been so many things to pay during the last two painful weeks, and her little funds were almost gone.

She stood with the telegram in her hand, watching the boy go whistling back to his wheel and riding off with a careless whirl out into the evening. His whistle lingered far behind, and her ears strained to hear it. Now if a whistle like that were coming home to her! Some one who would be glad to see her and want something she could do for him! Why, even little snubnosed, impudent Johnny Knox would be a comfort if he were all her own. Her arms suddenly felt empty and her hands idle because there was nothing left for her to do. Involuntarily she stretched them out to the gray dusk with a wistful motion. Then she turned, and went back to the window to read her telegram.

> DEAR CLOUDY JEWEL: Leslie and I are on our way East for a visit, and will stop over Wednesday night to see you. Please make us some caraway cookies if not too much trouble.
>
> Your loving nephew,
> Allison Cloud

A glad smile crept into Julia Cloud's lonely eyes. Leslie and Allison were her California brother's children, who had spent three happy months with her when they were five and seven while their father and mother went abroad. "Cloudy Jewel" was the pet name they had made up for her. That was twelve long years ago, and they had not forgotten! They were coming to see her, and wanted some caraway cookies! A glad light leaped into her face, and she lifted her eyes to the gray distance. Lo! the leaden clouds had broken and a streak of pale golden-rose was glowing through the bars of gray.

2

LESLIE and Allison!

Julia Cloud stood gazing out into the west, while the whole sky lightened and sank away into dusk with a burning ruby on its breast. The gloom of her spirit glowed into brightness, and joy flooded her soul.

Leslie and Allison! What round little warm bodies they had, and what delicate, refined faces! They had not seemed like Ellen's blowsy, obstreperous youngsters, practical and grasping to the last extreme after the model of their father. They had starry eyes and hair like tangled sunbeams. Their laughter rippled like brooks in summer, and their hands were like bands that bound the heart. Cookies and stories and long walks and picnics! Those had made up the beautiful days that they spent with her, roaming the woods and meadows, picking dandelions and violets, and playing fairy stories. It had been like a brief return of her old childish days with her boy comrade. She remembered the heartache and the empty days after they had gone back to their Western home, and the little printed childish letters that came for a few months till she was forgotten.

But not really forgotten, after all. For some link of tenderness must still remain that they should think of her now after all these years of separation, and want to visit her. They remembered the cookies! She smiled reminiscently. What a batch of delectable cookies she would make in the morning! Why, to-morrow would be Wednesday! They would be here to-morrow night! And there was a great deal to be done!

She turned from the belated sunset unregretting, and hastened to begin her preparations. There were the two front rooms upstairs to be prepared. She would open the windows at once, and let the air sweep through all night. They had been shut up a long time, for she had brought the invalid down-stairs to the little sitting-room the last few months to save steps and be always within hearing. The second story had been practically unused except when Ellen or the children were over for a day or two.

She hurried up-stairs, and lit the gas in the two rooms, throwing wide the windows, hunting out fresh sheets and counterpanes. She could dust and run the carpet-sweeper over the rooms right away, and have them in order; and that would save time for to-morrow. Oh, it was good to have something cheerful to do once more. Just supposing she had yielded—as once that afternoon she almost had—to Ellen's persistent urgings, and had gone home with her to-night! Why, the telegram might not have reached her till after the children had come, and found the house empty, and gone again!

Julia bustled around happily, putting the rooms into charming order, hunting up a little picture of the child Samuel kneeling in the temple, that Allison used to like, going to the bottom of an old hair trunk for the rag doll she had made for Leslie to cuddle when she went to sleep at night.

Mrs. Ambrose Perkins across the way looked uneasily out of her bedroom window at half-past nine, and said to her husband:

"Seems like Julia Cloud is staying up awful late to-night. She's got a light in both front rooms, too. There can't be company. I s'pose Ellen and some of her children have stayed down after all. Poor Ellen! She told me she simply couldn't spare the time away from home any longer, but Julia was set on staying there. I never thought Julia was selfish; but I s'pose she doesn't realize how hard it is for Ellen, living that way between two houses. Julia'll go to live with Ellen now, of course. It's real good of Herbert Robinson to ask her. Julia ought to appreciate having relatives like that."

"Relatives nothing!" said Mr. Ambrose, pulling off his coat and hanging it over a chair. "She'll be a fool if she goes! She's slaved all her life, and she deserves a little rest now. If she goes out to Herbert Robinson's, she won't be allowed to call her eyelashes her own; you mark my words!"

"Well, what else can she do?" said his wife. "She hasn't any husband or children, and I think she'll be mighty well off to get a good home. Men are awful hard on each other, Ambrose. I always knew that."

Julia Cloud meanwhile, with a last look at the neat rooms, put out her lights, and went to bed, but not to sleep. She was so excited that the darkness seemed luminous about her. She was trying to think how those two children would look grown up. Allison was nine-teen and Leslie nearly seventeen now. Their mother had been dead five years, and they had been in boarding-schools. Their guardian was an old gentleman, a friend of their mother's. That was about all she knew concern-ing them. Would they seem like strangers, she won-dered, or would there be enough resemblance to recall the dear girl and boy of the years that were gone? How she clung to those cookies with hope! There was some remembrance left, or they would not have put cookies in a telegram. How impetuous and just like Allison, the boy, that telegram had sounded!

It was scarcely daylight when Julia Cloud arose and went down to the kitchen to bake the cookies; and the preparations she made for baking pies and doughnuts and other toothsome dainties would lead one to suppose that she was expecting to feed a regiment for a week at least.

She filled the day with hard work, as she had been wont to do, and never once thought of gray sunsets or dreary futures. Not even the thought of her sister Ellen came to trouble her as she put the house in order, filled her pantry with good things to eat, and set the table for three with all the best things the house afforded.

At evening she stood once more beside the front window, looking out sunsetward. There was nothing gray about either sky or road or landscape now. There had been brilliant sunshine all day long, and the sky lay mellow and yellow behind the orchard, with a clear, transparent greenish-blue above and a hint of rosy light in the long rays that reached their fingers along the ground between the apple-trees. In a few minutes the evening train would be in, and there would be rose in the sunset. She knew the signs, and the sky would be glorious tonight. They would see it as they came from the train. In fifteen minutes it would be time for her to put on her hat and go down to meet them! How her heart throbbed with anticipation!

Forebodings came to shadow her brightness. Suppose they should not come! Suppose they were delayed, or had changed their minds and should send another telegram saying so! She drew a deep breath, and tried to brace herself for the shock of the thought. She looked fearfully down the road for a possible Johnny Knox speeding along with another telegram, and was relieved to see only Ambrose Perkins ambling home for supper followed by his tall, smiling Airedale.

There was a shadow, too, that stood behind her, though she ignored it utterly; it was the thought of the afterwards, when the two bright young things had been and gone, and she would have to face the gray in her life again without the rose. But that would be afterwards, and this was now! Ten minutes more, and she would go to the station!

At that minute a great blue automobile shot up to the front gate, and stopped. A big lump flew into Julia Cloud's throat, and her hand went to her heart. Had it then come, that telegram, saying they had changed their minds? She stood trembling by the window, unable to move.

But out from the front seat and the back as if ejected from a catapult shot two figures, and flew together up the front walk, a tall boy and a little girl, just as the sun dropped low and swung a deep red light into the sky, flooding the front yard with glory, and staining the heavens far up into the blue.

They had come! They had come before it was yet train-time!

Julia Cloud got herself to her front door in a tremor of delight, and instantly four strong young arms encircled her, and nearly smothered the life out of her.

"O you dear Cloudy Jewel! You look just the same. I knew you would. Only your hair is white and pretty," Leslie gurgled.

"Sure, she is just the same! What did I tell you?" cried Allison, lifting them both and carrying them inside.

"Now, who on earth can that be?" said Mrs. Ambrose Perkins, flying to her parlor window at the first sound of the automobile. "It isn't any of them folks from the city that were out to the funeral, for there wasn't a car like that there, I'm certain! I mean to run over and borrow a spoonful of soda pretty soon, just to find out. It couldn't be any of Tom's folks from out West, for they couldn't come all that way in a car. It must be some of her father's relations from over in Maryland, though I never heard they were that well off. A chauffeur in livery! The idea of all that style coming to see Julia Cloud!"

"No, we didn't come on the train," explained Leslie eagerly. "We came in Allison's new car. Mr. Luddington—that's our guardian—was coming East, and he said we might come with him. We've been dying to come for ages. And he'd been promising Allison he might get this new car; so we stopped in the city and bought it, and Allison drove it down. Of course Mr. Luddington made his man come along. He wouldn't let us come alone. He's gone up to Boston for three days; and, when he comes back, he's coming down here to see you."

Leslie was talking as fast as an express train, and Julia Cloud stood and admired her in wonder.

She was slim and delicately pretty as ever, with the same mop of goldy-brown curls, done up in a knot now and making her look quaintly like the little five-year-old on a hot day with her curls twisted on the top of her head for comfort. She wore a simple little straight frock of some dark silk stuff, with beaded pockets and marvellous pleats and belts and straps in unexpected places, such as one sees in fashion-books, but not on young girls in the town of Sterling; and her hat was a queer little cap with a knob of bright beads, wonderfully becoming, but quite different from anything that Julia Cloud had ever seen before. Her movements were darting and quick like a humming-bird's; and she wore long soft suède gloves and tiny high suède boots. The older woman watched her, fascinated.

"And you're sure we're not being an inconvenience, dropping down upon you in this unexpected way?"

asked Allison in a quite grown-up man's voice, and looking so tall and handsome and responsible that Julia Cloud wanted to take him in her arms and hug him to make sure he was the same little boy she used to tuck into bed at night.

"So soon after Grandma's death, too," put in Allison. "We didn't know, of course, till we got about a mile from Sterling and stopped to ask the way to the house, and a man told us about the funeral being Monday. We weren't sure then but it would be an intrusion. You see we left California about two weeks ago, and none of our mail has reached us yet; so we hadn't heard. You're sure we won't bother you a bit, you dear?"

Their aunt assured them rapturously that their coming was the most blessed thing that could have been just at this time.

"Oh! then I'm relieved," said Leslie, throwing off her hat and dropping into the nearest chair. "Allison, tell that man to put the car somewhere in a garage and get back to the city. They said there was a train back about this time. The man who directed us told us so. No, dear, he doesn't need any dinner. He's not used to it till seven, and he'll be in the city by that time. He's in a hurry to get back. Cookies? Well, yes, you might give him a cooky or two if you're sure there'll be enough left for us. I've just dreamed of those cookies all these years. I'm so anxious to see if they'll taste as they did when I was a child. May I come with you and see if I remember where the cooky-jar is? Oh, joy, Allison! Just look! A whole crock and a platter full! Isn't this peachy? Allison, do hustle up and get that man off so we can begin our visit!"

It was like having a couple of dolls suddenly come alive and begin to talk.

They talked so fast and they took everything so delightfully for granted that Julia Cloud was in a tremble of joy. It seemed the most beautiful thing in the world that these two strong, handsome, vivid young things should have dropped into her life and taken her into their hearts in this way as if she really belonged, as if they loved her! She was too excited to talk. She hardly knew what to do first. But they did not wait for her initiative. Allison was off with his car and his man, munching cookies as he went, and promising to return in fifteen minutes hungry as a bear.

"Now let's go up-stairs, you dear Cloudy Jewel, and I'll smooth my hair for dinner. I'm crazy to see if I remember things. There was a little red chair that I used to sit in—"

"It's here, in your room, dear, and the old rag doll, Betsey; do you remember her?"

"Well, I should say I did! Is Betsey alive yet? Dear old Betsey! How ducky of you to have kept her for me all these years! Oh, isn't it perfectly peachy that we could come? That we're really here at last, and you want us? You do, don't you, Cloudy, dear? You're sure you do?" Leslie's tone was anxious, and her bright brown eyes studied the older woman's face eagerly; but what she saw there was fully satisfactory, for she smiled, and rattled joyfully on in the old babbling-brook voice that reminded one so of years ago.

"I'm not to tell you what we've really come for till Allison comes, because I've promised; and anyway he's the man, and he wants to tell you himself; but it's the dandiest reason, perfectly peachy! It's really a plan. And say, Cloudy, dear, won't you promise me right here and now that you will say 'Yes' to what he asks you if you possibly, *possibly* can?"

Julia Cloud promised in a maze of delight.

She stood in hovering wonder, and watched the mass of curls come down and go up again with the swift manipulation of the slim white fingers, remembering how she used to comb those tangled curls with the plump little body leaning sturdily against her knee. It seemed to be the first time since she was a child that youth and beauty had come to linger before her. All her experience had been of sickness and suffering and death, not life and happiness.

There was stewed chicken and little biscuits with gravy for supper. It was a dish the children used to love. It was all dished up and everything ready when Allison came back. He reported that the car was housed but a block away, and the man had gone to his train, tickled to death with his cookies. Allison was so glad to be back that he had to take his aunt in his arms again and give her a regular bear-hug till she pleaded for mercy, but there was a happy light in her eyes and a bright color in her cheeks when he released her that made her a very good-looking aunt indeed to sit down at the table with two such handsome children.

Just at that moment Ellen Robinson in her own home was pouring her husband's second cup of coffee.

"Don't you think I'd better take the car and run down for Julia before dark?" she said. "I think she'll be about ready to come back with me by this time, and I need her early in the morning if I'm going to begin cleaning house."

"Better wait one more night," said Herbert stolidly. "Let her get her fill of staying alone nights. It'll do her good. We don't want her to be high and mighty when she gets here. I'm boss here, and she's got to understand that. She's so mighty independent, you know, it's important she should find that out right at the start. I'm not going to have her get bossy with these children, either. They aren't her children."

Four pairs of keen little Robinson eyes took in this saying with quick intelligence, and four stolid sets of shoulders straightened up importantly with four uplifted saucy chins. They would store these remarks away for future reference when the aunt in question arrived on the scene. They would come in well, they knew, for they had had experience with her in times past.

"Aunt Jule ain't goin' to boss me," swaggered the youngest.

"Ner me, neither!"

"Ner me!"

"I guess she wouldn't *dast* try it on *me*!" boasted the eldest.

3

"YOU haven't asked us what we came for," opened up Allison as soon as everybody was served with chicken, mashed potato, succotash, stewed tomatoes, biscuits, pickles, and apple-sauce.

"I thought you came for cookies," said Julia Cloud, with a mischievous twinkle in her gray eyes.

"Hung one on me, didn't you?" said Allison, laughing. "But that wasn't all. Guess again."

"Perhaps you came to see me," she suggested shyly.

"Right you are! But that's not all, either. That wouldn't last much longer than the cookies. Guess again."

"Oh, I couldn't!" said Julia Cloud, growing suddenly stricken with the thought of their going. "I give it up."

"Well, then I'll tell you. You see we've come East to college, both of us. Of course I've had my freshman year, but the Kid's just entering. We haven't decided which college it's to be yet, but it's to be co-ed, we know that much, because we're tired of being separated. When one hasn't but two in the family and has been apart for five years, one appreciates a home, I tell you that. And so we've decided we want a home. We're not just going to college to live there in the usual way; we're going to take a house, live like real folks, and go to school every day. We want a fireplace and a cooky-jar of our own; a place to bring our friends and have good times. But most of all we want a mother, and we've come all this way to coax you to come and live with us, play house, you know, as you used to do down on the mossy rocks with broken bits of china for dishes and acorns for cups and saucers. Play house and you be mother. Will you do it, Cloudy Jewel? It means a whole lot to us, and we'll try to play fair and make you have a good time."

Julia Cloud put her hand on her heart, and lifted her bewildered eyes to the boy's eager face.

"Me!" she said wonderingly. "You want *me!*"

"We sure do!" said Allison.

"Indeed we do, Cloudy, dear! That's just what we do want!" cried Leslie, jumping up and running around to her aunt's chair to embrace her excitedly. "And you promised, you know, that you would do what we wanted if you possibly, *possibly* could."

"You see, we put it up to our guardian about the house," went on Allison, "and he said the difficulty would be to get the right kind of a housekeeper that he could trust us with. Of course he's way off in California, and he has to be fussy. He's built that way. But we told him we didn't want any housekeeper at all, we wanted a mother. He said you couldn't pick mothers off trees, but we told him we knew where there was one if we could only get her. So he let us come and ask; and, if you say you'll do it, he's coming down to see you and fix it up about the money part. He said you'd have to have a regular salary or he wouldn't consider it, because there were things he'd have to insist upon that he had promised mother; and, if there wasn't a business arrangement about it, he wouldn't know what to do. Besides, he said it was worth a lot to run a couple of rough-necks like Les and me, and he'd make the salary all right so you could afford to leave whatever you were doing and just give your time to mothering us. Now it's up to you, Cloudy Jewel, to help us out with our proposition or spoil everything, because we simply won't have a house-keeper, and we don't know another real mother in the whole world that hasn't a family of her own."

They both left their delicious dinner, and got around her, coaxing and wheedling exactly as if she had already declined, when the truth was she was too dazed with joy to open her lips, even if they had given her opportunity to speak.

It was some time before the excitement quieted down and they gave her a chance to say she would go. Even then she spoke the words with fear and trembling as one might step off a common place threshold into a fairy palace, not sure but it might be stepping into space.

Outside the sky was still flooded with after-sunset glory, but there was so much glory in the hearts of the three inside the dining-room that they never noticed it at all. It might have been raining or hailing, and they would not have known, they were so happy.

Both the guests donned long gingham aprons and wiped the dishes when the meal was over, both talking with all their might, recalling the days of their childhood when they had had towels pinned around them and been allowed to dry the cups and pans; then suddenly jumping ahead and planning what they would do in the dear new home of the future. They were all three as excited about it as if they had been a bridal couple planning for their honeymoon.

"We shall want five bedrooms," said Leslie decidedly. "I've thought that all out, one for each of us and two guest-rooms, so we can have a boy and a girl home for overnight with us as often as we want to. And there simply must be a fireplace, or we won't take the house. If there isn't the right kind of a house in town, we'll choose some other college. There are plenty of colleges, but you can have only one home, and it must be the right kind. Then of course we want a big kitchen where we can make fudge as often as we choose in the evenings, and a dining-room with a bay window, with seats and flowers and a canary. Cloudy Jewel, you don't mind cats, do you? I want two at least. I've been crazy for a kitten all the time I was in school, and Al wants a big collie. You won't mind, will you?"

Suddenly Julia Cloud discovered that latent in her heart all these years there had also lain a desire for a cat and a dog; and she lifted guilty eyes, and confessed it. She felt a pang of remembrance as she recalled how her mother used so often to tell her she was nothing but an "old child."

"Perhaps your guardian will not think me a proper person to chaperon you," she suggested in sudden alarm.

"Well, he'd just better not!" declared Allison, bristling up. "I'd like to know where he could find a better."

"I've never been in society," said Julia Cloud thoughtfully. "I don't know social ways much, and I've never been considered to have any dignity or good judgment."

"That's just why we like you," chorused the children. "You've never grown up and got dull and stiff and poky like most grown folks."

"We were so afraid," began Leslie, putting a loving arm about her aunt's waist, "that you would have changed since we were children. We talked it all over on the way here. We had a kind of eyebrow code by which we could let each other know what we thought about it without your seeing us. We were to lift one eyebrow, the right one, if we were favorably impressed, and draw down the left if we were disappointed. But in case we were sure both eyebrows were to go up. And of course we were sure you were just the same dear the minute we laid eyes on you, and all four of our eyebrows went high as they'd go the first instant. Didn't you notice Allison? His eyebrows were almost up to his hair, and they pulled his eyes so wide open they were perfectly round like saucers. As for me I think mine went way up under my hair. I'm not sure if they've got back to their natural place even yet!" And Leslie laid a rosy finger over her brow, and felt anxiously along the delicate velvety line.

"I shall go out and telegraph Mr. Luddington that you are willing," announced Allison as he hung up the dish-towel. "He'll get it in the morning when he reaches Boston, and then he needn't fuss and fume any longer about what he's going to do with us. Besides, I like to have the bargain clinched somehow, and a telegram will do it." Allison slammed out of the house noisily to the extreme confusion of Mrs. Ambrose Perkins, who hadn't been able to eat her supper properly for watching the house to see what would happen next. Who could that young man be?

She simply couldn't get a clew; for, when she went over for the soda, though she knocked several times, and heard voices up-stairs, and altogether unseemly laughter for a house where there had just been a funeral, not a soul came to the door! Could it be that Julia Cloud heard her and stayed up-stairs on purpose? She felt that as the nearest neighbor and a great friend of Ellen's it would be rather expected of her to find out what was going on. She resolutely refrained from lighting the parlor lamp, and took up her station at the dark window to watch; but, although she sat there until after ten o'clock, she was utterly unable to find out anything except that the household across the way stayed up very late and there were lights in both front rooms again. She felt that if nothing developed by morning she would just have to get Ambrose to hitch up and drive out to Ellen's. Ellen ought to know.

But Julia Cloud was serenely unconscious of this espionage. She had entered an Eden of bliss, and was too happy to care about anything else.

Seated on the big old couch in the parlor with a child on either side of her, a hand in each of hers, often a head on each shoulder nestling down, they talked. Planned and talked. Now the brother would break in with some tale of his schooldays; now the sister would add a bit of reminiscence, just as if they had been storing it all up to tell her. The joyous happiness of them all seemed like heaven dropped down to earth. It was as she had sometimes dreamed mothers might talk with their own children. And God had granted this unspeakable gift to her! Was it real? Would it last? Or was she only dreaming? Once it vaguely passed through her mind that she would not be sure of the reality of the whole thing until she had seen Ellen. If she could talk with Ellen about it, tell her what she was going to do, show her the children, and then come back and find it all the same, it would last. But somehow she shrank unspeakably from seeing Ellen. She could not get away from the feeling that Ellen would dispel it all; that someway, somehow, she would succeed in breaking up all the bright plans and scattering them like soap-bubbles in the wind.

Nevertheless, it was a very beautiful illusion, if illusion it was; and one to be prolonged as late as possible.

She was horrified when at last she heard the rebuking strokes of the town clock, ten! eleven! *twelve!*

She started to her feet ashamed.

And even then they would not let her go to bed at once. She must turn out the lights, and sit in the hall between their rooms as she did long ago, and tell the story of "The Little Red Hen" just as she had told it night after night when they were children.

It was characteristic of the unfailing youth of the woman that she entered into the play with zest. Attired in a long kimono, with her beautiful white hair in two long silver braids down over her shoulders, she sat in the dark and told the story with the same vivid language; and then she stole on tiptoe first to the sister's bedside, to tuck her in and kiss her softly, and then to the brother's; and at each bedside a young, strong arm reached out and drew her face down, whispering "Good-night" with a kiss and "I love you, Cloudy Jewel," in tender, thrilling tones.

The two big children were asleep at last, and Julia Cloud stole to her own bed to lie in a tumult of wonder and joy, and finally sink into a light slumber, wherein she dreamed that she had fallen heir to a rose-garden, and all the roses were alive and could talk; until Ellen came driving up in her Ford and ran right over them, crushing them down and cutting their heads off with a long, sharp whip she carried that somehow turned out to be made of words strung together with biting sarcasm.

She awoke in the broad morning sunlight to find both children done up in bathrobes and slippers, sitting on each side of her on the bed, laughing at her and tickling her chin with a feather from the seam of the pillow.

"Now, Cloudy Jewel, you've just got to begin to make plans!" announced Leslie, curling up in a ball at her feet and looking very business-like with her fluffy curls around her face like a golden fleece. "There isn't much time, and Guardy Lud will be down upon us by to-morrow or the next day at least."

"Guardy Lud!" exclaimed Julia Cloud bewildered. "Who is that?"

"That's our pet name for Mr. Luddington," explained

Leslie, wrinkling up her nose in a grin of merriment. "Isn't it cute? Wait till you see him, and you'll see how it fits. He's round and bald with a shiny red nose, and spectacles; and he doesn't mind our kidding at all. He'd have made a lovely father if he wasn't married, but he has a horrid wife. We don't like her at all. She's like a frilly piece of French china with too much decoration; and she's always sick and nervous; and she jumps, and says 'Oh, mercy!' every time we do the least little thing. She doesn't like us any better than we like her. Her name is Alida, and Allison says we're always trying to 'elude' her. The only good thing she ever did was to advise Guardy Lud to let us come East to college. She wanted to get us as far away from her as possible. And it certainly was mutual."

"There, now, Leslie, you're chattering again," broke in Allison, looking very tall and efficient in his blue bathrobe. "You said you would talk business, and not bleat."

"Well, so I am," pouted Leslie. "I guess Cloudy has got to understand about our family."

"Well, now let's get down to business," said her brother. "Cloudy, what have you got to do before you leave? You know it isn't very long before the colleges open, and we've got to start out and hunt a home right away. Do you have to pack up here or anything?"

"Oh, I don't know!" gasped Julia Cloud, looking around half frightened. "I suppose I ought to ask Ellen. She will be very much opposed to anything I do, but I suppose she ought to be told first."

Allison frowned.

"Gee whiz! I don't see why Aunt Ellen has to butt into our affairs. She's got her own home and family, and she never did like us very much. I remember hearing her tell Grandma that we were a regular nuisance, and she would be glad when we were gone back to California."

"That was because you hid behind the sofa when Uncle Herbert was courting her, and kidded them," giggled Leslie.

A stray little twinkle of a dimple peeped out by the corner of Julia Cloud's mouth. It hadn't been out for a number of years, and she knew she ought not to laugh at such pranks now; but it was so funny to think of Herbert Robinson being kidded in the midst of his courting!

The dimple started the lights dancing in Leslie's eyes.

"There! Now you dear old Jewel, you know you don't want to talk to Aunt Ellen about us. She'll just mess things all up. Let's just *do* things, and get 'em all fixed up, and then tell her when it's too late for her to make a fuss," gurgled Leslie down close to Julia's ear, finishing up with a delicious bear-hug.

"I suppose she'll be mortally offended," murmured Julia Cloud in troubled hesitancy.

"Well, suppose she is; she'll get over it, won't she?" growled Allison. "And anyhow you're old enough to manage your own affairs, Cloudy Jewel. I guess you're older than she is, aren't you? I guess you've got a right to do as you please, haven't you? And you *do* want to go with us, don't you?" His voice was anxious.

"I certainly do, dear boy," said Julia Cloud eagerly; "but you know your guardian may not approve at all when he sees what a foolish 'young' aunt I am, allowing you to sit up late and talk fairy stories all the time."

They smothered her in kisses, compliments, and assurances; and it was some time before the conversation swung around again to the important subject of the morning.

"You don't have to do anything to the house but just shut it up, do you?" asked Allison, looking anxiously about in a helpless, mannish way. "Because, if you do, we ought to be getting to work."

"There's a man over at Harmony Village that wanted

to rent a house here," said Julia Cloud thoughtfully. "I might write a letter to him. I don't know whether he's found anything or not. He's the new superintendent of the high school. But it's time we got dressed and had breakfast."

"Write to him nothing!" said Allison eagerly. "I'll get the car, and we'll drive over to Harmony in no time, and get the thing fixed up. Hustle there, Leslie, and get yourself togged up. We don't need to wait for breakfast; we can eat cookies. Hurry everybody!" And he slammed over to his own room and began to stir about noisily.

Julia Cloud arose and made a hasty toilet, with a bright spot of excitement on each cheek; but she had no time to think what Ellen would say, for she meant that those children should have a real old-time breakfast before they began the day; and now that she was up her little round black clock on the bureau told her that it was high time the day had begun. She looked fearfully out of the window, half expecting to see Ellen's Ford bobbing down the hill already, and then hurried down to the kitchen. Allison soon came down, calling out to her to be ready when he came back with the car; but the delicious odors that had already begun to float out from the old kitchen made him lenient toward the idea of breakfast; and, when he came back with the full cut-out roaring the announcement of his arrival to the Perkinses, he was quite ready to wait a few minutes and eat some of Julia Cloud's flapjacks and sausages with maple-syrup and apple-sauce.

Julia Cloud herself ate little. She was in a tremor of delightful uncertainty and dread. Ought she to go ahead this way and manage her own affairs, leaving her sister out of the question? But then, if she consulted with Ellen that meant consulting with Herbert; for Herbert ran his wife most thoroughly, and Herbert could make things very unpleasant when he took the trouble.

So, when the children, unable at last to eat any more, pleaded with her to leave the dishes and go to see the man about the house at once, she gave one swift, apprehensive glance about, and assented. If Ellen should come to the house while they were away, and should look in at the window and see breakfast dishes standing! It would be appalling! But, as the children said, why worry? Somehow she felt like a little schoolgirl playing hookey as she carefully drew down the dining-room and kitchen window-shades that looked on the back porch, and locked the front door behind her. Well, perhaps she had earned the right to take this bit of holiday, and wash her dishes when she liked. Anyhow, hadn't God sent these blessed children to her in answer to her earnest prayer that He would show her what to do and save her if possible from having to spend the remainder of her days under Herbert Robinson's roof? Well, then she would just accept it that way and be grateful, at least until He showed her otherwise. So she drew a long breath of delight, and climbed into the luxurious back seat of the great blue car, utterly oblivious of the prying eyes behind the parlor shade across the way.

4

DOWN the little village street, past the station, and across the railroad toward Harmony swept the great blue car, with the villagers turning to stare at Miss Cloud taking a ride so early in the morning in so gaudy a car, so soon after the funeral, and even without a veil!

A few minutes later Ellen in her Ford rattled up to the door and got out with the air of one who had come to do things. She walked confidently up to the front door and tried it, rattled it, knocked, and then went angrily around to the back, trying all the doors and windows. Mrs. Perkins from her parlor window watched a minute; and, when she saw Ellen come around to the front again and look up at the second story, she threw a shawl around her shoulders and ran across the street to impart faithfully her story.

"For the land's sake!" said Ellen indignantly. "What can Julia be about? Mother always said she never would grow up, and I believe it. I was afraid when I went away she had some scheme in her mind. She's always getting up fool ideas. I remember that time when Mrs. Marsh died she wanted to adopt the twins and bring them up.

The idea! When there was a county poorhouse and no reason why they shouldn't go to it! But she'll have to come down off her independence and be sensible. Herbert says we can't have any of her foolishness. It's us that would have to suffer if she got into trouble and lost what little she's got, and I suppose I've got to have it out with her once and for all and get this thing settled. It's getting on all our nerves, and I've got the fall house-cleaning and jelly to do, and I can't fool around any longer. Well, I suppose I better try to get into this house. Have you got any keys that might fit?"

Mrs. Perkins hurried over for all her keys, including trunk-keys; and soon they had tried every door and every key with no effect, and had to call in the youngest Perkins and boost him up to the upper-hall window.

Under the guise of looking after Julia Cloud the two good ladies invaded her home and proceeded to investigate. The parlor and the hall gave forth no secrets except for a couple of handsome raincoats slung carelessly upon chairs. But the dining-room, oh, the dining-room! If Julia Cloud could have seen their faces as they swung open that carefully closed door and stood upon the threshold aghast, looking at the wreck of the breakfast, she would have cringed and shivered even on her way to Harmony.

But Julia Cloud could not see; she was safely over the bridge and out on the highway where she would not be likely to be followed, and the wine of the morning was rising in her veins. Such wonderful air, such clear blue sky and flying clouds! She felt like a flying cloud herself as she sped along in the great blue car with the chatter of the children in her ears and the silvery laughter of Leslie by her side. How could she help smiling and letting her cheeks grow pink and her eyes grow bright? Too soon after a funeral? The thought did come to her. But she knew by the thrill of her heart that her mother in heaven was gladder now than she had been for years of her bedridden life on earth, and, if she could look down to see, would no doubt be happy that some joy was coming to her hard-worked daughter at last. Julia would just enjoy this day and this delight to the full while it lasted. If it was not meant to last longer than the day, at least she would have this wonderful ride to remember always, this bird-like motion as if she were floating through a panorama! Not a thought of Ellen poking through her half-cleared house, finding unswept hearth and unmade beds and unwashed dishes, came to trouble her joy. It was as if the childhood of her life, long held in abeyance, had come back to her, and would not be denied.

Ellen and Mrs. Perkins in their inspection of the house came at last to the upper story and the guests' room strewn with brushes bearing silver monograms and elaborate appointments of travel that kept them guessing their use and exclaiming in wonder and horror that any one would spend so much on little details. Leslie's charming silk negligée and her frilly little night-gown with its lace and floating ribbons came in for a large amount of contempt, and it was some time before the good ladies arrived at Julia Cloud's room and found the open telegram on her bureau that gave the key to the mystery of the two visitors.

"H'm!" said Ellen. "So that's it! Well, I thought she had some bee in her bonnet. She must have written to them or they never would have come. Now, I suppose she means to keep them all winter, perhaps, and feed them, and baby them up; and, when she has spent all she has, she'll come back on us. Well, she'll find out she's much mistaken; and, when she gets back, I'll just tell her plainly that she can bundle up her company and send them home and come out to us now, to-day or to-morrow, or the offer is withdrawn, and she needn't think she can fall back on Herbert, either, when she's spent everything. Herbert is not a man to be put upon."

"I should say not!" said Mrs. Perkins sympathetically, looking over her friend's shoulder at the telegram. "So those were your brother's two children! He must 'uv been pretty well off for them to have a car like that. I must say I think it's a harm to children to be brought up wealthy."

"Their mother was rich," said Ellen sourly. It had always been a thorn in her flesh. "She was a snob, too, and her children'll likely be the limit by this time. But Julia is such a fool!"

They sat in Julia Cloud's parlor, one at each window, discussing the probabilities until half-past eleven. Then Ellen said she must go. She positively couldn't wait another minute; but she would return in the afternoon, and Mrs. Perkins must tell her sister that she was coming and wanted her to remain at home. That it was very important.

"I'll settle her!" she said with her thin lips set in a hard line. Then she stooped to crank her Ford.

Mrs. Perkins watched her away, than hurried to her own neglected work; and ten minutes later the big blue car sailed noiselessly up to the place. It was not until the Perkins children discovered it and told their mother that she knew it had arrived. This was very annoying. She had wanted to catch them quite casually on their arrival, and now she would have to make a special errand over, and as likely as not have them not come to the door again. Besides, she was getting dinner, and things were likely to burn. Nevertheless, she dared not wait with that big blue car standing so capably at the door, ready to spirit them away again at any moment. She wiped her hands on her apron, grabbed a teacup for an excuse, and ran over to borrow that soda once more.

Peals of laughter were echoing through the old house

when she knocked at the door, and a regular rush and scramble was going on, *so* unseemly just after a funeral! The door was on the latch, too, as if they did not care who heard; and to save her life she couldn't help pushing it a little with her foot, just enough to see in. And there was Julia Cloud, her white hair awry, and her face rosy with mirth, an ear of corn in one hand and a knife in the other, being carried—yes, actually *carried*—across the dining-room in the arms of a tall young man and deposited firmly on the big old couch.

"There, Cloudy Jewel! You'll lie right there and rest while Leslie and I get lunch. You're all tired out; I can see it in your eyes; and we can't afford to let you stay so. No, we don't need any succotash for lunch or dinner, either. I know it's good; but we haven't time now, and we aren't going to let you work," announced the young man joyously as he towered above her lying quiescent and weak with laughter.

"No, nor you aren't going to wash the dishes, either," gurgled the young girl who danced behind the young man; "Allison and I will wash them all while you take a nap, and then we're going to ride again."

Julia Cloud, her eyes bright with the joy of all this loving playfulness, tried to protest; but suddenly into the midst of this tumult came Mrs. Perkins's raucous assertion:

"H'm-m!"

The two young people whirled around alertly, and Julia Cloud sat up with a wild attempt to bring her hair into subjection as she recognized her neighbor. The color flooded into her sweet face, but she rose with gentle dignity.

"O Mrs. Perkins, we must have been making such a noise that we didn't hear your knock," she said.

As a matter of fact Mrs. Perkins hadn't knocked. She had been led on by curiosity until she stood in the open dining-room door, rank disapproval written on her face.

"It did seem a good bit of noise for a house of mourning," said Mrs. Perkins dryly.

Julia Cloud's sweet eyes suddenly lost their smile, and she drew herself up ever so little. There was just a ripple of a quiver of her gentle lips, and she said quite quietly and with a dignity that could not help impressing her caller:

"This is not a house of mourning, Mrs. Perkins. I don't think my dear mother would want us to mourn because she was released from a bed of pain where she had lain for nine long years, and gone to heaven where she could be young and free and happy. I'm glad for her, just as glad as I can be; and I know she would want me to be. But won't you sit down? Mrs. Perkins, this is my niece and nephew, Leslie and Allison Cloud from California. I guess you remember them when they were little children. Or no; you hadn't moved here yet when they were here—"

Mrs. Perkins with pursed lips acknowledged the introduction distantly, one might almost say insolently, and turned her back on them as if they had been little children.

"Your sister's been here all morning waiting for you!" she said accusingly. She gave a significant glance at the unwashed breakfast dishes, only part of which had been removed to the kitchen. "She couldn't imagine where you'd gone at that hour an' left your beds and your dishes."

A wave of indignation swept over Julia Cloud's sweet face.

"So you have been in my house during my absence!" she said quietly. "That seems strange since Ellen has no key!"

There was nothing in her voice to indicate rebuke, but Mrs. Perkins got very red.

"I s'pose your own sister has a right to get into the house where she was born," she snapped.

"Oh, of course," said Julia Cloud pleasantly. "And Ellen used to be a good climber before she got so fat. I suppose she climbed in the second-story window, although I hadn't realized she could. However, it doesn't matter. I suppose you have had to leave your dishes and beds once in a while when you were called away on business. You have a cup there; did you want to borrow something?"

Mrs. Perkins was one of those people who are never quite aware of it when they are in a corner; but she felt most uncomfortable, especially as she caught a stifled giggle from Allison, who bolted into the parlor hastily and began noisily to turn over the pages of a book on the table; but she managed to ask for her soda and get herself out of the house.

"Thank you for bringing my sister's message," called Julia Cloud after her. She never could quite bear to be unpleasant even to a prying neighbor, and Mrs. Perkins through the years had managed to make herself unpleasant many times.

"The old cat!" said Leslie in a clear, carrying voice. "Why did you thank her, Auntie Jewel? She didn't deserve it."

"Hush, Leslie, dear! She will hear you!" said Julia Cloud, hastily closing the door on the last words.

"I hope she did," said Leslie comfortably. "I *meant* she should."

"But, deary, that isn't right! It isn't—Christian!" said her aunt in distress.

"Then I'm no Christian," chanted Leslie mischievously. "Why isn't it right, I'd like to know? Isn't she an old cat?"

"But you hurt her feelings, dear. I'm afraid I was to blame, too; I didn't answer her any too sweetly myself."

"Well, didn't she hurt yours first? *Sweet!* Why you were honey itself, Cloudy, dear, thanking her for her old prying!"

"I hope it's the kind of honey that gets bitter after you swallow it!" growled Allison, coming out of the parlor. "If she'd said much more, I'd just have put her out of the house, talking to you like that, as if you were a little child, Cloudy!"

"Why, children! That didn't really hurt me any; it just stirred up my temper a little; but I'm ashamed that I let it, and I don't want you to talk like that. It isn't a bit right. It distresses me to have you think it's right to answer back that way and take vengeance on people."

"Well, there, Cloudy, let's lay that subject on the table for some of our night talks; and you can scold us all you like. We have a lot of work to do now, and let's forget the old pry. Now you lie down on that couch where I put you, and Leslie and I'll wash these dishes."

Julia Cloud lay obediently on the couch, but her mind was not at rest. She was in a tumult of indignation at her prying neighbor and an uncertainty of anxiety about Ellen and what she might do next. But beneath it all was a vague fear about these her dear children who were about to become her responsibility. Could she do it? Dared she do it? How differently they had been brought up from all the traditions which had controlled her life!

Take, for instance, that matter of Christianity. How would they feel about it? Would they be in sympathy with her ideas and ideals of right and wrong? They were no longer little children to obey her. They would have ideas of their own, yes, and ideals. Would there be constant clashing? Would she be haunted with a feeling that she was not doing her duty by them? There were so many questions, amusements, and Sabbath, and churchgoing, and how to treat other people. And doubtless she was old-fashioned, and they would chafe under her rule.

Take the little matter of Leslie's calling Mrs. Perkins a cat. She *was* a cat, but Leslie ought not to have told her so. It wasn't polite, and it wasn't Christian. And yet how could she, plain Julia Cloud, who had never been anywhere much outside of her home town, who had had no opportunity for study or wide reading, and who had only worked quietly all her life, and thought her plain little thoughts of love to God and to her neighbors, be able to explain all those things to this pair of lovable, uncontrolled children, who had always had their own way, and whose ideals were the ideals of the great wide unchristian world?

A little pucker grew between her brows, and a tired, troubled tear stole softly between her lashes. When the children, tiptoeing about and whispering, came to peek in at the door and see whether she was asleep, they discovered her expression at once, and, drawing near, sighted the tear. Then they went down upon their knees beside the couch, and noisily demanded the cause thereof.

Little by little they drew her fears from her.

"Why, Cloudy, dear! We'll do what you want. We'll let all the old cats in the community walk over you if that will make you happy," declared Leslie, patting her face.

"No, we won't!" put in Allison; "we'll keep 'em away from her, but we won't let 'em know how we despise 'em. Won't that do, Cloudy? And as for all those other things you are afraid about, why couldn't you just wait till we come to them? We're anything but angels, I admit, but we're going to try to do what you want us to if it busts the eye-teeth out of us, because we want you. And you always have been such a good scout. As for the church dope and all that, why, it's like that guy in the Bible you used to tell us about when we were children—or was she a lady? It's a case of 'Thy people shall be my people, and thy God my God,' or words to the effect. If we don't agree on our own account, we'll do it because you want it. Isn't that about the idea? Wouldn't that fill the bill?"

"You dear children!" said Julia Cloud, her eyes full of smiles and tears now as she gathered them both into a loving embrace. "I don't know how anybody could promise more than that. I wasn't afraid of you; it was myself. You know I'm not at all wise, and it's pretty late in life for me to begin to bring up children."

"Well, you're all right, anyhow, Cloudy; and you're the only person in the world we'll let bring us up; so it's up to you to do it the best you can, or it won't get done. Come on now; we've got lunch ready. There's cold chicken and bread and milk and pie and cake, and I've got the teakettle boiling like a house afire, so if you want any tea or anything you can have it."

So they had a merry meal, and Julia Cloud ate and laughed with them, and thought she never had been so happy since she was a little girl. Then, mindful of her prying neighbor and her imminent sister, she insisted on putting the house in order to the last bed and dish before she was ready for this afternoon.

"And now we're going to call on Aunt Ellen!" announced Allison as Julia Cloud hung up the clean dish-towels steaming from their scalding bath, and washed her hands at the sink.

"Why, she's coming here!" said his aunt, whirling around with a troubled look. "And, as she's left word she was coming, I suppose we'll have to wait for her. It's too bad, for she won't be here till three, and it's only a quarter of two. I'm sorry, because you wanted to go out in the car, didn't you?"

"We're going!" said Allison, again with a commanding twinkle in his eye. "We can't waste all that time; and, besides, don't you see if she comes here, she'll likely stay all the afternoon and argue? If we go there, we can come away when we like; and she'll feel we're more polite to come to her, anyhow, won't she, Cloudy?"

Julia Cloud looked into the boy's convincing eyes, and her trouble cleared away. Perhaps he was right. Anyhow, why should they spoil a whole day to conciliate Ellen? Ellen would be disagreeable about it, however they did; and they might as well rise above it, and just be pleasant, and let it go at that.

It was the first time in her long life of self-sacrifice that Julia Cloud had been able to rise above her anxiety about her sister's tantrums and go calmly on her way. It is scarcely likely that she would have managed it now if it hadn't been that she felt that Allison and Leslie ought not to be sacrificed.

She never did anything just for herself. It was not in her.

"All right," she said briskly, glancing at the clock; "then we must go at once, or we shall miss her. I'll be ready in five minutes. How about you, Leslie?"

"Oh, I'm ready now," said the girl, patting her curly hair into shape before the old mahogany-framed mirror in the hall.

In five minutes more they were stowed away in the big blue car again, speeding down the road, with Mrs. Perkins indignantly and openly watching them from her front porch.

"We put one over on Mrs. Pry, didn't we, Cloudy?" said Allison, turning around to wink a naughty eye back toward the Perkins house. "She thinks you've dared to run away after she gave you orders to stay at home."

Julia Cloud could not suppress a smile of enjoyment, and wondered whether she was getting childish that she should be happy with these children.

5

THE air was fine; the sky was clear without a cloud; and the spice of autumn flavored everything. Along the roadside blackberry vines were turning scarlet, and here and there in the distance a flaming branch proclaimed the approach of a frosty wooing. One could not ask anything better on such a day than to be speeding along this white velvet road in the great blue car with two beloved children.

But all too soon Herbert Robinson's ornate house loomed up, stark and green, with very white trimmings, and regular flower-beds each side of the gravel walk. It was the home of a prosperous man, and as such asserted itself. There had never been anything attractive about it to Julia Cloud. She preferred the ugly old house in which she had always lived, with its scaling gray paint and no pretensions to fineness. At least it was softened by age, and had the look of experience which saved its ugliness from being crude, and gave it the dignity of time.

And now Julia Cloud's heart began to beat rapidly. All at once she felt that she had done a most foolish thing in allowing the children to overrule her and bring her here. Ellen would not be dressed up nor have the children ready for inspection, and she would be angry at her sister for not having given warning of their coming. She leaned forward breathlessly to suggest turning back; but Allison, perhaps anticipating her feeling, said:

"Now don't you get cold feet, Cloudy Jewel. If Aunt Ellen is sore, just you talk up to her and smile a lot, and we'll back you up. Remember everything's going fine, and the whole thing's settled. It's too late to change it now. Is this the place? We'll turn right in, shall we?" And with the words he swept up under the elaborate wooden porte-cochère, and, swinging down, flung the door open for Julia Cloud to alight.

Leslie gave a quick disdainful glance about, fluttered out beside her aunt, and, catching the look of apprehension on her face, tripped up the steps and rang the bell, poising bird-like on the threshold and calling in a sweet, flute-like voice:

"Aunt Ellen! O Aunt Ellen! Where are you? Don't you know you've got company all the way from California?"

It was just like taking the bull by the horns, and Julia Cloud paused on the upper step in wonder. How winning a child she was! And how she had known by intuition just how to mollify her unpleasant relative!

What would Ellen say? How would she take it?

Ellen Robinson bustled frowning into the hall, whetting her sharp tongue for an encounter. She had seen the big blue car turn in at the gate, and knew from Mrs. Perkin's description who it must be. Julia Cloud had well judged her state of mind, for her four children could not have been caught in a worse plight so far as untidiness was concerned, and there had barely been time to marshal them all up the back stairs with order to scrub and dress or not to come down till the visitors were gone.

They were even now creeping shufflingly about overhead on their bare feet, hunting for their respective best shoes and stockings and other garments, and scrapping in loud whispers.

But Leslie, little diplomat that she was, wasted no time in taking stock of her aunt. She flung her arms joyously around that astonished woman, and fairly took her by storm, talking volubly and continuously until they were all in the house and seated in Ellen's best satin brocatelle parlor chairs, surrounded by crayon portraits of Herbert Robinson's ancestors and descendents. Allison too caught on to his sister's game, and talked a good deal about how nice it was to get East again after all the years, and how glad they were to have some relative of their own. Julia Cloud sat quietly and proudly listening; and Ellen forgot her anger, and ceased to frown. After all, it was something to have such good-looking relatives. For the first few minutes the well-prepared speech wherewith she had intended to dress down poor Julia lay idle on her lips, and a few sentences of grudging welcome even managed to slip by. Then suddenly she turned to her sister, and the sight of adoration for the visitors in Julia's transparent face kindled her anger. Never had such a look as this glowed in Julia Cloud's face for any little Robinson, save perhaps in the first few days of their tiny lives before the Robinson had begun to crop out in them.

"Where were you this morning, Jule? It certainly seems queer for you to be gadding around having a good time so soon after poor mother's death. And the dishes not washed, either! Upon my word, you have lost your head! You weren't brought up that way. I stood up-stairs and looked around on those unmade beds, and thought what poor mother would have said if she could see them. Such goings-on! I certainly was ashamed to have Mrs. Perkins see it."

Two rosy spots bloomed out on Julia Cloud's cheeks, and a tremble came in her lips, though one could see she was making a great effort to control herself; and the two long breaths that Leslie and Allison drew simultaneously were heavily threatening, much like the distant rumble of thunder.

"I'm sure I don't see what occasion Mrs. Perkins had to see it," she answered steadily.

"Well, she was there!" said her sister dryly. She seemed to have forgotten the presence of the two people, who, if they had been in the foreground, might have been noticed doing things with their eyebrows to their mutual understanding and agreement.

"Yes, so she told me," said Julia Cloud significantly. "But that was not what I came over to talk about, Ellen; I wanted to let you know that I've rented the house, and the tenant wants possession next week. I thought you might like to pick out some of mother's things to bring over here before I pack up. You spoke about wishing you had another couch for the sitting-room, and you might just as well have the dining-room one as not. Then I thought perhaps you could use mother's bedroom suit."

"You've rented the house!" screamed Ellen as soon as she got breath from her astonishment to interrupt. "You've rented the house without consulting me? Who to, I'd like to know? I had a tenant already for that house, I told you."

"Why, I had no time to consult you Ellen; and besides, why should I? The house is mine, and I knew you didn't want it. You have your own home."

"Well, you certainly are blossoming out and getting independent! I should think mere decency would have made you consult us before you did anything. What do you know about business? Herbert will be mad as anything when I tell him; and like as not you'll get into no end of trouble with a strange tenant, and we'll have to help you out. Herbert always says women make all the trouble they can for him before they call on him for assistance."

Julia smiled.

"I shall not be obliged to call on Herbert for assistance, Ellen. Everything is arranged. The contract was signed this morning, and I have promised to vacate as soon as possible. The tenant is the new school super-intendent, and he wants to come at once. I just heard last evening that he had been disappointed in getting the Harvey house. It's sold to the foreman of the mill. So I went over to Harmony to see him at once."

The news was so overwhelming and so unquestionably satisfactory from a business point of view that Ellen was speechless with astonishment. Allison gave Leslie a grave wink, and turned to look out of the window to prevent an outburst of giggles from his sister.

"Well, I think you might have let me know," Ellen resumed with almost her usual poise. "It's rather mortifying not to know what's going on in your own family when the neighbors ask. Here was I without any knowledge of the arrival of my own niece and nephew! Had to be told by Mrs. Perkins."

Then Allison and Leslie did laugh, but they veiled their mirth by talking about the two white chickens out in the yard which were contending for a worm. Suddenly Leslie exclaimed:

"O Allison! I hear the children coming down-stairs, and I forgot their presents! Run out to the car, and bring me that box."

Allison was off at once, and the entrance of the soapy and embarrassed children created a further diversion.

For a few minutes even Ellen Robinson was absorbed in the presents. There was a camera for Junior, a gold chain and locket for Elaine, and a beautiful doll for

Dorothy, and a small train of cars that would wind up and run on a miniature track for Bertie; so of course everything had to be looked at and tried. Elaine put on her chain and preened herself before the glass; Junior had to understand at once just how to take a picture; everybody had to watch the doll open and shut its eyes, and to try to unbutton and button its coat and dress; and then the railroad track had to be set up and the train started off on its rounds. Ellen Robinson really looked almost motherly while she watched her happy children; and Julia Cloud relaxed, and let the smile come around her lips once more.

But all things come to an end, and Ellen Robinson was not one to forget her own affairs for long at a time. She sat back from starting the engine on its third round, and fixed her eyes on her sister with that air of commander-general that was so intolerable.

"Well, then, I suppose you won't be over here till next week," she frowned thoughtfully. "I needed you to help with the crab-apple jelly. That makes it inconvenient. But perhaps I can hold off the fruit a little longer; I'll see. You ought to be able to get all your packing done this week, I should think. When do they go?" She nodded toward the niece and nephew quite indifferently as though as though they were deaf.

Julia Cloud's sensitive face flushed with annoyance, but the two pairs of bright eyes that lifted and fixed themselves upon their aunt held nothing but enjoyment of the situation.

"Why, we're not going until Aunt Jewel is ready to go with us, Aunt Ellen," announced Leslie, looking up from the doll she was reclothing. "You know we're all going to college together, Auntie, too!"

Ellen Robinson lifted an indignant chin. She had no sense of humor, and did not enjoy jokes, especially those practised upon herself.

"Going to college! At her age!" she snorted. "Well, I always knew she was childish, but I never expected her to want to go back to kindergarten!"

Leslie rose up straight as a rush, her strong young arms down at her sides, her fingers in their soft suède gloves working restively as if she wanted to rush at her aunt and administer corporal punishment. Her pretty red lips were pursed angrily, and her blue eyes fairly blazed righteous wrath. Julia Cloud caught her breath, and wondered how she was to control this young fury; but before she could say a word Allison stepped in front of her, and spoke coolly.

"That's the reason she's such a good scout, Aunt Ellen. That's why we want her to come and take care of us. Because she knows how to stay young."

He suddenly seemed to have grown very tall and quite mature as he spoke, and there was something about his manly bearing that held Ellen Robinson's tongue in check as he looked at his watch with a polite "Excuse me," and then turned to Julia Cloud. "Aunt Jewel, if we are to meet my guardian on that train, I think we shall have at hurry. It's quite a run into the city, you know." Julia Cloud arose with a breath of relief.

"The city!" gasped Ellen. "You're not going into the city this late in the afternoon, I hope! Do you know how long it takes?"

Allison glanced out to his high-powered machine confidently.

"We made it in an hour and a half coming over. I guess we shall have plenty of time to meet the five o'clock train if we go at once. I've got a peach of a car, Aunt Ellen. I'll have to come round and take you and the kids for a ride to-morrow or the next day if Aunt Jewel can spare me."

"Thank you! I have a car of my own!" snapped his aunt disagreeably.

"Oh! I beg your pardon! Well, Aunt Jewel, we really must go if we are to meet Mr. Luddington. Good-by, Aunt Ellen! Good-by, cousins! We'll see you again before we leave town, of course. Come on, Aunt Jewel!" And he took Julia Cloud lightly, protectingly by the elbow, and steered her out of the room, down the steps, and into the car, while Leslie danced gayly after, chattering away about how nice it was to get back East and meet real relatives.

But Ellen Robinson was not listening to Leslie. She hurried after her departing guests regardless of a noisy struggle that was going on between her two youngest over the railway train, and stood on her front steps, fairly snorting with indignation.

"Julia Cloud, what does all this mean? You shan't go away until you explain. Have you taken leave of your senses? What is this nonsense about going to college?"

Allison with his hand on the starter gave his aunt a swift, reassuring smile; and Julia Cloud from the safe vantage of the back seat leaned forward, smiling.

"Why, it's the children that are going to college, Ellen, not I. I'm only going along to keep house and play mother for them. Isn't it lovely? I'll tell you all about it to-morrow when you come down to pick out your things. Be sure to come early, because I want to get started packing the first thing in the morning. Mr. Luddington, the children's guardian, is coming to-night to complete the arrangements, and we expect to get away just as soon as I can get packed up. So come early."

The engine purred softly for a rhythmical second, and the car slid quickly away from the door.

"But—the very idea!" snorted Aunt Ellen. "Julia Cloud!" she fairly shouted. "Stop! You had no right in the world to go ahead and make plans without consulting me!"

But the car was beyond ear-shot now, and Leslie was waving a pretty, tantalizing hand from the back seat.

"The very idea!" Ellen Robinson gasped to the autumn landscape as she stood alone and watched the car, a mere speck down the road, on its way to town. "The idea!" And then as if for self-justification: "Poor mother! What would she think if she could know? Well, I wash my hands of her."

But Ellen Robinson did not wash her hands of her sister. Instead, she found that it was going to be very hard indeed to wash her hands of her own affairs without her sister's help. She had, in fact, been counting on that help for the last several years, after her mother became an invalid and she knew that it was only a matter of time before Julia's hands would be set free for other labor. It was quite too disconcerting now, after having got along all these years on the strength of the help that was to come, to find her capable sister snatched away from her by two young things in this ridiculous way.

They talked it over at supper, and Herbert was almost savage about it, as if in some way his wife had misrepresented the possibilities, and led him to expect the assistance that would come from her sister and save him from paying wages to a servant.

"Well, she'll be good and sick of it inside of three months, mark my words; and then she'll come whining back and want us to take her in—be glad enough to get a home. So don't you worry. But what I want understood is this: *She's not going to find it so easy to get back.* See? You make her thoroughly understand that. You better go down tomorrow and pick out everything you want. Take plenty. You can't tell but something may happen to the house, and the furniture burn up. We might as well have it as anybody. And you make it good and sure that she understands right here and now that if she goes she doesn't come back. Of course, I'm not saying she can't come back if she comes to her senses, and is real humble; but you needn't let her know that. Just give her to understand it is her last chance, that I can't be monkeyed with this way. I've offered her a very generous thing, and she knows it, and she's a fool, that's what she is, a *fool* I say!" He brought his big fist down heavily on the table, and jarred the dishes; and the children looked up in premature comprehension, storing up the epithet for future use. "She's no end of a fool, going off with those crazy kids. Some one ought to warn their guardian about her. Why, she has no more idea of how to take care of two high and mighty good-for-nothings like that than an infant in arms!"

Meantime the subject of their discussion was seated serenely at a table in one of the best hotels of the great city, having the time of her life. In the years that were to come there might be many more delightful suppers, even more elegantly served, perhaps; but none would ever rival this first time in her existence when she had sat among the wealthy and great of the land and been treated like one of them.

Mr. Luddington was a typical business man, elderly and kind, with wise eyes and a great smile. He turned his eyes keenly on Julia Cloud for an instant at their first meeting, then let his full smile envelop her, and she was somehow made aware of the fact that he had set his seal of approval to the contract already made by his two enthusiastic wards. All the forebodings she had entertained in the little intervals when Leslie and Allison allowed her to think at all were swept aside by his kind look and big, serious tone when he first took her hand and scanned her true face. "I'm glad they've picked such a woman!" he said. "You'll have your hands full, for they're a pair! But it's worth it!"

And, when they all rode home through the moonlight, Julia Cloud nestled under the soft, thick robes of the car, and listened to the pleasant talk between the young people and their guardian with a sense of peace. If this strong, wise business man thought the arrangement was all right, why, then she need not fear any longer. It was real, and not a dream, and she might rely upon the wisdom of her decision. And with that sense of being upheld by something wiser than her own wish she fell asleep that night, haunted by no dreams of her domineering sister.

6

THE pleasant aromas of coffee and sausages were mingling in the air when "Guardy Lud" woke up and looked about the old-fashioned room with a sense of satisfaction. The very pictures on the walls rested him, they reminded him so much of the rooms in his boyhood home. He had a feeling that old-fashioned things were best, and in spite of the fact that he owned a house most different from this one himself and knew that his wife would not for a minute have tolerated any old-fashioned things about unless they were so old-fashioned that they had become the latest rage, he could not help feeling that a woman brought up amid such simple surroundings would be the very best kind to mother these orphan children who had been left on his helpless hands. He would have loved to take them to his heart and his home; but his wife was not so minded, and that ended it. But it rolled a great burden from his shoulders to feel that he might leave them in such capable hands.

They had a rollicking time at breakfast, for Guardy Lud was delighted with the crisp brown sausages, fried potatoes, and buckwheats with real maple-syrup; and he laughed, and ate, and told stories with the children, and kept the old dining-room walls ringing with joy as they had not resounded within the memory of Julia Cloud. Then suddenly the door opened, and there stood Ellen Robinson, disapproval and hauteur written in every line of her unpleasant face! One could hardly imagine how those two, Julia and Ellen, could possibly be sisters.

Dismay filled Julia Cloud's heart for an instant, and brought a pallor to her cheek. How had she forgotten Ellen? What a fool she had been to tell Ellen to come early in the morning! But she had not realized that Mr. Luddington would be willing to come out to her humble home and stay all night. She had supposed that the arrangements would be made in the city. However, it could not be helped now; and a glance at the kind, strong face of the white-haired man gave her courage. Ellen could not really spoil their plans with him there. He felt that the arrangement was good, and with him to back her she felt she could stand out against any arguments her sister might bring forth.

So she rose with a natural ease, and introduced her. "My sister Mrs. Robinson, Mr. Luddington"; and Ellen stiffly and still disapprovingly acknowledged the introduction.

"I won't interrupt," she said disagreeably. "I'm just going up to look over some of my mother's things." And she turned to the back stairway, and went up, closing the door behind her.

Mr. Luddington gazed after her a second; and then, taking his glasses off and wiping then energetically, he remarked:

"Well, well, bless my soul! It must be getting late! We've had such a good time I didn't realize. Those certainly were good buckwheats, Miss Cloud. I shan't forget them very soon. And now I suppose we'd better get down to business. Could we just go into the other room there, and close the door for a few minutes, not to be interrupted?" and he cast an anxious glance toward the stair-door again.

Julia Cloud smiled understandingly, and ushered them into the little parlor ablaze with fall sunshine, its windows wreathed about with crimsoning woodbine; and, as she caught the flow and glint from the window, she remembered the gray evening when she had looked out across into her future as she supposed it would be. How beautiful and wonderful that the gray had changed to glow! As she sat down to enter into the contract that was to bind her to a new and wonderful life with great responsibilities and large possibilities, her heart, accustomed to look upward, sent a whisper of thanksgiving heavenward.

The details did not take long, after all; for Mr. Luddington was a keen business man, and he had gone over the whole proposition, and had the plan in writing for her to sign, telling just what were her duties and responsibilities with regard to his wards, just how much money she would have for housekeeping and servants and other expenses, and the salary she would receive herself for accepting this care.

"You're practically in a position of mother to them, you know," he said, beaming at her genially; "and I declare I never laid eyes on a woman that I thought could fill the part better!"

Julia Cloud was quite overwhelmed. But the matter of the salary troubled her.

"I think it should not be a matter of money," she demurred. "I would rather do it for love, you know."

"Love's all right!" said the old man, smiling; "but this thing has got to be on a business basis, or the terms of the will will not allow me to agree to it. You see what you are going to undertake means work, and it means sticking to it; and you deserve pay for it, and we're not going to accept several of the best years out of your life for nothing. Besides, you've got to feel free to give up the job if it proves too burdensome for you."

"And you to dismiss me if I do not prove capable for the position," suggested Julia Cloud, lifting meek and honest eyes to meet his gaze.

"Well, well, well, I can see there won't be any need of that!" sputtered the old gentleman pleasantly. "But, however that is, this is the contract I've made out. And I'm quite satisfied. So are the children. Are you willing to sign it? Of course there's a clause in there about reasonable notice if there is dissatisfaction on either side; that lets you out at any time you get tired of it. Only give me a chance to look after these youngsters properly."

Julia Cloud took the pen eagerly, tremblingly, a sense of wonder in her pounding heart, and signed her name just as Ellen's heavy footsteps could be heard pounding down the back stairs. Leslie seized Julia, and gave her a great hug as the last letter was finished, and then threw open the parlor door in the nick of time to save her Aunt Ellen from seeming to be deserted.

Ellen Robinson appeared on the scene just in time to witness the hearty handshake that Guardy Lud gave Julia Cloud as he picked up the papers and went upstairs for his suitcase while Allison went after the car to take him to the train.

"Is that man married? Because, if he isn't, I don't think it's respectable for you to go and live near him!" declared Ellen in a penetrating voice to the intense distress of Julia Cloud, who was happily hurrying the dishes from the breakfast table.

But Leslie came to the rescue.

"Oh, indeed, Aunt Ellen, he's very much married! Altogether too much married for comfort. He would be a dear if it wasn't for his silly little old bossy wife! But he doesn't intend to live anywhere near us. His home is off in California, and he's going back next week. He's only waiting to see us settled somewhere before he goes back; so you needn't worry about Aunt Jewel's morals. We'll take good care of her. But isn't he a dear? He was my Grandfather Leslie's best friend."

Leslie chattered on gayly till the visitor's footsteps could be heard coming down-stairs again, and Ellen Robinson could only shut her lips tight and go into the kitchen, from which her sister beat immediately a hasty retreat lest more unpleasant remarks should be forthcoming.

Julia Cloud bade Mr. Luddington good-by, standing on her own front steps, and then waited a moment, looking off toward the hills which had shut in her vision all her life. The two young people had rushed down to the car, and were pulling their guardian joyously inside. They seemed to do everything joyously, like two young creatures let out of prison into the sunshine. Julia Cloud smiled at the thought of them, but her soul was not watching them just then. She was looking off to the hills that had been her strength all the years through so many trials, and gathering strength now to go in and meet her sister in final combat. She knew that there would be a scene; that was inevitable. That she might maintain her calmness and say nothing unkind or regrettable she was praying earnestly now as her eyes sought the hills.

Across the road behind her parlor curtains Mrs. Perkins was keeping lookout, and remarking to a neighbor who had run in:

"Yes, I thought as much. There's always a man in the case when a woman acts queer! Now, doesn't that beat all? Do you suppose he's a long-lost lover or something, come back now he knows she's free? Seems to me I did hear there was somebody died or something before we came here to live, but she must have been awful young."

The car moved noisily away, and the old gentleman leaned out with a courteous lift of his hat toward Julia Cloud. She acknowledged it with a bow and a smile which Mrs. Perkins pounced on and analyzed audibly.

"Well, there's no fool like an old fool, as the saying is! Just watch her smirk! I'm mighty glad Ellen Robinson's there to relieve me of the responsibility. She'll be over after a while, and then we'll know who he is. There goes Julia in. She watched him out o' sight! Well, I wonder what her mother would think."

Julia Cloud went slowly back to the dining-room, where Ellen was seated on the couch, waiting like a visitor. Julia's smile was utterly lost on her glum countenance, which resembled an embattled tower under siege.

"Well!" she said as Julia began to gather up more dishes from the breakfast table. "I suppose you think you've done something smart now, don't you, getting that old snob here and fixing things all up without consulting any of your relatives?"

"Really, Ellen, this has all been so sudden that I had no opportunity," said Julia gently. "But it did not seem likely that you would object, for you suggested yourself that I rent the house, and you said you did not want me to stay here alone. This seemed quite providential."

"Providential!" sniffed Ellen. "Providential to take you away from your own home and your own people, and send you out into a world where nobody really cares for you, and where all they want of you is to make a drudge of you! You call that providential, do you? Well, *I don't!* And when I object, and try to save you from yourself, and offer you a good home where you will be cared for all the rest of your days, right among your own, where mother would have wanted to see you, you will probably get high-headed, and say I am interfering with your rights. But I can't help it. I've got to speak. I can't see you put the halter around your neck to hang yourself without doing everything I can to stop it. My own sister!"

"Why, Ellen, dear!" said Julia Cloud eagerly, sitting down beside her sister. "You don't understand. It isn't in the least that way. I'm sorry I had to spring it on you so suddenly and give you such a wrong impression. You know I couldn't think of coming to live on you and Herbert. It was kind of you to suggest it, and I am grateful and all that; but I know how it would be to have some one else, even a sister, come into the home, and I couldn't think of it. I have always resolved that I would never be dependent on my relatives while I had my health."

Ellen sat up bristling.

"And yet you are willing to go away to some strange place where nobody knows you, and slave for a couple of little snobs!"

"O Ellen!" said Julia pleadingly. "You don't understand. I am not going to slave. I'm just going to be a sort of mother to them. And you oughtn't to call them snobs. They are your own brother's children."

"Own brother's children, nothing!" sneered Ellen. "He's been away so many years he was just like a stranger when he came back the last time, and as for the children they are just like his stuck-up wife and her family. Yet you'll leave the children that were born and raised close beside you, and go and slave for them. Mother! Fiddlesticks! You'll slave all right. I know you. In six weeks you'll be a drudge for them the way you've been all your life! I know how it is, and you may not believe it; but I have feelings for my sister, and I don't like to see her put upon."

Ellen fumbled for her handkerchief, and managed a comely tear or two that quite touched Julia's heart. Affection between them even when Ellen was a child had been quite one-sided; for Ellen had always been a self-ish, spoiled little thing, and Julia had looked in vain for any signs of tenderness. Now her heart warmed toward her younger sister in this long-delayed thoughtfulness, and her tone grew gentler.

"That's dear of you, Ellen, and I appreciate it; but I haven't been able to make you understand yet, I see. I'm not to be a worker nor even a housekeeper. I'm to be just a sort of mother, or aunt, if you please, to see that the house runs all right, to be with the children and have a happy time with them and their young friends, and to see that they are cared for in every way necessary; just a housemother, you understand. I am to have servants to do the work, although I'm sure one servant will be all that I shall want in a little household like that. But Mr. Luddington quite insisted there should be servants, and that no work of any sort should fall upon me. He said that as their nearest relative I was to be in the position of mother and guardian to them, and to preside over their home."

"That's ridiculous!" put in Ellen. "Why don't they go to college and board like any other reasonable young folks if they must go to college at all? I think it's all non-sense for 'em to go. What do they do it for? They've got money, and don't have to teach or anything. What do they need of learning? They've got enough now to get along. That girl thinks she's too smart to live. I call her impudent, for my part!"

"They want a home," said Julia, waiving the subject of higher education; "and they have chosen me, and I mean to do my best."

There was a quiet finality in her tone that impressed her sister. She looked at her angrily.

"Well, if you will, you will, I suppose. Nobody can stop you. But I see just what will come of it. You'll fool away a little while there, and find out how mistaken you were; and then you'll come back to Herbert to be taken care of. And you don't realize how offended Herbert is going to be by your actions, and how he'll feel about letting you come back after you have gone away in such high feather. You haven't anything to speak of to support yourself, of course, and how on earth do you expect to live anyway after these children get through their college and get married or something? They won't want you then."

Julia arose and went to the window to get calmed. She was more angry than she had been for years. The thought of Herbert's having to take care of her ever was intolerable. But she was able to hold her tongue until she could get her eyes on those hills out of the window. "I will lift up mine eyes unto the hills, from whence cometh my help." That had been the verse which she had read from her little Bible before leaving her room in the early morning and she was grappling it close to her heart, for she had known it would be a hard day.

Ellen was watching her silently. Almost she thought she had made an impression. Perhaps this was the time to repeat Herbert's threat.

"Herbert feels," she began, "that if you refuse his offer now he can't promise to keep it open. He can't be responsible for you if you take this step. He said he wanted you to understand thoroughly."

Julia Cloud turned and walked with swift step to the little parlor where lay the paper she and Mr. Luddington had just signed, and a copy of which he had taken with him. She returned to her astonished sister with the paper in her hand.

"Perhaps it would be just as well for you to read this," she said with dignity, and put the paper into Ellen's hands, going back to her clearing of the table.

There was silence in the dining-room while Ellen read, Julia moving on quiet feet about the table, putting things to rights. She had finished her part of the argument. She was resolutely putting out of her mind the things her sister had just said, and refusing altogether to think of Herbert. She knew in her heart just how Herbert had looked when he had said those things, even to the snarl at the corner of his nose. She knew, too, that Ellen had probably not reported the message even so disagreeably as the original, and she knew that it would be better to forget.

"Well," said Ellen, rising after a long perusal, laying the paper on the table, "that sounds all very well in writing. The thing is to see how it comes out. The proof of the pudding is in the eating, and you needn't tell me that any man in his senses will pay all that salary merely for a 'chaperon,' as he calls it. If he does, he's a fool; that's all I've got to say. But I suppose nothing short of getting caught in a trap will make you see it; so I better save my breath. I'm sure I hope you won't go to the poor-house through your stubbornness. I've done all I could to keep you from it, and it's pretty hard to have my only sister leave me—so soo-oo-on after mother's—death."

"Well, Ellen," said Julia Cloud, looking at her speculatively, "I'm sure I never dreamed you cared about having me away from here. You've never shown much interest in being with me. But I'm sorry if you feel it that way, and I'm sure I'll write to you and try to do little things for the children often, now that I shall have something to do with." But her kindly feeling was cut short by Ellen interrupting her.

"Oh, you needn't trouble yourself! We can look after the children ourselves. You better save what you get to look after yourself when those two get over this whim!"

And then to her great relief Julia Cloud heard the car returning from the station, and the two young people rushing into the hall.

7

"I'M going up-stairs to put on that calico wrapper you loaned me, Aunt Jewel," shouted Leslie, putting a rosy face into the dining-room for an instant and then vanishing.

"I bought a pair of overalls at the store, as you suggested, Cloudy," put in Allison, waving a pair of blue jeans at her and vanishing also.

Ellen Robinson stood mopping her eyes and staring out from the dining-room window—not at the hills—and sniffing.

"I should think you'd stop them calling you that ridiculous name!" she snorted. "It isn't respectful. It sounds like making fun of the family."

Poor Ellen Robinson! She had her good points, but a sense of humor wasn't one of them. Also it went against the grain to give up her own way, and she couldn't remember when she hadn't planned for the freedom she would have when Julia came to live with her. Having an entirely different temperament from Julia's and no spiritual outlook whatever on life, she was unable to understand what thraldom she had been preparing and planning for her patient elder sister. A little of this perhaps penetrated to Julia Cloud's disturbed consciousness as she watched her sister's irate back; for, when she spoke again, it was in a gentle, soothing tone.

"There now, Ellen, let's forget it all, and just put it away. I shall be coming back to see you now and then, perhaps, and you can come and see me. That'll be something new to look forward to. Suppose now we just get to work and see what's to be done. Have you decided what you want to have taken over to the house?"

It is doubtful whether Ellen would have succumbed so easily, had not the two young people returned just then and demanded that they have something to do.

As quietly as if she were used to packing and moving every year of her life, Julia Cloud gave them each a pile of newspapers, and set them to wrapping and packing dishes in a big barrel; and Ellen was forced to join in and say what she wanted to have of her mother's things.

Without a word Julia set aside anything Ellen asked for, even when it was something she would have liked to keep herself; and Ellen, her lips pursed and her eyes bright with defeat, went from room to room, picking and choosing as if she were at an auction.

Allison still in overalls rushed out in the car, and got a man with a moving-wagon; and before twelve o'clock Ellen Robinson saw a goodly load of house-hold furniture start for her own home; and, being somewhat anxious as to how it would be disposed on its arrival, she took the car, and sped away to placate Herbert. She really felt quite triumphant at the ease with which she secured several valuable pieces of mahogany which she knew had always been favorites with Julia.

"Gee!" said Allison as the car vanished out of sight, "isn't Aunt Ellen some depressor? Was she always so awfully grown up? I say, Cloudy, you won't get that way, will you when we get you off in our house? If you do, take poison, or get married, or something. Say, Cloudy Jewel, you're twenty years younger than she is, do you know it? Now what'll I do next? That closet is all empty. Shall I begin on this one? You want this barrel up in the attic, you say? All right; here goes! No, I won't hurt my back; I'm strong as a horse. I know how to lift things without hurting myself. Open that door, Leslie, and move that chair out of my way. Which corner shall I stow it, Cloudy? Southwest? All right!" and he vanished up the stairs with his barrel.

At half-past twelve a man and a woman arrived whom Julia Cloud had hired to help; and the house was like a busy hive, not a drone among them. It really was wonderful how short a time it took to dismantle a home that had been running for years. But the hands were wonderfully eager that took hold of the work, and they went at things with a will. Moreover, Julia Cloud's domain was always in perfect order, which made a big difference.

They ate their lunch from the pantry shelf, because Ellen had taken the dining-room table. But it was a good lunch, bread and butter, apple butter, cookies, half a custard pie, and glasses of rich, foamy milk. Then they went to work again. The children were smudged with dust and tumbled and happy. They were doing real things for the first time in their lives, and they liked it. Moreover, they were bringing to pass a beloved plan that had seemed at first impossible; and they wanted to hustle it through before anything spoiled or delayed it. There was Aunt Ellen. There was no telling what she might not do to hinder, and Julia Cloud was easily troubled by her sister, they could see that, wise children that they were; so they worked with all their might and main.

Two more men were requisitioned, and the furniture began a steady march up to the attic, where it was to be stored.

Leslie developed a talent for finding the place where she was most needed and getting to work. She put the sideboard drawers in order, and then went to packing away garments from the closets in drawers and trunks and chests, until by four o'clock a great many little nooks and corners in the house were absolutely clear and empty, ready for the cleaning before the new tenants arrived, although, to tell the truth, there was scarcely a spot in Julia Cloud's house that needed much cleaning, because it had always been kept immaculate.

When Ellen Robinson in her car arrived in sight of the house at half-past four she identified the parlor and dining-room carpets hanging on a line strung across the back yard, and two bedroom carpets being beaten in the side yard. Mrs. Perkins from her patient watch-tower had also identified them, and hurried out to greet her friend and get more accurate information; but Ellen was in too much of a hurry to get inside and secure several other articles, which she had thought of and desired to have, to spend much time in gossip. Besides, if Julia was really going, it was just as well to make as much of it as possible, so she greeted Mrs. Perkins as one too busy with important affairs to tell details, and hurried into the house. Standing within the old hallway, she gazed about, startled. How on earth had Julia managed to tear up things in such a hurry? The pictures had all vanished from the walls. The books were gone from the old bookcase; the furniture itself was being carried away, the marble-topped table being the last piece left. The woman was washing the parlor floor, slopping on the soapy water with that air of finality that made Ellen Robinson realize that the old home was broken up at last. Grimly she walked into the dining-room, and saw immaculate empty closets and cleanly shining window-panes. As far as the work had progressed it had been done thoroughly.

Up-stairs a cheery chatter came from the rooms, and Ellen Robinson experienced a pang of real jealousy of these two young things who had swept in and carried her neglected sister by storm. Somehow it seemed to her that they had taken something that belonged to her, and she began to feel bereft. Julia ought to love her better than these two young strangers; why didn't she? Why didn't those two children make such a fuss over her as they did over Julia? It certainly was strange! Perhaps some gleam of perception that it might all be her own fault began to filter to Ellen Robinson's consciousness as she stood there on the stairs and listened to the pleasant chatter.

"O Cloudy, dear! Is this really Daddy's picture when he was a little boy? What a funny collar and necktie! But wasn't he a darling? I love the way his hair curls around his face. I can remember Daddy quite well. Mother used to say he was a wonderful man. I think he must have been a good deal like you. Our old nurse used to say that families went in streaks. I guess you and Daddy were off the same streak, weren't you? I hope Allison and I will be too. Say, Cloudy, can't I have this picture of Daddy to hang in my room in our new house? I love it."

Ellen Robinson wondered whether they had classified her as another "streak," and somehow the thought was unpleasant. It was like one of those little rare mirrors that flash us a look now and then in which we "see ourselve's as others see us," and are warned to take account of stock. As she climbed the old stairs, Ellen Robinson took account of herself, as it were, and resolved to show a better side to these children than she had shown heretofore; and so, when she appeared among them, she put aside her grim aspect for a while, and spoke in quite an affable tone:

"Well, you certainly can work!"

The contrast was so great that both the young people blinked at her in wonder, and a smile broke out on Leslie's lovely face. Somehow it warmed Aunt Ellen's heart, and she went on:

"But you all must be tired. You better come up to our house for supper to-night. You won't have any chance to get it here."

"Oh, we don't mind picnicking," said Leslie hastily. Then she caught a glimpse of her aunt's face, and her natural kindliness came to the front. "But of course that would be lovely if it won't be too much trouble for you," she added pleasantly with one of her brilliant smiles, although she could see Allison making violent motions and shaking his head at her from the other room, where he was out of his Aunt Ellen's sight. Leslie really had a lovely nature, and was always quick to discern it when she had hurt any one. Ellen Robinson looked at her suspiciously, alert for the insult always, but yielded suddenly and unexpectedly to the girl's loveliness. Was it something in Leslie's eyes that reminded Ellen of her big brother who used to come home now and then, and tease her, and bring her lovely gifts? She watched Leslie a moment wistfully, and then with a sigh turned away. She wished one of her little girls could look like that.

"Well, I'd better go right home and get supper ready," she said alertly; and there was a note of almost pleased eagerness in her voice that she was included in this function of packing and moving that seemed somehow to have turned into a delightful game in which weariness and care were forgotten.

"I'll have supper ready to dish up by seven o'clock," she admonished her astonished sister as she swept past the bedroom where she was at work putting away blankets and pillows in camphor. "You won't be ready much before that; but don't you be a minute later, or the supper will be spoiled."

By which admonition Julia Cloud became aware that Ellen was going to favor them with some of her famous chicken potpie. She stood still for a whole minute with a light in her eyes and a smile on her face, listening to Ellen's retreating footsteps down the stairs; then, as the Ford set up its churning clatter, she turned back to her task, and murmured softly, "Poor Ellen!"

The supper passed off very well. Herbert was a trifle gruff and silent; but it was plain that Allison's stories amused him, for now and then a half-smile crept into his stolid countenance. Julia Cloud was so glad that she could have cried. She hated scenes, and she dreaded being at outs with her relatives. So she ate her chicken potpie and fresh pumpkin pie thankfully, and forgot how weary she was. After supper Leslie sat down at the piano, and rattled off rag-time; and she and Allison sang song after song, while the children stood about admiringly, and even Herbert sat by as at a social function and listened. The atmosphere was really quite clear when at last they prepared to leave, and Julia Cloud had an inkling that the big blue car had something to do with it.

"That's some car you've got," said Herbert patronizingly as he held a lantern for them to get down the steps. "Get it this year? What do you have to pay for that make now? I'm thinking of getting a new one myself pretty soon."

Down upon their knees in the lantern-light went the two men of the party, examining this and that point of interest, their noses turned to the mysterious inner workings of the wonderful mechanism, while Julia Cloud sat and marveled that here at last was something which Herbert Robinson respected.

And Ellen stood upon the steps, really smiling and

saying how nice it had been to have them, for all the world as if they were company, all the hard lines of her rapidly maturing face softened by kindliness! It seemed like a miracle. Julia Cloud settled back into the deep cushions, and lifted her eyes to the dark line of the hills against the sky. "From whence cometh my help," trailed the words through her tired brain; and her heart murmured, "God, I thank Thee!"

8

THEY all slept very late the next morning, being utterly worn out from the unaccustomed work; and, when they finally got down-stairs, they took a sort of a lunch-breakfast off the pantry shelves again. It was strange how good even shredded-wheat biscuit and milk can taste when one has been working hard and has a young appetite, although Leslie and Allison had been known to scorn all cereals. Still, there were cookies and wonderful apples from the big tree in the back yard for dessert.

"When are those men coming back to finish up?" suddenly demanded Leslie, poising a glass of milk and a cooky in one hand and taking a great bite from her apple.

"Not till to-morrow," said Julia Cloud, looking around the empty kitchen speculatively, and wondering how in the world she was going to cook with all the cooking-utensils packed in the attic.

"We ought to have left the kitchen till last," she added with a troubled look. "You crazy children! Didn't you know we had to eat? I told that man not to take any of those things on the kitchen-table, that they were to stay down until the very last thing, and now he has taken the table even! I went up-stairs to see if I could get at things, and I find he has put them away at the back, and piled all the chairs and some bed-springs in front of them. I'm afraid we shall have to get some things out again. I don't see how we can get along."

"Not a bit of it, Cloudy!" said Leslie, giving a spring and perching herself on the drain-board of the sink, where she sat swinging her dainty little pumps as nonchalantly as if she were sitting on a velvet sofa. "See! Here's my plan. I woke up early, and thought it all out. Let's see," consulting her wee wrist-watch, "it's nine o'clock. That isn't bad. Now we'll work till twelve; that's long enough for to-day, because you got too tired yesterday; and, besides, we've got some other things to attend to. Then we'll hustle into the car, and get to town, and do some shopping to get ready for our trip. That will rest you. We'll get lunch at a tea-room, and shop all the afternoon. We'll go to a hotel for dinner, and stay all night. Then in the morning we can get up early, have our breakfast, and drive back here in time before the men come. Now isn't that perfectly spick-and-span for a plan?"

"Leslie! But, dear, that would cost a lot! And, besides, it isn't in the least necessary."

"Cost has nothing to do with it. Look!" and Leslie flourished a handful of bills. "See what Guardy Lud gave me! And Allison has another just like it. He said particularly that we were not to let you get all worked out and get sick so you couldn't go with us, and he particularly told us about a lot of things he wanted us to buy to make things easy on the way. After he leaves us and goes back to California we're in your charge, I know; but just now you're in ours, you dear, unselfish darling; and we're going to run you. Oh, we're going to run you to beat the band!" laughed Leslie, and jumped down from her perch to hug and squeeze the breath out of Julia Cloud.

"But child! Dear!" said that good woman when she could get her breath to speak. "You mustn't begin in that extravagant way!"

But they put their hands over her lips, and laughed away her protests until she had to give up for laughing with them.

"Well, then," she said at last, when they had subsided from a regular rough-house frolic for all the world as if they were children, "we'll have to get to work in good earnest; only it doesn't seem right to let you work so hard when you are visiting me."

"Visiting, nothing!" declared Allison; "we're having the time of our lives. I haven't been in a place where I could do as I pleased since I was eight years old. This is real work, and I like it. Come now, don't let's waste any time. What can I do first? Wouldn't you like to have me take down all the pictures on the second floor, stack them in the attic, and sweep down the walls the way we did down here yesterday?"

"Yes," said their aunt with an affectionate homage in her eyes for this dear, capable boy who was so eager over everything as if it were his own.

"And those big bookcases. What are you going to do with the books? Do you want any of them to go with you, or are they to be packed away?"

"No, I won't take any of those books. They'll need to be dusted and put in boxes. There are a lot of boxes in the cellar, and there's a pile of papers to use for lining the boxes. But you'll have your hands full with the pictures, I think. Let the books go till to-morrow."

Allison went whistling up-stairs, and began taking down the pictures; but anybody could see by the set of his shoulders that he meant to get the books out of the way too before noon.

"Now, what can I do?" said Leslie, whirling around from wiping the last cup and plate they had used. "There's one more bureau besides yours. Does it need emptying out?"

"No, dear. That has your grandmother's things in it, and is in perfect order. She had me fix up the things several months ago. Everything is tied up and labelled. I don't think we need to disturb it. The men can move it up as it is. But we need to get the rest of the bed-clothes out on the line for an airing before I pack them away in the chest up-stairs. You might do that."

So Leslie went back and forth, carrying blankets and quilts, and hanging them on the line, till Mrs. Perkins had to come over to see what was going on. She came with a cup in her hand to ask for some baking-powder and Julia Cloud gave her the whole box.

"No, you needn't return it," she said, smiling. "I shall not need it. I've rented the house, and am going away for a while." Mrs. Perkins was so astonished that she actually went home without finding out where Julia Cloud was going, and had to come back to see whether there was anything she could do to help, in order to get a chance to ask.

It was really quite astonishing what a lot could be done in three hours. When twelve o'clock came, the two children descended upon their aunt with insistence that she wash her hands and put on her hat. The rooms had assumed that cleared-up, ready look that rests the tired worker just to look around and see what has been accomplished. With a conviction that she was being quite a child to run away this way when there was still a lot to be done, but with an overwhelming desire to yield to the pressure, Julia Cloud surrendered.

When she came down-stairs five minutes later in her neat black suit and small black hat with the mourning veil about it that Ellen had insisted upon for the funeral, the car was already at the door, and she felt almost guilty as she locked the door and went down the path. But the beauty of the day intoxicated her at once, and she forgot immediately everything but the joy of riding out into the world.

Leslie was a bit quiet as they glided down the road out of town, and kept eyeing her aunt silently. At last, as Julia Cloud was calling attention to a wonderful red woodbine that had twined itself about an old dead tree and was setting the roadside ablaze with splendor, Leslie caught her eye.

"What is it, dear? Does something trouble you? Is anything wrong with me?" asked Julia Cloud, putting up a prospecting hand to her hair and hat.

Leslie's cheeks went rosy red.

"O Cloudy, dear," said Leslie, "I was just wondering. But I'm afraid to say it. Maybe it will make you feel bad."

"Not a bit, deary; what is it?"

"Well, then, Cloudy, do you think Grandmother would care very much if you didn't wear black? Do you like it yourself, or feel it wouldn't be right not to wear it? I don't mean any disrespect to Grandmother; but oh, you would look so sweet in gray, gray and lavender and soft pink, or just gray now for a while. Are you very mad at me for saying it?"

Julia Cloud reached over and patted the young hand that lay near her on the seat.

"Why, no dear! I'm not mad, and I don't care for black myself. I don't believe in wearing black for the people who have left us and gone to heaven. It seems to me white would be a great deal better. But I put on these things to please Ellen. She thought it would be showing great disrespect to mother if I didn't, and rather than argue about it I did as she wanted me to. But I don't intend to darken the place around me by dressing in mourning, child; and I'm glad you don't want me to. I like bright, happy things. And, besides, Leslie, dear, your grandmother was a bright, happy woman herself once when she was young, before she was sick and had trouble; and I like to remember her that way, because I'm sure that is the way she looks now in heaven."

"Oh, I'm so glad!" sighed Leslie. "That makes the day just perfect."

"I think I'll wait until I get away to change, however," said Julia Cloud thoughtfully. "It would just annoy Ellen to do it now, and might make such people as Mrs. Perkins say disagreeable things that would make it unpleasant for your aunt."

"Of course!" said Leslie, nestling closer, her eyes dancing with some secret plans of her own. "That's all right, Cloudy. How dear and sort of 'understanding' you are, just like a real mother."

And somehow Julia Cloud felt as if she was entering into a new world.

Allison seemed to know by intuition just where to find the right kind of tea-room. He ushered them into the place, and found a table in a secluded nook, with a fountain playing nearby over ferns, and ivy climbing over a mimic pergola. There were not many people eating, for it was past one o'clock. There were little round tables with high-backed chairs that seemed to shut them off in a corner by themselves.

"This is nice!" he sighed. "We're a real family now, aren't we?" and he looked over at Julia Cloud with that fine homage that now and then a boy just entering manhood renders to an older woman.

"Creamed chicken on toast, fruit-salad, toasted muffins, and ice-cream with hot chocolate sauce," ordered

Allison after studying the menu-card for a moment. "You like all those, don't you, Cloudy?"

"Oh, but my dear! You mustn't order all that. A sandwich is all I need. Just a tongue sandwich. You must not begin by being extravagant."

"This is my party, Cloudy. This goes under the head of expenses. If you can't find enough you like among what I order, why, I'll get you a tongue sandwich, too; but you've been feeding us out of the cooky-jar, and I guess I'll get the finest I can find to pay you back. I told you this was my time. When we get settled, you can order things; but now I'm going to see that you get enough to eat while you're working so hard."

Leslie's eyes danced with her dimples as Julia Cloud appealed to her to stop this extravagance.

"That's all right, Cloudy. I heard Guardy Lud tell Al not to spare any expense to make things comfortable for you while you were moving."

So Julia Cloud settled down to the pleasure of a new and delicious combination of foods, and thoroughly enjoyed it all.

"Now," said Leslie as the meal drew to a close, "we must get to work. It's half-past two, and the stores close at half-past five. I've a lot of shopping to do. How about you, Cloudy?"

"I must buy a trunk," said Julia Cloud thoughtfully, "and a hand-bag and some gloves. I ought to get a new warm coat, but that will do later."

Leslie eyed her thoughtfully, and raised one brow intensively at her brother as she rose from the table.

Allison landed them at a big department store, and guided his aunt to the trunk department with instructions to stay there until he and Leslie came back. Then they went off with great glee and many whisperings.

It is a curious thing how easily and quickly young people can shop provided they have plenty of money and no older person by to hamper them. Allison and Leslie were back within the time they had set, looking very meek and satisfied. Leslie carried a small package, which she laid in Julia Cloud's lap.

"You said you needed a hand-bag," she said; "and I came on a place where they were having a sale. I thought this was a peach; so I bought it. If you don't like it, we can give it to Aunt Ellen or some one."

Julia Cloud's cheeks grew pink with pleasure, and she felt like a very young, happy child as she opened the parcel to find a lovely gray suède handbag with silver clasp and fittings, containing quite a little outfit of toilet articles and brushes in neat, compact form. She caught her breath with delight as she touched the soft white leather lining, and noticed the perfection and finish of the whole. It seemed fit for a queen, yet was plain and quiet enough on the outside for a dove to carry. She looked up to see the two pairs of eager eyes upon her, and could hardly refrain from throwing her arms about the children right there in the store; but she stopped in time and let her eyes do the caressing, as she said with a tremble in her low, sweet voice:

"O you dear children! How you are going to spoil me! I see I must get settled quickly so that I shall have the power to restrain you."

They rollicked forth then, and bought several things, a big steamer rug for the car, a pair of long gray mocha gloves to match the handbag, a silk umbrella, and for Aunt Ellen a shiny black hand-bag with a number of conveniences in it, and a pair of new black gloves with long, warm wrists tucked inside of it. Then Allison thoughtfully suggested a handsome leather wallet for Uncle Herbert, and Julia Cloud lingered by the handkerchief-counter, and selected half a dozen new fine handkerchiefs. It all seemed just like a play to her, it was so very long since she had been shopping herself. Ellen had bought everything for her for years, because she was always too busy or too burdened to get away.

When they were out in the street again, it was still too early to think of going to the hotel for dinner.

"How about a movie, Cloudy?" asked Allison shyly. "There's a pippin down the street a ways. I saw it as we came by. Or don't you like movies? Perhaps you'd rather go to the hotel and lie down. I suppose you are maybe worn out. I ought to have thought of that."

"Not a bit of it!" said the game little woman. "I should love to go. Maybe you won't believe it, but I never went to a movie in my life, and I've been wanting to know what they were like for a long time."

"Never went to a movie in your life! Why, Cloudy, you poor dear!" said Allison, who had been fairly fed on movies. "Why, how did it happen? Don't they have moving pictures in your town?"

"Yes, they have them now, though only a year or so ago. But you know I've never been able to get away, even if they had been all about me. Besides, I suppose I should have been considered crazy if I had gone, me, an oldish woman! If there had been children to take, it would have been different. I suppose it is a childish desire, but I always loved pictures."

"Well, we're going," said Allison. "Get in quick, and I'll have you there before you say Jack Robinson!"

And so in the restful cool of a flower-laden atmosphere, on one of the finest moving-picture places in the city, Julia Cloud sat with her two children and saw her first moving picture, holding her breath in wonder and delight as the people on the screen lived and moved before her.

"I'm afraid I'm having too good a time," she said quietly as she settled back in the car again, and was whirled away to the hotel. "I feel as if I were a child again. If this keeps on, I won't have dignity enough left to chaperon you properly."

"Oh, but Cloudy, dear, that's just why we want you, because you know how to be young and play with us," clamored both of them together.

Then after a good dinner they went up to their rooms, and there was Julia Cloud's shining new trunk that had to be looked over; and there on the floor beside it stood two packages, big boxes, both of them.

"This must be a mistake," said Julia Cloud, looking at them curiously. "Allison, you better call the boy and have him take them away to the right room."

Allison picked up the top package, a big, square box.

"Why, this is your name, Cloudy Jewel!" he exclaimed. "It must be yours. Open it!"

"But how could it be?" said Julia Cloud perplexedly.

"Open it, Cloudy. I want to see what's in it."

Julia Cloud was bending over the long pasteboard box on the floor and finding her name on that, too.

"It's very strange," she said, her cheeks beginning to grow pink like those of a child on her first Christmas morning. "I suppose it's some more of your extravagant capers. I don't know what I shall do with you!"

But her eager fingers untied the string, while Leslie and Allison executed little silent dances around the room and tried to stifle their mirth.

The cover fell off at last, and the tissue-paper blew up in a great fluff; and out of it rolled a beautiful long, soft, thick gray cloak of finest texture and silken lining, with a great puffy collar and cuffs of deep, soft silver-gray fox.

"Oh-h!" was all Julia Cloud could say as the wonderful garment slipped out and spread about over the box and floor. And then the two children caught it up, and enveloped her in it, buttoning it down the front and turning the collar around her ears.

"It's yours, Cloudy, to keep you warm on the journey!" cried Leslie, dancing around and clapping her hands. "Doesn't she look lovely in it, Allison? Oh, isn't she dear?" and Leslie caught her and whirled her around the room.

Then Allison brought the big square box, and demanded that it be opened; and out of it came a small gray hat in soft silky beaver, with a close gray feather curled quietly about it, that settled down on Julia Cloud's lovely white hair as if it had been made for her.

"You don't mind, do you, Cloudy, dear? You don't think I'm officious or impertinent?" begged Leslie anxiously. "It was Allison's idea to get the hat to match the coat, and it was such a dear we couldn't help taking it; but, if there is anything about them you don't like, we got special permission for you to exchange them tomorrow morning."

"Like them!"

Julia Cloud settled down in a chair, and looked at herself in helpless joy and admiration. Like them!

"But O children! You oughtn't to have got such wonderful, expensive things for me. I'm just a plain, simple woman, you know, and it's not fitting."

Then there arose a great clamor about her. Why was it not fitting? She who had given her life for others, why should she not have some of the beautiful, comfortable things of earth? It wasn't sensible for her to talk that way. That was being too humble. And, besides, weren't these things quite sensible and practical? Weren't they warm, and wouldn't they be convenient and comfortable and neat? Well, then, "Good-night," finished Allison.

And so at last they said, "Good-night," and went to their beds; but long after the children were asleep Julia Cloud lay awake and thought it out. God had been good to her, and was leading her into green pastures beside quiet waters; but there were things He was expecting of her, and was she going to be able to fulfil them? These two young souls were hers to guide. Would she have the grace to guide them into the knowledge of God in Christ? And then she lay praying for strength for this great work until the peace of God's sleep dropped down upon her.

9

THE next two days were busy ones. There were a
great many last little things to be done, and Julia Cloud
would have worked herself out, had not the children in-
terfered and carried her off for a ride every little while.
The intervening Sabbath was spent at Ellen Robinson's.
The handsome handbag and wallet served to keep Ellen
from being very disagreeable. In fact, at the last, when
she began to realize that Julia was really going away, and
would not be down at the old house any more for her
to burden and torment, she really revealed a gleam of
affection for her, and quite worried poor Julia with
thinking that perhaps, after all, she ought not to go
away so far from her only sister. When Ellen sat down
on the bare stairs in the old hall Monday morning, and
gave vent to a real sob at parting, Julia had a swift vision
of her little sister years ago sitting on that same stair
weeping from a fall, and herself comforting her; and she
put her arms around Ellen, and kissed her for the first
time in many reticent years.

But at last they were off, having handed over the keys
to the new tenant, and Julia Cloud leaned back on the

luxurious cushions and laughed. Not from mirth, for there were tears in her eyes; and not from nervousness, for she was never subject to hysteria; but just from sheer excitement and joy to think that she was really going out in the world at last to see things and live a life of her own.

The two young people felt it, and laughed with her, until the blackbirds, swirling in a rustling chorus overhead on their way south, seemed to be joining in, and a little squirrel whisked across the road and sat up inquiringly on a log framed in scarlet leaves.

They went straight to the city, for Mr. Luddington had promised to meet them there and confer with them further about their plans. But, when they reached the hotel, they found only a telegram from him saying that business had held him longer than he expected and that he should have to arrange to meet them farther along in their journey. He suggested three colleges, either one of which he should favor, and outlined their journey to take in a stop at each. He promised to communicate with them later, and gave his own address in case they decided to remain at either the first or the second place visited.

"Now," said Julia Cloud after the telegram was disposed of, "I want to get a new dress and a few things before we go any farther. I know you children don't like these old black things, and we might as well start out right. It won't take me long, and I shall be ready to go on my way right after lunch."

Leslie was delighted, and the two spent two hours of happiness in shopping, while Allison drove to a garage to have his car looked over thoroughly, and laid in a supply of good things for the journey. He also spent a profitable half-hour studying a road-map and asking questions concerning the journey.

They tried to make Julia Cloud take a nap before they

started, but she declared she would rather rest in the car; and so they started off, feeling like three children going to find the end of the rainbow.

It was a wonderful afternoon. The air was like wine, and the autumn foliage was in all its glory. As they flew along, it seemed as if they were leaving all care behind. A soft pink color grew in Julia Cloud's cheeks, and she sat with her hands folded and her eyes bright with the beauty of the day.

"Oh, but you're a beauty, Cloudy, dear!" exclaimed Leslie suddenly. "See her, Allison! Just look at her. Isn't she great? She was all right in those black things, of course, but she's wonderful in the gray things!"

For Julia Cloud had laid aside in the very bottom of her new trunk the prim black serge that Ellen had bought, and the black funeral goves and coat and hat; and she was wearing a lovely soft gray wool jersey dress with white collar and cuffs. The big gray coat was nestled by her side ready for use when the wind grew colder, and she was wearing the new gray hat and gloves, and looked a lady every inch. Allison turned slowly, and gave her a look that made her blush like a girl.

"I should say she *is* great! She's a peach!" he agreed. "That hat is a crackerjack! It looks like a pigeon's wing. I like it; don't you, Cloudy? But say, Leslie, she's something more than a beauty. She's a good scout. That's what she is. Do you realize she hasn't opened her lips about the car once? 'Member the time I took Mrs. Luddington down to the office for Guardy, how she squeaked every time another car went by, and cautioned me to be careful and go slow, and asked me how many times I had ever driven before, and if I wasn't exceeding the speed-limit, and no end of things? But Cloudy hasn't batted an eye. She just sits there as if she was riding a cloud and enjoyed it."

"Well, I do," said Julia Cloud, laughing; "and I never

thought of being afraid. I didn't know enough to. Ought I to? Because I'm having such a good time that I'm afraid I'd forget to be frightened."

"That's what I said. You're a good sport. I believe you like to go fast."

Julia Cloud admitted shamedly that she did.

"He's a splendid driver, and so am I," Leslie explained earnestly. "Guardy had us taught ages ago, and we've driven a lot; only of course we didn't have our own car. We just had the regular car that belongs to the house. But we made that work some. And Allison took a full course in cars. He knows how to repair them, and put them together, and everything."

"Shall I let her go, Cloudy?" asked Allison eagerly. "Will you be afraid?"

"I should love it," said Julia Cloud eagerly, and then with a sober look at the boy: "Don't do anything crazy, dear! Don't do anything that you oughtn't to do."

"Of course not!" said Allison gravely, sitting up with a manly look in his handsome young face. And by the look he gave her she knew that she had put him upon his honor, and she knew that he would take no risks now that she had trusted him. If she had been a squealing, hectoring kind of woman, he might have been challenged into taking risks, but not here, when she trusted him and the responsibility was all his.

Julia Cloud, as she drew a long breath and prepared to enjoy the flight down the white ribbon of road, up a hill and down another, registered the thought that here was a clew to the boy's character. Trust him, and he would be faithful. Distrust him, and you wouldn't be anywhere. It did not come to her in words that way, but rather as a subconscious fact that was incorporated into her soul, and gave her a solid and sure feeling about her boy. She had seen all that in his eyes.

He turned around presently, and told her how fast

they had been going; and her eyes were shining as brightly as Leslie's.

"You're a pretty good pard, Cloudy," he said. "We'll make you a member of the gang and take you everywhere. See! You're being initiated now, and you're making good right along. I knew we did a good thing when we came after you. Didn't we, Les?"

And Leslie turned and flung herself into Julia Cloud's arms with one of her enthusiastic hugs.

It was just evening when they entered the little town about twenty miles from a larger city, where was located a seat of learning, co-educational, which had been highly recommended to Mr. Luddington, and which seemed to him to have a great many good points in its favor.

The sign-posts warned them of their approach; and the three sat silently watching, judging the place from the outskirts. Big square houses and lawns multiplied as they progressed. Some streets had fences. Substantial churches rose here and there, and the college grounds became visible as they neared the centre of the town. The buildings were spacious and attractive, with tall old elms and maples shading the broad walks. There was an ideal chapel of dark-red stone with arches and a wonderful belfry, and one could easily imagine young men and maidens fitting here and there.

The two young people studied the scene as the car drove slowly by, and said nothing. Allison went on to the other end of town till the houses grew further apart, and nothing had been said. Then Leslie drew a big sigh.

"Turn around, brother, and let's go back past there again."

Allison turned around, and drove slowly by the college grounds again.

"There are tennis-courts at the back," said Leslie,

"and that looks like a gym over there. Do you suppose that's the athletic field over at the back?"

They drove slowly around the block, and Julia Cloud sat silently, trying to think of herself in this strange environment, and feeling suddenly chilly and alone. There would be a lot of strange people to meet, and the children would be off at college all day. She hadn't thought of that.

"Try some of the side streets," ordered Leslie; "I haven't seen our house yet."

They came to the business part of the town, and found the stopping-place suggested in Mr. Luddington's directions.

"We can't tell much about it tonight," said Allison gravely. "I guess we better get some supper and let Cloudy Jewel get rested for a while. Then to-morrow we can look around."

They were wise words, and Julia Cloud assented at once; but it was quite plain that neither he nor Leslie was much elated at the place.

Allison slipped out for a walk through the college grounds after the others had gone to their rooms, and came back whistling gravely.

"He doesn't like it, Cloudy," whispered Leslie as the sound floated in through the transom. "He won't have anything to do with it. You see!"

"What makes you think so, dear? He's whistling. That sounds as if he liked it."

"Yes, but look what he's whistling. He always begins on 'The Long, Long Trail' if he isn't pleased or has to wait when he's in a hurry to get anywhere. Now, if he had been pleased, you would have heard 'One grasshopper hopped right over th' other grasshopper's back.' I can always tell. Well, I don't care; do you, Cloudy? There's plenty of other colleges, and I didn't see our house in any of the streets we went through, did you?"

Julia Cloud had to confess that she had not been in love with anything she had seen yet.

"Well, then, what's the use of going over the old college? I say let's beat it in the morning."

But Julia Cloud would not hear to that. She said they must be fair even to a college, and Mr. Luddington would want them to look the place over thoroughly while they were there. So after breakfast the two reluctant young people went with Julia Cloud to make investigation.

They went through the classrooms and the chapel and the library and gymnasiums. They visited the science halls and workshops. They even climbed up to the observatory, and took a squint at the big telescope, and then they came down and went with a real-estate dealer to see some houses. But at twelve o'clock they came back to their boarding-house with a sigh of relief, ate a good dinner, and, climbing into their car, shook the dust of the town, as it were, from their feet.

"It may be a very nice town, but it's not the town for me," chanted Leslie, nestling back among the cushions.

"Here, too!" said Allison, letting the car ride out under full power over the smooth country road. But, though Julia Cloud questioned several times, she could get no explanation except Allison's terse "Too provincial," whatever he meant by that. She doubted whether he knew himself. She wondered whether it were that they each felt the same homesick feeling that she had experienced.

They stayed that night at a little country inn, and started on their way again at early morning, for they had a long journey before them to reach the second place that Mr. Luddington had suggested. Late that afternoon they stopped in a small city, and decided to rest until morning; for the children wanted to stretch their limbs, and they felt that their aunt was very weary, though she declared she was only sleepy.

The sun had quite gone down the next evening, and the twilight was beginning to settle over everything as they drove at last into the second college town of their tour, and the church bells were pealing for prayer meeting. Church bells! The thought of them sent a thrill through Julia Cloud's heart. There was somehow a familiar, home-like sound to them that made her think of the prayer meetings that had cheered her heart through many lonely days.

It had really been for many years her one outing to go to prayer meeting. Even after her mother had become bedridden she had always insisted on Julia's going off to prayer meeting, and a neighbor who was lame and sometimes stayed with her would come hobbling in and send her off. The old cracked church bell at home had always sounded sweet to her ears because it meant that this hour was her own quiet time to go away alone and rest. And it had been real heart-rest always, even though sometimes the meetings themselves had been woefully prosy. There had always been the pleasant little chat and the warm handshake afterwards, and then the going home again beneath the stars with a bit of the last hymn in one's soul to sing one to sleep with,

> *Nearer, my God, to Thee,*
> *Nearer to Thee;*
> *E'en though it be a cross*
> *That raiseth me;*

and the burden had grown less, and her heart had grown light with the promise of her Father. Those meetings had been to Julia Cloud very real meetings with her Christ; and now, as the evening bells pealed out, her heart leaped to meet and answer the call.

"Oh! I'd like to go to prayer meeting!" she said impulsively as they passed the lighted church, and saw a few faithful going in at the door.

"Do you mean it?" asked Allison, bringing the car to a stop. "Do you *mean* it, Cloudy? Then let's go. We can size the people up, and see if we like their looks. I guess we can stand a prayer meeting unless you are too tired."

With the eagerness of a child Julia Cloud got out of the car and went into the house of the Lord. It was like a bit of heaven to her. She didn't realize what a bore it might be to her two companions.

It was a good little meeting as such meetings go. Very little enthusiasm, very few present, mostly elders and their wives, with an old saint or two almost at the journey's end, and a dignified white-haired minister, who said some good things in a drony, sleepy tone. The piano was played by a homely young woman who wore unfashionable clothes, and made frightful mistakes in the bass occasionally; but that did not seem to trouble the singers, who sang with the heart rather than with their voices.

Allison sat solemnly, and refrained from looking at his sister; but both stole occasional glances at their aunt, and admired her new clothes and the beautiful light on her face. For Julia Cloud felt as if she were glimpsing into heaven and seeing her Lord in this bit of communion with some of His saints; and, when she bowed her head in the closing prayer, she was thanking Him for all His mercies in bringing this wonderful change into her gray life, and giving her these two dear children to love her and be loved by her. As she rose to come out, her face was glorified by that vision on the mount.

The gentle-faced minister came and spoke to them, and welcomed them to the church, although Allison told him quite curtly that they were only passing through the town; but Julia Cloud trod the neat brown ingrain carpet of the aisle as if it were golden pavement.

"Of all the stupid places!" said Allison as they got into the car. "What do they have prayer meetings for, anyway? Did you manage to keep awake, Cloudy?"

And suddenly like a pall there fell upon Julia Cloud's bright soul the realization that these children did not, would not, feel as she did about such things. They had probably never been taught to love the house of God, and how was she ever to make them see? Perhaps it had been prosy and dull to one who did not hear the Lord's voice behind the Bible words. Perhaps the old minister had been long and tiresome, and the children were weary with the journey and sleepy; she ought not to have let them stop now; and she began to say how sorry she was. But, when they saw from her words that she had really enjoyed that dull little meeting, they were silent.

"Well, Cloudy, I'll hand it to you," said Allison at last. "If you could stand that meeting and enjoy it, you're some Christian! But I'm glad for one that we went if you liked it; and I guess, if you can go a football game now and then, I ought to be able to stand a prayer meeting. So now here goes for seeing the town. It's only nine o'clock, and I believe that's the college up there on the hill where all those lights are. Shall we drive up there?"

The car slipped through the pleasant evening streets, turning a corner, slowing up at a crossing to take a view of the town, and keeping all the time in view the clusters of lights on the hill, which Allison conceived to be the college. Suddenly Leslie leaned forward, and cried:

"O Allison, stop! Stop! There it is, just there on the right. And it's for sale, too! Oh, let's get right out and get the name of the agent, so we won't lose it again."

Allison stopped the car suddenly, and turned to look. There in the full blaze of an electric arc-light, nestled among shrubbery and tall trees, with a smooth terrace in front, was a beautiful little cottage of white stone, with a pink roof, and windows everywhere.

"Why, that's not the college, Les; what's the matter with you?" said Allison, putting his hand on the starter again. "Better wake up. Don't you know a college when you don't see one?"

"College nothing!" said his sister. "That's our house. That's our *home*, Allison. The very house I've dreamed of. It looks a little like the houses in California, and it is the very thing. Now, there's no use; you've got to get out and get that agent's name, or I'll jump out myself, and get lost, and walk the rest of the way!"

"It is lovely!" said Julia Cloud, leaning over to look. "But it looks expensive, and you wouldn't want to *buy* a house, you know, dear; for you might not stay."

"Oh, yes, we would if we liked it. And, besides, houses can be sold again when you get done with them, though I'd never want to sell that! It's a perfect little duck. Allison, will you get out or shall I?"

"Oh, I'm game," said Allison, getting out and jumping the hedge into the pretty yard.

He took out his pencil, and wrote down the address in his note-book, stepped up the terrace and glanced about, then went close to the street sign, and found out what corner it was near.

"It is a pippin, sure thing," he said as he sprang into the car again; "but, Leslie, for the love of Mike, don't find any more houses to-night. I'm hungry as a bear. That prayer meeting was one too many for me; I'm going to make for the nearest restaurant; and then, if you want to go house-hunting after that, all right; but I'm going to find the eats first."

They asked a group of boys where the restaurant was, and one pointed to an open door from which light was streaming forth.

"There's the pie-shop," they said, and the party descended hungry and happy with the delicious uncertainty of having found a dream of a house in the dark, and wondering what it would turn out to be in the daytime. They inquired the way to the inn, and decided to stop further investigations until morning.

10

THEY were all very weary, and slept well that night; but, strange to say, Allison, who was the sleepy-head, awoke first, and was out looking the town over before the others had thought of awaking. He came back to breakfast eager and impatient.

"We don't need to go any farther," he declared. "It's a peach of a place. There's a creek that reaches up in the woods for miles; and they have canoes and skating and a swimming-hole; and there are tennis-courts everywhere; and it's only eleven miles from the city. I say we just camp here, and not bother about going on to the other place. I'm satisfied. If that house is big enough, it's just the thing."

"But have you been to the college?"

"No, but I asked about it. They have inter-collegiate games and frats, and I guess it's all right. It has a peach of a campus, too, and a Carnegie library with chimes—"

"Well, but, dear, you aren't going to college just for those things."

"Oh, the college'll be all right. Guardy wouldn't have

suggested it if it wasn't. But we'll go up there this morning and look around."

"Now, children, don't get your heart set on it before you know all about it. You know that house may be quite impossible."

"Now, Cloudy!" put in Leslie. "You know Allison told you you were a good sport. You mustn't begin by preaching before you find out. If it isn't all right, why, of course we don't want it; so let's have the fun of thinking it is till we prove it isn't—or it is."

Julia Cloud looked into the laughing, happy eyes, and yielded with a smile.

"Of course," she said, "that's reasonable. I'm agreed to that. But there's one thing: you know we're bound to go on to the other college, because Mr. Luddington expects us; and we can come back here again if we like this better."

"Oh, we can wire him to come here," said Leslie. "Now, let's go! First to that house, please, because I'm so afraid somebody will buy it before we get the option on it. I've heard that houses are very scarce in the East just now, and people are snapping them up. I read that on the back of that old man's paper at the next table to ours this morning."

All three of them having the hearts of children, they went at once to hunt up the agent before ever they got even a glimpse of the halls of learning standing brave and fair on the hillside in the morning sunshine. "Because there are plenty more colleges," said Leslie; "but there is only one home for us, and I believe we've found it, if it looks half as pretty in the daylight as it did at night."

It took only a few minutes to find the agent and get the key of the house, and presently they were standing on the terrace gazing with delight at the house.

It was indeed a lovely little dwelling. It was built of stone, and then painted white, but the roof and gables were tiled with great pink tiles, giving an odd little foreign look to it, something like Anne Hathaway's cottage in general contour, Leslie declared.

The top of the terrace was pink-tiled, too, and all the porches were paved with tiles. The house itself seemed filled with windows all around. Allison unlocked the door, and they exclaimed with pleasure as he threw it wide open and they stepped in. The sun-shine was flooding the great living-room from every direction, it seemed. To begin with, the room was very large, and gave the effect of being a sun-parlor because of its white panelled walls and its many windows. Straight across from the front door on the opposite side of the room opened a small hallway or passage with stairs leading up to a platform where more windows shed a beautiful light down the stairs on walls papered with strange tropical birds in delicate old-fashioned tracery.

To the right through a wide white arch from the living-room was a charming white dining-room with little, high, leaded-paned windows over the spot for the sideboard and long windows in front.

To the left was an enormous stone fireplace with high mantel-shelf of stone and the chimney above. The fire-opening was wide enough for an old Yule log, and on either side of it were double glass doors opening into a long porch room, which also had a fireplace on the opposite side of the chimney, and was completely shut in by long casement windows.

Up-stairs there were four large bedrooms and a little hall room that could be used for a sewing-room or den, or an extra bedroom, besides a neat little maid's room in a notch on the half-way landing, and two bathrooms, white-tiled and delightful, tucked away in between things. Then Leslie opened a glass door in the very prettiest room of all, which she and Allison immediately decided must belong to their aunt, and exclaimed in delight; for here nestled between the gables, with a tiled wall all about it, was a delightful housetop or uncovered porch, so situated among the trees that it was entirely shut in from the world.

It was perfect! They stood and looked at one another in delight, and for the time the college was forgotten. Then Allison dashed away, and came back eagerly almost immediately.

"There's a garage!" he said, "just behind the kitchen, a regular robin's nest of a one, white with pink tiles just like the house, and a pebbled drive. Say, it must be some fool of a guy that would sell this. Isn't it just a cracker-jack?"

"My dear," put in Julia Cloud, "it can't help being very expensive—"

"Now, Cloudy, remember!" said Leslie, holding up her finger in mock rebuke. "Just wait and see! And, anyhow, you don't know Guardy Lud. If he could see us located in a peach of a home like this, he'd go back to his growley old dear of a wife with happy tears rolling down his nice old cheeks. Allison, you go talk to that agent, and you give him a hundred dollars if you've got it left—here, I guess I've got some, too—just to bind the bargain till Guardy gets here. And say, you go see if you can't get Guardy on the 'phone. I don't want to go a step farther. Couldn't you be happy here, Cloudy, with that fireplace, and that prayer meeting to go to? I wouldn't mind going with you sometimes when I didn't have to study."

Julia Cloud stooped, and kissed the eager face, and whispered, "Very happy, darling!"

And then they went to the agent again and the telephone. "Guardy Lud" proved himself quite equal to the occasion by agreeing to come on at once and approve their choice, and promised to be there before evening.

"I knew he would," said Leslie happily, as they seated themselves in the car again for the pleasant run to the college.

They found the dean in his office, and Allison was taken with him at once.

"He isn't much like that musty little guy in the other college. He looked like a wet hen!" growled Allison in a low tone to his sister and aunt, while the dean was out in the hall talking to a student. "I like him, don't you?" and Julia Cloud sat wondering what the boy's standards could be that he could judge so suddenly and enthusiastically. Yet she had to admit herself that she liked this man, tall and grave with a pleasant twinkle hidden away in his wine-brown eyes and around the corners of his firm mouth. She felt satisfied that here was a man who would be both wise and just.

They made the rounds of the college buildings and campus with growing enthusiasm, and then drove back to the inn to lunch with hearty appetites.

"Let's go down to the house, and measure things, and look around once more," proposed Leslie. "Then we can come back and wait here for Guardy. We mustn't be away when he arrives, for he'll want to get everything fixed up and get away. I know him. Allison, did you get a time-table?"

Allison produced one from his coat-pocket, and they studied the trains, and decided that there was no possibility of the arrival of their guardian until three o'clock, and probably not until five.

"That's all right," said Leslie. "Cloudy and I'll stay here from three to five, and you can meet the trains; but first I want the dimensions of those rooms, so Cloudy and I can plan. We've got a whole lot to do before college opens, and we can't spare a minute. O Cloudy! I'm so happy! Isn't that house just a duck?"

They went to the village store, bought a foot-rule, a yardstick, and a tape-measure, and repaired to the house. Allison took the foot-rule by masculine right; Julia Cloud said she felt more at home with the tape-measure; and Leslie preferred the yardstick. With pencil and paper they went to work, making a diagram of each room, with spaces between windows and doors for furniture, taking it room by room.

"We've got to know about length of curtains, and whether furniture will fit in," declared Leslie wisely. "I've thought it all out nights in the sleeper on the way over here. Just think! Isn't it going to be fun furnishing the whole house? You know, Cloudy, I didn't have hardly anything sent, because it really wasn't worth while. We sort of wanted to leave the house at home just as it was when Mamma was living, to come back to sometimes; and so we let it to an old gentleman, a friend of Grandfather's and Guardy's, who has only himself and his wife and servants, and will take beautiful care of it. But I went around and picked out anything I wanted, rugs and pictures and some bric-à-brac, and a few bits of old mahogany that I love, just small things that would pack easily. Guardy said we might buy our own things. He set a limit on our spending, of course; but he said it would be good experience for us to learn how to buy wisely inside a certain sum."

Julia Cloud went around like one in a dream with her new tape-measure, setting down careful figures, and feeling like a child playing dolls again. It was almost three o'clock when they finally finished their measurements, and Allison hurried them back to the inn, and repaired to the station to meet trains.

Leslie made her aunt lie down on the bed, supposedly for a nap; but no one could have taken a nap even if he had wanted to—which Julia Cloud did not—with an eager, excited girl sitting beside the bed, just fluttering with ideas about couches and pillows and furniture and curtains.

"We'll have a great deep couch, with air-cushions on the seat and back, and put it in the middle of the living-room facing the fireplace, won't we, Cloudy? And what color do you think would be pretty for the cushions? I guess blue, deep, dark-blue brocaded velvet, or something soft that will tone well with the mahogany wood-work. I love mahogany in a white room, don't you, Cloudy? And I had a great big blue Chinese rug sent over that I think will do nicely for there. You like blue, don't you, Cloudy?" she finished anxiously. "Because I want to have you like it more even than we do."

"Oh, I love it!" gasped Julia Cloud, trying to set her mind to revel in extravagant desires without compunction. She was not used to considering life in terms of Chinese rugs or mahogany and brocade velvet.

"I'd like the curtains next the windows to be all alike all over the house, wouldn't you? Just sheer, soft, creamy white. And then inner curtains of Chinese silk or something like that. We'd want blue in the living-room, of course, if we had the blue rugs and couch, and oh! old rose, I guess, in the dining-room, or perhaps mahogany color or tan. Green for that sun-porch room! That's it, and lots of willow chairs and tables! And rush mats on the tiled floor! Oh! Aren't we having fun, Cloudy, dear? Now, I'll write out a list of things we have to buy while you take a nap."

And so it went on the whole afternoon, until the sound of a distant whistle warned them that the five o'clock train was coming in and they must be prepared to meet Mr. Luddington.

According to programme they hurried into their wraps, and went down to the piazza to wait for the car. None too soon, for Allison was already driving around the curve in front of the door, and Mr. Luddington sat beside him, radiating satisfaction. Anything that pleased his adorable wards pleased him, but this especially so, for he was in a hurry to respond to the many telegrams summoning him home to California, and the quicker this little household was settled, the sooner he might leave them.

They drove at once, of course, to the house, Allison and Leslie talking fast and eagerly every minute of the way, their eyes bright and their faces beautiful with enthusiasm; and Mr. Luddington could only sit and listen, and smile over their heads at Julia Cloud, who was smiling also, and who in her new silvery garments looked to him all the more a lady and fit to play mother to his wards.

"Well, now, now, now!" said Guardy Lud after they had gone carefully over every room and were coming down-stairs again. "This is great! This certainly is great. I couldn't have had it better if I'd made it to order, could I? And I certainly wish you were settled here, and I could stay long enough to take breakfast with you and enjoy some more of your excellent buckwheat cakes, Miss Cloud." He turned with a gallant bow to Julia. "I hope you'll teach my little girl here to bake them just like that, so she can make me some when she comes back to California to visit us again."

They rode him around the town, through the college grounds, and then back to the inn for dinner. That evening they spent in discussion and business plans for the winter. The next morning they took Mr. Luddington up to the college, where he made final arrangements for the young people to be entered as students, and afterwards drove to the city. Mr. Luddington had one or two friends there to whom he wished to introduce them, that they might have some one near at hand to call upon in a time of need. He also took them all to a bank, and arranged their bank accounts so that they might draw what they needed at any time. After lunch he went with them to several of the largest stores, and opened a charge account for them. Then, with a warm hand-shake for Julia Cloud and an emotional good-by for the young people, he left them to rush for his train.

"We might stay in town tonight, and be ready to shop early in the morning," proposed Leslie.

"No," said Allison decidedly. "Cloudy looks worn to a frazzle, and I'm sick to death of the city. Let's beat it back to where they have good air. We can go right to bed after dinner, and get up good and early, and be here as soon as the stores are open. They don't open till nine o'clock. I saw the signs on the doors everywhere."

So back they went for a good night's rest, and were up and at it early in the morning, scarcely noticing the way they rode, so interested were they in deciding how many chairs and beds and tables they needed to buy.

"Let's get the curtains first, and then we can have the windows washed, and put them right up," said Leslie, "and nobody can see in. I'm crazy to be shut into our own house, and feel that it belongs to us. We can select them while Allison's gone to see what's the matter with his engine."

But, when Julia Cloud heard the stupendous price that was asked for ready-made curtains or curtains made to order, with fixtures and installation, she exclaimed in horror:

"Leslie! This is foolish. We can easily make them our-selves, and put them up for less than half the price. If I had only brought my sewing-machine! But it was all out of repair."

"Could we really make them ourselves, Cloudy? Wouldn't that be fun? We'll get a sewing-machine, of course. We'll need it for other things, too, sometimes, won't we? Of course we'll get one. We'll buy that next.

Now, how many yards of each of these do we need?"

In a few minutes the salesman had figured out how much was needed, counted the number of fixtures for doorways and windows, and arranged to send the package down to the car at a certain time later in the morning. Then they went at once and bought a sewing-machine, one that Julia Cloud knew all about and said was the best and lightest on the market. Leslie was as pleased with the idea of learning to run it as if it had been a new toy and she a child.

"We'll have it sent right to the little new house, and then we can go there evenings after we are through shopping, and sew. You can cut, and I can put in the hems, if you think I can do them well enough. We must get scissors and thread, a lot of it, and silk to match the colored curtains, too."

They took the rooms one at a time, and furnished them, Allison joining them, and taking as much interest in the design of the furniture as if he had been a young bridegroom just setting up housekeeping for himself.

They had set aside a certain sum for each room so that they would not overstep their guardian's limit, and with Julia Cloud to put on the brakes, and suggest simplicity, and decide what was in good taste for such a small village house, they easily came within the generous limit allowed them.

It was a great game for Julia Cloud to come out of her simple country life and plunge into this wholesale beautiful buying untroubled by a continual feeling that she must select the very cheapest without regard to taste or desire. It was wonderful; but it was wearying in spite of the delight, and so the little house was not all furnished in a day.

"Well, the living-room's done, anyway, and the willow set for the porch room!" sighed Leslie, leaning back with a fling of weariness. "Now to-morrow we'll do the dining-room."

"To-morrow's Sunday, Les; the stores aren't open. Use your bean a little, child."

"Sunday!"

Leslie's beautiful face drew itself into a snarl of impatience, the first, really, that Julia Cloud had seen.

"Oh, darn!" said Leslie's pretty lips. "Isn't that too horrid? I forgot all about it. I wonder what they have to have Sunday for, anyway. It's just a dull old bore!"

"O Leslie, darling!" said Julia Cloud, aghast, something in her heart growing suddenly heavy and sinking her down, down, so that she felt as if she could hardly hold her head up another minute.

"Well, Cloudy, dear, don't you think it's a bore yourself, truly? Come, now, own up. And I'm sure I don't see what's the use of it, do you? One can't do a thing that's nice. But I'll tell you what we can do!" her eyes growing bright with eagerness again. "We'll measure and cut all the curtains, and turn the hems up. And, Allison, you can put up the fixtures. If only the machine could have been sent up today, we could have had the curtains all done, couldn't we, Cloudy?"

But Julia Cloud's lips were white and trembling, and her sweet eyes had suddenly gone dark with trouble and apprehension.

"O Leslie, darling child!" she gasped again. "You don't mean you would work on the Sabbath day!"

"Why, why not, Cloudy, dear? Is there anything wrong about that?"

JULIA Cloud had a sudden feeling that everything was whirling beneath her—the very foundations of the earth. She drew a deep breath, and tried to steady herself, thinking in her heart that she must be very calm and not make any mistakes in this great crisis that had arisen. It flashed across her consciousness that she was a simple, old-fashioned woman, accustomed to old-fashioned ideas, living all her life in a little town where the line between the church and the world was strongly marked, where the traditions of Christianity were still held sacred in the hearts of many and where the customs of worldliness had not yet noticeably invaded. All the articles she had read in the religious press about the worldliness of the modern Sabbath, the terrible desecration of the day that had been dear and sacred to her all her life as being the time when she came closest to her Lord; all the struggle between the church and the world to keep the old laws rigidly; and all the sneers she had seen in the secular press against the fanatics who were trying to force the world back to Puritanism, came shivering to her mind in one great thrill of agony as she recognized that she was face to face with one of the biggest religious problems of the day, and must fight it out alone.

The beautiful life that had seemed to be opening out before her was not, then, to be all beauty. Behind the flowers of this new Eden there hid a serpent of temptation; and she, Julia Cloud, disciple of the Lord Christ, was to be tried out to see what faith there was in her. For a moment she faltered, and closed her eyes, shuddering. How could she face it, she, who knew so little what to say and how to tell her quiet heart-beliefs? Why had she been placed in such a position? Why was there not some one wiser than she to guide the feet of these children into the straight and narrow way?

But only a moment she shrank thus. The voice of her Master seemed to speak in her heart as the wind whirled by the car and stirred the loose hair on her forehead. The voice that had been her guide through life was requiring her now to witness to these two whom she loved, as no other could do it, be they ever so wise; just because she loved them and loved Him, and was not pretending to be wise, only following. Then she drew a deep breath, reminded herself once more that she must be careful not to antagonize, and sat up gravely.

"Dear, it is God's day, and I have always felt that He wanted us to make it holy for Him, keep worldly things out of it, you know. I wouldn't feel that I could work on that day. Of course I have no right to say you shall not. I'm only your adviser and friend, you know. But I'd rather you wouldn't, because I know God would rather you wouldn't."

Leslie pouted uneasily.

"How in the world could you know that?" she said almost crossly. She did love to carry out her projects, and hitherto Julia Cloud had put no hindrance in her way.

"Why, He said so in His book. He said, 'Thou shalt

not do any work, thou, nor thy son, nor thy daughter—"

"Oh, those are the old commandments, Cloudy, dear; and I've heard people, even ministers, say that they are out of date now. They don't have anything to do with us nowadays."

Julia Cloud looked still graver.

"God doesn't change, Leslie. He is the same yesterday and to-day and forever. And He said that whoever took away from the meaning of the words of His book would have some terrible punishment, so that it were better that a millstone were hanged about his neck and that he were drowned."

"Well, I think He'd be a perfectly horrid God to do that!" said Leslie. "I can't see how you can believe any such old thing. It isn't like you, Cloudy, dear; it's just some old thing you were taught. You don't like to be long-faced and unhappy one day in the week, you know you don't."

"Long-faced! Unhappy! Why, dear child, God doesn't want the Sabbath to be that. He wants it to be the happiest day of all the week. I'm never unhappy on Sunday. I like it best of all."

Suddenly Allison turned around, and looked at Julia Cloud, saw the white, strained look around her lips, the yearning light in her eyes, and had some swift man's intuition about the true woman's soul of her. For men, especially young men, do have these intuitions sometimes as well as women.

"Leslie," he said gently, as if he had suddenly grown much older than his sister, "can't you see you're hurting Cloudy? Cut it out! If Cloudy likes Sunday, she shall have it the way she wants it."

Leslie turned with sudden compunction.

"O Cloudy, dear, I didn't mean to hurt you; indeed I didn't! I never thought you'd care."

"It's all right, dear," said Julia Cloud with her gentle

voice, and just the least mite of a gasp. "You see—I—Sunday has been always very dear to me; I hadn't realized you wouldn't feel the same."

She seemed to shrink into herself; and, though the smile still trembled on her lips, there was a hovering of distress over her fine brows.

"We *will* feel the same!" declared Allison. "If you feel that way so much, we'll manage somehow to be loyal to what you think. You always do it for us; and, if we can't be as big as you are, we haven't got the gang spirit. It's teamwork, Leslie. Cloudy goes to football games, and makes fudge for our friends; and we go to church and help her keep Sunday her way. See?"

"Why, of course! Sure!" said Leslie, half bewildered. "I didn't mean not to, of course, if Cloudy likes such things; only she'll have to teach me how, for I never did like those things."

"Well, I say, let's get Cloudy to spend the first Sunday telling us how she thinks Sunday ought to be kept, and why. Is that a bargain, Cloudy?"

"But I'm afraid I wouldn't be wise enough to explain," faltered Julia Cloud, distress in her voice. "I could maybe find something to read to you about it."

"Oh, preserve us, Cloudy! We don't want any old dissertations out of a book. If we can't have your own thoughts that make you live it the way you do, we haven't any use for any of it. See?"

Julia Cloud forced a trembling little smile, and said she saw, and would do her best; but her heart sank at the prospect. What a responsibility to be put upon her ignorant shoulders. The Lord's Sabbath in her bungling hands to make or to mar for these two young souls! She must pray. Oh, she must pray continually that she might be led!

And then there came swiftly to her mind one of the verses that had become dear and familiar to her through the years as she read and reread her Bible, "And when they bring you unto the synagogues, and unto magistrates, and powers, take ye no thought how or what thing ye shall answer, or what ye shall say; for the Holy Ghost shall teach you in the same hour what ye ought to say."

This was not exactly being brought before magistrates; but it was being challenged for a reason for the hope that was in her, and perhaps she could claim the promise. Surely, if the Lord wanted her to defend His Sabbath before these two, He would give her wise words in which to speak. Anyhow, she would just have to trust Him, for she had none of her own.

"Now see what you've done, Leslie!" said her brother sharply. "Cloudy hasn't looked that way once before. Next thing you know she'll be washing her hands of us and running off back to Sterling again."

"O Cloudy!" said the penitent Leslie, flinging herself into her aunt's arms and nestling there beseechingly. "You wouldn't do that, would you, Cloudy, dear? No matter how naughty I got? Because you would know I wouldn't mean it ever. Even if I was real bad."

"No, dear," said Julia Cloud, kissing her fair forehead. "But this is just one of those things that I meant when I was afraid to undertake it. You see there may be a great many things you will want to do on Sunday that I would not feel it right for me to do, and I may be a hindrance to you in lots of ways. I shouldn't like to get to be a sort of burden to you, and it isn't as if they were things that I could give up, you know. This is a matter of conscience."

"That's all right, Cloudy," put in Allison. "You have your say in things like that. We aren't so selfish as all that. And besides, if it's wrong for you, who knows but it's wrong for us, too? We'll look into it."

Julia Cloud went smiling through the rest of the evening, but underneath was a tugging of strange dread and fear at her heart. It was all so new, this having responsibility with souls. She had always so quietly trusted her Bible and tried to follow her Lord. She had never had to guide others. There had not been time for her even to take a class in Sunday school, but she knew her religion only as it applied to her one little narrow life, she thought, not realizing that, when one has applied a great faith to the circumstances of even a narrow life, and applied it thoroughly through a lifetime, one has learned more theology than one could get in years of a theological seminary. Theories, after all, are worth little unless they have been worked out in experience; and when one has patiently, even happily, given up much of the joy of living to serve, has learned to keep self under and love even the unlovable, has put to the test the promises of the Bible and found them to hold true in time of need, and has found the Sabbath day an oasis in the desert of an otherwise dreary life, even an old theologian wouldn't have much more to go on in beginning a discussion on Sabbath-keeping.

Quite early the next morning, before Leslie had awakened, Julia Cloud had slipped softly to her knees by the bedside, and was communing with her heavenly Father concerning her need of guidance.

When Leslie awoke, her aunt was sitting by the window with her Bible on her knee and a sweet look of peace on her face, the morning sunlight resting on the silvery whiteness of her hair like a benediction. It was perhaps the soft turning of a leaf that brought the girl to wakefulness, and she lay for some time quietly watching her aunt and thinking the deep thoughts of youth. Perhaps nothing could have so well prepared her for the afternoon talk as that few minutes of watching Julia Cloud's face as she read her Bible, glancing now and then from the window thoughtfully, as if considering something she had read. Julia Cloud was reading over everything that her Bible said about the Sabbath, and with the help of her concordance she was being led through a very logical train of thought, although she did not know it. If you had asked her, she would have said that she had not been thinking about what she would say to the children; she had been deep in the meaning that God sent to her own soul.

But when Leslie finally stirred and greeted her, Julia Cloud looked up with a smile of peace; and there was no longer a little line of worry between her straight brows.

The peace lasted all through the morning, and went with her down to breakfast; and something of her enjoyment of the day seemed to pervade the atmosphere about her and extend to the two young people. They hovered about her, anxious to please, and a trifle ill at ease at first lest they should make some mistake about this day that seemed so holy to their aunt and had always been to them nothing but a bore to get through with in the jolliest way possible.

There was no question about going to church. They just went. Leslie and Allison had never made a practice of doing so since they had been left to themselves. It had not been necessary in the circle in which they moved. When they went to school, and had to go to church, they evaded the rule as often as possible. But somehow they felt without being told that if they tried to remain away now it would hurt their aunt more than anything else they could do; and, while they were usually outspoken and frank, they both felt that here was a time to be silent about their habits.

"We're going to church," said Allison in a low tone as he drew his sister's chair away from the breakfast-table. His tone had the quality of command.

"Of course," responded Leslie quietly.

It was so that Julia Cloud was spared the knowledge that her two dear young people did not consider it necessary to attend church every Sabbath, and her peace was not disturbed.

The sermon in the little stucco church where they had gone to prayer meeting that first night was not exceedingly enlivening nor uplifting. The minister was prosy with dignity, soaring into occasional flights of eloquence that reminded one of a generation ago. There was nothing about it to bring to mind the sweetness of a Sabbath communion with Christ, nothing to remind a young soul that Christ was ready to be Friend and Saviour. It was rather a dissertation on one of the epistles with a smack of modern higher criticism. The young people watched the preacher a while listlessly, and wished for the end; but a glance at the quiet, worshipful face of their aunt kept them thoughtful. Julia Cloud evidently had something that most other people did not have, they said to themselves, some inner light that shone through her face, some inner finer sight and keener ear that made her see and hear what was not given to common mortals to comprehend; and because she sat thus with the light of communion on her face they, too, sat with respectful hearts and tried to join lustily in the hymns with their fresh voices.

The minister came down and shook hands with them, welcoming them kindly. He seemed more human out of the pulpit, and asked quite interestedly where they were to live and whether he might call. He mentioned Sunday school and Christian Endeavor, and said he hoped they would "cast in their lot" among them; and the young people gave him cold little smiles and withdrew into themselves while their aunt did the talking. They were willing she should have her Sabbath, and they would do all in their power to make it what she wanted; but they were hostile toward this church and this minister and all that it had to do with. It simply did not interest them. Julia Cloud saw this in their eyes as she turned to go away, and sighed softly to herself. How much there was to teach them! Could she ever hope to make them feel differently? In two short weeks the college would open, and they would be swept away on a whirl of work and play and new friends and functions. Was she strong enough to stem the tide of worldliness that would engulf them? No, not of herself. But she had read that very morning the promises of her Lord, "Surely I will be with them," "I will help thee"; and she meant to lay hold on them closely. She could do nothing of herself, but she with her Lord helping could do anything He wanted done. That was enough.

Leslie turned longing eyes toward the winding creek and an alluring canoe that lolled idly at the bank down below the inn as she stood on the piazza after dinner waiting for her aunt; but Allison saw her glance, and shook his head.

"Better not suggest it," he said. "There are a lot of picnickers down there carrying on high. She would not like it, I'm sure. If it were all quiet and no one about, it would be different."

"Well, there are a lot of people around here on the piazzas," said Leslie disconsolately. "I don't see the difference."

But, when Julia Cloud came with her Bible slipped unobtrusively under her arm, she suggested a quiet spot in the woods; and so they wandered off through the trees with a big blanket from the car to sit on, and found a wonderful place, high above the water, where a great rift of rocks jutted out among drooping hemlocks, and was carpeted with pine-needles.

"It would please me very much," said Julia Cloud as she sat down on the blanket and opened her Bible, looking up wistfully at the two, "if you two would go to that Christian Endeavor meeting to-night. I hate to ask you to do anything like that right away, but that minister begged me to get you to come. He said they were having such a struggle to make it live and that they needed some fresh young workers. He asked me if you didn't sing, and he said singers were very much needed."

There was a heavy silence for a moment while the two young things looked at each other aghast across her, and Julia Cloud kept her eyes on the floating clouds above the hemlocks. She still had that softened look of being within a safe shelter where storms and troubles could not really trouble her; yet there was a dear, eager look in her eyes. Both children saw it, and with wonderful intuition interpreted it; and because their hearts were young and tender they yielded to its influence.

Leslie swooped down upon her aunt with an overwhelming kiss, and Allison dropped down beside her with a "Sure, we'll go, Cloudy, if that will do you any good. I can't say I'm keen about pleasing that stiff old parson guy, but anything *you* want is different. I don't know just what you're letting us in for, but I guess we can stand most anything once."

Julia Cloud put out a hand to grasp a hand of each; and, looking up, they saw that there were tears in her eyes.

"Are those happy tears, Cloudy, or the other kind? Tell us quick, or we'll jump in the creek and drown ourselves," laughed Leslie; and then two white hand-kerchiefs, one big and one little, came swiftly out and dabbed at her cheeks until there wasn't a sign of a tear to be seen.

"I think I'm almost too happy to talk," said Julia Cloud, resting back against the tree and looking up into its lacy green branches. "It seems as if I was just beginning my life over and being a child again."

For a few minutes they sat so, looking up into the changing autumn sky, listening to the soft tinkle of the water running below, the dip of an oar, the swirl of a blue heron's wing as it clove the air, the distant voices of the picnickers farther down the creek, the rustle of the yellow beech-leaves as they whispered of the time to go, and how they would drift down like little brown boats to the stream and glide away to the end. Now and then a nut would fall with a tiny crisp thud, and a squirrel would whisk from a limb overhead. They were very quiet, and let the beauty of the spot sink deep into their souls. Then at last Julia Cloud took up her Bible, and began to talk.

12

THERE were tiny slips of paper in Julia Cloud's well-worn Bible, and she turned to the first one shyly. It was such new work to her to be talking about these things to any but her own worshipful soul.

The two young people settled back in comfortable attitudes on the blanket, and put their gaze upon the far sky overhead. They were embarrassed also, but they meant to carry this thing through.

"Thus the heavens and the earth were finished, and all the host of them," read Julia Cloud; and straightway the shining blue above them took on a personality, and became a witness in the day's proceedings. It was as if some one whom they had known all their lives, quite familiar in their daily life, should suddenly have stood up and declared himself to have been an eye-witness to most marvellous proceedings. The hazy blue with its floating clouds was no longer a diversion from the subject in hand. Their eyes were riveted with mysterious thoughts as they lay and listened, astonished, fascinated. It was the first time it had ever really entered into their consciousness that there had been a time when there was no blue, no firm earth, no anything. Whether it were true or not had not as yet become a question with them. They were near enough to their fairy-story days to accept a tale while it was being read, and revel in it.

The quiet voice went on:

"And on the seventh day God ended his work which he had made; and he rested on the seventh day from all his work which he had made. And God blessed the seventh day, and sanctified it: because that in it he had rested from all his work which God created and made."

"What did He have to rest for? A God wouldn't get tired, would He?" burst forth Leslie, turning big inquiring eyes on Julia Cloud.

"I don't know, unless He did it for our sakes to set us an example," she answered slowly, "although that might mean He rested in the sense of stopped doing it, you know. And that would imply that He had some reason for doing so. I'm not very wise, you know, and because I may not be able to answer your questions doesn't mean they can't be answered by some one who has studied it all out. I've often wished I could have gone to college and studied Greek and Hebrew, so I could have read the Bible in the original."

"H'm!" said Allison thoughtfully. "That would be interesting, wouldn't it? I always wondered why they did it, but I don't know but I'll study them myself. I think I'd enjoy it if there was a real reason besides just the discipline of it they are always talking about when you kick about mathematics and languages."

"Well," said Leslie, sitting up interestedly, "is that all there is to it? Did some one just up and say we had to keep Sunday because God did? I think that is a kind of superstition. I don't see that God would want to make us do everything He did. We couldn't. I *wouldn't* unless *He* said to, anyhow."

"O Les! You're way off," laughed her brother. "God

did. He said, 'remember the sabbath day to keep it holy. Six days shall thou labor, and do all thy work, but the seventh day is the sabbath of the Lord thy God; in it thou shalt not do any work, thou, nor thy son, nor thy daughter, thy man servant nor thy maid servant—' Don't you remember the Ten Commandments? No, I guess you were too little to learn them. But I got a Testament for learning them once. Say, Cloudy, when did He give that command? Right away after He made Adam and Eve?"

"I'm not sure," said Julia Cloud, fluttering the leaves of her Bible over to the second slip of paper. "I don't find any reference to it in my concordance till way over here in Exodus, after the children of Israel had been in Egypt so many years, and Moses led them out through the wilderness, and they got fretful because they hadn't any bread such as they used to have in Egypt, so God sent them manna that fell every morning. But He told them not to leave any over for the next day because it would gather worms and smell bad, except on Saturday, when they were to gather enough for the Sabbath. Listen: 'And they gathered it every morning, every man according to his eating; and when the sun waxed hot, it melted. And it came to pass, that on the sixth day they gathered twice as much bread, two omers for one man; and all the rulers of the congregation came and told Moses. And he said unto them, This is that which the Lord hath said, To-morrow is the rest of the holy sabbath unto the Lord; bake that which ye will bake to-day, and seethe that ye will seethe; and that which remaineth over lay up for you to be kept until the morning. And they laid it up till the morning, as Moses bade; and it did not stink, neither was there any worm therein. And Moses said, Eat that to-day; for to-day is a sabbath unto the Lord: to-day ye shall not find it in the field. Six days ye shall gather it; but on the seventh day, which is the sabbath, in it there shall be none. And it came to pass, that there went out some of the people on the seventh day for to gather, and they found none. And the Lord said unto Moses, How long refuse ye to keep my commandments and my laws? See, for that the Lord hath given you the sabbath, therefore he giveth you on the sixth day the bread of two days; abide ye every man in his place, let no man go out of his place on the seventh day. So the people rested on the seventh day.' It looks as though the people had been used to the Sabbath already, for the commandments given on the mount come three whole chapters later. It looks to me as if God established the Sabbath right at the beginning when He rested from His own work, and that's what it means when it says He sanctified it."

"What do you suppose He said, 'I have given *you* a sabbath' for? It looks as if it were meant for a benefit for the people and not for God, doesn't it?" said Allison, sitting up and looking over his aunt's shoulder. "Why, I always supposed God wanted the Sabbath for His own sake, so people would see how great He was."

Julia Cloud's cheeks grew red with a flash of distress as if he had said something against some one she loved very much.

"Oh, no!" she said earnestly. "God isn't like that. Why, He loves us! He wouldn't have given a Sabbath at all if it hadn't been quite necessary for our good. Besides, in the New Testament, Jesus said, " 'The sabbath was made for man, and not man for the sabbath'! Oh, He made it for us to be happy in, I'm sure. And perhaps He rested Himself so that we might understand He had set apart that time of leisure in order to be everything to us on the day when we had most time for Him. I have read somewhere that God had to teach those early people little by little just as we teach babies, a few things each year; and over in the New Testament it says that all these things that happened in the Old Testament to those children of Israel happened and were written down for an example to us who should live in the later part of the world. So, little by little, by pictures and stories He taught those people what He wanted all of us to know as a sort of inheritance. And He took the things first that were of the most importance. It would seem as if He considered this matter of the Sabbath very important, and as if He had it in mind right away at the first when He made the world, and intended to set apart this day out of every seven, because He stopped right off the very first week Himself to establish a precedent, and then He 'sanctified' it, which must mean He set it apart in such a way that all the world should understand."

"What is a precedent?" asked Leslie sharply.

"Oh, you know, Les, it's something you have to do just because you always have done it that way," said Allison, waving her aside. "But, Cloudy, what I can't get at all is why He wanted it in the first place if He didn't want it just entirely for His own glorification."

"Why, dear, I am not sure; but I think it was just so that He and we might have a sort of a trysting-time when we could be sure of having nothing to interfere between us. And He meant it, too, to be the sign between Himself and those who really loved Him and were His children, a sign that should show to the world who were His. He said so in several places. Listen to this." She turned the leaves quickly. "'And the Lord spake unto Moses, saying: Speak thou also unto the children of Israel, saying, Verily my sabbaths ye shall keep; for it is a sign between me and you throughout your generations; that ye may know that I am the Lord that doth sanctify you. Ye shall keep the sabbath therefore; for it is holy unto you; every one that defileth it shall surely be put to death; for whosoever doeth any work therein, that soul shall be cut off from among his people. Six days may work be done; but in the seventh is the sabbath of rest, holy to the Lord; whosoever doeth any work in the sabbath day, he shall surely be put to death. Wherefore the children of Israel shall keep the sabbath, to observe the sabbath throughout their generations, for a perpetual covenant. It is a sign between me and the children of Israel forever; for in six days the Lord made heaven and earth, and on the seventh day he rested, and was refreshed.' "

"There! Now!" said Leslie, sitting up. "That's just what I thought! That was only for the children of Israel. It hasn't the leastest bit to do with us. Those were Jews, and they keep it yet, on Saturday."

"Wait, dear!" Julia Cloud turned the leaves of her Bible rapidly to Corinthians.

"Listen! 'Moreover, brethren, I would not that ye should be ignorant, how that all our fathers were under the cloud, and all passed through the sea; and were all baptized unto Moses in the cloud and in the sea; and did all eat the same spiritual meat; and did all drink the same spiritual drink; for they drank of that spiritual Rock that followed them; and that Rock was Christ. But with many of them God was not well pleased; for they were overthrown in the wilderness. Now these things were our examples, to the intent we should not lust after evil things, as they also lusted. Neither, be ye idolators, as were some of them; as it is written, The people sat down to eat and drink, and rose up to play. . . . Neither let us tempt Christ, as some of them also tempted, and were destroyed of serpents. Neither murmur ye, as some of them also murmured, and were destroyed of the destroyer. Now all these things happened unto them for ensamples: and they are written for our admonition, upon whom the ends of the world are come. Wherefore

let him that thinketh he standeth take heed lest he fall.'
Doesn't that look as though God meant the Sabbath for
us, too, Leslie?"

Leslie dropped back on her pillow of moss with a
sigh. "I s'pose it does," she answered somewhat disconsolately. "But I never did like Sundays anyhow!" and
she drew a deep breath of unrest.

"But, dear,"—Julia Cloud's hand rested on the bright
head lovingly,—"there's a closer sense than that in
which this belongs to us if we belong to Christ; we are
Israel ourselves. I was reading about it just this morning, how all those who want to be Christ's chosen
people, and are willing to accept Him as their Savior, are
Israel just as much as a born Jew. I think I can find it
again. Yes, here it is in Romans: 'For they are not all Israel which are *of* Israel: neither, because they are the seed
of Abraham, are they all children; but, In Isaac shall thy
seed be called. That is, they which are children of the
flesh, these are not the children of God: but the children
of the promise are counted for the seed.' That means the
promise that was given to Abraham that there should be
a Messiah sometime in his family who would be the
Saviour of the world, and the idea is that all who believe
in that Messiah are the real chosen people. It was to the
chosen people God gave these careful directions—com-
mands, if you like to call them—to help them be what a
chosen people ought to be. And the Sabbath rest and
communion seems to be the basis of the whole idea of a
people who were guided by God. It is the coming home
to God after the toil of the week. They had to have a
time when other things did not call them away from
spending a whole day with Him and getting acquainted,
from getting to know what He wanted and how to
shape their lives, or they would just as surely get interested in the world and forget God."

"Well, I don't see why we have to go to church, anyway," declared Leslie discontentedly. "This is a great deal better out here under the trees, reading the Bible."

"Yes," said Allison. "Cloudy, that minister's dull. I know I wouldn't get anything out of hearing him chew the rag."

"O Allison, dear! Don't speak of God's minister that way!"

"Why not, Cloudy? Maybe he isn't God's minister. How did he get there, anyway? Just decided to be a minister, and studied, and got himself called to that church, didn't he?"

"Oh, no, dear! I trust not. That is terrible! Where ever did you get such an idea? There may be some unworthy men in the ministry. Of course there must be, for the Bible said there would be false leaders and wolves in sheep's clothing; but surely, *surely* you know that most of the men in the pulpit are there because they believe that God has called them to give up everything else and spend their lives bringing the message of the gospel to the souls of men. The office is a holy office, and must be reverenced even if we do not fancy the man who occupies it. He may have a message if you listen for it, even though he may seem dull to you. If you knew him better, you could look into his life and see the sacrifices he has made to be a minister, see the burdens of the people he has to bear!"

"O Cloudy, come now. Most of the ministers I ever saw have automobiles and fine houses, and about as good a time as anybody. They get big salaries, and don't bother themselves much about anything but church services and getting people to give money. Honestly, now, Cloudy Jewel, I think they're putting it over on you. I'll bet not half of them are sincere in that sacrifice stuff they put over. It may have been so long ago; but ministers have a pretty soft snap nowadays, in cities anyhow."

"Allison! Didn't you ever see any true, sincere ministers, child? There are so many, many of them!"

"To tell you the truth, Cloudy, I never saw but one that didn't have shifty eyes. He was a little missionary chap that worked in a slum settlement and would have taken his eye-teeth out for anybody. Oh, I don't mean that old guy to-day looked shifty. I should say he was just dull and uninteresting. He may have thought he had a call long ago, but he's been asleep so long he's forgotten about it."

"O Allison! This is dreadful!"

Julia Cloud closed her Bible, and looked down in horror at the frank young face of the boy who minced no words in saying what he thought about these holy things that had always been so precious and sacred to her. She felt like putting her hands over her ears and running away screaming. Her very soul was in agony over the desecration. The children looked into her face, saw the white, scared look, and took warning.

"There now, Cloudy, don't worry!" said Allison, leaning over and patting her hand awkwardly. "I didn't mean to hurt you; honest I didn't. Perhaps I'm wrong. Of course I am if you say so. I don't really know any ministers, anyhow. I was just saying what is the general impression among the fellows. I didn't realize you would *care*."

"Do the young men all think that?" Julia Cloud's lips were white, and an agonized expression for the church of God had grown in her eyes. She searched the boy's face with a look he did not soon forget. It made an impression that stayed with him always. At least, there was something in religion if it could make her look like that to hear it lightly spoken of. At least this one woman was a sincere follower of Christ.

"There now, Cloudy! I tell you I'm sorry I said that; and just to prove it I'll go to that old Christian Endeavor to-night, and try to find something interesting. I will truly. And Les will go, too!"

"Of course!" said Leslie, nestling close. "Forget what he said, and tell us why we have to go to church, Cloudy, dear."

Julia Cloud tried to recall her troubled thoughts to the subject in hand.

"Well, God had them build the tabernacle for worship, you know, dear; told them how to make everything even to the minutest details, and established worship. That was to be part of the Sabbath day, a place to worship, and a promise that He would be there to meet any one who came. That promise holds good to-day. You needn't ever think about the minister. Just fancy you see Christ in the pulpit. He is there, come to meet His own, you know. He'll be in that Christian Endeavor to-night. He was in the tabernacle of old. There was a brightness in the cloud of His presence to show the people that God had come down to meet them. They were children, and had to be helped by a visible manifestation."

"Yes, that would be something like!" said Allison. "If we could see something to help us believe—"

"Those who truly believe with the heart will have the assurance," said Julia Cloud earnestly. "I *know*."

There was something in her tone and the look of her eye that added, "For I have experienced it." The young people looked at her, and were silent. There was a long, quiet pause in which the sounds of the falling nuts and the whispering of the hemlocks closed in about them, and made the day and hour a sacred time. At last Leslie broke the silence.

"Well, Cloudy, suppose we go to church and Christian Endeavor. What can we do the rest of the day? We don't have to go to church every minute, do we? I don't really see how it's going to do me any good. I don't, indeed."

Julia Cloud smiled at her wistfully. It was so wonder-fully sweet to have this bright, beautiful young thing asking her these vital questions.

"Why, deary, it's just a day to spend with God and get to enjoy His company," she said. "Let me read you this verse in Isaiah: 'Blessed'—that means, 'O the happiness of the man that doeth this, and the son of man that layeth hold on it; that keepeth the sabbath from pollut-ing it, and keepeth his hand from doing any evil. Neither let the son of the stranger that hath joined him-self to the Lord'—there, Leslie, that means us, or any Gentiles that want to be Christ's—'speak, saying, The Lord hath utterly separated us from his people. . . . For thus saith the Lord to' them 'that keep my sabbaths, and choose the things that please me, and take hold of my covenant; even unto them will I give in mine house and within my walls a place and a name better than of sons and of daughters; I will give them an everlasting name, that shall not be cut off. Also the sons of the stranger that join themselves to the Lord, to serve him, and to love the name of the Lord, to be his servants, every one that keepeth the sabbath from polluting it, and taketh hold of my covenant; even them will I bring to my holy mountain, and make them joyful in my house of prayer'—you see, Allison, there's a promise that will secure you from feeling the service dull and dry if you are willing to comply with its conditions—'their burnt offerings and their sacrifices shall be accepted upon mine altar; for mine house shall be called a house of prayer for all people.'"

She turned the leaves quickly again.

"And now I want to read you the verse that seems to me to tell how God likes us to keep the Sabbath. 'If thou turn away thy foot from the sabbath, from doing thy pleasure on my holy day; and call the sabbath a de-light'—you see, Leslie, He doesn't want it to be a dull, poky day. He wants us to call it a delight. And yet we are to find our pleasure in Him, and not in the things that belong just to ourselves. Listen: 'a delight, the holy of the Lord, honorable; and shalt honor him, not doing thine own ways, nor finding thine own pleasure, nor speaking thine own words: then shalt thou delight thyself in the Lord; and I will cause thee to ride upon the high places of the earth, and feed thee with the heritage of Jacob thy father; for the mouth of the Lord hath spoken it.' "

Leslie suddenly threw her head in Julia Cloud's lap right over the Bible, and looked up into her face with an exquisite earnestness all her own.

"Cloudy Jewel, it sounds all different from anything I ever heard of, and I don't know how to do it; but something inside says it ought to be true, and I'm going to try it!" she said. "Anyhow, we've had a grand time this afternoon, and it hasn't been a bit dull. Do you suppose maybe we've been 'delighting' in Him this afternoon? But there goes the supper bell, and I'm hungry as a bear. How about that, Cloudy? Is it right to cook on Sunday? That place you read about the man who picked up sticks to make a fire in camp doesn't sound like it."

"Well, dear, you know in the old times we always got the Sunday cooking and baking done on Saturday, just as the Lord told the Israelites to do. I haven't any business to judge other people, and every one must decide for himself what is necessary and what is not, I suppose; but, as for me, I like to do as mother always did. I always have the cake-box and bread-box full of nice fresh things, and make a pie, perhaps, and cook a piece of meat, or have some salad in the ice-box; and then it is the work of but a few minutes to get the nicest kind of a meal on Sunday. It is easy to have a beefsteak to broil, or cold meat, or something to warm up in a minute if one cares enough to get it ready; and it really makes a lovely, restful time on Sunday to know all that work is done. Besides, it isn't any harder. I like it."

Allison gathered up the rug and books, and they walked slowly toward the inn, watching the wonderful colorings of the foliage they passed, and drinking in all the woodsy odors and gentle sounds of dying leaves and dropping nuts.

"Say, Cloudy," said Allison suddenly out of the midst of his thoughtfulness, "why don't the ministers preach about all this? I had to go to church a lot when I was in prep school, and I never yet heard a sermon on it. Or, if I did, it was so dull I didn't get the hang of it. But I should think if they preached about it just as you've done, made it plain so people could understand, that most folks, that is, the ones who wanted to do half right, would see to it that Sunday wasn't so rotten."

"Well, Allison," said Julia Cloud, a soft smile playing dreamfully about her lips, "Perhaps they don't realize the need. Perhaps it's 'up to you,' as you say, to somehow wake them up and set them at it."

Allison drew a long whistle and grinned as they went into the house.

13

A few minutes later Julia Cloud watched them go off into the dusk to the Christian Endeavor meeting. She was to follow them in a little while and meet them for the evening service. She wondered as she saw them disappear into the shadows of the long maple-lined avenue whether perhaps she was not overdoing the matter a little in the way of meetings, and was almost sorry she had not suggested staying home from the evening service. It would not do to make them weary of it all on this first Sunday.

As they walked along together, the brother and sister were thinking deeply.

"Say, Allison, isn't this the very funniest thing we ever did, going off like this to a prayer meeting alone? What did we do it for?" asked the sister.

"Well, I guess just because Cloudy wanted it," replied the brother. "She's given up her home and everything for us; we ought to. But say, Les, there's a whole lot in what Cloudy was reading this afternoon. If it's all true, it's a wonder more people don't try it. I've often wondered why we were alive, anyway, haven't you? There doesn't seem much sense to it unless there's something like this."

"Oh, I don't know, Allison; it's nice to be alive. But of course we never will feel quite as if this is the only place since Mother and Dad aren't here any more. Aren't things queer, anyway? I wish there was some way to be sure."

"Well, I s'pose the Bible claims to be sure. Perhaps we could find out a lot if we read it."

"We're likely to read it quite a good deal, don't you think?" asked the sister archly. "But really, now, it was interesting, and isn't Cloudy a dear? If Christians were all like that, I'd believe in them."

"Perhaps they are, real Christians. Perhaps the ones we mean aren't anything but shams."

"Well, there's a good many shams, then."

The big, noisy bell began to bang out a tardy summons now; but the two young people did not feel the same antipathy toward it that they had felt the night they heard it first. It seemed somehow to have a homely, friendly sound. As they neared the open door, they grew suddenly shy, however, and drew back, lingering on the corner, watching the few stragglers who walked into the pathway of light that streamed from the doorway.

"Some bunch!" growled Allison. "I should say they did need waking up, but I don't hanker for the job."

They slipped in, and followed the sound of voices, through a dimly-lighted hall, smelling of moldy ingrain carpet, into a wide, rather pleasant, chapel room. There were branches of autumn leaves about the walls, reminiscent of some recent festivity, and a bunch of goldenrod in a vase on the little table by the leader's chair.

Two girls were turning over the hymn-book, picking out hymns for the evening; and a tall, shy, girlish young fellow was making fancy letters on a blackboard up in front. Three more girls with their arms about one another had surrounded him, and were giggling and gurgling at him after the manner of that kind of girl. Another plain-faced, plainly-dressed young woman sat half-way up at one side, her hands folded and a look of quiet waiting on her face. That was all that were in the room.

Allison and Leslie found a seat half-way up on the other side from the plain-faced girl, and sat down. No one noticed them save for furtive glances, and no one came near them. The three giggling girls began to talk a little louder. One with her hair bobbed and a long view of vertebrae above her blue dress-collar began to prattle of a dance the night before.

"I thought I'd die!" she chortled. "Bob had me by the arm; and here was my dress caught on Archie's button, and he not knowing and whirling off in the other direction; and the georgette just ripped and tore to beat the band, and me trying to catch up with Archie, and Bob hanging on to me, honest.—You'd uv croaked if you could uv seen me. Oh, but Mother was mad when she saw my dress! She kept blaming me, for she knew I hated that dress and wanted a new one. But me, *I'm* glad. Now I'll get after Dad for a new one. Say, when's Mary's surprise? Is it true it's put off till next week?"

"I'm going to have a new dress for that and silver slippers," declared the girl next her, teetering back and forth on her little high-heeled pumps. "Say, Will, that letter's cock-eyed. What are you giving us? What's the old topic, anyway? I don't see any use in topics. They don't mean anything. I never can find a verse with the words in. I just always ask for a hymn, and half the time I give out any old number without knowing what it is, just to see what it'll turn out."

"Oh, say! Did you hear Chauncey Cramer singing last Sunday night?" broke out the third girl with a side glance at the strangers. "He was perfectly killing. He was twisting the words all around in every hymn. He had girls' names and fellers' all mixed up, and made it rhyme in the neatest way. I thought I'd choke laughing, and Dr. Tarrant was just coming in, and looked at me as if he'd eat me. Oh, my goodness! There he comes now. We better beat it, Hattie. Come on, Mabel. Let's sit back in the last row."

The three girls toppled down the aisle on their high-heeled pumps, and rustled into the back row just as the pastor entered and looked about the room. His eyes brightened when he saw the brother and sister, and with a pleasant "Good-evening" to the three whispering misses in the back seat he came over to shake hands with Allison and Leslie. But, when he expressed a most cordial hope that the two would come in and help in the young people's work, Allison was wary. He said they would have to see how much time they had to spare after college opened. It was altogether likely that they would be exceedingly busy with their college work.

The minister, watching their bright faces wistfully, and knowing their kind, sighed, and thought how little likelihood there was that his Christian Endeavor society would see much of them.

A few more people straggled in, and one of the girls who had been picking out hymns went and sat down at the piano. The other girls sat near her. The young man at the blackboard took his place at the little table in front of the desk, and the elaborate colored letters which he had just made were visible as a whole for the first time.

THE GREAT COMPANION: HOW TO LIVE WITH HIM

There was something startling and solemn in the words as they stood out in blue and gold and crimson and white on the little blackboard. Allison and Leslie looked and turned wonderingly toward the young leader. He had corn-colored hair, light, ineffective blue eyes, and a noticeably weak chin. He did not look like a person who would be putting forth a topic of that sort and attempting to do anything about it. His face grew pink, and his eyelashes seemed whiter in contrast as he stood up to give out the first hymn. It was plain that he was painfully embarrassed. He glanced now and then deprecatingly toward the visitors with an anxious gasp as he announced that they would open the meeting by singing number twenty-nine. The two young strangers opened their hymn-books and found the place, marveling how such a youth had ever been persuaded to get himself into such a trying situation. Allison found himself thinking that there must be some power greater than the ordinary influences of life that made him do it. He seemed so much out of his element, and so painfully shy.

"All to Jesus I surrender!" chirped the little gathering gayly. They had good voices, and the harmony was simple and pleasing. Allison and Leslie joined their beautiful voices in with the rest, and liked it, felt almost as if they were on the verge of doing something toward helping on the kingdom of heaven.

They sang another hymn, and more young people came in until there were twenty-four in the room. Then the leader called upon Tom Forbes to read the Scripture, and a boy about fourteen years old read in a clear voice the story of the walk to Emmaus. To the brother and sister whose Bible knowledge was limited to the days of their very young childhood, it was most interesting. They listened intently, but were surprised to notice a tendency to whisper on the part of some, especially the girls in the back seat, who had been joined by three young fellows of about their own age and caliber. Leslie, glancing over her shoulder at the whisperers, saw they had no thrill over the story, no interest save in their own voluble conversation. The story went on to the point where Jesus at the table blessed the bread, and the two men knew Him, and He vanished out of their sight, without an interruption in the whispering. The Great Companion had come into the room and gone, and they had not even known it.

The leader rose, and cleared his voice with courage; and then in a tone of diffidence he recited the few words he had learned for the occasion.

"Our topic to-night is 'The Great Companion: How to Live with Him.' It seems hard to realize that Christ is still on the earth. That He is with us all the time. We ought to realize this. We ought to try to realize it. It would make our lives different if we could realize that Christ is always with us. I expect some of us wouldn't always feel comfortable if we should find Him walking along with us, listening to our talk. We ought to try to live so we would feel all right if we should find Christ walking with us some day. And I heard a story once about a boy who had been a cripple, and he had been a great Christian; and, when he came to die, they asked him if he was afraid; and he said no, he wasn't afraid, that it was only going into another room with Jesus. And I think we ought to all live that way. We will now listen to a solo by Mame Beecher, after which the meeting will be open, and I hope that all will take part."

It was a crude little speech, haltingly spoken, and the speaker was evidently relieved when it was over. Yet there had been amazing truth in what he had said, and it came to the two visitors with the force of newness. As he mopped his perspiring brow with a large handkerchief and sat down, adjusting his collar and necktie nervously, they watched him, and marvelled again that he had been willing to be put in so trying a position. There had been a genuineness about him that brought convic-

tion. This young man really believed in Christ and that
He walked with men.

Allison, always ready to curl his lips over anything
sissified, sat watching him gravely. Here was a new
specimen. He didn't know where to place him. Did he
have to lead a meeting? Was he a minister's son or something, or did he just do it because he wanted to, because
it seemed his duty to do it? Allison could not decide. He
knew that he himself could have made a much better
speech on the subject, but he would not want to. He
would hate it, talking about sacred things like that out
to the world; yet he was frank enough to see that a better speech might not have been so acceptable to God as
this halting one full of repetition and crudities.

The girl up by the piano was singing the solo. Why
did she let herself be called "Mame" in that common
way? She was a rather common-looking girl, with loud
colors in her garments and plenty of powder in evidence
on her otherwise pretty face; but she had a good voice,
and sang the words distinctly.

> In the secret of His presence how my soul delights to
> hide!
> Oh, how precious are the lessons which I learn at Jesus'
> side!

The words were wonderful. They somehow held you
through to the end. The girl named Mame had that quality of holding attention with her voice and carrying a
message to a heart. There were two lines that seemed
particularly impressive,

> And whene'er you leave the silence of that happy meet-
> ing-place,
> You must mind and bear the image of the Master in your
> face.

Leslie found herself looking around the room to see whether any one person bore that image, and her eyes lingered longest on the quiet girl in the plain garments over on the other side of the room. She had a face that was almost beautiful in its repose, if it had not worn that air of utter reticence.

There was a long pause after the soloist was done, and much whispering from the back row, which at last terminated in a flutter of Bible leaves and the reading of three Bible verses containing the word "companion," without much reference to the topic, from the three girls on the back seat, passing the Bible in turn, with much ado to find their respective places. Another hymn followed, and a prayer from a solemn-looking boy in shell-rimmed spectacles. It was a good prayer, but the young man wore also that air of reticence that characterized the girl on the other side of the room, as if he were not a part of these young people, had nothing in common with them. Allison decided that they were all dead, and surely did need some one to wake them up; but the task was not to his liking. What had he in common with a bunch like that? In fact, what had any of them in common that they should presume to form themselves into a society? It was rank nonsense. You couldn't bring people together that had nothing in common and make them have a good time. These were his thoughts during another painful pause, during which the pastor in the back seat half rose, then sat down and looked questioningly toward the two visitors. The young leader seemed to understand the signal; for he grew very red, looked at Allison and Leslie several times, cleared his throat, turned over his hymn-book, and finally said with painful embarrassment:

"We should be glad to hear from our visitors tonight. We'd like to know how you conduct things in your society."

He lifted agonized eyes to Allison, and broke down in a choking cough.

Allison, chilled with amazement, filled with a sudden strange pity, looked around with growing horror to see whether it was really true that he had been called upon to speak in meeting. Then with the old nonchalance that nothing ever quite daunted he rose to his feet.

"Why, I," he began, looking around with a frank smile, "I never was in a Christian Endeavor meeting before in my life, and I don't know the first thing about it. My sister and I only came tonight because somebody wanted us to; so I can't very well tell about any other society. But I belong to a college frat, and I suppose it's a good deal the same thing in the long run. I've been reading that pledge up there on the wall. I suppose that's your line. You've got good dope all right. If you live up to that, you're going some.

"I remember when I first went to college the fellows began to rush me. I had bids from two or three different frats, and they had me going so hard I got bewildered. I didn't know which I wanted to join. Then one day one of the older fellows got hold of me, and he saw how it was with me; and he said: 'You want to look around and analyze things. Just you look the fellows over, and see how they size up in the different frats. Then you see what they stand for, and how they live up to it; and lastly you look at their alumni.' So I began to size things up, and I found that one frat was all for the social doings, dances, and dinners, and always having a good time; and another was pretty wild, had the name of always getting in bad with the faculty, and had the lowest marks in the college; three fellows had been expelled the year before for drunkenness and disorderliness. Then another one was known as ranking highest in scholarship and having the most athletes in it. I looked over their alumni, too, for they used to come around a good bit and get in with us boys; and you could see just which were making good out in the world, and which were just in life for what they could get out of it; and I made my decision one day just because of one big man who had been out of college for ten years; but he had made good in the world, and was known all over as being a successful man and a wonderful man, and he used to come back to every game and everything that went on at the college, and sit around and talk with the fellows, and encourage them; and, if anybody was falling down on his job, he would show him where he was wrong and how to get into line again, and even help him financially if he got in a tight place. And so I thought with men like that back of it that frat was a pretty good thing to tie up to, and I joined it, and found it was even better than I expected.

"And I was thinking as I looked at the blackboard, and heard you talking about the Great Companion, it was something like that man. If all that's true that you've been reading and saying tonight, why, you've got pretty good things back of you. With an Alumnus like that"—nodding toward the blackboard—"and a line of talk like that pledge, you sure ought to have a drag with the world. All you've got to do is to make everybody believe that it is really so, and you'd have this room full; for, believe me, that's the kind of dope everybody wants, especially young people, whether they own it or not."

Allison sat down abruptly, suddenly realizing that he had just made a religious speech and had the interest of the meeting in his hands. His speech seemed to set loose something in the heart of the young leader; for he rose eagerly, alertly, his embarrassment departed, and began to speak:

"I'm glad our friend has spoken that way. I guess it's all true what he has just said. We've got the right dope;

only we aren't using it. I guess it looks mighty like to the world as if we didn't really believe it all, the way we live; but believe me, I'm going to try to make things different in my life this week, and see if I can't make at least one person believe we have something here they want before next Sunday."

He seemed about to give out another hymn, but the plain girl spoke up and interrupted him. She was sitting forward in her chair, an almost radiant look upon her face that quite changed it; and she spoke rapidly, breathlessly, like a shy person who had a great message to convey. She was looking straight at Allison as if she had forgotten everyone else in the room.

"I've got to speak," she said earnestly. "It isn't right to keep still when I've had such a wonderful experience, and you spoke as if it might not all be true about Christ's being our companion every day." In spite of himself Allison met her eyes as though they were talking alone together, and waited for what she should tell.

"I've always been just a quiet Christian," she went on; "and I don't often speak here except to recite a Bible verse. I'm sort of a stranger myself. But you all ought to know what Christ has done for me. When my people died and everything in my life was changed, and troubles came very thick and fast, there wasn't anybody in the world I could turn to for every-day help and companionship but Jesus; and one day it came to me how my mother used to feel about Him, and I just went to Him, and asked Him to be my companion, as He used to be hers. I didn't half believe He would when I asked Him; but I was so hurt and alone I had to do something; and I found out it was all true! He helped me in so many little everyday ways, you wouldn't believe it, perhaps, unless you could have lived it out yourself. I guess you really have to live it out to know it, after all. But I found that I could go to Him just as if I could see Him, and I was so surprised the first day when He answered a prayer in a perfectly wonderful way. It all came over me, 'Why, He loves me!' And at first I thought it was just happening; but I tried it again and again, and every day wonderful things began to come into my life, and it got to be that I could talk with Him and feel His answer in my heart. If it were not for Him, I couldn't stand life sometimes. And I'm sure He'll talk with any one that way who wants Him enough to try and find Him," she finished; and then, suddenly conscious of herself, she sat back, white and shy again, with trembling lips.

The meeting closed then; but, while they were singing the last hymn Allison and Leslie were watching the face of the quiet girl with the holy, uplifted light on it.

"I think she is lovely, don't you?" whispered Leslie after the benediction, as they turned to go out. "I'd like to know her."

"H'm!" assented Allison. "Cloudy would like her, I guess."

"I mean to find out who she is," declared Leslie.

The minister came up just then with cordial greeting and urgent appeal that the young people would at once join their Christian Endeavor.

"That was a great talk you gave us tonight," he said with his hand resting admiringly on Allison's shoulder. "We need young blood. You are the very one to stir up this society."

"But I'm not a Christian," said Allison, half laughing. "I don't belong here."

"Oh, well," answered the smiling minister, "if you take hold of the Endeavor, perhaps you'll find you're more of a Christian than you think. Come, I want you to meet some of our young people."

The young people were all gathered in groups, looking toward the strangers, and came quite willingly to have a nearer glimpse of them. Last of all, and by herself, came the plain-faced girl; and the minister introduced her as Jane Bristol. He did not speak to her more than that, and it occurred to Allison that she seemed as if she came more at the instigation of some higher power than at the call of her pastor; for she passed quietly on again in a pleasant dignity, and did not stop to talk and joke with her pastor as some of the other young people had done.

"Who is she?" asked Allison, hardly aware that he was asking.

"Why, she is the daughter of a forger who died in prison. Her mother, I believe, died of a broken heart. Sad experience for so young a girl. She seems to be a good little thing. She is working at housework in town, I believe. I understand she has an idea of entering college in the fall. You are entering college here? That will be delightful. My wife and I will take pleasure in calling on you as soon as you are ready to receive visitors."

Leslie's eyes were on Jane Bristol as she moved slowly toward the door, lingering a moment in the hall. None of the other girls seemed to have anything to do with her. With her usual impulsiveness Leslie left Allison, and went swiftly down the aisle till she stood by Jane Bristol's side.

"We are going to meet my aunt and stay to church. Would you come and sit with us to-night?" she asked eagerly. "I'd like to get acquainted with you."

Jane Bristol shook her head with a wistful smile.

"I'm sorry," she said. "I wish I could. But I take care of a little girl evenings, and I only get off long enough for Christian Endeavor. It's dear of you to ask me."

"Well, you'll come and see me when I get settled in my new home, won't you?"

Jane looked at her thoughtfully, and then gave her a beautiful smile in answer to Leslie's brilliant one.

"Yes, if you find you want me when you get settled,

I'll come," she answered, and giving Leslie's little gloved hand an impulsive squeeze, she said, "Good-night," and went away.

Leslie looked after her a minute, half understanding, and then turned to find her brother beside her.

"She thinks I won't want her because she works!" she said. "But I do. I shall."

"Sure you will, kid," said her brother. "Just tell Cloudy about her. She'll fix things. That old party—I mean, the reverend gentleman—"

"Look out, Allison, that isn't any better; and there comes Cloudy. Don't make her feel bad again."

"Well, parson, then—doesn't seem to have much use for a person who's had the misfortune to have her father commit forgery and her mother die of a broken heart, or is it because she has to work her way through college? He may be all right, sister; but I'd bank on that girl's religion over against his any day in the week, Sundays included."

Then Julia Cloud came up the steps, and they went in to a rather dreary evening service with a sparse congregation and a bored-looking choir, who passed notes and giggled during the sermon. Allison and Leslie sat and wondered what kind of a shock it would be to them all if the Great Companion should suddenly become visible in the room. If all that about His being always present was true, it certainly was a startling thing.

14

THE next morning dawned with a dull, dreary drizzle coming noisily down on the red and yellow leaves of the maple by the window; but the three rose joyously and their ardor was not damped.

"Six days shalt thou labor and do all thy work," quoted Allison at the breakfast-table. "Cloudy, we've got to hustle. Do you mind if it does rain? We've got our car."

But Julia Cloud smiled unconcernedly.

"I should worry," she said with a gay imitation of Leslie's inimitable toss of the head, and the two young people laughed so hilariously that the other staid couples already in the dining-room turned in amazement to see who was taking life so happily on a day like this.

They piled into the car, and hied themselves to town at once, chattering joyfully over their list as to which things they would buy first.

"Let's begin with the kitchen," said Leslie. "I'm crazy to learn how to make cookies. Cloudy, you'll teach me how so I can make some all myself, won't you?"

"And waffles!" said Allison from the front seat.

"Um-mmm-mmmm! I remember Cloudy's waffles. And buckwheat cakes."

"We're going to have everything for the kitchen to make things easy, so that when we can't get a maid Cloudy won't be always overdoing," said Leslie. "Guardy told me especially about that. He said we were to get every convenience to make things easy, so the cook wouldn't leave; for he'd rather pay any amount than have Cloudy work herself to death and have to break down and leave us."

So it was the house-furnishing department of the great store to which they first repaired, and there they hovered for two hours among tins and aluminum and wooden ware, discussing the relative charms of white-enamel refrigerators and gas-ranges, vacuum cleaners and dish-washers, the new ideas against the old. Julia Cloud was for careful buying and getting along with few things; the children were infatuated with the idea of a kitchen of their own, and wanted everything in sight. They went wild over a new kind of refrigerator that would freeze its own ice, making ice-cream in the bargain, and run by an electric motor; but here Julia Cloud held firm. No such expensive experiment was needed in their tiny kitchen. A small white, old-fashioned kind was good enough for them. So the children immediately threw their enthusiasm into selecting the best kind of ice-cream freezer.

When they finally went to the tea-room for lunch, everything on Julia Cloud's list was carefully checked off by Allison with its respective price; and, while they were waiting to be served, he added the column twice to make sure he was right.

"We're shy five dollars yet of what we planned to spend on our kitchen, Cloudy," he announced radiantly. "What did I tell you?"

"But where would you have been if I had let you get that refrigerator?" she retorted.

"Well, there were a lot of things we didn't really need," he answered.

"Such as what?"

"Oh, clothes-pins and—well, all those pans. Did you need so many?" he answered helplessly.

They laughed his masculine judgment out of countenance, and chatted away about what they should do next, until their order arrived.

They were like three children as they ate their lunch, recalling now and then some purchase which gave them particular pleasure.

Suddenly Julia Cloud lifted her hands in mock distress. "I know what we've forgotten! Dish-towels!" she said.

"Dish-towels! Why, sure. We have to have a lot so we can all wipe dishes when the cook goes out. Will five dollars buy them, Cloudy?" asked Leslie distressingly.

"Well, I certainly should hope so!" said Julia Cloud, laughing "The idea! Five dollars' worth of dish-towels!"

"Well, we'll go and get them at once," said Leslie; "and after that we'll do the bedrooms."

Five o'clock found them wending their way homeward once more, tired but happy.

"Now, to-morrow," said Julia Cloud, leaning back on the soft cushions, "I think we had better stay at home and receive the things. The house must be cleaned at once, and then we can put things right where they are going to belong. Allison, you ought to be able to get a man to wash windows. I'll ask the chambermaid about a woman to help clean, and Leslie and I will make curtains while you put up the rods."

They were so interesting a trio at their table in the inn

dining-room that night that people around began to ask who were those two charming young people and their beautiful mother. Little ripples of query went around the room as they entered, for they were indeed noticeable anywhere. The young people were bubbling over with life and spirits and kindliness, and Julia Cloud in her silvery robes and her white hair made a pleasant picture. But they were so wholly wrapped up in their own housekeeping plans that they were utterly unaware of the interest they excited in their fellow-boarders. Just at present they had no time to spare on other people. They were playing a game, just as they used to play house when they were little, with their aunt; and they wanted no interruption until they should have completed the home and were ready to move in and begin to live. After that other people might come in for their attention.

The next morning bright and early Allison was up and out, hunting his man, and announced triumphantly at the breakfast-table that he was found and would be down at the house and ready for work in half an hour. Breakfast became a brief ceremony after that. For Julia Cloud also had not been idle, and had procured the address of a good woman to clean the house. Allison rushed off after the car, and in a few minutes they were on their way, first to leave Julia Cloud and Leslie at the house to superintend the man, and then to hunt the woman. He presently returned with a large colored woman sitting imposingly in the back seat, her capable hands folded in her lap, a look of intense satisfaction on her ample countenance.

Julia Cloud had thoughtfully brought from home a large bundle of cleaning-rags, and a little canned-alcohol heater presently supplied hot water. Leslie made a voyage of discovery, and purchased soap and scouring-powder; and soon the whole little house was a hive of workers.

"Now," said Julia Cloud, opening the bundle of curtain material, "where shall we begin?"

"Right here," said Leslie, looking around the big white living-room with satisfaction. "I'm just longing to see this look like a home; and you must admit, Cloudy, that this room is the real heart of the house. We'll eat and sleep and work and study in the other rooms; but here we'll really live, right around that dear fireplace. I'm just crazy to see it made up and burning. Oh, won't it be great?"

Busy hands and shining scissors went to work, measuring, cutting, turning hems; and presently a neat pile of white curtains, the hems all turned ready for stitching, lay in the wide back window-seat. Then they went at the other rooms, the sun-porch room and the dining-room. But before that was quite finished a large furniture-truck arrived, and behold the sewing-machine had come! Leslie was so eager to get at it that she could hardly wait until the rest of the load was properly disposed.

She was not an experienced sewer, but she brought to her work an enthusiasm that stood loyally beside her aunt's experience, and soon some of the curtains were up.

They could not bear to stop and go back to the inn for lunch; so Allison ran down to the pie-shop with the car, and brought back buns cut into halves and buttered, with great slices of ham in them, a pail of hot sweetened coffee, a big cocoanut pie, a bag of cakes, and a basket of grapes; and they made a picnic of it.

"Our first meal in our own house! Isn't it great?" cried Leslie, dancing around with a roll sandwich in one hand and a wedge of pie in the other.

By night every clean little window in that many-windowed house was curtained with white drapery, and in some rooms also with inner curtains of soft silk. The house began to look cozy in spite of its emptiness, and they could hardly bear to leave it when sunset warned them that it was getting near dinner-time and they must return to the inn to freshen up for the evening.

Another day at the little house completed the cleaning and curtaining, and by this time all the furniture so far purchased had arrived, and they had no need to be there to watch for anything else; so another day of shopping was agreed upon.

"And I move we pick out the piano first of all," said Leslie. "I'm just crazy to get my fingers on the keys again, and you don't know how well Allison can sing, Cloudy. You just ought to hear him. Oh, boy!"

Julia Cloud smiled adoringly at the two, and agreed that the piano was as good a place as any to begin.

That day was the best of all the wonderful shopping to Julia Cloud. To be actually picking out wonderful mahogany furniture such as she had seen occasionally in houses of the rich, such as she had admired in pictures and read of in magazine articles, seemed too wonderful to be true. For the first time in her life she was to live among beautiful things, and she felt as if she had stepped into at least the anteroom of heaven. It troubled her a little to be allowing the children to spend so much, even though their guardian had made it plain that they had plenty to spend; for it did not seem quite right to use so much on one's self when so many were in need; but gradually her viewpoint began to change. It was true that these things were only relative, and what seemed much to her was little to another. Perhaps coming directly from her exceedingly limited sphere she was no fit judge of what was right and necessary. And of course there was always the fact that good things lasted, and were continually beautiful if well chosen. Also much good might be done to a large circle of outsiders by a beautiful home.

So Julia Cloud, because the matter of expenditure was not, after all, in her hands, decided just to have a good time and enjoy picking out these wonderful things, interfering only where she thought the article the children selected was not worth buying, or was foolish and useless. But on the whole they got along beautifully, and agreed most marvellously about what fitted the little pink-and-white stone "villa," as Leslie had named it. " 'Cloudy Villa,' that's what we'll call it," she cried one day in sudden inspiration; and so it was called thereafter in loving jest.

Two days more of hard work, and their list was nearly finished. By this time they were almost weary of continually trying to decide which thing to get. A bewildering jumble of French gray bedsteads and mahogany tables and dining-room chairs swung around in their minds when they went to sleep at night, and smilingly met their waking thoughts. They were beginning to long for the time when they could sit down in the dining-room chairs, and get acquainted with their beds and tables, and feel at home.

"I wish we could get in by Sunday," grumbled Allison. "It's fierce hanging around this hotel with nothing to do."

"Well, why not?" assented Julia Cloud as she buttered her breakfast muffin. "The bedding was promised to come out this morning, and I don't see why we couldn't make up the beds and sleep there tonight, although I don't know whether we can get the gas-range connected in time to do much cooking."

"Oh, we can come back here for our meals till next week," declared Leslie. "Then we'll have time to get the dishes unpacked and washed and put in that lovely china-closet. Perhaps we'll be able to get at that today. The curtains are every blessed one up, inside and out, now; and, if we succeed in getting that maid that you heard of, why, we'll be all fixed for next week. I do wish those California things would arrive and we could get the rugs down. It doesn't look home without rugs and pictures."

And, sure enough, they had not been at work ten minutes before the newly-acquired telephone bell rang, and the freight agent announced that their goods were at the station, and asked whether they wanted them sent up today, for he wanted to get the car out of his way. In two hours more the goods arrived, and right in the midst of their unloading the delivery-wagons from the city brought a lot more articles; and so the little pink-and-white house was a scene of lively action for some time.

When the last truck had started away from the house, Allison drove the car up.

"Now, Cloudy, you jump in quick, and we're going back to the inn for lunch. Then you lie down and rest a whole hour, and sleep, or I won't let you come back," he announced. "I saw a tired look around your eyes, and it won't do. We are not going to have you worked out, not if we stay in that old inn for another month. So there!"

He packed them in, and whirled them away to the inn in spite of Julia Cloud's protest that she was not tired and wanted to work; but, when they came back at two o'clock, they all felt rested and fit for work again.

"Now, I'm the man, and I'm going to boss for a while," said Allison. "You two ladies go up-stairs, and make beds. Here, which are the blankets and sheets? I'll take the bundles right up there, and you won't have any running up and down to do. These? All of them? All right. Now come on up, and I'll be undoing the rugs and boxes from California. When you come down, they'll be all ready for you to say where they shall go."

Leslie and her aunt laughingly complied, and had a

beautiful time unfolding and spreading the fine white sheets, plumping the new pillows into their cases, laying the soft, gay-bordered blankets and pretty white spreads, till each bed was fair and fit for a good night's sleep. And then at the foot of each was plumped, in a puff of beauty, the bright satin eiderdowns that Leslie had insisted upon. Rose-color for Julia Cloud's, robin's-egg blue for Leslie's, and orange and brown for Allison's, who had insisted upon mahogany and quiet colors for his room. Leslie's furniture was ivory-white, and Julia Cloud's room was furnished in French gray enamel, with insets of fine cane-work. She stood a moment in the open doorway, and looked about the place; soft gray walls, with a trellis of roses at the top, filmy white draperies with a touch of rose, a gray couch luxuriously upholstered, with many pillows, some rose, some gray, a thick, gray rug under her feet, and her own little gray desk drawn out conveniently when she wanted to write. Over all a flood of autumn sunshine, and on the wall a great water-color of a marvellous sunset that Leslie had insisted belonged in that room and must be bought or the furnishing would not be complete.

It filled Julia Cloud's eyes with tears of wonder and gratitude to think that such a princess's abode should have come to be her abiding-place after her long years of barren living in dreary surroundings. She lifted her eyes to the sunset picture on the wall, and it reminded her of the evening when she had stood at her own home window in her distress and sorrow, looking into the gray future, and had watched it break into rose-color before her eyes. For just an instant after Leslie had run down-stairs she closed her door, and dropped upon her knees beside the lovely bed to thank her Lord for this green and pleasant pasture where He had led her tired feet.

Allison had all the rugs spread out on the porch and lawn, and he and Leslie were hard at work giving them a good sweeping. They were wonderful rugs, just such as one would expect to come from a home of wealth where money had never been a consideration. Julia Cloud looked at them almost with awe, recognizing by instinct the priceless worth of them, and almost afraid of the idea of living a common, daily life on them. For Julia Cloud had read about rugs. She knew that in far lands poor peasant people, whole families, sometimes wove their history into them for a mere pittance; and they had come to mean something almost sacred in her thoughts.

But Allison and Leslie had no such reverence for them; and they swept away gayly, and slammed them about familiarly, in a happy hurry to get them in place. So presently the big blue Chinese rug covered the living-room, almost literally; for it was an immense one, and left very little margin around it. A handsome Kermanshah in old rose and old gold with pencillings of black was spread forth under the mahogany dining-table, and a rich dark-red and black Bokhara runner fitted the porch-room as if it had been bought for it. The smaller rugs were quickly disposed here and there, a lovely little rose-colored silk prayer rug being forced upon Julia Cloud for her bedroom as just the finishing touch it needed, and Leslie took possession of two or three smaller blue rugs for her room. Then they turned their attention to pictures, bits of jade and bronze, a few rare pieces of furniture, a wonderful old bronze lamp with a great dragon on a sea of wonderful blue enamel, with a shade that cast an amber light; brass andirons and fender, and a lot of other little things that go to make a lovely home.

"Now," said Allison, "when we get our books unpacked, and some magazines thrown around, it will look like living. Cloudy, can we sleep here to-night?"

"Why, surely," said Julia Cloud with a child-like delight in her eyes. "What's to hinder? I feel as if I was in a dream, and if I didn't go right on playing it was true I would wake up and find it all gone."

So they rode back to the inn for their supper, hurried their belongings into the trunk, and moved bag and baggage into the new house at nine o'clock on Saturday night.

While Leslie and her aunt were up-stairs putting away their clothes from the trunk into the new closets and bureau-drawers, Allison brought in a few kindlings, and made a bit of a fire on the hearth; and now he called them down.

"We've got to have a housewarming the first night, Cloudy," he called. "Come down and see how it all looks in the firelight."

So the two came down-stairs, and all three sat together on the deep-blue velvet settee in front of the fireplace, Julia Cloud in the middle and a child on either side.

They were all very tired and did not say much, just sat together happily, watching the wood blaze up and flicker and fall into embers. Presently both children nestled closer to her, and put down a head on each of her shoulders. So they sat for a long time quietly.

"Now," said Julia Cloud, as the fire died down and the room grew dusky with shadows, "it is time we went to bed. But there is something I wish we could do this first night in our new home. Don't you think we ought to dedicate it to God, or at least thank God for giving it to us? Would you be willing to kneel down with me, and—we might just all pray silently, if you don't feel like praying out loud. Would you be willing to do that?"

There was a tender silence for a moment while the children thought.

"Sure!" growled Allison huskily. "You pray out, Cloudy. We'd like it."

"Yes," whispered Leslie, nestling her hand in her aunt's.

And so, trembling, half fearful, her heart in her throat, but bravely, Julia Cloud knelt with a child on either side, hiding wondering, embarrassed, but loyal faces.

There was a tense silence while Julia Cloud struggled for words to break through her unwilling lips, and then quite softly she breathed:

"O dear Christ, come and dwell in this home, and bless it. Help us to live to please Thee. Help me to be a wise guide to these dear children—"

She paused, her voice suddenly giving way with a nervous choke in her throat, and the two young hands instantly squeezed her hands in sympathy.

Then a gruff young voice burst out on one side,

"Help me to be good, and not hurt her or make it hard for her."

And Leslie gasped out, "And me, too, dear God!"

Then a moment more, and they all rose, tears on their faces. In the dying firelight they kissed Julia Cloud fervently, and said good-night.

15

LESLIE and Allison did not go to the Christian Endeavor meeting that second Sunday. They were tired out, and wanted to stay at home all the evening, and Julia Cloud felt that it would be unwise to urge them; so they sat around the fire and talked. Leslie sat down at the new piano, and played softly old hymns that Julia Cloud hummed; and they all went to bed early, having had a happy Sabbath in their new home.

But Monday evening quite early, just after they had come back from supper and were talking about reading a story aloud, there came a knock at the door. Their first caller! And behold, there stood the inefficient-looking young man who had led the Christian Endeavor meeting, the boy with the goggles who had prayed, and the two girls who had sat by the piano.

"We're a committee," announced the young man, quite embarrassed. "My name's Herricote, Joe Herricote. I'm president of our Christian Endeavor Society, and this is Roy Bryan; he's the secretary. This is Mame Beecher. I guess you remember her singing. She's chairman of our social committee, and Lila Cary's our pianist and chairman of the music committee. We've come to see if you won't help us."

"Come in," said Allison cordially, but with a growing disappointment. Now, here were these dull people coming to interrupt their pleasant evening, and there wouldn't be many of them, for college would soon begin, and they would be too busy then to read stories and just enjoy themselves.

Leslie, too, frowned, but came forward politely to be introduced. She knew at a glance that these were not people of the kind she cared to have for friends.

"We're a committee," repeated young Herricote, sitting down on the edge of a chair, and looking around most uncomfortably at the luxurious apartment. He had not realized it would be like this. He was beginning to feel like a fish out of water. As for the rest of the committee, they were overawed and dumb, all except the little fellow with the tortoise-rimmed glasses. He was not looking at anything but Allison, and was intent on his mission. When he saw that his superior had been struck dumb, he took up the story.

"They appointed us to come and interview you, and see if you wouldn't give us some new ideas how to run our society so it would be a success," he put in. "They all liked your speech so much the other night they felt you could help us out of the rut we've got into."

"Me?" asked Allison, laughing incredulously. "Why, I told you I didn't know the first thing about Christian Endeavor."

"But we've gotta have your help," said the young secretary earnestly. "This thing's gotta go! It's needed in our church, and it's the only thing in the town to help some of the young people. It's just *gotta* go!"

"Well, if you feel that way, you'll make it go, I'm sure," encouraged Allison. "You're just the kind of a fellow to make it go. You know all about it. Not I. I never heard of the thing till last week, except just in a casual way. Don't know much about it yet."

"Well, s'pose it was one of your frats, and it wasn't succeeding. What would you do? You saw what kind of a dead-and-alive meeting we had, only a few there, and nobody taking much interest. How would you pull up a frat that was that way?"

"Well," said Allison, speaking at random, "I'd look around, and find some of the right kind of fellows, and rush 'em. Get in some new blood."

"That's all right," said Bryan doggedly. "I'm rushin' you. How do you do it? I never went to college yet; so I don't know."

Allison laughed now. He rather liked this queer boy.

"He's a nut!" he said to himself, and entered into the talk in earnest.

"Why, you have parties, and rides, and good times generally, and invite a fellow, and make him feel at home, and make him want to belong. See?"

"I see," said Bryan, with a twinkling glance at the rest of his committee. "We have a party down at my house Friday night. Will you come?"

Allison saw that the joke was on him, and his reserve broke down entirely.

"Well, I guess it's up to me to come," he said. "Yes, I'm game. I'll come."

Bryan turned his big goggles on Leslie.

"Will you come?"

"Why, yes, if Allison does, I will," agreed Leslie, dimpling.

"That's all right," said Bryan, turning back to Allison. "Now, what do you do when you rush? You'll have to teach us how."

"Well," said Allison thoughtfully, "we generally pick out our best rushers, the ones that can talk best, and put them wise. We never let the fellow that's rushed know what we're doing. Oh, if he has brains, he always knows, of course; but you don't say you're rushing him in so many words. At college we meet a fellow at the train, and show him around the place, and put him onto all the little things that will make it easy for him; and we invite him to eat with us, and help him out in every way we can. We appoint some one to look after him specially, and a certain group have him in their charge so the other frats won't have a chance to rush him—"

"I see. The other frats being represented by the devil, I suppose," said the round-eyed boy keenly without a smile.

Allison stared at him, and then broke into a laugh again.

"Exactly," he cried; "you've got onto the idea. It's your society over against the other things that can draw them away from what you stand for. See? And then there's another thing. You want to have something ready to show them when you get them there. That's where our alumni come in. They often run down to college for a few days and help us out with money and influence and experience. If you've got good working alumni, you're right in it, you see. We generally appoint a committee to talk things over with the alumni."

"You mean," said Bryan, drawing his brows together in a comical way behind his goggles, "you mean—pray, I suppose."

"Why," said Allison, flushing. "I suppose that would be a good idea. I hadn't thought of it just in that way."

"You called Christ our alumnus the other night," reminded the literal youth solemnly.

"So I did," acknowledged Allison embarrassedly. "Well, I guess you're right. But I don't know much about that kind of line."

"I'm afraid there don't many of us," put in the bashful president. "I wouldn't hardly know who to appoint on

such a committee. There's only two or three like to pray
in our meetings. There's Bryan; we always ask him because he doesn't mind, and I—well, I do sometimes
when there's no one else, but it comes hard; and there's
old Miss Ferby, but she always prays so long, and gets
in the president and all the missionary stations—"

"I should think you'd ask that Jane Bristol," spoke up
Leslie earnestly. "I know she must be able to. She talked
that way."

"I suppose she would," responded the president hes-
itatingly, looking toward the two ladies of the committee with a half apology. "What do you girls think about
it?"

"Oh, I suppose she could *pray*," said the girl called
Mame, with a shrug. "She does, you know, often in
meeting."

Then with a giggle toward Leslie she added as if in
explanation, "She works *out*, you know."

"It must be very hard for her," said Leslie, purposely
ignoring the inference.

"Well, you know she isn't in our set. Nobody has
much to do with her."

"Why not? I think she is very unusual," said Leslie
with just the least bit of hauteur.

"Well, it wouldn't be wise to get her into things. It
might keep some others out if we made her prominent,"
put in Lila Cary with some asperity. "We must have
some social distinction, you know."

"In our frat one fellow is as good as another if he has
the right kind of character," remarked Allison dryly.
"That girl sounded to me as if she had some drag with
your alumni. But of course you know her better than I."

"She is a good girl all right and real religious," hastened Lila to amend. "I suppose she'd be real good on a
prayer committee, and would help to fill up there, as
you haven't many."

"Well, I'll tell you one thing," said Allison, "if you really want to succeed, you've got to pull together, every member of you, or you won't get anywhere. And I should think that you'd have to be careful now at first whom you get in. Of course after you're pretty strong you can take in a few just to help them; but, if you get in too many of that lame kind, your society'll go bad. The weak kind will rule, and the mischief will be to pay. I shouldn't think it would help you any just now to get in any folks that would feel that way about a good girl just because she earns her living."

Mame Beecher and Lila Cary looked at each other in alarm, and hastened to affirm that they never felt that way about Jane Bristol. *They* thought she was a real good sort, and had always meant to get acquainted with her; only she always slipped out as soon as meeting was over.

Back in the dining-room behind the rose-lined blue-velvet hangings Julia Cloud lingered and smiled over the way her two children were developing opinions and character. How splendid of them to take this stand! And who was Jane Bristol? Assuredly she must be looked up and helped if that was the way the town felt about her, poor child!

"Well," said Bryan in a business-like tone, "I'm secretary. Joe, you call that prayer committee together Thursday night at your house at half-past seven, and I'll send a notice to each one. You make Jane Bristol chairman, and I'll be on the committee; and I'll go after her and take her home. Now, who else are you going to have on it?"

The president assented readily. He was one not used to taking the initiative, but he eagerly did as he was told when a good idea presented itself.

"We want you on it," he said, nodding to Allison, and then, looking shyly at Leslie, added, "And you?"

"Oh!" said Leslie, flushing in fright, "what would we have to do? I never prayed before anybody in my life. I'm not sure I even know how to pray, only just to say 'Thank you' to God sometimes. I think you could find somebody better."

"We've got to have you this time," said the president, shaking his head. "You needn't pray if you don't want to, but you must come and help us through."

"But I couldn't go and be a—a sort of slacker!" said Leslie, her cheeks quite beautifully red.

"That's all right! You come!" said Bryan, looking solemnly at her.

When the visitors finally took themselves away, Allison, polite to the last, closed the door with a courteous "Good-night," and then stood frowning at the fire.

Julia Cloud came softly into the room, and went and stood beside him with loving questions in her eyes. He met her gaze with a new kind of hardness.

"Now, you see what you let me in for, Cloudy, when you made me go to that little old dull Christian Endeavor! But I won't do it! That's all there is to it. You needn't think I'm going to. The idea! Why, what did we come here to college for? To run an asylum for sick Sunday schools, I'd like to know? As if I had time to monkey with their little old society! It's rank nonsense, anyhow! What good do they think they can do, a couple of sissies, and two or three kid vamps, setting up to lisp religion? It's ridiculous!"

He was working himself up into a fine frenzy. Julia Cloud stood and watched him, an amused smile growing on her sweet lips. He caught the amusement, and fired up at it.

"What are you looking like that at me for, Cloudy? You know it is. You know it's all foolishness. And you know I couldn't help them, anyhow. Come, now, don't you? *What* are you looking like that for, Cloudy? I believe you're laughing at me! You think I'll go and get into this thing, but I'll show you. I *won't!* And that's an end of it. Cloudy, I insist on knowing what you find to laugh at in this situation."

"Why, I was just thinking how much you reminded me of Moses," said Julia Cloud sweetly.

"Of *Moses!*" screamed Allison half angrily. "Why, he was a meek man, and I'm not meek. I'm mad! Out and out *mad*, Cloudy. What do you mean?"

"Oh, no, he wasn't always meek," said his aunt thoughtfully; "and he talked just as you are doing when God called on him first to lead the children of Israel out of Egypt. He said he couldn't and he wouldn't and he shouldn't, and made every excuse in the calendar; and finally God had to send along Aaron to help him, although God had said *He* would be with him and make him perfectly able alone to do what He wanted done."

"I suppose I'm Aaron," sighed Leslie, settling into a big chair by the fire. "But I don't like those girls one bit! And I don't care if they stay in seven Egypts."

"Now, look here, Cloudy Jewel," pleaded Allison. "You're not going to get me into any such corner as that. The idea that God would call me to do any of His work when I never had anything at all to do with the church in my life, and I don't want to. How should I know what to do? Why should He ever call me, I'd like to know, when I don't know the first thing about churches? You're all off, Cloudy. Think again. Why, I'm not even what you'd call a Christian. He surely wouldn't call people that haven't—well, what you'd call enlisted with Him, would He?"

"He might," answered Julia Cloud reflectively. She was sitting on the end of the big blue couch, and the firelight played over her white hair with silvery lights, and cast a lovely rose tint over her sweet face. "There were several instances where He called people who had never known Him at all, who, in fact, were worshipping idols and strange gods, and told them to go and do something for Him. There was Paul; he was actually against Him. And there was Abraham; he lived among regular idol-worshippers, and God called him to go into a strange land and founded a new family for him, the beginning of the peculiar people through whose line was to come Jesus, the Saviour of the world. And Abraham went."

"Oh, nonsense, Cloudy! That was in those times. Of course. There wasn't anybody else, I suppose; and He had to take some one. But now there are plenty of people who go to church all the time and like that sort of thing."

"How do you know, Allison? Perhaps you are the only one in this town, and God has sent you here just to do this special work."

"Well, I won't, and that's flat, Cloudy; so you can put the idea right out of your head. I won't, not even for you. Anything that has to do with your personal comfort I wouldn't say that about, of course; but this belongs entirely to that little old ratty church, and I haven't anything at all to do with it; and I want you to forget it, Cloudy, for *I'm not going to do it!*"

"Why, Allison, you're mistaken about me. It isn't my affair, and I don't intend to make it so. I didn't get this up. It's between you and God. If God really called you, you'll have to say no to Him, not to me. I don't intend to make excuses to God for you, child. You needn't think it. And, besides, there's another thing you're very much mistaken about, and that is that you haven't anything to do with the church. When you were a little baby six months old, your father and mother brought you home to our house; and the first Sunday they were there they took you to the old church where all the children and grandchildren had been christened for years, and they stood up and assented to the vows that gave you to God. And they promised for themselves that they would do their best to bring you up in the nurture and admonition of the Lord until you came to years and could finish the bond by giving yourself to the Lord. I shall never forget the sweet, serious look on the face of your lovely girl-mother when she bowed her head in answer to the minister's question, 'Do you thus promise?'"

Allison had stopped in his angry walk up and down the room, and was looking at her interestedly.

"Is that right, Cloudy? Was I baptized in the old Sterling church? I never knew that. Tell me about it," and he seated himself on the other end of the couch, while Leslie switched off the light and nestled down between them, scenting a story.

"Wasn't I, too, Cloudy?" she asked hungrily.

"No, dear, I think you were baptized in California in your mother's church, and I'm sorry to say I wasn't there to see; so I can't tell you about it; but I remember very distinctly all about Allison's christening, for we were all so happy to have it happen in the East, and he was the first grandchild, and we hadn't seen your father for over two years, nor ever seen his young wife before, so it was a great event. It was a beautiful bright October day, and I had the pleasure of making the dress you wore, Allison, every stitch by hand, hemstitching and embroidery and all. And right in the midst of the ceremony you looked over your father's shoulder, and saw me sitting in the front seat, and smiled the sweetest smile! Then you jumped up and down in your father's arms, and patted your little pink hands together, and called out 'Ah-*Jah!*' That's what you used to call me then, and everybody all over the church smiled. How could they help it?"

"Gee, I must 'a' been some kid!" said Allison, slipping

down into a comfortable position among the pillows. "Say, Cloudy, I knew a good thing when I saw it even then, didn't I?"

"You know, Allison, that ceremony wasn't just all on your father's and mother's part; it entailed some responsibility upon you. It was part of your heritage, and you've no right to waste it any more than if it were gold or bank stock or houses and lands. It was your title to a heavenly sonship, and it gave God the right to call upon you to do whatever He wants you to do. It's between you and God now, and you'll have to settle it yourself. It's not anything I could settle for you either way, much as I might want it, because it is you who must answer God, and you must answer Him from the heart either way; so nobody else has anything to do with it."

"Oh, good-*night!* Cloudy, you certainly can put things in an awkward way. Oh, hang it! Now this whole evening's spoiled. I wish I hadn't gone to the front door at all. I wish I'd turned out the lights and let 'em knock. And there was that story you were going to read, and now it's too late!"

"Why, no; it's not too late at all," said Julia Cloud, consulting her little watch in the firelight. "It's only quarter to nine, and I'm sure we can indulge ourselves a little tonight, and finish the story before we go to bed. Turn the light on, and get the magazine."

With an air of finality Julia Cloud put aside the debated question, and settled herself in the big willow chair by the lamp with her book. Leslie went back to her chair by the fire, and Allison flung himself down on the couch with a pillow half over his eyes; but anybody watching closely would have seen that his eyes were wide open and he was studying the calm, quiet profile of his aunt's sweet face as she read in a gentle, even tone, paragraph after paragraph without a flicker of disturbance on her brow. Allison was not more than half listening to the story. He was thinking hard. Those things Julia Cloud had said about obligations and Moses and Abraham and Paul stuck hard in his mind, and he couldn't get away from them.

16

JULIA Cloud said nothing more to her boy about that Christian Endeavor Society, but she said much to her Lord, praying continually that he might be led to see his duty and want to do it, and that through it he might be led to know Christ.

In the meantime she went sunnily about setting the new home to rights and getting the right maid to fit into their household régime. Julia Cloud had never had a maid in her life, but she had always had ideas about one, and she put as much thought and almost as much care into preparing the little chamber the maid was to occupy as she had put upon the other rooms. To begin with, the room itself was admirably adapted to making the right maid feel at home and comfortable. It had three windows looking into gardens on the next block, and a blaze of salvia and cosmos and geraniums would greet her eyes the first time she looked out from her new room. Then it had a speck of a bathroom all its own, which Julia Cloud felt would go a long way toward making any maid the right maid, for there would be no excuse for her not being clean and no excuse for her keeping her tooth-brush down on the edge of the kitchen sink or taking a bath in the laundry tubs, as she had heard that some of her neighbors' maids had done at various times.

The windows were shrouded with white curtains of the same kind as those all over the house, and within were draperies with bright flower borders. The bureau was daintily fitted out, and the bed was spotless and inviting-looking. A cushioned rocking-chair stood beside a small table, with a dainty work-basket on the shelf below; and against the wall were some shelves with a few interesting books and magazines. A drop-light with a pretty shade gave a home-like air, and the room was as attractive as any other in the house. Any maid might think her lines had fallen in pleasant places who was fortunate enough to occupy that room. As a last touch Julia Cloud laid a neat coarse-print Testament on the table, and then knelt beside the rocking-chair and asked God to make the unknown comer a blessing to their house, and help them all to be a blessing to her. Then she went down to the car, and let Allison take her out to the addresses that had been given her. As a result, by Wednesday the little gay chamber half-way up the stairs was occupied by a pleasant-faced, sturdy colored girl about eighteen years old, who rejoiced in the name of Cherry, and was at once adopted as part of the new household with the same spirit with which everything else had been done. Perhaps if every household would go about it in the same way it would go far toward settling the much-mooted servant question.

When Cherry was introduced into her bedchamber the look on her face was worth seeing. It was in the early evening when she arrived, riding on the front seat of the wagon that brought her trunk; and, when she was ushered in by Julia Cloud, with Leslie in the offing to see what the newcomer would say to it, the girl stepped in, gave a wild glance around, then backed off, and rolled her eyes at her new mistress.

"This ain't—you'all ain't puttin' me into dis year fine bedroom!" she exclaimed in a kind of horror.

"Yes, this is your room," said Julia Cloud kindly, stepping in and moving a chair a little farther from the bed, that there might be room for the girl's trunk. "You can put your trunk right here, I should think; and here is your closet," swinging open the closet door and showing a plentitude of hooks and hangers, "and that is your bathroom." She pushed back the crash curtain that shut off the tiny bathroom, and stood back smiling. But the girl was not looking at her. She had cast one wild look around, and then her eyes had been riveted on the little vase on her bureau, containing a single late rose that Leslie had found blooming in the small garden at the rear, and put there for good luck, she said. Could it be that any one had cared to pick a flower for a servant's room? Her eyes filled with tears; she dropped her bundles on the floor, and came over to where her new mistress stood.

"Oh!" she said in a choked voice. "If you-all is goin' to treat me like comp'ny, I'se jest goin' to wuk my fingahs to de bone for youse!"

After the advent of Cherry things began to settle down into something like routine. The inn was abandoned entirely, and each meal was a festive occasion. Cherry took kindly to the cooking-lessons that Julia Cloud knew well how to give. Light, wonderful white bread came forth from the white-enamel gas-range oven, sweet, rich, nutty loaves of brown bread, even more delectable. Waffles and muffins and pancakes vied with one another to make one meal better than another; apple dumpling, cherry pie, and blackberry roly-poly varied with chocolate steamed pudding, lemon custard, and velvet whip made the desserts an eagerly awaited surprise.

Leslie hovered over everything new that was made,

and wanted to have a hand in it. Each day she learned some new and wholesome fact about housekeeping, and seemed to take to the knowledge readily. Her first attempt at real cooking was learning to make bread; and, when she succeeded so well that Allison thought it was his aunt's baking, she declared her intention of making it once a week just to keep her hand in.

Allison had said no more about Christian Endeavor; and, when Thursday afternoon came, he asked his aunt to ride to the city after a few little articles that were still needed to make the house complete. They had a pleasant trip, and Julia Cloud entirely forgot that the young people had been asked to attend the committee meeting that evening. Perhaps Allison was waiting for her to speak about it; for he looked at his watch uneasily several times, and glanced back at his aunt suspiciously; but she sat serenely enjoying the ride, and said nothing. At last, just as they were nearing home he burst forth with, "Cloudy, do you really think we ought to go to that blooming thing tonight?"

Julia Cloud lifted quiet eyes and smiled.

"I didn't say you ought to go; did I, dear?"

"Well, yes, you sorta did, Cloudy."

Julia Cloud shook her head.

"I don't think I did. I said it wasn't a matter for me to meddle with."

"Well, don't you?"

"No, Allison; not unless you feel that God has called you and you are willing to do what He wants you to. If you just went because you thought I wanted you to go, I don't believe it would be worth while, because you wouldn't be working with the right spirit. But, as I said before, that is something you have got to account for to God, not to me."

Allison drew his brows in a frown, and said no more; but he was almost silent at supper, and ate with an abstracted air. At quarter to eight he flung down the magazine he had been reading, and got up.

"Well, I s'pose I've got to go that bloomin' thing," he said half angrily. "Come on, kid; you going?"

Leslie hurried into her hat and cape, and they went off together, Allison grumbling in a low, half-pleasant voice all the time. Julia Cloud sat apparently reading, watching the little byplay, and praying that God would strengthen the young heart.

"Dear Moses!" she murmured with a smile on her lips as the front door banged behind the children and she was left reading alone.

Two hours later the two returned full of enthusiasm. Leslie was brimming over.

"O Cloudy, we're going to give this sleepy old town the surprise of a lifetime! We're going to have a grand time to-morrow night, just getting all the members together and doping it out what to do. And you ought to hear Allison talk! He's just like a man! He made a wonderful speech telling them how they ought to get together, and everybody do teamwork and all that, like they do in football; and they asked him to make it over again to-morrow night, and he's going to!"

Leslie's eyes were shining with pride, and she looked at her brother lovingly. He flushed embarrassedly.

"Well, what could you do, Cloudy? There they were sitting like a lot of boobs, and nobody knowing what to do except that Jane Bristol. She's the only sensible one of the bunch, and they don't listen to her. They made me mad, ignoring her suggestions the way they did; so I had to speak up and say she was right; and I guess I talked a lot more when I got started, because she really had the right dope, all right, and they ought to have had sense enough to know it. She's been in this work before, and been to big State conventions and things. Say, Cloudy, that Christian Endeavor stuff must be a pretty big thing. It seems to have members all over the world, and it's really a kind of international fraternity. I rather like their line. It's stiff all right, but that's the only way if you're going into a thing like that."

"And how did the praying go?" asked Julia Cloud, watching her boy's handsome, eager face as he talked.

"All right," he evaded reticently.

"*He* prayed, Cloudy!" announced Leslie proudly. "It was *regular!*"

"Well, what could a fellow do?" said Allison apologetically, as if he had done something he was half ashamed of. "That poor girl prayed something wonderful, and then they all sat and sat like a parcel of boobs until you could feel her cheeks getting red, and nobody opening their mouths; so I started in. I didn't know what to say, but I thought somebody ought to say something. I did the best I knew how."

"It was regular, Cloudy!" repeated Leslie with shining eyes.

"Well, it got 'em started, anyhow," said Allison. "That was all that mattered."

Julia Cloud with lips trembling joyously into a smile of thanksgiving listened, and felt her heart glad. Somehow she knew that her boy had yielded himself to the call of his God to lead this band of young people out of an Egypt into a promised land, and she saw as by faith how he himself would be led to talk with God on the mount before the great work was completed.

"It really was regular, Cloudy," reiterated Leslie. "I didn't know my brother could pray like that, or talk either. After he prayed everybody prayed, just a sentence or two, even that little baby doll Lila that was here the other night. They didn't say much, but you could see they wanted to do the right thing and be right in it. But everybody was in earnest; they really were, Cloudy. That Jane Bristol is wonderful! The president had told her she was chairman, and all about the meeting; and she read some verses out of the Bible about Christ's being always in a meeting where there were just two or three, and about two or three agreeing to ask for something and always getting it. I never knew there were such verses in the Bible, did you? Well, and after that it seemed awfully solemn, just as if we had all come into God's reception-room and were waiting to ask Him as a big favor to help this little Christian Endeavor Society to be worth something in His kingdom. Those aren't my words, Cloudy; you needn't look surprised. That's the way Jane Bristol put it, and it made me feel queer all down my back when she said it, as it did the first time I went to hear some great music. And—why, after that you couldn't help praying just a little, so the promise would hold good. It wasn't square not to help them out, you see."

"And we're not going to have anybody to-morrow night but the regular members until we get them all to understand and be ready to help," went on Allison.

"Yes, they asked Allison to take charge and help plan it all out; and Allison is going to hunt up some of the big Christian Endeavor people in the city, and get them to come out one or two at a time to our meetings,"—Julia Cloud noted the pronoun "our" with satisfaction,—"and stir things up on Sundays; and we'll drive in and get them, and bring them to our house to supper, maybe, and put them wise to things so they'll know best how to help and then we'll drive them home after church that night, see? And Allison suggested that we have pretty soon a series of parties or receptions, just for the young people to get together and bring new ones in one at a time, just as the boys in college have rushing-parties, you know. We'll have a reception, real formal, with regular eats from a caterer, and flowers and invitations and everything, for the first one; and a Hallowe'en

party for the October meeting, and a banquet for the
November meeting, just about Thanksgiving time, you
know. Oh, it's going to be lots of fun. And, Cloudy, I
told them we'd make a hundred sandwiches for to-morrow night; you don't mind, do you? We can buy the
bread, and it won't take long to make them. I know
how to cut them in pretty shapes, and I thought I'd tie
them with ribbons to match the lemonade."

Julia Cloud with radiant face entered into the plans eagerly, and to have heard them talk one would never
have imagined that twenty-four hours before these two
young people had been exceedingly averse to having
anything to do with that little dying Christian Endeavor
Young People's Society.

"And, Cloudy, that Jane Bristol is real pretty. She had
on a charming collar to-night, and her hair fixed all soft
around her face. She has beautiful hair! I think they were
all surprised at the easy way she talked; I don't believe
she is a day older than I am, either. And she *is* going to
college. I'm awfully glad, for I want to get to know her.
We'll invite her down here sometimes, won't we? I want
you to know her, Cloudy. You'll like her, I'm sure."

So Julia Cloud went to her pretty gray bed that night,
and lay marvelling at the goodness of God to answer her
prayers. As for the children, they could hardly settle
down to sleep, so full of plans were they for the revivi-
fying of that Christian Endeavor Society. They kept
calling back and forth from room to room, and after everything had been quiet for a long time and Julia Cloud
was just dropping off to sleep, Leslie woke them all up
calling to know if it wouldn't be a good plan to have the
Hallowe'en party there at the house and have everybody
come in costume. Then they had to begin all over again,
and decide what they would wear and who they would
be. Allison declared he was going to be a firecracker;
he had a "dandy" costume for it in California, and he

would write to-morrow morning to the housekeeper to look it up.

Leslie wanted to have a candy-pull, with apples and nuts and raisins for refreshments. Julia Cloud began to wonder whether it was just as acceptable to God to have play mixed up with the religion as these children were doing it.

"You must look out that your festivities don't get ahead of your righteousness," she warned half laughingly; but Allison took her in earnest.

"You're right there, Cloudy. That's one of the things we have to look out for in frats. We have to see we don't have too many social things. If we do, the marks suffer; and right away we lose ground. We'll have to keep those Sunday meetings up to the mark—see, kid?—or the other things will only bring in a lot of dead-wood that won't count. They must come to the Sunday meetings, or they don't get invited to the parties. That's the way we'll fix 'em."

"There's no use saying 'must,' " said Leslie wisely. "If you don't have your meetings interesting, they won't come anyhow you fix it."

"That's a girl for you!" scorned Allison. "No loyalty to the whole bunch. They've got to *like* everything. Now, the real spirit is to come and *make* the meetings good, just because they're *your* meetings. See, kid?"

"Yes, I see," snapped Leslie; "But I don't come to your old meetings at all if you are going to talk that way about girls. I guess I've always been loyal to everything, especially you, and I won't stand for that!"

"Oh, I didn't mean you, kid; I was talking about girls in general," soothed the brother. "You're all right, of course. But those little fluffy-ruffles that sat in the back seat, now, you'll have to teach them what loyalty means. See?"

Finally the household settled to sleep.

The next day the little house saw little else done save the making of marvellous dainty sandwiches in various forms and shapes.

Even Cherry entered into the work with zest, and Julia Cloud proved herself rich in suggestions for different fillings, till great platters of the finished product reposed in the big white refrigerator, neatly tucked about with damp napkins to keep them from drying.

All that day Allison flew hither and yon in his car, carrying some member of the committee on errands connected with the evening social. Never had such a stir been made about a mere church social in all the annals of the society. Every remotest member was hunted out and persuaded to be present, and Allison agreed to go around in the evening and pick up at least a dozen who had professed their inability to get there alone. So the big blue car was enlisted in Christian Endeavor service, and the young people were as busy and as happy as ever they had been in getting their little new home settled. They drove away about seven o'clock after a hasty supper, with their platters of sandwiches safely guarded on the back seat; and Julia Cloud watched them, and smiled and was glad. She wondered whether this work would get such a hold upon them that it would last after they started their college work, and fervently hoped that it might, so that there would be another link to bind them to God's house and His work. She sighed to think how many things there would likely be to draw them away.

About ten o'clock Leslie telephoned. She wanted to bring Jane Bristol home for the night, as the people where Jane was living were away, and she would otherwise have to stay alone in a big house. Julia Cloud readily assented, and she and Cherry had a pleasant half-hour putting one of the guest-rooms in order. It was while she was doing this that she began to wonder seriously what Jane Bristol would be like. Who was brought intimately into their new home might mean so much to her two children. And in this room, too, after Cherry had gone to bed, she knelt and breathed a consecrating prayer. Then she went down-stairs to wait for the coming of her children, building up the fire and lighting the porch light so that all would be cheery and attractive for them and their guest. Only a little, lonesome child who did housework for her living, but it was good to be able to give her a pleasant welcome.

In a few minutes the car arrived, and the two girls came chattering in, while Allison put the car away. At least, Leslie was chattering.

"I think you look so lovely in that soft blue dress!" she was saying. "It is so graceful, and the color just fits your eyes."

"It's only some ole accordion-pleated chiffon I had," answered the guest half ashamed. "I had to wash it and dye it and make it myself, and I wasn't sure the pleats would iron out, or that it would do at all. You know I don't have much use for evening dresses, and I really couldn't afford to get one. That's the reason I hesitated at your suggestion about having receptions and parties. But I guess you have to have them."

"You don't mean to say you made it all yourself! Why, you're a wonder! Isn't she, Cloudy? Just take her in and look for yourself! She made that dress all herself out of old things that she washed and dyed. Why, it looks like an imported frock. Doesn't it look like one, Cloudy? And that girdle is darling, all shirred that way!"

That was Julia Cloud's introduction to the guest as she stood in the open door and watched the two trip along the brick terrace to the entrance.

Leslie snatched away the long, dark cloak that covered Jane Bristol's dress; and she stood forth embarrassed in the firelight, clad in soft, pale-blue chiffon in simple straight lines blending into the white throat in a little round neck, and draping the white girlish arms. The firelight and lamplight glimmered and flickered over the softly waved brown hair, the sweet, serious brow, the delicate, refined face; and Jane Bristol lifted two earnest deep-blue eyes, and looked at Julia Cloud. Then between them flashed a look of understanding and sympathy, and each knew at once that she liked the other.

"Isn't she a dear, Cloudy Jewel?" demanded Leslie.

"She is!" responded Julia Cloud, and put her arms softly around the slender blue-clad shoulders. Then she looked up to see the eyes of Allison resting upon them with satisfaction.

They turned down the light and sat before the fire for a little while, telling about the success of the evening and talking of this and that, just getting acquainted; and, when they finally took Jane Bristol up to the pretty guestroom, it was with a sense that a new and lasting friendship had been well begun. Julia Cloud as she lay down to sleep found herself wondering whether her children would always show so much good sense in picking out their friends as they had done this time.

17

THE day when college opened was a great day. The children could hardly eat any breakfast, and Allison gave Leslie a great many edifying instructions about registering.

"Now, kid, if you get stuck for anything, just you hunt me up. I'll see that you get straightened out. If you and Jane Bristol could only get together, you could help each other a lot. I'll get some dope from some of the last-year fellows. That's the advantage I get from finding a chapter of my frat here. They'll put me wise as to the best course-advisers, and you stick around near the entrance till I give you the right dope. It doesn't pay to get started wrong in college."

Leslie meekly accepted all these admonitions, and they started off together in the car with an abstracted wave of good-by to Julia Cloud, who somehow felt suddenly left out of the universe. To have her two newly-acquired children suddenly withdrawn by the power of a great educational institution and swept beyond her horizon was disconcerting. She had not imagined she would feel this way. She stood in the window watching them, and wiped away a furtive tear, and then laughed to herself.

"Old fool!" she said softly to the window-pane. "The trouble with you is, you'd like to be going to college yourself, and you know it! Now put this out of your mind, and go to work planning how to make home doubly attractive when they get back, so that they will want to spend every minute possible here instead of being drawn away from it. They love it. Now keep them loving it. That's your job."

When the two came back at noon, they were radiant and enthusiastic as usual, albeit they had many a growl to express. One would have thought to hear Allison that he had been running colleges for some fifty years the way he criticized the policy and told how things ought to be run. At first Julia Cloud was greatly distressed by it all, thinking that they surely had made a mistake in their selection of a college, but it gradually dawned upon her that this was a sort of superior attitude maintained by upper-class men toward all institutions of learning, particularly those in which they happened to be studying, that it was really only an indication of growing developing minds keen to see mistakes and trying to think out remedies, and as yet inexperienced enough to think they could remedy the whole sick world.

The opening days of college were turbulent days for Julia Cloud. Her children were so excited they could neither eat nor sleep. They were liable to turn up unexpectedly at almost any hour of the morning or afternoon, hungry as bears, and always in a hurry. They had so many new things to tell her about, and no time in which to talk. They mixed things terribly, and gave her impressions that took months to right; and they could not understand why she looked distressed at their flightiness. They were both taken up eagerly by the students and invited hither and yon by the various groups and societies, which frequently caused them to be absent from meals while they were being dined and lunched and breakfasted. Of course, Julia Cloud reflected, two such good-looking, well-dressed, easy-mannered young people, with a home in the town where they could invite people, a car in which to take friends out, and a free hand with money, would be popular anywhere. Her anxiety grew as the first week waxed toward its end and finished up Saturday night with invitations to two dances and one week-end party at a country house ten miles away.

Leslie rushed in breathless about six o'clock Saturday evening, and declared she was too much in a hurry to eat anything; she must get dressed at once, and put some things in her bag. She rattled on about the different social functions she was expected to attend that evening until Julia Cloud was in hopeless confusion, and could only stand and listen, and try to find the things that Leslie in her hurry had overlooked. Then Allison arrived, and wanted some supper. He talked with his mouth full about where he was going and what he was going to do, and at the end of an hour and a half Julia Cloud had a very indefinite idea of anything. She had a swift mental vision of church and Sabbath and Christian Endeavor all slipping slowly out of their calculation, and the WORLD in large letters taking the forefront of their vision.

"You are going to a dance!" she said in a white, stricken way she had when an anxiety first bewildered her. "To *two* dances! O my dear Leslie! You—*dance*, then? I—hadn't thought of that!"

"Sure I dance!" said Leslie gayly, drawing up the delicate silk stocking over her slim ankles and slipping on a silver slipper. "You ought to see me. And Allison can dance, too. We'll show you sometime. Don't you like dancing, Cloudy? Why, Cloudy! You couldn't mean you don't approve of dancing? Not *really!* But where would we be? *Everybody* dances! Why, there wouldn't be anything else to do when young people went out. Oh, do you suppose Cherry would press out this skirt a little bit? It's got horribly mussed in that drawer."

Julia Cloud had dropped into a chair with an all-gone feeling and a lightness in the top of her head. She felt as if the world, the flesh, and the devil had suddenly dropped down upon the house and were carrying off her children bodily, and she was powerless to prevent it. She could not keep the pain of it out of her eyes; yet she did not know what to say in this emergency. None of the things that had always seemed entirely convincing in forming her own opinions seemed adequate to the occasion.

Leslie turned suddenly, and saw her stricken face.

"What's the matter, Cloudy? Is something wrong? Aren't you well? Don't you like me to go to a dance? Why, Cloudy! Do you really *object?*"

"I have no right to object, I suppose, dear," she said, trying to speak calmly; "but—Leslie, I can't bear to think of you dancing; it's not nice. It's too—too intimate! My little flower of a girl!"

"Oh, but we have to dance, Cloudy; that's ridiculous! And you aren't used to dances, or you wouldn't say so. Can't you trust me to be perfectly nice?"

Julia Cloud shuddered, and went to the head of the stairs to answer a question Allison was calling up to her; and, when she came back, she said no more about it. The pain was too great, and she felt too bewildered for argument. Leslie was enveloped in rose-colored tulle, with touches of silver, and looked like a young goddess with straps of silver over her slim shoulders and a thread of pearls about her throat. The white neck and back that the wisp of rose-color made no attempt to conceal were very beautiful and quite childish, but they shocked the sweet soul of Julia Cloud inexpressibly. She stood aghast when Leslie whirled upon her and demanded to know how she liked the gown.

"O my dear!" gasped her aunt. "You're not going out before people—*men*—all undressed like that!"

Leslie gave her one glance of hurt dismay, whirled back to her glass, and examined herself critically.

"Why, Cloudy!" Her voice was almost trembling, and her cheeks were rosier than the tulle with disappointment. "Why, Cloudy, I thought it was lovely! It's just like everybody's else. I thought you would think I looked *nice!*" The child drooped, and Julia Cloud went up to her gently.

"It is beautiful, darling, and you are—exquisite! But, dear! It seems terrible for my little girl to go among young men so sort of nakedly. I'm sure if you understood life better, you wouldn't do it. You are tempting men to wrong thoughts, undressed that way, and you are putting on common view the intimate loveliness of the body God gave you to keep holy and pure. It is the way cheap women have of making many men love them in a careless, physical way. I don't know how to tell you, but it seems terrible to me. If you were my own little girl, I never, *never* would be willing to have you go out that way."

"You've said enough!" almost screamed Leslie with a sudden frenzy of rage, shame, and disappointment. "I feel as if I never could look anybody in the face again!" And with a cry she flung herself into the jumble of bright garments on her bed, and wept as if her heart would break. Julia Cloud stood over her in consternation, and tried to soothe her; but nothing did any good. The young storm had to have its way, and the slim pink shoulders shook in convulsive sobs, while the dismayed elder sat down beside the bed, with troubled eyes upon her, and waited, praying quietly.

In the midst of it all Allison appeared at the door.

"What in thunder is the matter? I've yelled my head off, and nobody answers. What is the matter with you, kid? It's time we started, and you doing the baby act! I never thought you'd get hystericky."

Leslie lifted a wet and smeary face out of her pillow and addressed her brother defiantly:

"I've good reason to cry!" she said. "Cloudy thinks I'm not decent to go out in this dress, and she won't believe everybody dresses this way; and I'm *not going!* I'm *never* going *anywhere* again; I'm *disgraced!*" And down went her head in the pillow again with another long, convulsive sob.

Her brother strode over to her, and lifted her up firmly but gently.

"There, kid, quit your crying and be sensible. Stand up and let's look at you."

He stood her upon her feet; and she swayed there, quivering, half ashamed, her hands to her tear-stained face, her pink shoulders heaving and her soft, pink chest quivering with sobs, while he surveyed her.

"Well, kid, I must say I agree with Cloudy," he said half reluctantly at last. "The dress is a peach, of course, and you look like an angel in it; but, if you could hear the rotten things the fellows say about the way the girls dress, you wouldn't want to go that way; and I don't want them to talk that way about my sister. Couldn't you stick in a towel or an apron or something, and make a little more waist to the thing? I'm sure you'd look just as pretty, and the fellows would think you a whole lot nicer girl. I don't want you to get the nickname of the Freshman Vamp. I couldn't stand for that."

Poor Leslie sank into a chair, and covered her face for another cry, declaring it was no use, it would utterly spoil the dress to do anything to it, and she couldn't go, and wouldn't go and wear it; but at last Julia Cloud came to the rescue with needle and thread and soft rose drapery made from a scarf of Leslie's that exactly matched the dress; and presently she stood meek and sweet, and quite modest, blooming prettily out of her pink, misty garments like an opening apple-blossom in spite of her recent tears.

"But when are you coming back?" asked Julia Cloud in sudden dismay, her troubles returning in full force as she watched them going out the door to the car, Allison carrying two bags and telling Leslie to hurry for all she was worth.

The two children turned then, and faced their aunt, with a swift, comprehending vision of what this expedition of theirs meant to her. It had not occurred to them before that they were deliberately planning to spend most of the night, Saturday night, in mirth, and stay over Sunday at a house-party where the Sabbath would be as a thing unknown. Nobody had ever talked to them about these things before. They had accepted it as a part of the world of society into which they had been born, and they had never questioned it. They were impatient now that their tried and true friend and comrade did not comprehend that this occasion was different from most, and that it must be an exception. They were willing to keep the Sabbath in general, but in this particular they felt they must not be hampered. The whole idea shone plainly in their faces, and the pain and disappointment and chagrin shone clearly, emphatically in Julia Cloud's eyes as she faced them and read the truth.

"Why, we don't know, just for sure, Cloudy," Allison tried to temporize. "You see, they usually dance to all hours. It's Saturday night, and no classes to-morrow, and this is an unusual occasion. It's a week-end party, you know—"

"Then—you won't be back to-night! You are not going to church to-morrow! You will spend the Sabbath at a party!"

She said these things as if she were telling them to herself so that she could better take in the facts and not cry out with the disappointment of it. There was no quality of fault-finding in her tone, but the pain of her voice cut to the heart the two young culprits. Therefore, according to the code of loving human nature, they got angry.

"Why, of course!" chirped Leslie. "Didn't you expect that? That's what week-end parties are!"

"Oh, cut this out, Leslie," cried Allison. "We've gotta beat it. We're way late now! Cloudy, you can expect us when we get here. Don't bother about anything. There's no need to. We'll telephone you later when we expect to come back. Nightie, nightie, Cloudy. You go rest yourself. You look tired."

He gave her a hurried, deprecatory kiss, and swept his sister out into the night. Julia Cloud heard the purring of the engine, saw the lights of the car glide away from the door down the street and out of sight. They were gone! She felt as though a piece of herself had been torn away from her and flung out for the world to trample upon. For a long time she stood staring from the window into the darkness, unshed tears burning behind her eyes and throat, trying to steady the beating of her heart and get used to the gnawing trouble that somehow made her feel faint and weak.

It came over her that she had been a fool to attempt to fill the place of mother to these two modern young things. Their own ideas were fully made up about all questions that seemed vital to her. She had been a fossil in a back-country place all her life, and of course they felt she did not know. Well, of course she did not know much about modern society and its ways, save to dread it, and to doubt it, and to wish to keep them away from it. She was prejudiced, perhaps. Yes, she had been reared

that way, and the world would call her narrow. Would
Christ the Lord feel that way about it? Did He like to
have His children dressing like abandoned women and
making free with one another under the guise of polite
social customs? Did He want His children to spend their
Sabbaths in play, however innocent the play might be?
She turned with a sigh away from the window. No, she
could not see it any other way. It was the way of the
world, and that was all there was to it. Leslie had made
it plain when she said they had to do it or be left out.
And wasn't that just what it meant to be a "peculiar
people" unto the Lord, to be willing to give up doubtful
things that harmed people for the sake of keeping pure
and unspotted from the world? "If ye were of the world,
the world would love its own; but because I have chosen
you out of the world, therefore the world hateth you,"
came the familiar old words. Well, and what should she
do now? It wouldn't do to rave and fuss about things.
That never did any good. She couldn't say she wouldn't
stay if they danced and went away over the Sabbath.
Those were things in which she might advise, but had
no authority. They were old enough to decide such matters for themselves. She could only use her influence, and
trust the rest with the Lord. Yes, there was one thing she
could do. She could pray!

So Julia Cloud gave her quiet orders to Cherry, and
went up to her rose-and-gray room to kneel by the bed
and pray, agonizing for her beloved children through
the long hours of that long, long evening.

It was a quiet face that she lifted at last from her vigil,
for it bore the brightness of a face-to-face communion
with her Lord; and she rose and went about her preparations for the night. Then, just as she had taken
down her hair and was brushing it in a silver cloud
about her shoulders, she heard a car drive up. A moment

more a key turned in the latch, and some one came in.

Julia Cloud stood with the hair-brush poised half-way down a strand of hair, and listened. Yes, the car had gone on to the garage. What could have happened.?

18

IT was all still below stairs, then a soft, stealthy, silken movement, cautiously coming up the stairs. Julia Cloud went quickly to the hall door, and switched on the light. On the landing stood Leslie, lovely and flushed, with her hair slightly ruffled and her velvet evening cloak thrown back, showing the rosy mist of her dress. She stood with one silver slipper poised on the stairs, a sweet, guilty look on her face.

"O Cloudy! I thought you were asleep, and I didn't want to waken you," she said, penitently; "but you haven't gone to bed yet, have you? I'm glad. We wanted you to know we were home."

"Is anything the matter?" Julia Cloud asked with a stricture of emotion in her throat.

"No; only we got tired, and we didn't want to stay to their old party, anyway, and we'd rather be home." Leslie sprang up the stairs, and caught her aunt in her arms with one of her sweet, violent kisses.

"O my dear!" was all Julia Cloud could say. And then they heard Allison closing the door softly below, and creaking across the floor and up the stairs.

"Oh, you waked her up!" he said reproachfully as he caught sight of his sister in Julia Cloud's arms.

"No, you're wrong. She hadn't even gone to bed yet. I knew she wouldn't," said Leslie, nestling closer. "Say, Cloudy, we're not going to trouble you that way again. It isn't worth it. We don't like their old dancing, anyway. I couldn't forget the way you looked so hurt—and the things you said. Won't you please come down to the fire awhile? We want to tell you about it."

Down on the couch, with Allison stirring up the dying embers and Leslie nestled close to her, Julia Cloud heard bits about the evening.

"It wasn't bad, Cloudy, 'deed it wasn't. They dance a lot nicer in colleges than they do other places. I know, for I've been to lots of dances, and I never let men get too familiar. Allison taught me that when I was little. That's why what you said made me so mad. I've always been a lot carefuller than you'd think, and I never dance with anybody the second time if I don't like the way he does it the first time. And everybody was real nice and dignified to-night, Cloudy. The boys are all shy and bashful, anyway; only I couldn't forget what you had said about not liking to have me do it; and it made everything seem so—so—well, not nice; and I just felt uncomfortable; and one dance I sent the boy for a glass of water for me, and I just sat it out; and, when Allison saw me, he came over, and said, 'Let's beat it!' and so I slipped up to the dressing-room, and got my cloak, and we just ran away without telling anybody. Wasn't that perfectly dreadful? But I'll call the girl up after a while, and tell her we had to come home and we didn't want to spoil their fun telling them so."

They sat for an hour talking before the fire, the young people telling her all about their experiences of the last few days, and letting her into their lives again with the

196

old sweet relation. Then they drifted back again to the subject of dancing.

"I don't give a whoop whether I dance or not, Cloudy," said Allison. "I never did care much about it, and I don't see having my sister dance with some fellows, either. Only it does cut you out of lots of fun, and you get in bad with everybody if you don't do it. I expected we'd have to have dances here at the house, too, sometimes; but, if you don't like it, we won't; and that's all there is to it."

"Well, dear, that's beautiful of you. Of course I couldn't allow you to let me upset your life and spoil all your pleasure; but I'm wondering if we couldn't try an experiment. It seems to me there ought to be things that people would enjoy as much as dancing, and why couldn't we find enough of them to fill up the evenings and make them forget about the dancing?"

"There'll be some that won't come, of course," said Leslie; "but we should worry! They won't be the kind we'll like, anyway. Jane Bristol doesn't dance. She told me so yesterday. She said her mother never did, and brought her up to feel that she didn't want to, either."

"She's some girl," said Allison irrelevantly. "She entered the sophomore class with credits she got for studying in the summer school and some night-work. Did you know that, kid? I was in the office when she came in for her card, and I heard the profs talking about her and saying she had some bean. Those chumps in the village will find out some day that the girl they despised is worth more than the whole lot of them put together."

Julia Cloud leaned forward, and touched lightly and affectionately the hair that waved back from the boy's forehead, and spoke tenderly.

"Dear boy, I'll not forget your leaving your friends and coming back to me and to the Sabbath and church and all that. It means a lot to me to have my children observe those things. I hope that some day you'll do it because you feel you want to please God instead of me."

"Sure!" said Allison, trying not to look embarrassed. "I guess maybe I care about that, too, a little bit. To tell the truth, Cloudy, I couldn't see staying away from that Christian Endeavor meeting after I've worked hard all the week to get people to come to it. It didn't seem square."

The moment was tense with deep feeling, and Julia Cloud could not bring herself to break it by words. She brought the boy's hand up to her lips, and pressed it close; and then just as she was about to speak the telephone rang sharply again and again.

Allison sprang up, and went to answer.

"Hello. Yes. Oh! Miss Bristol! What? Are you sure? I'll be there at once. Lock yourself in your room till I get there."

He hung up the receiver excitedly.

"Call up the fire department quick, Leslie! Tell them to hurry. There's some one breaking into the Johnson house, and Jane Bristol is there alone with the children. It's Park Avenue, you know. Hustle!"

He was out the door before they could exclaim, and Leslie hastened to the telephone.

"He went without his overcoat," said Julia Cloud, hurrying to the closet for it. "It will be very cold riding. He ought to have it."

Leslie hung up the receiver, and flung her velvet cloak about her hurriedly, grabbing the overcoat.

"Give it to me, Cloudy; I'm going with him!" she cried, and dashed out the door as the car slid out of the garage.

"O Leslie! Child! You *oughtn't* to go!" she cried, rushing to the door; but Leslie was already climbing into the car, moving as it was.

"It's all right, Cloudy!" she called. "There's a revolver in the car, you know!" and the car whirled away down the street.

Julia Cloud stood gasping after them; the horrible thought of a revolver in the car did not cheer her as Leslie had evidently hoped it would. What children they were, after all, plunging her from one trouble into another, yet what dear, tender-hearted, loving children! She went in, and found a heavy cloak, and went out again to listen. Then it came to her that perhaps Leslie had not made the operator understand; so she went back to the telephone to try to find out whether any one had been sent. Suppose those children should try to face a burglar alone! There might be more than one for aught they knew. Oh, Leslie *should not* have gone! A terrible anxiety took possession of her, and she tried to pray as she worked the telephone hook up and down and waited for the operator. Then into the quiet of the night there came the loud clang of the fire-bell, and a moment later hurried calls and voices in the distance, sounding through the front door that Julia Cloud had left open. For an instant she was relieved, and then she reflected that this might be a fire somewhere else, and not the call for the Johnson house at all; so she kept on trying to call the operator. At last a snappy voice snarled into her ear. "We don't tell where the fire is; we're not allowed any more," and snap! The operator was gone again.

"But I don't want to know where the fire is!" called Julia Cloud in dismay. "I want to ask a question."

No answer came, and the dim buzz of the wire sounded emptily back to her anxious ear. At last she gave it up, and went out to the street to look up and down. If she only knew which way was Park Avenue! She could hear the engine now, clattering along with the hook and ladder behind; and dark, hurrying forms crossed the street just beyond the next corner, but no one came by. She hurried out to the corner, and called to a boy who was passing; and he yelled out: "Don't know, lady. Up Park Avenue somewhere." Then the street grew very quiet again, and all the noise centred away in the distance. A shot rang out, and voices shouted, and her heart beat so loud she could hear it. She hurried back to the house again, and tried to get the telephone operator; but nothing came of it, and for the next twenty minutes she vibrated between the street and the telephone, and wondered whether she ought not to wake up Cherry and do something else.

It seemed perfectly terrible to think of those two children handling a burglar alone—and yet what could she do?

Pretty soon, however, she heard the fire-engine returning, with the crowd, and she hurried down to the corner to find out.

"It wasn't no fire at all, lady," answered a boy whom she questioned. "It was just two men breakin' into a house, but they ketched 'em both an' are takin' 'em down to the lockup. No, lady, there wasn't nobody killed. There was some shootin', sure! A girl done it! Some college girl in a car. She see the guy comin' to make a get-away in her car, see? And she let go at him, and picked him off the first call, got him through the knee; an' by that time the fire comp'ny got there, and cinched 'em both. She's some girl, she is!"

Julia Cloud felt her head whirling, and hurried back to the house to sit down. She was trembling from head to foot. Was it Leslie who had shot the burglar? Leslie, her little pink-and-silver butterfly, who seemed so much like a baby yet in many ways? Oh, what a horrible danger she had escaped! If she had escaped. Perhaps the boy did not know. Oh, if they would but come! It seemed hours since they had left. The midnight train was just pulling into the station! How exasperating that telephone did not respond! Something must be out of order with it. Hark! Was that the car? It surely was!

19

HOW welcome a sound was the churn of the engine as it came flying up the road and turned into the driveway!

Julia Cloud was at the door, waiting to receive them, straining her eyes into the darkness to be sure they were both there.

Leslie sprang out, and dashed into her arms.

"O Cloudy! You waited up, didn't you? We thought you must be asleep and didn't hear the telephone. We tried to call you up and explain. You see, Jane was there alone, and of course she didn't much enjoy staying after what had happened; so we waited till the Johnsons got back from the city. They had been to the theatre, and they just came on that midnight train. If I lived in a lonely place like that, I wouldn't leave three babies with a young girl all alone in the house. It seems the servants were all away, or left, or something. I guess they were pretty scared when they got back. I wanted to bring the children up here to stay all night with us, and let them *be* scared when they got home; but she wouldn't, of course; so we stayed with her."

Leslie tossed aside her velvet cloak as she talked.

"It was awfully exciting, Cloudy. I'm glad I went. There's no telling what might have happened to Allison if somebody hadn't been there. You see he shut down the motor as we came up to the house. We'd been going like a streak of lightning all the way, and we tried to sneak up so they wouldn't hear us and get away; but there was one man outside on the watch, and he gave the word; and just as Allison got out of the car he disappeared into the shadows. The other one came piling out of a window, and streaked it across the porch and down the lawn. Allison made for him; but he changed his course, and came straight toward the car. I guess they thought it was empty. And then the other one came flying out from behind the bushes, and made for Allison; so I just leaned out of the car and shot. I don't know how I ever had the nerve, for I was terribly frightened; but he would have got Allison in another minute, and Allison didn't see him coming. He had a big club in his hand. I saw it as he went across in front of the window, and I knew I must do something; so I aimed right in front of him, and I saw him go down on his knees and throw up his hands; and then I felt sick, and began to think what if I had killed him. I didn't, Cloudy; they say I only hit his knee; but wouldn't it have been awful all my life to have to think I had killed a man? I couldn't have stood it, Cloudy!" and with sudden breaking of the tension the high-strung child flung herself down in a little, brilliant heap at Julia Cloud's lap, and burst into tears.

"You brave little darling!" Julia Cloud caressed her, and folded her arms about her.

"She's all of that, Cloudy! She saved my life!" It was Allison who spoke, standing tall and proud above his sister and looking down at her tenderly. "Come now, kiddie, don't give way when you've been such a trump.

I knew you could shoot, but I didn't think you could keep your head like that. Cloudy, she was a little winner, the cool way she aimed at that man with the other one coming right toward her and meaning plainly to get in the car and run away in it. He'd have taken her, too, of course, and stopped at nothing to get away. But, when he saw the good shot she was, and heard his pal groaning, he threw up his hands, and turned sharp about for me. He knew it was his only chance, and that whoever was shooting wouldn't shoot at him while he was all tangled up with me; so he made a spring at me before I knew what he was doing, and threw me off my feet, and got a half Nelson on me, you know—"

"Yes, Cloudy, he was fiendish, and I couldn't do a thing, for fear of hitting Allison; and just then I heard a motor-cycle chugging by the car. I hadn't heard it before, there was so much going on; and a big, strong fellow with his hair all standing up in the wind jumped off, and ran toward them where they were rolling on the ground. Then I thought of the flash-light, and turned it on them; and that motor-cycle man saw just how things were, and he jumped in, and grabbed the burglar; and then all of a sudden the yard was full of men and boys and a terrible noise and clanging, and the fire-engine and hook and ladder came rushing up, Cloudy! You didn't tell them there was a fire, did you? I didn't. I told that telephone girl there was a burglar and to send a policeman. But somehow she got it that the house was on fire. And Jane Bristol was in the house, with the baby in her arms and the other little children asleep in their cribs; and she didn't know what was happening because she didn't dare to open the window."

Into the midst of the excitement and explanations there came a loud knock on the door, and Allison sprang up, and went to see who was there. A young man with disheveled garments, hair standing on end, and face much streaked with mud and dust stood there. A motor cycle leaned against the end of the porch.

"Pardon me," he said half shyly. "I saw the light, and thought some one was up yet. Did the lady drop this? I found it in the grass when I went back to hunt for my key-ring. It was right where she stood."

He held forth his hand, and there dropped from his fingers a slender white, gleaming thing.

Allison flashed on the porch-light, and looked at it.

"Leslie, is this yours?"

The motor-cycle man looked up, and there stood the princess, her rosy garments like the mist of dawn glowing in the light of fire and lamp, her tumbled golden curls, her eyes bright with recent tears, her cheeks pink with excitement. He had seen her dimly a little while before in a long velvet cloak and a little concealing head-scarf, standing in a motor-car shooting with a steady hand, and again coming with swift feet to her brother's side in the grass after he was released from the burglar's hold; but he had not caught the look of her face. Now he stood speechless, and stared at the lovely apparition. Was it possible that this lovely child had been the cool, brave girl in the car?

Leslie had put her hand to her throat with a quick cry, and found it bare.

"My string of pearls!" she said. "How careless of me not to have noticed they were gone! I'm so glad you found them! They are the ones that mamma used to have." Then, looking up for the first time, she said:

"Oh, you are the young man who saved my brother's life. Won't you please come in? I think you were perfectly splendid! I want my aunt to meet you, and we all want to thank you."

"Oh, I didn't do anything," said the stranger, turning as if to go. "It was you who saved his life. I got there just in time to watch you. You're some shot, I'll tell the world. I sure am proud to meet you. I didn't know any girl could shoot like that."

"Oh, that's nothing!" laughed Leslie. "Our guardian made us both learn. Please come in."

"Yes, we want to know you," urged Allison. "Come in. We can't let you go like that."

"It's very late," urged the young man.

But Allison put out a firm arm, and pulled him in, shutting the door behind him.

"Cloudy," he said, turning to his aunt, "this man came in the nick of time, and saved me just as I was getting woosey. That fellow sure had a grip on my throat, and something had hit my head and taken away all the sense I had, so I couldn't seem to get him off."

"That's all right. I noticed you were holding your own," put in the stranger. "It isn't every man would have tackled two unknown burglars alone." He spoke in a voice of deep admiration.

"Well, I noticed you were the only man on the spot till the parade was about over," said Allison, slapping him heartily on the shoulder. "Say, I think I've seen you before riding that motor-cycle; tell me your name, please. I want to know you next time I see you."

"Thanks, I'm not much to know, but I have an idea you are. My name's Howard Letchworth. I have a room over the garage, and take my meals at the pie-shop. My motor-cycle is all the family I have at present."

Allison laughed, and held out his hand with a warm grip of admiration.

"I'm Allison Cloud; and this is my sister, Leslie Cloud, and my aunt, Miss Cloud; and this house we call Cloudy Villa. You'll always be welcome whenever you are willing to come. You've saved my life and brought back my sister's pearls, and put us doubly in your debt. I'm sure no one in this town has a better right to be welcome here. Please sit down a minute, and tell us who you are. You don't belong to the church bunch, and I don't think I've seen you about the college."

"No," said Letchworth, "not this year. I'm a laboring man. I work over at the ship-building plant. If everything goes well with me this winter, I may get back to college next fall. I was a junior last year, but I couldn't quite make the financial part; so I had to go to work again."

There was a defiance in his tone as he told it, as if he had said, "Now perhaps you won't want to know me!" and he had not taken the offered chair, but was standing, as if he would not take their friendship under false pretences.

But trust Allison to say the graceful thing.

"I somehow felt you were my superior," he said with his eyes full of real friendship. "Sit down just a minute, so we can be sure you really mean to come again."

"Yes, do sit down," said Julia Cloud. "I was just going to get these children a bite to eat, and I'm sure they'd like to have you share it with them. It's a long time since supper, and you have been through a good deal. Aren't you hungry? The pie-shop won't be open this time of night."

She smiled that welcoming home smile that no young person could resist, and the young man sat down with a swift, furtive glance at Leslie. She seemed too bright and wonderful to be true. He let his eyes wander about the charming room; the fire, the couch, the lamp-light on the books, the little home touches everywhere, and then he sank into the big cushions of the chair gratefully.

"Say, this is wonderful!" he said. "I haven't known what home was like for seven years."

"Well, it's almost that long since we had a real home, too," said Leslie gravely; "and we love this one."

"Yes," said Allison, "we've just got this home, and

we sure do appreciate it. I hope, if you like it, you'll often share it with us."

"Well, I call that generous to an utter stranger!"

Then Julia Cloud entered with a tray, and Allison and Leslie both jumped up to help her. Leslie brought a plate with wonderful frosted cakes and little sandwiches, which somehow Julia Cloud always managed to have just ready to serve; Allison passed the cups of hot chocolate with billows of whipped cream on the top, and they all sat down before the fire to eat in the coziest way. Suddenly, right in the midst of their talk the big grandfather clock in the corner chimed softly out a single clear, reminding stroke.

"Why, Cloudy! It's one o'clock! Sunday morning, and here we are having a Sunday-morning party, after all, right at home!" laughed Leslie teasingly.

The stranger stood up with apology.

"Oh, please don't go for a minute," said Leslie. "I want you to do one more thing for me. Now, Allison, I can see it in your eyes that you mean to get ahead of me, but I have first chance. He's my find. Mr. Letchworth, you don't happen to belong to a Christian Endeavor Society anywhere, do you?"

The startled young man shook his head, a look of being on his guard suddenly coming into his eyes.

"Do I look like it?" he asked half comically, suddenly glancing down at his muddy, greasy garments and old torn sweater.

"Well, then I want you to come to the meeting to-morrow night—no, to-night, at seven o'clock, down at that little brick church on the next street. Everybody had to promise to bring some one who has never come before, and I didn't have anybody to ask because all the college people I know are off at a house-party; and I ran away from it, and came home; so I couldn't very well ask them. Will you go?"

The young man looked at the lovely girl with a smile on his lips that might easily have grown into a sneer and a curt refusal; but somehow the clear, true look in her eyes made refusal impossible. Against all his prejudices he hesitated, and then suddenly said:

"Yes, I'll go if you want me to. I'm not in the habit of going to such places, but—If you want me, I'll go."

She put her slim, cool hand into his, and thanked him sweetly; and he went out into the starlight feeling as if a princess had knighted him.

"There!" sighed Leslie as the sound of his motor-cycle died away in the distance. "I think he's a real man. It's queer; but he and Jane Bristol are the nicest people we've met in this town yet, and they both work for their living."

"I was just thinking that, too," said Allison, vigorously poking the fire into a shower of ruby sparks. "Don't you like him, Cloudy?"

"Yes," said Julia Cloud emphatically. "He looks as if he took life in earnest. But come, don't you think we better go to bed?"

So they all lay down to sleep at last, Julia Cloud too profoundly thankful for words in the prayer her heart fervently breathed.

THE routine of college classes became settled at last, and gradually the young people found bits of leisure for the family life which they craved and loved. Allison came in one day, and announced that he had bought a canoe.

"It's a peach, Cloudy, and I got it cheap from a fellow that has to leave college. His father has got a job out in California, and they are going to move, and want to transfer him to a Western college so he won't be so far away from them. I got it for fifteen dollars with all the outfit, and it's only been used one season. But he couldn't take it with him. There are three paddles and two cushions and some rugs belonging to it, and I've arranged to keep it down behind the inn so it won't be far for us to go to it. Now, I want you to be ready to take a trial trip this afternoon at three when Leslie and I get through our classes."

With much inward questioning but entire loyalty Julia Cloud yielded herself to the uncertainties of canoeing, but it needed but that first trip to make her an ardent admirer of that form of recreation. Re-creation it really seemed to her to be, as she sank among the pillows in the comfortable nest the children had prepared for her, and felt herself glide out upon the smooth bosom of the creek into the glow of the autumn afternoon. For in the shelter of the winding ravine where the creek wandered the frost had not yet completed its work, and the trees were still in glowing colors, blending brilliantly with the dark green of the hemlock. A few stark trunks were bare and bleak against the sky in unsheltered places, but for the most part the banks of the creek still set forth a most pleasing display to the nature-lover who chose to come and see. Winding dark and soft and still, with braided ripples here and there, and little floating brown leaves that slithered against the boat as they passed, the creek meandered between the hills, now turning almost upon itself around a mossy, grassy stretch of meadowland, skirting a chestnut-grove, or slipping beneath great rocks that cropped out on the hillside, where moss had crept in a lovely carpet, and graceful hemlocks found a foothold and leaned over to dip in the water and brush the faces of those who passed. Up, up, and up, through the frantic little rapids that bubbled and fought and were conquered, into the stiller water above, between banks all dark and green and quiet, most brilliantly and cunningly embroidered with exquisite strawberry vines and scarlet berries. It was most entrancing, and Julia Cloud was reluctant to come home. No need ever to coax her any more. She was ready always to go in that canoe, jealous of anything that prevented a chance to go.

Often she and Cherry, instead of getting a hot lunch at home, would put up the most delectable lunch in paper boxes, and when the children came home she would be ready to go right down to the canoe and spend two delightful hours floating up and down the creek and eating an unconscionable number of sandwiches and cakes. This happened most often on Wednesdays, when the children had no classes from eleven o'clock until three and there was time to take the noon hour in a leisurely way. Not even cool weather coming on could daunt them. Steamer-rugs and warm sweaters and gloves were requisitioned, and the open-air lunches went on just the same. One day they took a pot of hot soup and three small bowls and spoons. They landed at the great rocks, and, climbing up, built a fire and gave their soup another little touch of heat before they ate it. Such experiences welded their hearts more and more together, and Julia Cloud came to be more and more a part of the lives of these two young people who had taken her for their mother-in-love.

It was on these outings that they talked over serious problems: whether Leslie should join one of the girls' sororities, what they should do about the next Christian Endeavor meeting, why it was that Howard Letchworth and Jane Bristol were so much more interesting than any of their other friends, why Cloudy did not like to have Myrtle Villers come to the house, and what Allison was going to do in life when he got through with college. They were absolutely one in all their thoughts and wishes just at this time, and there was not anything that any one of them would not willingly talk over with the others. It was a beautiful relation, and one that Julia Cloud daily, tremblingly prayed might last, might find nothing to break it up.

By this time the young people had begun to bring their college mates to the house, and everybody up there was crazy for an invitation to the little lunches and dinners and pleasant evening gatherings that had begun to be so popular. There were not wanting the usual "boy-crazy" girls, who went eagerly trailing Allison, literally begging him for rides and attention, and making up to Julia Cloud and Leslie in the most sickening of silly girl fashions.

And of these Myrtle Villers was at once the most subtle and least attractive. Julia Cloud had an intuitive shrinking from her at the start, although she tried in her sweet, Christian way to overcome it and do as much for this girl as she was trying to do for all the others who came into their home. But Myrtle Villers was quick to understand, and played her part so well that it was impossible to shake her off as some might have been shaken. She studied Leslie like an artist, and learned how to play upon her frank, emotional, impulsive nature. She confided in her, telling the sorrows of an unloved life, and her longings for great and better things, and fell to attending Christian Endeavor most strenuously. She was always coming home with Leslie for overnight and being around in the way.

Allison did not like her in the least, and Julia Cloud barely tolerated her; but, as the weeks went by, Leslie began to champion her, to tell the others they were unfair to the girl, and that she really had a sincere heart and a lovely nature, which had been crushed by loneliness and sorrow. Allison always snorted angrily when Leslie got off anything like that, and habitually absented himself whenever he knew "the vamp," as he called her, was to be there.

It was one day quite late in the fall, almost their last balmy picnic before the cold weather set in, that they were sitting up on the rocks around a pleasant, resinous pine-needle fire they had made, discussing this. Allison was maintaining that it was not good for Leslie to go with a girl like that, that all the fellows despised; and Leslie was pouting and saying she didn't see why he had to be so prejudiced and unfair; and Julia Cloud was looking troubled and wondering whether her heart and her head were both on the wrong side, or what she ought to do about it, when a step behind them made them all turn around startled. It was the first time they had been interrupted by an intruder in this retreat, and it had come to seem all their own. Moreover, the cocoa on the fire was boiling, and the lunch was about to be served on the little paper plates.

There stood a tall man with a keen, care-worn face, a scholarly air, and an unmistakably wistful look in his eyes.

"Why, is this where you spend your nooning, Cloud? It certainly looks inviting," he said, with a comprehensive glance at the wax-papered sandwiches and the little heap of cakes and fruit.

Allison arose with belated recognition.

"O Dr. Bowman," he said, "let me introduce you to my aunt, Miss Cloud, and my sister Leslie."

The scholarly gentleman bowed low in acknowledgment of the introduction, and fairly seemed to melt under the situation.

"Well, now, this certainly is delightful!" he said, still eyeing the generously spread rock table. "Quite an idea! Quite an idea! Is this some special occasion, some celebration or something?" He glanced genially round on the group.

"Oh, no, we often bring our lunch out here," said Julia Cloud in a matter-of-fact tone. "It keeps us out-of-doors, and makes a pleasant change." There was finality in her tone, and a sensitive-minded professor would have moved on at once, for the cocoa was boiling over, and had to be rescued, and he might have seen they did not want him; but he lingered affably.

"Well, that certainly is an original idea. Quite so. It really makes one quite hungry to think of it. That certainly looks like an attractive repast."

There was nothing for it but to invite him to partake, which Allison did as curtly as he dared, considering that the intruder was one of his major professors, and hoping sincerely that he would refuse. But Professor Bowman did not refuse. No such good chance, and quite to Julia Cloud's annoyance—for she wanted to have the talk out with her children—he sat himself down on the rock as if he were quite acclimated to picnics in November, and accepted so many sandwiches that Leslie, seated slightly behind and out of his sight, made mock signs of horror lest there should not be enough to go around.

It appeared that he had started out to search for his pocket-knife, which his young son had borrowed and lost somewhere in that region as nearly as he could remember, and thus had come upon the picnickers.

"Old pill!" growled Allison gruffly when at last the unwelcome guest had departed hastily to a class, with many praises for his dinner and a promise to call to see them in the near future. "Old pill! Now we'll never dare to come here again as long as he's around. Bother him. I wish I'd told him to go to thunder. We don't want him. He lives right up here over that bluff. His wife's dead, and his sister or aunt or something keeps house for him. She looks like a bottle of pickles! Say, Cloudy, we'll just be out evenings for a while till he forgets it."

But Dr. Bowman did not forget it as Allison had hoped. He came the very next week on a stormy night when no one in his senses would go out if he could help it; and there were the gay little household, with the addition of Jane Bristol and Howard Letchworth, down on their knees before the fire, roasting chestnuts, toasting marshmallows, and telling stories. His grim, angular presence descended upon the joyous gathering like a wet blanket; and the young people subsided into silence until Leslie, rising to the occasion, went to the piano and started them all singing. A wicked little spirit seemed to possess her, and she picked out the most jazzy ragtime she could find, hoping to freeze out the unwelcome guest, but he sat with patient set smile, and endured it, making what he seemed to think were little pleasantries to Julia Cloud, who sat by, busy with some embroidery. She, poor lady, was divided between a wicked delight at the daring of the children and a horror of reproach that they would be treating a college professor in this rude manner. She certainly gave him no encouragement; and, when he at last rose to go, saying he had spent a very pleasant and profitable evening getting acquainted with his students, and he thought he should soon repeat it, she did not ask him to return. But he was a man of the kind who needs no encouragement, and he did return many times and often, until he became a fixed institution, which taxed all their faculties inventing ways of escape from him. The winter went, and Dr. Bowman became the one fly in the pleasant ointment of Cloudy Villa.

"We'll just have to send Cloudy away awhile, or put her to bed and pretend she is sick every time he comes, or something!" said Leslie one night, after his departure had made them free to express their feelings. "We've tried everything else. He just won't take a hint! What do you say, Cloudy; will you play sick?"

"My dear!" said Julia Cloud aghast, "he doesn't come to see me! What on earth put that in your head?" Her face was flaming scarlet, and distress showed in every feature.

The children fairly shouted.

"You dear, old, blind Cloudy, of course he does! Who on earth else would he come to see?"

"But," said Julia Cloud, tears coming into her eyes, "he mustn't. I don't want to see him! Mercy!"

"That's all right, Cloudy; you should worry! I'll go tell him so if you want me to."

"Allison! You wouldn't!" said Julia Cloud, aghast.

"No, of course not, Cloudy, but we'll find a way to get rid of the old pill if we have to move away for a while."

Nevertheless, the old pill continued to come early and often, and there seemed no escape; for he was continually stealing in on their privacy at the most unexpected times and acting as if he were sure of a welcome. The children froze him, and were rude, and Julia Cloud withdrew farther and farther; but nothing seemed to faze him.

"It's too bad to have so much sweetness wasted," mocked Leslie one night at the supper-table when their unwelcome visitor had been a subject of discussion. "Miss Detliff is eating her heart out for him. She's always noseying round in the hall when his class is out, and it's about time for hers to begin, just to get a word with him. She kept us waiting for our papers ten whole minutes the other day while she discussed better classroom ventilation with him. 'O Doctah, don't you think we might do something about this mattah of ventilation?'" she mimicked, convulsing Allison with her likeness to her English teacher.

"That's an idea!" said Allison suddenly. "No, don't ask me what it is. It would spoil things. Cloudy, may I bring a guest to dinner to-morrow night?"

"Certainly, anybody you please," replied Julia Cloud innocently; and the incorrigible Allison appeared the next afternoon with Miss Detliff, smiling and pleased, sitting up in the back seat of the car. Julia Cloud received her graciously, and never so much as suspected anything special was going on until later in the evening, when Dr. Bowman arrived and was ushered in to find his colaborer there before him. He did not look especially pleased, and Julia Cloud caught a glance of intelligence passing between Leslie and Allison, with a sudden revelation of a plot behind it all. During the entire evening she sat quietly, saying little, but her eyes dancing with the fun of it. What children they were, and how she loved them! Yes, and what a child she was herself! For she couldn't help loving their pranks as well as they did.

However, though Dr. Bowman had to take Miss Detliff home, and got very little satisfaction out of his call that evening, it did not discourage him in the least; and Julia Cloud decided that extreme measures were necessary to rid them of his presence.

"We might go away during Thanksgiving week; only there's the Christian Endeavor banquet," said Leslie. "We couldn't be away from that. And then I wanted to have Jane to dinner. She's gone up to college this week to live. She's doing office work there, and she'll be alone on Thanksgiving Day."

"Yes, and there's Howard. I thought we'd have him here," put in Allison dubiously.

"Of course!" said Julia Cloud determinedly. "And we don't want to go away, anyway. You children run up to your rooms this evening and study. Stay there, I mean, no matter who comes. Do you understand?"

With a curious look at her they both obeyed; and a little later, when the knocker sounded through the house, they sat silently above, not daring to move, and heard their aunt open the door, heard Dr. Bowman's slow, scholarly voice and Julia Cloud's even tones, back and forth for a little while, and then heard the front door open and shut again, and slow steps go down the brick terrace and out to the sidewalk.

What passed in that interview no one ever knew. Julia Cloud came to the foot of the stairs, and called them down, and her eyes were shining and confident as she sat by the lamp and sewed while they studied and joked in front of the fire; but the unwelcome guest came no more, and whenever they met him in the street, or at receptions, or passing at a college game, he gave them a distant, pleasant bow; that was all. Julia Cloud had done the work well, however she had done it. The little Bowmans need not look to her to fill their mother's place, for she was not so minded.

Meantime, the winter had been going on, and the little pink-and-white house was becoming popular among the students at college as well as among the members of the Christian Endeavor Society of the little brick church. Many an evening specially picked groups of girls or boys or both spent before that fire, playing games, and talking, and singing. Sometimes the college glee-club came down and had dinner. Again it was the football team that was feasted. Another time Allison's frat came for his birthday, aided and abetted by his sister and aunt.

Jane Bristol became a frequent visitor, though not so frequent as they would have liked to have her, for her time was very much taken up with her work and her studies. Julia Cloud often wished she might lift the financial burden from the young shoulders and make things easier for her, both for her own sake and Leslie's, who would have liked to make her her constant companion; but Jane Bristol was too independent to let anybody help her, and there seemed no way to do anything about it. Meantime, Myrtle Villers improved each idle hour, and kept Leslie busy inventing excuses to get away from her, and Julia Cloud busy worrying. Leslie was so dear, but she was also self-willed. And she would go off with that wild girl in the car for long rides. Not that Julia Cloud worried about the driving; for Leslie was most careful, and handled a car as if she had been born with the knowledge, as indeed she did all things athletic; but her aunt distrusted the other girl.

And then one clear, cold afternoon in December Leslie went off for a ride in the car with Mrytle. Of course Julia Cloud did not know that the girl had pestered the life out of Leslie for the ride, and had finally promised that, if she would go, she would stop going with a certain wild boy in the village of whom Leslie disapproved. Neither did she know that Leslie had resolved never to go again without her aunt along. So she sat at the window through the short winter afternoon, and watched and waited in vain for the car to return; and Allison came back at half-past six after basketball practice, and still Leslie had not appeared.

21

THERE had been a little friction between Allison
and Leslie about the use of the car. Allison had always
been most generous with it until his sister took up this
absurd intimacy with Myrtle Villers. It had been rather
understood between them that Leslie should use the car
afternoons when she wanted it, as Allison was busy
with basket-ball and other things; but several times Allison had objected to his sister's taking her new friend
out, and Leslie told him he was unfair. After a heated
discussion they had left the question still unsettled. In
fact, it did not seem that it could be settled, for Leslie
was of such a nature that great opposition only made
her more firm; and Julia Cloud advised her nephew to
say nothing more for a time. Let Leslie find out for herself the character of the girl she had made her friend. It
was really the only way she would learn not to be carried away by flattery and high-sounding words. Allison, grumbling a little, assented; but in his heart he still
boiled with rage at the idea of that girl's winding his
sister around her little finger just for the sake of using
the car when she wanted it. It was not, perhaps, all

happening that for two or three days Allison had left the switch-key where his sister could not find it, and a hot war of words ended in Leslie's quietly ordering a new switch-key so that such a happening would be impossible in future. She would have one of her own. A card had come that very morning from the express office, notifying Leslie that there was a package there waiting for her; so, when she started out with Myrtle, she stopped and got it. She tossed it carelessly into the car with a feeling of satisfaction that now Allison could not hamper her movements any longer by his carelessness.

"Which way shall we go?" she asked as she always did when taking her friends out, and Myrtle named a favorite pike where they often drove.

Out upon the smooth, white road they sped, rejoicing in the clear beauty of the day and in the freedom with which they flew through space. Myrtle had chosen to sit in the back seat, and lolled happily among rugs and wraps, keeping a keen eye out on the road ahead and chattering away like a magpie to Leslie, telling her what a darling she was—she pronounced it "dolling"—and how this ride was just the one thing she needed to recuperate from her violent study of the night before, incident to an examination that morning. Myrtle professed to be utterly overcome and exhausted by the physical effort of writing for three whole hours without a let-up. If Leslie could have seen her meagre paper, through which a much-tortured professor was at that moment wearily plodding, she would have been astonished. Leslie herself was keen and thorough in her class work, and had no slightest conception of what a lazy student could avoid when she set herself to do so.

Five miles from home two masculine figures came in sight ahead, strolling leisurely down the road. Any one watching might have seen Myrtle suddenly straighten up and cast a hasty glance at Leslie. But Leslie with brighter cheeks and shining eyes was forging ahead, regardless of stray strollers.

At exactly the right moment Myrtle leaned forward, and clutched Leslie's shoulder excitedly:

"O Leslie! That's my cousin Fred Hicks! And that must be his friend, Bartram Laws! They're out for a hike. How lucky! Stop a minute, please; I want to speak to my cousin."

At the same moment the two young men turned, with a well-timed lifting of surprised hats in response to Myrtle's violent waving and shouting.

Leslie of course slowed down. She could not carry a girl past her own cousin when she asked to stop to speak to him; besides, it never occurred to her not to do so.

Myrtle went through the introductions glibly.

"Mr. Laws, meet my friend Miss Cloud; My cousin, Fred Hicks, Leslie. Pile in, boys! Isn't this great that we should meet? Out for a hike? We'll give you a lift. Which way are you going? Fred, you can sit in front with Leslie. I want Bart back here with me."

Leslie caught her breath in a troubled hesitancy. This wasn't the kind of thing she had bargained for. It was the sort of thing that her aunt and brother would object to most strenuously. Yet how could she object when her guest had asked them? Of course Myrtle didn't realize that it was not quite the thing for them to be off here in the country unchaperoned, with two strange young men, though of course they weren't strangers really, both of them friends of Myrtle's, and one her cousin. Myrtle could not be expected to think how it would seem to her.

But the young men were not waiting for Leslie's invitation. They seemed to feel that their company would be ample compensation for any objections that might be had. They scrambled in with alacrity.

The color flew into Leslie's cheeks. In her heart she said they were altogether too "fresh."

"Why, I suppose we could give you a lift for a little way," said Leslie, trying to sound patronizing. "How far are you going? We turn off here pretty soon."

"Oh, that's all right," said Cousin Fred easily; "any old road suits us so it's going in this direction. Want me to take the wheel?"

"No, thank you," said Leslie coldly, "I always drive myself. My brother doesn't care for me to let other people use the car."

"That's all right; I thought you might be tired, and I'm a great driver. People trust me that won't trust any one else."

"That's right, Leslie," chimed in Myrtle. "Fred can drive like a breeze. You ought to see him!"

Leslie said nothing, but dropped in the clutch, and drove on. She was not prepossessed in Fred Hicks's favor. She let him make all the remarks, and sat like a slim, straight, little offended goddess. But Fred Hicks was not disturbed in the least. He started in telling a story about a trip he took from Washington up to Harrisburg in an incredibly brief space of time, and he laughed uproariously at all his own jokes. Leslie was a girl of violent likes and dislikes, and she took one of them now. She fairly froze Cousin Fred, though he showed no outward sign of being aware of it.

"Here's a nice road off to the right," he indicated, reaching out a commanding hand to the wheel suddenly, "Turn here."

Leslie with set lips bore on past the suggested road at high speed.

"Please don't touch my wheel," was all she said, in a haughty little voice. She was very angry indeed.

They were nearing an old mansion, closed now

for the winter, with a small artificial lake between the grounds and the highway.

Leslie felt a passing wish that she might dump her undesired cargo in that lake and fly away from them.

"I think you will have to get out at the next crossroads," she said with more dignity. "I have to go home now."

"Why, Leslie Cloud! You don't any such thing!" broke in Myrtle. "You told me you could be out till quarter of six. It's only half-past four! I thought you were a good sport."

"I've changed my mind," said Leslie coldly, bringing the car to a standstill. "I'm going back right now. Do you and your friend want to get out here, Mr. Hicks?"

Fred Hicks lolled back in the car, and leered at Leslie.

"Why, no, I can't say I'm particularly anxious to get out, but I think I'd like to change around a little. If you'll just step over here, I'll run the car for you, my dear. I don't think Myrtle is ready to go back yet. How 'bout it, Myrt?" He turned and deliberately winked at Myrtle, who leaned over with a light laugh, and patted Leslie on the shoulder.

"There, there, Leslie, don't get up in the air," she soothed. "I'll explain all about it if you'll just turn around and go up that road back there. It won't take you much longer, and we'll be back in plenty of time. The fact is, I had a little plan in the back of my head when I came out this afternoon; and I want you to help me out. Now be a good girl and let Fred run the car a little while. He won't do it any harm, and your brother will never know a thing about it."

Leslie's eyes were flashing, and her head was held haughtily; but she kept her hands firmly on the wheel.

"Your friends will have to get out, Myrtle," she said coldly. "I can't help you out in any scheme I don't understand. You'll have to go to some one else for that kind of help."

Myrtle pouted.

"I must say I don't think you're very nice, Leslie Cloud, speaking in that way before my friends; but of course you don't understand; I'll have to tell you. Bart Laws and I are engaged, and we're going to a town down in the next State to get married. Bart has the license and the minister, and it's all arranged nicely. His aunt will be there for a chaperon. If you behave yourself and do as we tell you, the whole thing will go off quietly and no one will know the difference. You and I will go back home before dark, and everything will be lovely. You see, dear, I've been engaged all this time; only I couldn't tell you, because my guardians don't approve of my getting married until I'm through college. You didn't understand why I had so much to do with Rich Price, but he was just a go-between for Bart and me. Now, do you understand why I wanted you to go this afternoon?"

Myrtle's voice was very soft and insinuating. She had tears always near the surface for ready use. "You never have been in love, Leslie; you don't know what it is to be separated from the one who is all the world to you. Come, now, Leslie; I'll do anything in the world for you if you'll only help me out now."

"And if I won't?" asked Leslie calmly, deliberately, as if she were really weighing the question.

"Well, if you won't," put in the person called Fred Hicks, "why, Bart and I will just fix you up perfectly harmlessly in the back seat there, where you can't do any damage"—and he put his hand in his pocket, and brought out the end of an ugly-looking rope—"and then we'll take charge of this expedition and go on our way. You can take it or leave it as you please. Shut up there, Myrt; we haven't any more time to waste. We're behind schedule now."

Leslie's mouth shut in a pretty little tight line, and her eyes got like two blue sparks, but her voice was cool and steady.

"Well, I *won't!*" she said tensely; and with a sudden motion she grabbed the switch-key and, springing to her feet, flung it far out across the road, across a little scuttled canoe that lay at the bank, and plunk into the water, before the other occupants of the car could realize what she was doing.

Fred Hicks saw just an instant too late, and sprang for her arm to stop it, then arose in his seat with curses on his lips, watching the exact location of the splash and calling to his mate to go out and fish for it.

Leslie sank back in her seat, tense and white, and both young men sprang out and rushed to the shore of the little lake, leaving a stream of unspeakable language behind them. Myrtle began to berate her friend.

"You little *fool!*" she said. "You think you've stopped us, don't you? But you'll suffer for this! If you make us late, I'll see that you don't get back to your blessed home for a whole week; and, when you do, you won't have such a pretty reputation to go on as you have now! It won't do a bit of good, either, for those two men can find that switch-key; or, if they can't, Fred knows how to start a car without one. You've only made a lot of trouble for yourself, and that's all the good it will do you. You thought you were smart, but you're nothing but an ignorant little kid!"

But the ignorant little kid was not listening. With trembling fingers she was pulling off the wrappings from a small package, and suddenly a warning whir cut short Myrtle's harangue. She lurched forward, and tried to pull Leslie's hands away from the wheel.

"Bart! Come quick! She's got another! Hurry, boys!"

22

THE two young men had shoved the old canoe up on the bank, turned it over, emptied it, and put it back in the water. Fred Hicks was holding it at arm's length now in the water; and the would-be bridegroom had crawled out to the extreme end, and with rolled-up sleeves was pawing about in the water, which did not appear to be very deep. At the cry they turned; and Fred Hicks, forgetting the other man's plight, let go the boat, and dashed back to the road. Young Laws, arising too hastily, rolled into the water completely, and came splashing up the bank in a frothy state of mind. But suddenly, as they came, while Myrtle's best efforts were put forth to hinder Leslie's movements, something cold and gleaming flashed in her face that sent her crouching back in the corner of her seat and screaming. Leslie had slipped her hand into the little secret pocket of the car door and brought out her revolver, hoping fervently that it was still loaded, and that Allison had not chosen to shoot at a mark or anything with it the last time he was out.

"You'd better sit down and keep quiet," she said coolly. "I'm a good shot."

Then she put her foot on the clutch, and the car started just as Fred Hicks lit on the running-board.

Leslie's little revolver came promptly around to meet him, and he dropped away with a gasp of surprise as suddenly as he had lit. Suddenly Leslie became aware of the other young man dripping and breathless, but with a dangerous look in his eye, bearing down upon her from the lake side of the road; and she flashed around and sent a shot ringing out into the road, the bullet ploughing into the dust at his very feet. The car leaped forward to obey her touch, and in a second more they had left the two young men safely behind them.

Myrtle was crouched in the back seat, weeping; and Leslie, cool and brave in the front seat, was trembling from head to foot. This was a new road to her; at least, she had never been more than two or three miles on in, and she did not know where she would bring up. She began to wonder how long her gasoline would hold out, for she had been in such a hurry to get away with Myrtle before Allison should come home that she had forgotten to look to see if everything was all right; and she now remembered that Allison had had the car out late the night before. Everything seemed to be falling in chaos about her. The earth rose and fell in front of her excited gaze; the sun was going down; and the road ahead seemed endless, without a turning as far as she could see.

A great burying-ground stretched for what seemed like miles along one side of the road. The polished marble gleamed red and bleak in the setting sun. The sky had suddenly gone lead-color, and there was a chill in the air. Leslie longed for nothing so much as to hide her head in Julia Cloud's lap and weep. Yet she must go on and on till this awful road came to an end. Would it *ever* come to an end? Oh, it *must* somewhere! A great tower of bricks loomed ahead with a wide paved driveway leading to it through an arched gateway, and over the arch some words. Leslie got only one of them. "Crematory." She shuddered, and put on speed. It seemed that she had come to the place of death and and desolation. It was lonely everywhere, and not a soul in sight. What horror if her gasoline should give out in a place like this, and they have to spend the night here, she and that poor, weak creature sobbing behind! What contempt she felt for her former friend! What contempt she felt for herself! Oh, she was well punished for her willfulness! To think she should have presumed to hope she could help her to better ways, she, a little innocent, who never dreamed of such depths of duplicity as had been shown her that afternoon! Oh, to think of that loathsome Hicks person daring to touch her! To try to take her car away from her! and to *smile* at her in that disgusting way!

On and on went the car, and the road wound away into the dusk up a high hill and down again, up another, past an old farmhouse with one dim light in the back window and a great dog howling like one in some old classic tale she had read; on and on, till at last a cross-road came, and she knew not which way to take, to right or to left. There was a sign-board; but it was too dark to read, and she dared not get out and leave Myrtle. There was no telling but she might try to run off with the car. It was at the crematory that she began to pray, and, when she reached the crossing, her heart put up a second plea for guidance. "O God, if You will just help me home, I will try, *try,* TRY to be what You want me to be! Please, please, *please!*" It was the old vow of a heart bowed down and brought to the limit. It was the first time Leslie had ever realized that there could be a situation in which Leslie Cloud would not find some way out. It was the first time, too, perhaps, when she realized herself as being a sinner in the sense of having a will against God and having exercised it for her own pleasure rather than for His glory.

Down the road to the left the car sped, and after a mile and a half of growing darkness, with woods and scattered farmhouses, the lights of a village began to appear. But it was no village that Leslie knew, and nothing anywhere gave her a clew. A trolley line appeared, however; and after a little a car came along with a name that showed it was going cityward. Leslie decided to follow the trolley track.

In the meantime the girl in the back seat roused up, and began to look about her, evidently recognizing something familiar in the streets or town.

"You can put me out here, Leslie; I'm done with you," she said haughtily. "I don't care to go any farther with you. I'll go back on the train."

"No!" said Leslie sharply. "You'll go home with me. I took you away without knowing what you intended, but I mean to put you back where you were before I'm done. Then my responsibility for you will be over. I was a fool to let you deceive me that way, but I'm not a fool any longer."

"Well, I *won't* go home with you, so! and that's flat, Leslie Cloud. You needn't think you can frighten me into going, either. We're in a village now, and my aunt lives here. If you get out that revolver again, I'll scream and have you arrested, and tell them you're trying to murder me; so there!"

For answer Leslie turned sharply into a cross-road that led away from the settled portion of the town, and put on all speed, tearing away into the dusk like a wild creature. Myrtle screamed and stormed behind her, all to no purpose. Leslie Cloud had her mettle up, and meant to take her prisoner home. Out of the town she turned into another road that ran parallel to the trolley track, from which she could see the lights of the trolleys passing now and again, as it grew darker; and by and by when they came to another cross-road, Leslie got back to the trolley track, and followed it; but whenever they came into a town she kept to its outskirts.

Leslie had a pretty good general sense of direction, and she knew just where the sun went down. If it had not been for a river and some hills that turned up and bewildered her, she would have made a pretty direct course home; but, as it was, she went far out of her way, and was long delayed and much distressed besides, being continually harassed by the angry girl in the back seat. The gasoline was holding out. It was evident that Allison had looked after it. Blessed Allison, who always did everything when he ought to do it, and never put off things until the next day! How cross she had been with him for the last six weeks, and how good and kind he always was to her! How she had deceived dear Cloudy and troubled her by going off this afternoon! Oh, what would they think? Would they ever forgive her, and take her back into their hearts, and trust her again? The tears were blurring her eyes now as she stared ahead at the road. It seemed as if she had been tearing on through the night for hours like this. Her arms ached with the nervous strain; her back ached; her head ached. Perhaps they were going around the world, and would only stop when the gasoline gave out!

They swept around a curve. Could it be that those were the lights of the college ahead on the hill? Oh, joy at last! They were! Up this hill, over across two blocks, and the little pink-and-white house would be nestled among the hemlocks; and rest and home at last! But there was something to be done first. She turned toward the back seat, where sat her victim silent and angry.

"Well, you can let me out now, Leslie Cloud," said Myrtle scornfully. "I suppose you won't dare lord it over me any longer, and I'll take good care that the rest of the town understands what a dangerous little spitfire you are. You ought to be arrested for this night's work! That's all *I've* got to say."

"Well, I have one more thing to say," said Leslie slowly, as she swerved into her own street and her eyes hungrily sought for the lights of Cloudy Villa. "You're coming into the house with me first, before you go anywhere else, and you're going to tell this whole story to my Aunt Jewel. After that—*I should worry!*"

"Well, I rather guess I am not going into your old house and tell your old aunt anything! I'm going to get right out here this minute; and you're good and going to *let* me out, too, or I'll scream bloody murder, and tell it all over this town how you went out there to meet those boys. You haven't got any witnesses, and *I* have, remember!" said Myrtle, suddenly feeling courageous now that she was back among familiar streets.

But Leslie turned sharply into the little drive, and brought up the car in a flood of light at the end of the terrace.

"Now, get out!" she ordered, swinging the door open and flashing her little revolver about again at the angry girl.

"O Leslie!" pleaded the victim, quickly quelled by the sight of the cold steel, and thrilled with the memory of that shot whistling by her into the road a few hours before.

"Get out!" said Leslie coolly as the front door was flung open and Julia Cloud peered through the brightness of the porch light into the darkness.

"Get out!" Leslie held the cold steel nearer to Myrtle's face, and the girl shuddered and got out.

"Now go into the house!" she ordered; and shuddering, shivering, with a frightened glance behind her and a fearful glance ahead, she walked straight into the wondering, shocked presence of Julia Cloud, who threw the door open wide and stepped aside to let them in. Leslie, with the revolver still raised, and pointed toward the other girl, came close behind Myrtle, who sidled hastily around to get behind Miss Cloud.

"Why, Leslie! What is the matter?" gasped Julia Cloud.

"Tell her!" ordered Leslie, the revolver still pointed straight at Myrtle.

"What shall I tell?" gasped the other girl, turning a white, miserable face toward Miss Cloud as if to appeal to her leniency. But there was a severity in Julia Cloud's face now after her long hours of anxiety that boded no good for the cause of all her alarm.

"Tell her the whole story!" ordered the fierce young voice of Leslie.

"Why, we went out to take a ride," began Myrtle, looking up with her old braggadocio. There had seldom been a time when Myrtle had not been able to get out of a situation by use of her wily tongue.

"Tell it all," said Leslie, looking across the barrel of her weapon. "Tell who wanted to go on that ride."

"Why, yes, I asked Leslie to take me. I—we—well, that is—I wanted to meet a friend."

"Tell it straight!" ordered Leslie.

"Why, of course I didn't tell Leslie I expected to meet them—him. I wasn't just sure he could make the arrangements. I meant to tell her when we got out. And when we met him—and my cousin—it was my cousin I was to meet—you see I'm—we—he—"

Myrtle was getting all tangled up with her glib tongue under the clear gaze of Julia Cloud's truth-compelling eyes. She looked up and down, and twisted the fringe on her sash, and turned red and white by turns, and seemed for the first time a very young, very silly child. But Leslie had suffered, and just now Leslie had no mercy. This girl had been a kind of idol to whom she had sacrificed much, and now that her idol had fallen she wanted to make the idol pay. Or no, was that it? Leslie afterwards searched her heart, and felt that she could truly say that her strongest motive in compelling this confession had been to get the burden of the knowledge of it off her own shrinking soul.

"Tell the rest!" came the relentless voice of Leslie, and Myrtle struggled on.

"Well, I'm engaged to Mr. Bartram Laws; and my guardian won't let us get married till I'm through college, and we fixed it up to get married to-day quietly. I knew it would be all right after he found out he couldn't help himself, and so—"

"Tell how you asked the boys to get in the car!" ordered the fierce voice again; and Myrtle, recalled from another attempt to pass it all off pleasantly, went step by step through the whole shameful story until it was complete.

Then Leslie with a sudden motion of finality flung the little weapon down upon the mahogany table, and dashed into Julia Cloud's arms in a storm of tears. "O Cloudy, I'll never, never do any such thing again! And I hate her! I *hate* her! I'll never forgive her! Can you ever forgive *me?*"

No one had heard a sudden, startled exclamation from the porch room as Leslie and Myrtle came into the house; but now Myrtle suddenly looked up, thinking the time had come for her to steal away unseen; and there in the two doorways that opened on either side of the fireplace stood, on one side Allison Cloud and the dean of the college, and on the other side two members of the student executive body, all looking straight at her! Moreover, she read it in their eyes that they had heard every word of her confession. Without a word she dropped white and stricken into a chair, and covered her face with her hands. For once her brazen wiles were gone.

23

IT happened that Miss Myrtle Villers had not con-
fined her affections to Mr. Bartram Laws. She had been
seen wandering about the campus with other youths at
odd hours of the evening when young-lady students
were supposed to be safely within college halls or properly chaperoned at some public gathering. The "student
exec" had had her in tow for several weeks, and she had
already received a number of reproofs and warnings. A
daring escapade the evening before had brought matters
to a head, and it was very possibly because of some suspicion that they might have found her out that Myrtle
had made her plans to be absent on that afternoon.
However that was, when the executive body in consultation with the dean sent for her, they traced her to the
Clouds' house. At least, they came there about seven
o'clock to inquire and hoping to take her unaware. They
had found Allison in a great state of excitement, tele-
phoning hither and yon to try to get some clew to his
sister's whereabouts. They had remained to advise and
suggest, greatly worried at the whole situation, the

more so because it involved Leslie Cloud, whose bright presence had taken great hold upon everybody.

And now, without knowing it, Leslie Cloud had taken the one way to put the whole matter into the right hands and to exonerate herself. If she had known that any member of the faculty was in that room listening, if she had dreamed that even her brother was there, she would not have thought it right or honorable to put even an enemy in such a position, either for her own sake or for the girl's. She had only wanted some wise, true adviser to know the truth, so that the girl might learn what was right and have the responsibility taken from her own shoulders. She thought, too, that she had a right to be exonerated before her aunt. So now, while she wept out her contrition in Julia Cloud's arms, retribution was coming swiftly to Myrtle Villers; and her career in that college was sealed with finality. It was only too plain that such a girl was a menace to the other students, and needed to be removed.

Presently Leslie, feeling something strange in the atmosphere, lifted frightened, tear-filled eyes, and saw the grave faces of the dean and his companions! She held her breath with suspense. How terrible! How public and unseemly! She had brought all this upon herself and her family by her persistent friendship with this silly girl! And she fell to trembling and shuddering, all her fine, sweet nerve gone now that the strain was over.

Julia Cloud drew her down upon the couch and soothed her, covering her with an afghan and trying to comfort her. Then the dean stepped over to the couch and spoke to Leslie.

"Miss Cloud, you must not feel so bad," he said gently, as if she had been his own child. "You have acted nobly, and no one will blame you. You have perhaps saved Miss Villers from great shame and sorrow, and you certainly have been brave and true. Don't worry, child," and he patted Leslie's heaving shoulder kindly.

Presently the dean and his committee were gone, taking the cowering Myrtle with them, and Leslie lay snuggled up on the couch, with Allison building up the fire and Cherry bringing a tray with a nice supper. Julia Cloud fixed a hot-water bag to warm the chilled hands and feet. It was so good to be at home! The tears rushed into her eyes again, and her throat filled with sobs.

"O Cloudy!" She caught her aunt's hands. "I'll never, never do anything again you don't want me to!" she sobbed out, and then burst into another paroxysm of tears.

"There! Now, kid! Don't cry any more!" pleaded Allison, springing to her side and kneeling by her, smoothing her hair roughly. "You were a little winner! You had every bit of your nerve with you. Why, you did a great thing, kid! Outwitting those two brutes and bringing that girl back in spite of herself. But the greatest thing of all was your making her confess. Now they've got something to go on. If you hadn't done that, it would have been her word against yours; and I imagine she's always managed to keep things where she could get around people with her wiles. Now she's got to face facts; and believe me, kid, it'll be better for her in the end. She was headed straight for a bad end, and no mistake. All the fellows knew it, and the faculty suspected it; and it was making no end of trouble. But now the girl may be saved, for that dean never lets a student go to destruction, they say, if he can help it. Oh, of course he'll fire her. She isn't fit to be around here. But he'll keep an eye on her, and he'll fire her in such a way that she'll have another chance to make good if she's willing to take it. Don't you worry about spoiling her life. She'd set out to spoil it in the first place, and the best thing that could possibly happen to her was to get stopped before she went too far. From all you say I

shouldn't think a marriage with that fellow would have
been any advantage to her."

"Oh, he was *awful*, Allison!" shuddered Leslie. "He
smelled of liquor; and he had great, coarse lips and eyes;
and he put his arms around her, and kissed her right
there before us all; and they acted perfectly disgusting!
I'm almost sure from things I heard them say that
she hadn't been engaged to him at all, she hadn't even
known him till last week. She met him in town—just
picked him up on the street! And that Fred Hicks! I don't
believe now he was her cousin at all."

"Probably not. But leave that all to the dean. He'll fer-
ret it out. He went in there to the telephone before he
left, and from what I heard I imagine he's got detectives
out after those two guys, and they may sleep in the lockup to-night. They certainly deserve to. And I shall have
a hand in settling with them, too. I can't have my sister
treated that way and let it go easily. They've got to answer to me. There, kid!"

He stooped down, and kissed her gently on her hot,
wet forehead; and Leslie caught his hand and nestled her
own in it.

"O Allison! It's so good to be home!" she murmured,
squeezing his hand appreciatively. "I'll never, never,
never go with a girl again that you don't like. I'm just
going to stick to Jane. She's the only one up there I
really love, anyway."

Allison seemed quite satisfied with these sentiments,
and they had a beautiful time eating their supper before
the fire, for no one had had any appetite before; and
Cherry was as pleased to have the anxiety over and wait
upon them all as if Leslie had been her own sister.

Into the midst of their little family group broke a hurried, excited knock on the door, and there stood Howard Letchworth with anxious face.

"I heard that your sister and one of the college girls

had gone off in a car and got lost. Is it true? I came right around to see if I could help."

Leslie sat up with her teary eyes bright and eager, and her cheeks rosy with pleasure, all her pretty hair in a tumble about her face and the firelight playing over her features in a most charming way.

"Oh, it's awfully good of you," she called eagerly. "But I'm perfectly all right and safe."

He came over to the couch, and took her offered hand most eagerly, expressing his delight, and saying he had been almost sure it was some town gossip, but he could not rest satisfied until he was positive.

But Allison would not let it go at that.

"I'm going to tell him, Leslie," he said. "He won't let any one be the wiser; and, if people are saying anything like that, he can help stop their mouths." So Allison told the whole story. When it came to the part about Fred Hicks and Bartram Laws, Howard's face grew dark, and he flashed a look that boded no good to the two young ruffians.

"I know who that Laws fellow is," he said gravely. "He's rotten! And I shouldn't wonder if I could locate his friend. I get around quite a bit on my motor-cycle. May I use your 'phone a minute? I have a friend who is a detective. They ought to be rounded up. Miss Leslie, would you tell me carefully just what roads you took, as nearly as you know?"

So Leslie told in detail of the wild ride once more. Julia Cloud watched the young man's face as he listened, and knew that Leslie had a faithful friend and champion, knew also that here was one whose friendship was well worth cultivating, a clean, fine, strong young soul, and was glad for her little girl. Something stirred in her memory as she watched his look, and she went back to her childish days and the boy friend who had kissed her when he went away never to return. There was the same look in Howard Letchworth's eyes when he looked at Leslie, the age-old beauty of a man's clean devotion to a sweet, pure woman soul.

Of course Leslie was a mere child yet, and was not thinking of such things; but there need be no fear that that fine, strong young man would be unwise enough to let the child in her be frightened away prematurely. They were friends now, beautiful friends; and that would be enough for them both for a long time. She was content.

She watched them all the evening, and listened to their talk about the Christian Endeavor Society. How beautiful it was that Leslie had been able to bring the boy to a degree of interest in that! Of course it was for her sake, but he was man enough to be interested on his own account now; and from their talk she could see that he had gone heart and soul with Allison into the plans for the winter work. He had a fine voice, and was to sing a solo at the next meeting. Presently Leslie so far recovered her nerves as to smooth out her hair and go to the piano to practise with him.

> *O Jesus, Thou art standing*
> *Outside the fast-closed door,*

rang out the rich, sweet notes; and the tender, sympathetic voice brought out each word with an appeal. The boy could not sing like that and not feel it himself sometime. Julia Cloud found herself praying; praying, as if she whispered to a dear Companion sitting close beside her at the hearthside: "Dear Christ, show this boy. Teach him what Thou art. Make him Thy true disciple."

Suddenly the young fellow turned to Allison with a smile.

"I like the way you take your religion with you into college, Cloud. It makes it seem real. I haven't met many fellows that had any before, or perhaps I shouldn't have been such a heathen as I am. But I say, why don't you try to get some of your frat brothers to come down to the meeting? They ought to be willing to do that for you, and it would be great to have them sing. You've got a lot of the glee club in your crowd."

"That's so!" said Allison. "I don't know but I'll try it. I'd like to have them come the night you sing. Guess I'll have to hunt around and get a speaker. No, I won't either. Just the meeting itself is good enough now for anybody. They're a pretty good little bunch down there. They've been working like beavers. Jane Bristol gets the girls together, and coaches them for every meeting. She's some girl, do you know it?"

Howard Letchworth agreed that she was, but he cast a side glance down at the bright head of the girl who was playing his accompaniment as if he felt there were others. Julia Cloud was watching her darling girl, wondering, hoping, praying that she might always stay so sweet and unspoiled.

But when the young man was gone home, and Leslie came back to the couch again, she suddenly drooped.

"Cloudy Jewel," she said wearily, "it isn't right. I don't deserve people to be so nice to me, the dean, and you all, and Howard and everybody. It was a lot my fault that all this happened. I thought I could make that girl over if I just stuck to her. She had promised me she would come to Christian Endeavor, and join; and I wanted to show you all what a power I had over her. I was just conceited; that was all there was about it. Now I see that she was only fooling me. I couldn't have done anything at all alone. I needed God. I didn't ask Him to help. You've talked a lot about that in our Sunday meetings, but it never went down into my heart until I was driving past that old crematory, and I felt as if I was all alone and Death all in black trailing robes was going along fast beside me. Then I knew God was the only one who could help, and I began to pray. I hope maybe I've learned my lesson, and I'll not be so swelled-headed next time. But you oughtn't to forgive me, Cloudy, not so easy. Cloudy, you're just like God!"

It was several days before Leslie recovered fully from the nervous strain she had been under. She slept long the next day, and Julia Cloud would not waken her. For a week there were dark circles under the bright eyes, and the rose of her cheek was pale. She went about meekly with downcast eyes, and the bright fervor of her spirit seemed dimmed. It was not until one afternoon when Allison suggested that they get Jane Bristol and Howard Letchworth and go for bittersweet-berry vines and hemlock-branches to decorate for the Christian Endeavor social that her spirits seemed to return, and the unwholesome experience was put away in the past at last.

Howard Letchworth had been most thoughtful about the matter in the village, and had managed so that the tragic had been taken out of the story that had started to roll about, and Leslie could go around and not feel that all eyes were upon her wondering about her escapade. Gradually the remembrance of it died out of her thoughts, although the wholesome lesson she had learned never faded.

More and more popular in the college grew the gatherings down at Cloudy Villa. Sometimes Leslie brought home three or four girls for Friday and Saturday, not often any on Sunday, unless it was Jane; for Sundays were their very own day for the little family, and they dreaded any who might seem like intruders.

"It is our time when we catch up in our loving for all the week," Leslie explained with a quaint smile to one girl who broadly hinted that she would not mind being asked for over Sunday. "And, besides, you mightn't like the way we keep Sunday. Everybody who comes has to go to church and Christian Endeavor with us, and enjoy our Bible-reading, singing hour around the fire; and I didn't think you would."

"Well, I like your nerve!" answered the girl; but she sat studying Leslie afterwards with a thoughtful gaze, and began to wonder whether, after all, a Sunday spent in that way might not be really interesting.

"She's a kind of a nut, isn't she?" she remarked to another friend of Leslie's.

"She's a pretty nice kind of a nut, then, Esther," was the response. "If that's a nut, we better grow a whole tree of them. I'm going down there all I can. I like 'em!"

Julia Cloud seemed to have a fertile brain for all kinds of lovely ways to while away a holiday. As the cold weather came on, winter picnics became the glory of the hour. Long walks with heavy shoes and warm sweaters and mittens were inaugurated. A kettle of hot soup straight from the fire, wrapped in a blanket and carried in a big basket, was a feature of the lunch. When the party reached a camping-spot, a fire would be built and the soup-kettle hung over an improvised crane to put on its finishing touches, while the rest of the eatables were set forth in paper plates, each portion neatly wrapped in waxed paper ready for easy handling. Sometimes big mince pies came along, and were stood on edge near the fire to get thawed out. Bean soup, corned-beef sandwiches, and hot mince pie made a hearty meal for people who had tramped ten or fifteen miles since breakfast.

Oh, how those college-fed boys and girls enjoyed these picnics, with Julia Cloud as a kind of hovering angel to minister with word or smile or in some more practical way, wherever there was need! They all called her "Cloudy Jewel" now whenever they dared, and envied those who got closest to her and told her their troubles. Many a lad or lassie brought her his or her perplexities; and often as they sat around the winter camp, perhaps on a rock brushed free from snow, she gave them sage advice wrapped up in pleasant stories that were brought in ever so incidentally. There was nothing ever like preaching about Julia Cloud; she did not feel that she knew enough to preach. And sometimes, as they walked homeward through the twilight of a long, happy afternoon, and the streaks of crimson were beginning to glow in the gray of the horizon, some one or two would lag behind and ask her deep, sweet questions about life and its meaning and its hereafter. Often they showed her their hearts as they had never shown them even to their own people, and often a word with her sent some student back to work harder and fight stronger against some subtle temptation. She became a wholesome antidote to the spirit of doubt and atheism that had crept stealthily into the college and was attacking so many and undermining what little faith in religion they had when they came there.

It came to be a great delight to many of the young college people to spend an evening around the hearth at Cloudy Villa. There never had been any trouble about that question of dancing, because they just did not do it; and there was always something else going on, some lively games, sometimes almost a "roughhouse," as the boys called it, but never anything really unpleasant. Julia Cloud was "a good sport," the boys said; and the girls delighted in her. The evenings were filled with impromptu programmes thought out carefully by Julia Cloud, but proposed and exploited in the most casual manner.

"Allison, why wouldn't it be a good idea for you to act out that story we were reading the other day the next time you have some of the young people down? You and Leslie and Jane with the help of one or two others could do it, and there wouldn't be much to learn. If you all read it over once or twice more, you'd have it so you could easily extemporize. Do you know, I think there's a hidden lesson in that story that would do some of those boys and girls good if they could see it lived out, and perhaps set them to reading the book?"

Again they would be asked suddenly, soon after their arrival, each one to represent his favorite character in Shakespeare, or to reproduce some great public man so that they all could recognize him; and they would be sent up-stairs to select from a great pile of shawls, wraps, and all sorts of garments any which they needed for an improvised costume.

Another evening there would be brought forth a new game which nobody had seen, and which absorbed them all for perhaps two hours until some delicious and unique refreshments would be produced to conclude the festivities. At another time the round dining-table would be stretched to take in all its leaves, and the entire company would gather around it with uplifted thumbs and eager faces unroariously playing "up Jenkins" for an hour or two. Any little old game went well under that roof, though Julia Cloud kept a controlling mind on things, and always managed to change the game before anybody was weary of it.

Also there was much music in the little house. Allison played the violin well; two or three others who played a little at stringed and wind instruments were discovered; and often the whole company would break loose into song until people on the street halted and walked back and forth in front of the house to listen to the wild, sweet harmonies of the fresh young voices.

At the close of such an evening it was not an uncommon happening for a crowd of the frat boys to gather in a knot in front of the house and give the college yell, with a tiger at the end, and then "CLOUD! CLOUD! CLOUD!" The people living on that street got used to it, and opened their windows to listen, with eyes tender and thoughtful as they pondered on how easily this little family had caught the hearts of those college people, and were helping them to have a good time. Perhaps it entered into their minds that other people might do the same thing if they would only half try.

In return for all her kindness a number of the young people would often respond to Julia Cloud's wistful invitation to go to church, and more and more they were being drawn by twos and threes to come to the Christian Endeavor meetings in the village. It seemed as if they had but just discovered that there was such a thing, to the equal amazement of themselves and the original members of the Christian Endeavor Society, who had always responded to any such suggestions on the part of their pastor or elders with a hopeless "Oh, you can't get those college guys to do anything! They think they're it!" The feeling was gradually melting away, and a new brotherhood and sisterhood was springing up between them. It was not infrequent now for a college maiden to greet some village girl with a frank, pleasant smile, and accept invitations to lunch and dinner. And college boys were friendly and chummy with the village boys who were not fellow-students, and often took them up to their frat rooms to visit. So the two elements of the locality were coming nearer to each other, and their bond was the village Christian Endeavor Society.

So passed the first winter and spring in the little pink-and-white house. And with the first week of vacation there came visitors.

24

"GUARDY Lud" was the first visitor, just for a night
and a day. He had come East for a flying business trip,
and could not pass by his beloved wards without at least
a glimpse. He dropped down into their midst quite unexpectedly the night before college closed, and found
them with a bevy of young people at the supper-table,
who opened their ranks right heartily, and took him in.
He sat on the terrace in the moonlight with them afterwards, joking, telling them stories, and eating choco-
lates with the rest. When they gathered about the piano
for a sing, he joined in with a good old tenor, surprising
them all by knowing a lot of the songs they sang.

After the young people were gone he lingered, wiping his eyes, and saying, "Bless my soul!" thoughtfully.
He told Julia Cloud over and over again how more than
pleased he was with what she had done for his children,
and insisted that her salary should be twice as large. He
told her she was a big success, and should have more
money at her command to do with as she pleased, and
that he wanted the children to have a larger allowance
during the coming year. Allison had spoken of his work

among the young people of the church, and he felt that it would have been the wish of their father and mother both that the young people should give liberally toward church-work. He would see that a sum was set aside in the bank for their use in any such plans as they might have for their Christian Endeavor work.

They talked far into the night, for he had to hear all the stories of all their doings, and every minute or two one or the other of the children would break in to tell something about the other or to praise their dear Cloudy Jewel for her part in everything.

The next day they took him everywhere and showed him everything about the college and the place, introduced him to their favorite professors, at least those who were not already gone on their vacations, and took him for a long drive past their favorite haunts. Then he had to meet Jane Bristol and Howard Letchworth. Julia Cloud was greatly relieved and delighted when he set his approval upon both these young people as suitable friends for the children.

"They are both poor and earning their own living," said Julia Cloud, feeling that in view of the future and what it might contain she wanted to be entirely honest, that the weight of responsibility should not rest too heavily upon her.

"All the better for that, no doubt," said Guardy Lud thoughtfully, watching Jane Bristol's sweet smile as she talked over some committee plans with Allison. "I should say they were about as wholesome a couple of young people as could be found to match your two. Just keep 'em to that kind for a year or two more, and they'll choose that kind for life. I'm entirely satisfied with the work you're doing, Miss Cloud. I couldn't have found a better mother for 'em if I'd searched heaven, I'm sure."

And so Julia Cloud was well content to go on with her beloved work as home-maker.

But the day after Guardy Lud left, just as the three were sitting together over a great State map of roads, perfecting their plans for a wonderful vacation, which was to include a brief visit to Ellen Robinson at Sterling, a noisy Ford drew up at the door, and there was Ellen Robinson herself, with the entire family done up in linen dust-coats and peering curiously, half contemptuously, at the strange pink-and-white architecture of the many-windowed "villa."

Allison arose and went down the terrace to do the honors, showing his uncle where to drive in and put his car in the little garage, helping his aunt and the little cousins to alight.

"For mercy's sake, Julia, what a queer house you've got!" said Ellen the minute she arrived, gazing disapprovingly at the many windows and the brick terrace. "I should think 'twould take all your time to keep clean. What's the idea in making a sidewalk of your front porch? Looks as if some crazy person had built it. Couldn't you find anything better than this in the town? I saw some real pretty frame houses with gardens as we came through."

"We like this very well," said Julia Cloud with her old patient smile and the hurt flush that always accompanied her answers to her sister's contempt. "Cherry doesn't seem to mind washing windows. She likes to keep them bright. We find it very comfortable and light and airy. Come inside, and see how pretty it is."

Once inside, Ellen Robinson was somewhat awed with the strangeness of the rooms and the beauty of the furnishings, but all she said after a prolonged survey was: "Um! No paper on the wall! That's queer, isn't it? And the chimney right in the room! It looks as though they didn't have plaster enough to go around."

Leslie took the children up-stairs to wash their faces and freshen up, and Julia Cloud led her sister to the lovely guest-room that was always in perfect order.

"Well, you certainly have things well fixed," said Ellen grudgingly. "What easy little stairs! It's like child's play going up. I suppose that's one consolation for having such a little playhouse affair to live in; you don't have to climb up far. Well, we've come to stay two days if you want us. Herbert said he could spare that much time off, and we're going to stop in Thayerville on the way back and see his folks a couple of days; and that'll be a week. Now, if you don't want us, say so, and we'll go on to-night. It isn't as if we couldn't go when we like, you know."

But Julia Cloud was genuinely glad to see her sister, and said so heartily enough to satisfy even so jealous a nature as Ellen's; and so presently they were walking about the pretty rooms together, and Ellen was taking in all the beauties of the home.

"And this is your bedroom!" she paused in the middle of the rose-and-gray room, and looked about her, taking in every little detail with an eye that would put it away for remembrance long afterwards. "Well, they certainly have feathered your nest well!" she declared as her eyes rested on the luxury everywhere. "Though I don't like that painted furniture much myself," she said as she glanced at the French gray enamel of the bed; "but I suppose it's all right if that's the kind of thing you like. Was it some of their old furniture from California?"

"Oh, no," said Julia Cloud quickly, the pretty flush coming in her cheeks. "Everything was bought new except a few little bits of mahogany down-stairs. We had such fun choosing it, too. Don't you like my furniture? I love it. I hovered around it again and again; but I didn't dream of having it in my room, it was so expensive. It's real French enamel, you know, and happens to be a craze of fashion at present. I thought it was ridiculous to buy it, but Leslie insisted that it was the only thing for my room; and those crazy, extravagant children went and bought it when I had my head turned."

"You don't say!" said Ellen Robinson, putting a hard, investigating finger on the foot-board. "Well, it does seem sort of smooth. But I never thought my cane-seat chairs were much. Guess I'll have to get 'em out and varnish 'em. What's that out there, a porch?"

Julia Cloud led her out to the upper porch with its rush rugs, willow chairs, and table, and its stone wall crowned with blooming plants and trailing vines. She showed her the bird's nest in the tree overhead.

"Well," said Ellen half sourly, "I suppose there's no chance of your getting sick of it all and coming back, and I must say I don't blame you. It certainly is a contrast from the way you've lived up to now. But these children will grow up and get married, and then where will you be? I suppose you have chances here of getting married, haven't you?"

The color flamed into Julia Cloud's cheeks in good earnest now.

"I'm not looking for such chances, Ellen," she said decidedly. "I don't intend ever to marry. I'm happier as I am."

"Yes, but after these children are married what'll you do? Who'll support you?"

"Don't let that worry you, Ellen. There are other children, and I love to mother them. But as far as support is concerned I'm putting away money in the bank constantly, more than I ever expected to have all together in life; and I shall not trouble anybody for support. However, I hope to be able to work for a good many years yet, and what I'm doing now I love. Shall we go downstairs?"

"Have Allison and Leslie got any sweethearts yet?" she asked pryingly as she followed her sister down the stairs. "I suppose they have by this time."

"They have a great many young friends, and we have beautiful times together. But you won't see many of them now. College closed last week."

For two long days Allison and Leslie devoted themselves religiously to their relatives, taking them here and there in the car, showing them over the college and the town, and trying in all the ways they knew to make them have a good time; but when at last the two days and two nights were over, and the Robinsons had piled into their car and started away with grudging thanks for the efforts in their behalf, Leslie sat on the terrace musingly; and at last quite shyly she said:

"Cloudy, dear, what makes such a difference in people? Why are some so much harder to make have a good time than others? Why, I feel as if I'd lived years since day before yesterday, and I don't feel as if they'd half enjoyed anything. I really wanted to make them happy, for I felt as if we'd taken so much from them when we took you; but I just seemed to fail, everything I did."

Julia Cloud smiled.

"I don't know what it is, dear, unless it is that some people have different ideals and standards from other people, and they can't find their pleasure the same way. Your Aunt Ellen always wanted to have a lot of people around, and liked to go to tea-parties and dress a great deal; and she never cared for reading or study or music. But I think you're mistaken about their not having had a good time. They appreciated your trying to do things for them, I know, for Aunt Ellen said to me that you were a very thoughtful girl. And the children enjoyed the victrola, especially the funny records. Herbert liked it that Allison let him drive his car when they went out. They enjoyed the eating, too, I know, even though Ellen did say she shouldn't care to have her meals cooked by a servant; she should want to be *sure* they were clean."

"Did she truly say that, Cloudy?" twinkled Leslie. "Isn't she funny?" They both broke down and laughed.

"But I'm glad they came, Cloudy. I truly am. It was nice to play with the children, and nice to have a home to show our relatives, and nicest of all to have them see you—how beautiful you are at the head of the house."

"Dear, flattering child!" said Julia Cloud lovingly. "It is so good to know you feel that way! But now here comes Allison, and we must finish up our plans for the trip and get ready to close the house for the summer."

They had a wonderful trip to mountains and lakes and seaside, staying as long as they pleased wherever they liked, and everywhere making friends and having good times; but toward the end of their trip the children began to get restless for the little pink-and-white cottage and home.

"We really ought to get back and see how the Christian Endeavor Society is getting along," said Allison one day as they glided through a little village that reminded them of home. "I don't see any place as nice as our town, do you, Cloudy? And I don't feel quite right anywhere but home on Sunday, do you? For, really, all the Christian Endeavor societies I've been to this summer acted as if their members were all away on vacations and they didn't care whether school kept or not."

And so they went home to begin another happy winter. But the very first day there came a rift in their happiness in the shape of the new professor of chemistry, a man about Julia Cloud's age, whom Ellen Robinson had met on her visit to Thayerville, and told about her sister. Ellen had suggested that maybe he could get her sister to take him to board!

To this day Julia Cloud has never decided whether Ellen really thought Julia would take a professor from the college to board, or whether she just sent him there as a joke. There was a third solution, which Julia Cloud kept in the back of her mind and only took out occasionally with an angry, troubled look when she was very much annoyed. It was that Ellen was still anxious to have her sister get married, and she had taken this way to get her acquainted with a man whom she thought a "good match." If Julia had been sure that this idea had entered into her sister's thoughts, she might have slammed the door in Professor Armitage's face that night when he had the audacity to come and ask to be taken into Cloudy Villa as a boarder.

"Why, the very idea!" said Leslie with snapping eyes. "As if we wanted a *man* always around! No, indeed! *Horrors!* Wouldn't that be *awful?*"

But Professor Armitage, like everybody else who came once to Cloudy Villa, liked it, and begged a thousand pardons for presuming, but came again and again, until even the children began to like him in a way, and did not in the least mind having him around.

But the day came at last, about the middle of the winter, or nearer to the spring, when Leslie and Allison began to realize that Professor Armitage came to see their Cloudy Jewel, and they met in solemn conclave to talk it over.

25

IT was out on a lonely road in the car that they had chosen to go for their conference, where there was no chance of their being interrupted; and they whirled away through the town and out to the long stretch of whiteness in glum silence, the tears welling to overflow in Leslie's eyes.

At last they were past the bounds where they were likely to meet acquaintances, and Leslie broke forth.

"Do you really think it's true that we've got to give her up? Are you sure it has come to that, Allison? It seems perfectly preposterous!"

"Well, you know if she cares for him," said Allison gravely, "we've no right to hold on to her and spoil her life. You know it was different when it was old Pill Bowman. This is a real man."

"Care for him! How *could* she possibly care for him?" snapped Leslie. "Why, he has a wart on his nose, and he snuffs! I never thought of it before till last night, but he does; he snuffs every little while! Ugh!"

"Why, I thought you liked him, Leslie!"

"So I did until I thought he wanted Cloudy, but I

can't see that! I hate him. I always thought he was about the nicest man in the faculty except the dean, and he's married; but since I got onto the idea that he wants Cloudy I can't bear the sight of him. I went way round the block to-day to keep from meeting him. He isn't nice enough for Cloudy, Allison."

"What's the matter with him? Warts and snuffing don't count if you love a person. I like him. I like him ever so much, and I think he's lonesome. He'd appreciate a home like ours. You know what a wonderful wife Cloudy would make."

Leslie fairly screamed.

"O Allison! To think you have come to it that you're *willing* to give up our lovely home, and have Cloudy go off, and we go the dear knows where, and have to board at the college or something."

"Some day we'll be getting married, too, I suppose," said Allison speculatively.

His sister flashed a wise, curious look up at him, and studied his face a minute. Then a shade came over her own once more.

"Yes, I s'pose *you* will, pretty soon. You're almost done with college. But poor me! I'll have to board for two whole years more, and I'm not sure I'll ever get married. The man I like might not like me. And you may be very sure I'm not going to live on any sister-in-law, no matter how much I love her, so there!"

Allison smiled, and put his arm protectingly around his sister.

"There, kid, you needn't get excited yet awhile. It's me and thee always, no matter how many wives I have; and you won't ever have to board. But, kid, I'm not willing to give up our house and Cloudy and all; I'm just thinking that maybe we *ought* to, you know. I guess we're not pigs, are we? Cloudy has had a mighty hard life, and missed a lot of things out of it."

"Well, isn't she having 'em now, I'd like to know? I think Cloudy likes us, and wants to stay with us. I think she's just loved the house and everything about it."

"Yes, I think so, too; but this is something bigger than anything else in the world if she really cares. Don't you think we ought to give her the chance?"

"I s'pose so, if she really wants it; but how can we find out?"

"That's it; just give her the chance. When Armitage comes in, just sneak out and stay away, and let her have a little time alone with him. It isn't right, us kids always sticking around. We ought to go out or up-stairs or something."

Leslie was still for a long time; and then she heaved a big sigh, and said, "All right!" in a very small voice. As they sped on their way toward home, there was hardly a word more between them.

It was after supper that very night that Leslie, having almost frightened Julia Cloud out of her happy calm by refusing to eat much supper, went off to bed with a headache as soon as the professor came in. Allison, too, said he had to go up to the college for a book he had forgotten; and for the first time since his advent the professor had a clear evening ahead of him with Julia Cloud, without anybody else by.

But Julia Cloud was distraught, and gave him little attention at first, with an attitude of listening directed toward the floor above. Finally she gently excused herself for a moment, and hurried up to Leslie's room, where she found a very damp and tearful Leslie attempting to appear wonderfully calm.

"What is it, dear child? Has something happened?" she begged. "I know you must be sick, or you wouldn't have gone to bed so early. Please tell me what is the matter. I shall send for the doctor at once if you don't."

Then Leslie, knowing that her brother would blame

her if she spoiled the test, sat up bravely, and tried to laugh, assuring her aunt that she was only tired from studying and a little stiff from playing hockey too long, and she thought it would be better to rest to-night so she could be all right in the morning.

Julia Cloud, only half reassured by this unprecedented carefulness for her health on the part of the usually careless Leslie, went down abstractedly to her professor, and wished he would go home. He was well into the midst of a most heartfelt and touching proposal of marriage before she realized what was coming.

His voice was low and pleading; and Leslie, lying breathless above, not deigning to try to listen, yet painfully aware of the change of tones, was in tortures. Then Julia Cloud's pained, gentle tones, firmly replying, and more entreaty, with brief, simple answers. Most unexpectedly, before an hour passed Leslie heard the front door open and the professor go out and pass slowly down the walk. Her heart was in her throat, beating painfully. What had happened? A quick intuition presented a possible solution. Cloudy would not leave them while they were in college, and had bid him wait, or perhaps turned him down altogether! How dear of her! And yet with quick revulsion of spirit she began to pity the poor, lonely man who could not have Cloudy when he loved her.

A moment later Julia Cloud came softly up the stairs and tiptoed into her own room, and, horror of horrors! Leslie could hear her catch her breath like soft sobbing! Did Cloudy care, then, and had she turned down a man she loved in order to stick to them and keep her promise to their guardian?

Quick as a flash she was out of bed and pattering barefoot into Julia Cloud's room.

"Cloudy! Cloudy! You are crying! What is the matter? Quick! Tell me, please!"

Julia Cloud drew the girl down beside her on the bed, and nestled her lovingly and close.

"It's nothing, dear. It's only that I had to hurt a good man. It always makes me sorry to have to hurt any one."

Leslie nestled closer, smoothed her aunt's hair, and tried to think what to say; but nothing came. She felt shy about it. Finally she put her lips up, and touched her aunt's cheek, and whispered, "Don't cry, Cloudy dear!" and just then she heard Allison's key in the lock. She sprang up, drew her bathrobe about her, and ran down to whisper to him on the stairs what had happened.

"Well, it's plain she cares," whispered Allison sadly, gravely, turning his face away from the light. "I say, Les, we ought to do something. We ought to tell her it's all right for her to go ahead."

"I can't, Allison; I'd break down and cry, I know I would. I tried up there just now, but the words wouldn't come."

"Well, then, let's write her a letter! And we'll both sign it."

"All right. You write it," choked Leslie. "I'll sign it."

They slipped over to the desk in the porch room, and Leslie cuddled into a big willow cushioned chair, and shivered and sniffed while Allison scratched away at a sheet of paper for a few minutes. Then he handed it to her to read and sign. This was what he had written:

"DEAR CLOUDY: We see just how it is, and we want you to know that we are willing. Of course it'll be awfully hard to lose you; but it's right, and we wouldn't be happy not to have you be happy; and we want you to go ahead and not think of us. We'll manage all right somehow, and we love you and want to see you happy."

Leslie dropped a great tear on the page when she signed it; but she took the soft, embroidered sleeve of her nightgown, and dabbled it dry, so that it didn't blur the writing; and then together they slipped upstairs. Leslie went into her aunt's room in the dark, and in a queer little voice said, "Cloudy, dear, here's a note for you." Laying it in her hand, Leslie hurried into her own room, shut her door softly, and hid in the closet so that Julia Cloud would not hear her sob.

A moment later Julia Cloud came into the hall with a dear, glad ring in her voice, and called: "Children! Where are you? Come here quick, you darlings!" and they flocked into her arms like lost ducklings.

"You blessed darlings!" she said, laughing and crying at the same time. "Did you think I wanted to get married and go away from you forever? Well, you're all wrong. I'll never do that. You may get married and go away from me; but I'll never go away from you till you send me, and I won't ever get married to any one on this earth at any time! Do you understand? I don't want to get married, *ever!*"

They all went into Julia Cloud's room then, and sat down with her on her couch, one on either side of her.

"Do you really mean it, Cloudy Jewel?" asked Leslie happily. "You *don't want* to get married, not even to that nice Professor Armitage?"

"Look here! Leslie, you said he had a wart!" put in her brother.

"Now keep still, Allison. He was nice all the time; only I didn't like him to want our Cloudy. He didn't seem to be quite nice enough for her. He didn't quite fit her. But if she wanted him—"

"But I don't, Leslie," cried Julia Cloud in distress. "I *never* did!"

"Are you really true, Cloudy, dear? You're such a dear, unselfish Cloudy. How shall we ever quite be sure she isn't giving him up just for us, Allison?"

"Children, listen!" said Julia Cloud, suddenly putting

a quieting hand on each young hand in her lap. "I'll tell you something I never told to a living soul."

There was that in her voice that thrilled them into silence. It was as if she suddenly opened the door of her soul and let them look in on her real self as only God saw her. Their fingers tightened in sympathy as she went on.

"A long time ago—a great many years ago—perhaps you would laugh and think me foolish if you knew how many—"

"Oh, no, Cloudy, never!" said Leslie softly; and Allison growled a dissenting note.

"Well—there was some one whom I loved—who died. That is all; only—I never could love anybody that way again. Marriage without a love like that is a desecration."

"O Cloudy! We never knew—" murmured Leslie.

"No one ever knew, dear. He was very young. We were both scarcely more than children. I was only fourteen—"

"O Cloudy! How beautiful! And you have kept it all these years! Won't you—tell us just a little about it? I think it is wonderful; don't you, Allison?"

"Yes, wonderful!" said Allison in that deep, full tone of his that revealed a man's soul growing in the boy's heart.

"There is very little to tell, dear. He was a neighbor's son. We went to school together, and sometimes took walks on Saturdays. He rode me on his sled, and helped me fasten on my skates, and carried my books; and we played together when we had time to play. Then his people moved away out West; and he kissed me good-by, and told me he was coming back for me some day. That was all there was to it except a few little letters. Then they stopped, and one day his grandmother wrote that he had been drowned saving the life of a little child. Can you understand why I want to wait and be ready for him over there where he is gone? I keep feeling God will let him come for me when my life down here is over."

There was a long silence during which the young hands gripped hers closely, and the young thoughts grew strangely wise with insight into human life and all its joys and sorrows. They were thinking out in detail just what their aunt had missed, the sweet things that every woman hopes for, and thinks about alone with God; of love, strong care, little children, and a home. She had missed it all; and yet she had its image in her heart, and had been true to her first thought of it all the years. Now, when it was offered her again, she would not give up the old love for a new, would not take what was left of life. She would wait till the morning broke and her boy met her on the other shore.

Suddenly, as they thought, strong young arms encircled her, and held her close in a dear embrace.

"Then you're ours, Cloudy, all ours, for the rest of down here, aren't you?" half whispered Leslie.

"Yes, dear, as long as you need me—*want* me," she finished.

"We shall want you always, Cloudy!" said Allison in a clear man's voice of decision. "Put that down forever, Cloudy Jewel. You are our mother from now on and we want you always."

"That is dear," said Julia Cloud; "but"—a resignation in her voice—"some day you will marry, and then you will not need me any more and I shall find something to do somewhere."

Two fierce young things rose up in arms at once.

"Put that right out of your head, Cloudy Jewel!" cried Leslie. "You shan't say it again! If I thought any man could be mean enough not to feel as I do about you, I would never marry him; so there! I would never marry anybody!"

"My wife will love you as much as I do!" said Allison with conviction. "I shall never love anybody that doesn't. You'll see!"

And so with loving arms about her and tender words of fierce assertion they convinced her at last, and the bond that held them was only strengthened by the little tension it had sustained.

Professor Armitage came no more to the little pink-and-white house; but Julia Cloud was happy with her children, and they were content together. The happy days moved on.

"I don't see how you get time for that Christian Endeavor Society of yours, Cloud," said one of the professors to Allison. "I hear you're the moving spirit in it; yet you never fall down on your class work. How do you manage it? I'd like to put some of my other students onto your ways of planning."

"Well, there's all of Sunday, you know, professor," answered Allison promptly. "I don't give so very much more time, except a half-hour here and there to a committee meeting, or now and then a social on Friday night, when I'd otherwise be fooling, anyway. My sister and I cut out the dances, and put these social parties in their place."

"But don't you have to study on Sundays?"

"*Never* do!" was the quick reply. "Made it a rule when I started in here at this college, and haven't broken it once, not even for examinations. I find I'm fresher for my work Monday morning when I make the Sabbath *real*."

The professor eyed him curiously.

"Well, that certainly is interesting," he said. "I'll have

to try it. Though I don't see how I'd quite manage it. I usually have to spend the whole Sunday correcting papers."

"Save 'em up till early Monday morning, and come over to our Christian Endeavor meeting. See if it isn't worth while, and then see how much more you can do Monday morning at five o'clock, when you're really rested, than you could all day Sunday hacking at the same old job you've had all the week. I'll look for you next Sunday night. So-long!" And with a courteous wave he was off with a lacrosse stick, gliding down the campus like a wild thing. The professor stood and watched him a moment, and then turned thoughtfully up the asphalt path, pondering.

"They are a power in the college and in the community, that sister and brother," he said. "I wonder why."

Down at the church they wondered also as they came in crowds to the live Christian Endeavor meetings, and listened to the clear, ringing words of the young man who had been president before him; as the praises sounded by his admiring friends, especially the young man who had been president before him; as they saw the earnest spirit that went out to save, and had no social distinctions or classes to hinder the fraternal interest. The pastor wondered most of all, and thanked God, and told his wife that that Endeavor Society was making his church all over. He didn't know but it had converted him again, too. The session wondered as it listened to the earnest, simple gospel sermons that the pastor now preached, and saw his zeal for bringing men to the service of Christ.

Oh, they pointed out the four young people, the Clouds, Jane Bristol, and Howard Letchworth, as the moving spirits in the work; and they admitted, some of them, that prayer had made the transformation, for there were not many of the original bunch of young people who by this time had not been fully trained to understand that if you wanted anything in the spiritual world you must take time and give energy to getting acquainted with God. But, if they could have gone with some spirit guide to find out the true secret of all the wonderful spiritual growth and power of that young people's society, they must have looked in about Julia Cloud's fireplace on Sabbath afternoon, and seen the four earnest young people with their Bibles, and Julia Cloud in the midst, spending the long, beautiful hours in actual spiritual study of God's word, and then kneeling and communing with God for a little while, all of them on intimate terms with God. They were actually learning to delight themselves in the Lord. It was no wonder that other people, even outside the church and the Christian Endeavor Society, were beginning to notice the difference in the four, just as they noticed the shining of Moses's face when he came down from the mountain after communing with God.

Julia Cloud stood at the window of her rose-and-gray room one Sabbath evening after such an afternoon, watching the four children walk out into the sunset to their Christian Endeavor meeting, and smiled with a tender light in her eyes. She had come to call them her *four* children in her heart now, for they all seemed to love and need her alike; and for many a month, though they seemed not yet openly aware of it, they had been growing more and more all in all to one another; and she was glad.

She watched them as they walked. Allison ahead with Jane, earnestly discussing something. Jane's sweet, serious eyes looking up so trustfully to Allison, and he so tall and fine beside her; Leslie tripping along like a bird behind with Howard, and pointing out the colors in the sunset, which he watched only as they were reflected in her eyes.

26

HOWARD Letchworth settled himself comfortably by an open window in the 5:12 express and spread out the evening paper, turning, like any true college man, first to the sporting page. He was anxious to know how his team had come out in the season's greatest contest with another larger college. He had hoped to be there to witness the game himself, and in fact the Clouds had invited him to go with them in their car, but unfortunately at the last minute a telegram came from a firm with whom he expected to be located during the summer, saying that their representative would be in the city that afternoon and would like to see him. Howard had been obliged to give up the day's pleasure and see his friends start off without him. Now, his business over, he was returning to college and having his first minute of leisure to see how the game came out.

The train was crowded, for it was just at closing time and every one was in a rush to get home. Engrossed in his paper, he noticed none of them until someone dropped, or rather sprawled, in the seat beside him, taking far more room than was really necessary, and making a lot of fuss pulling up his trousers and getting his patent leather feet adjusted to suit him around a very handsome sole-leather suitcase which he crowded unceremoniously over to Howard's side of the floor.

The intruder next addressed himself to the arrangement of a rich and striking necktie, and seemed to have no compunctions about annoying his neighbor during the process. Howard glanced up in surprise as a more strenuous knock than before jarred his paper out of focus. He saw a young fellow of about his own age with a face that would have been strikingly handsome if it had not also been bold and conceited. He had large dark eyes set off by long curling black lashes, black hair that crinkled close to his head in satiny sleek sheen, well-chiselled features, all save a loose-hung, insolent lip that gave the impression of great self-indulgence and selfishness. He was dressed with a careful regard to the fashion and with evidently no regard whatever for cost. He bore the mark at once of wealth and snobbishness. Howard, in spite of his newly-acquired desire to look upon all men as brothers, found himself disliking him with a vehemence that was out of all proportion to the occasion.

"Don't they have any pahlah cars on this road?"

The question was addressed to him in a calm, insolent tone as if he were a paid servitor of the road. He looked up amusedly and eyed the stranger pityingly:

"Not so as you'd notice it," he remarked crushingly as he turned back to his paper. "People on this road too busy to use 'em."

But the stranger did not crush easily:

"Live far out?" he asked, turning his big, bold eyes on his seatmate and calmly examining him from the toe of a well-worn shoe to the crown of a dusty old hat that Howard was trying to make last till the end of the season. When he had finished the survey his eyes travelled complacently back to his own immaculate attire, and his well-polished shoes fresh from the hands of the city station bootblack. With a well-manicured thumb and finger he flecked an imaginary bit of dust from the knee of his trousers.

Howard named the college town brusquely.

"Ah, indeed!" Another survey brief and significant this time. "I don't suppose you know any people at the college." It was scarcely a question, more like a statement of a deplorable fact. Howard was suddenly amused.

"Oh, a few," he said briefly. (He was just finishing his senior year rather brilliantly and his professors were more than proud of him.)

Another glance seemed to say: "In what capacity?" but the elegant youth finally decided to voice another question:

"Don't happen to know a fellah by the name of Cloud, I suppose? Al Cloud?"

"I've met him," said Howard with his eyes still on his paper.

"He's from my State!" announced the youth with a puff of importance. "We live next door in California. He's a regular guy, he is. Got all kinds of money coming to him. He'll be of age in a month or two now, and then you'll see him start something! He's some spender, *he* is."

Howard made no comment, but something in him revolted at the idea of talking over his friend in such company.

"I've got to hunt him up," went on the young man, not noticing that his auditor appeared uninterested. "I'm to stay with him to-night. I was to send a telegram, but didn't think of it till it was almost train time. Guess it won't make much difference. The Clouds always used to keep open house. I suppose they have a swell place out here?"

"Oh, it's quite comfortable, I believe." Howard turned

over a page of the paper and fell to reading an article on the high price of sugar and the prospect of a fall.

"You ought to see their dump out in Cally. It's some mansion, believe me! There wasn't anything else in that part of the State to compare with it for miles around. And cahs! They had cahs to burn! The old man was just lousy with gold, you know; struck a rich mine years ago. His wife had a pile, too. Her father was all kinds of a millionaire and left every bit to her; and Al and his sister'll get everything. Seen anything of *her?* She ought to be a winner pretty soon. She was a peach when she was little. She's some speedy kid! We used to play together, you know, and our folks sorta fixed it up we were just made for each other and all that sorta thing, you know—but I don't know—I'm not going to be bound by any such nonsense, of course, unless I like. One doesn't want one's wife to be such an awfully good shot, fer instance, you know—!"

A great anger surged up in Howard's soul, and his jaw set with a fierce line that those who knew him well had learned to understand meant self-control under deep provocation. He would have liked nothing better than to surprise the insolent young snob with a well-directed blow in his pretty face that would have sent him sprawling in the aisle. His hands fairly twitched to give him the lesson that he needed, but he only replied with a slight inscrutable smile in one corner of his mouth:

"It *might* be inconvenient for *some people*." There was an aloofness in his tone that did not encourage further remarks, but the young stranger was evidently not thin-skinned, or else he loved to hear himself babbling.

"I'm coming on heah, you know, to look this college ovah—!" he drawled. "If it suits me, I may come heah next yeah. Got fired from three institutions out West for larking, and father thought I better go East awhile. Any fun doing out this way?"

"I suppose those that go to college looking for it can find it," answered Howard noncommittally.

"Well—that's what I'm looking for. That's about all anybody goes to college for anyway, that and making a lot of friends. Al Cloud used to be a lively one. I'll wager he's into everything. See much of the college people down in town—do you?" He eyed his companion patronizingly. "S'pose you get in on some of the spoahts now and then?"

"Oh, occasionally," said Howard with a twinkle in his eye. He was captain of the football team and forward in basketball, but it didn't seem to be necessary to mention it.

"Any fellows with any pep in them out here? I suppose there must be or Al wouldn't stay unless he's changed. He used to keep things pretty lively. That's one reason why I told dad I'd come out here. I like a place with plenty of ginger. It gets my goat to be among a lot of grinds and sissies! This is a co-ed college, isn't it? That suits me all right if the girls have any pep and aren't too straitlaced. Any place around here where you can go off and take a girl for a good dinner and a dash of life? I couldn't stand for any good-little-boy stuff. Know any place around here where you can get a drink of the real thing now and then, some place near enough to go joy-riding to, you know? I shall bring my cah of course—! One can get away with a lot more stuff if they have their own cah, you know—especially where there's girls. You can't pull off any devilment if you have to depend on hired cahs. You might get caught. I suppose they have some pretty spicy times down at the frat rooms, don't they? I understood the frats were mostly located down in the town."

Howard suddenly folded his paper, looking squarely in the limpid eyes of his seatmate for the first time, with a cold, searching, subduing gaze.

"I really couldn't say," he answered coldly.

"Oh, I s'pose you're not interested in that sort of thing, not being in college," said the other insolently. "But Al Cloud'll put me wise. He's no grind, I'll wager. He's always in for a good time, and he's such a good bluff he never gets found out. Now I, somehow, always get caught, even when I'm not the guilty one."

The boy laughed uproariously as if it were a good joke, and his weak chin seemed to grow weaker in the process.

Howard was growing angry and haughty, but it was his way to be calm when excited. He did not laugh with the stranger. Instead, he waited until the joke had lost its amusement and then he turned soberly to the youth with as patronizing an air as ever the other had worn:

"Son, you've got another guess coming to you about Allison Cloud. You'll have the surprise of your young life when you see him, I imagine. Why, he's been an A student ever since he came to this college, and he has the highest average this last semester of any man in his class. As for bluff, he's as clear as crystal, and a prince of a fellow; and if you're looking for a spot where you can bluff your way through college you better seek elsewhere. Bluff doesn't go down in *our* college. We have student government, and I happen to be chairman of the student exec just now. You better change your tactics if you expect to remain here. Excuse me, I see a friend up at the front of the car!"

With which remarks Howard Letchworth strode across the sprawling legs of his fellow-traveler and departed up the aisle, leaving the elegant stranger to enjoy the whole seat and his own company.

Thus did Clive Terrence introduce himself to Howard Letchworth and bring dismay into the little clique of four young people who had been enjoying a most unusually perfect friendship. Howard Letchworth, as he stood the rest of the ride on the front platform of the car conversing with apparent interest with a fraternity brother, was nevertheless filled with a growing dismay. Now and then he glanced back and glared down the aisle at the elegant sprawling youth and wondered how it was that a being as insignificant as that could so upset his equilibrium. But the assured drawl of the stranger as he spoke of Leslie and called her a "speedy kid" had made him boil with rage. He carried the mood back to college with him, and sat gloomily at the table thinking the whole incident over, while the banter and chaffing went on about him unnoticed. Underneath it all there was a deep uneasiness that would not be set aside. The young man had said that the Clouds were very wealthy. That Leslie was especially so. That when she was of age she would have a vast inheritance. There had been no sign of great wealth or ostentation in their living but if that were so then there was an insuperable wall between him and her.

It was strange that the question of wealth had never come up between them. Howard had known that they were comfortably off, of course. They had a beautiful car and wore good clothes, and were always free with their entertaining, but they lived in a modest house, and never made any pretences. It had not occurred to him that they were any better off than he might be some day if he worked hard. They never talked about their circumstances. Of course, now he came to think about it, there were fine mahogany pieces of furniture in the little house and wonderful rugs and things, but they all fitted in so harmoniously with their surroundings that it never occurred to him that they might have cost a mint of money. They never cried out their price to those who saw them, they were simply the fitting thing in the fitting place, doing their service as all right-minded things both animate and inanimate in this world should do. It was the first serpent in the Eden of this wonderful friendship at Cloudy Villa and it stung the proud-spirited young man to the soul.

Alone in his room that night he finally gave up all pretence at study and faced the truth. He had been drifting in a delightful dream during the last two years, with only a vague and alluring idea of the future before him, a future in which there was no question but that Allison Cloud AND his sister Leslie should figure intimately. Now he was suddenly and roughly awakened to ask himself whether he had any right to count on all this. If these young people belonged to the favored few of the world who were rolling in wealth, wasn't it altogether likely that when they finished college they would pass out of this comradely atmosphere into a world of their own, with a new set of laws whereby to judge and choose their friends and life companions? He could not quite imagine Allison and Leslie as anything but the frank, friendly, enthusiastic comrades they had been since he had known them—and yet—he knew the world, knew what the love of money could do to a human soul, for he had seen it many times before in people he had come to love and trust who had grown selfish and forgetful as soon as money and power were put into their hands. He had to confess that it was possible. Also, his own pride forbade him to wish to force himself into a crowd where he could not hold his own and pay his part. They would simply not be in his class, at least not for many years to come, and his heart sank with desolation. It was then, and not till then, that the heart of the trouble came out and looked him in the face. It was not that he could not be in their class, that he could not keep pace with Allison Cloud and come and go in his company as freely as he had done; it was that he loved the bright-haired Leslie, the sweet-faced, eager, earnest, wonderful girl. She held his future happiness in her little rosy hand, and if she really were a rich girl he couldn't of course tell her now that he loved her, because he was a poor man. He didn't expect to stay poor always, of course, but it would be a great many years before he could ever hope to compete with anything like wealth, and during those years who might not take her from him? Was it conceivable that such a cad as that youth who had boasted himself a playmate of her childhood could possibly win her?

Howard went out and sat on the campus under a great shadowing tree. He watched a sliver thread of a moon slip down between the branches and dip behind the hill, and while he sat there he went through all the desolation of a lonely life; the bitterness of having Leslie taken from him by one who was unworthy!—He persuaded himself that he loved her enough to be willing to step aside and give her up to a man who was better than himself—but this little whiffet—ugh!

The chimes on the library pealed out nine o'clock, reminding him of his work half done, yet the shadow of engulfing sorrow and loss hung over him. With a jerk he drew himself up and tried to grasp at common sense. How ridiculous of him to get up all this nightmare out of a few minutes' talk with a fellow who used to be the Clouds' old neighbor. He might not have been telling the truth. And anyhow it was a libel on friendship to distrust them all this way, as though riches were some kind of a disease like leprosy that set people apart. It wasn't his night to go down to the village, but just to dispel this nonsense and bring back his normal state of mind he would go and drop in on the Clouds for a few minutes. A sight of them all would reassure him and clear his brain for the work he must do before midnight. Leslie Cloud was very young yet, and much can happen in a year or two. He might even be in a fair way to make a fortune himself somewhere, who knew? And as for that little cad, it was nonsense to suppose he was anything to fear. Besides, it wasn't time yet to think about being married when he wasn't even out of college. He would forget it and work the harder. Of course he could never quite go back and forget that he had admitted to himself that he was in love with Leslie, but he would keep it like a precious jewel hid far in his heart, so carefully locked that not even for his own delight would he take it out to look at now at this time.

Having thus resolved, a weight seemed to have rolled from his shoulders and he sprang up and walked with a quick tread down to the village. There was a cheerful clang of victrolas, player-pianos and twanging guitars as he passed the fraternity rooms, and he went whistling on his way toward Cloudy Villa.

But as he neared the tall arched hedge, and looked eagerly for the welcome light, he saw that the big living-room windows were only lit by a soft play of firelight. Did that mean they were all sitting in the firelight around the hearth? A fearful thought of the stranger intruded just here upon his fine resolves, and to dispel it he knocked noisily on the little brass knocker.

It was very still inside, but a quick electric light responded to his knock and in a moment he could hear someone coming down-stairs to the door. His heart leaped. Could it be Leslie? Ah! He must not—yet how wonderful it was going to be to look at her this first time after really knowing his own heart in plain language. Could he keep the joy of her out of his eyes, and the wonder of her from his voice? Then the door opened and there stood Cherry in a negligée of flaring rosy cotton crepe embroidered with gorgeous peacocks, and her pigtails in eclipse behind an arrangement of cheap lace and pink ribbons.

"No, sir, Mister Howard, dey ain't none ob 'em heah! Dey got cumpney—some young fellah fum back to Californy way. Dey done tuk him out to see de town."

Howard's heart sank and he turned his heavy foot-steps back to college. The worst fear had come to pass. Of course reason asserted itself, and he told himself that he was a fool, a perfect fool. Of course they had to be polite to an old neighbor whether they liked him or not. And what was he to presume to judge a stranger from a five-minute conversation, and turn him down so completely that he wasn't willing to have his old friends even like him? Well, he was worse than he had thought himself and something would have to be done about it.

What he did about it was to stay away from Cloudy Villa for almost a week, and when Leslie at last, after repeated efforts to get hold of him by telephone, called him up to say there was an important committee meeting at the church which he ought to attend, he excused his long absence by telling how busy he had been. Of course he had been busy, but Leslie knew that he had always been busy, and yet had found time to come in often. She was inclined to be hurt and just the least bit stand-offish. Of course if he didn't *want* to come he needn't! And she took Clive Terrence driving in the car and showed him all the wonders of the surrounding neighborhood with much more cordiality than she really felt. It was her way of bearing her hurt. At last she got Allison by himself and asked him quite casually why Howard hadn't been down. But Allison, in haste to keep an appointment with Jane, and knowing that Howard enjoyed being down as much as they wanted him, hadn't even noticed the absence yet.

"Oh, he's up to his eyes in work," responded Allison. "He's likely busy as a one-armed paperhanger with fleas! He's a senior, you know. Wait till next year and you'll see me in the same boat!" and he hurried away whistling.

27

CLIVE Terrence hung around. He calmy took it for granted that the Clouds wanted him as long as he condescended to stay. In fact, it wouldn't have troubled him whether they wanted him or not if he wanted to stay. He had discovered that Leslie was the very same kind of a "peach" which her younger days had promised her to be, and there was plenty of good fun, so he stayed. He said he wanted to see what the college was like before he made his decision, and day after day went by with apparently no plans whatever for leaving in the near future.

Julia Cloud didn't like him. She admitted that much to herself the very first evening, and for that reason she was twice as cordial to him as she might have been if she had liked him better. She reasoned that it was unfair to take a sudden dislike that way, and perhaps it was only a sign he needed a bit of their home all the more. So she made him welcome and treated him as she did any other boys who came. But more and more as the days slipped by she did not like him. At first she was a bit worried about his influence on Allison, till she saw that he merely annoyed Allison. Then she began to be annoyed by his constant attendance on Leslie. And finally she grew exceedingly restless and anxious as day succeeded day and Howard came no more. Finally, one evening just before dinner, she went to the 'phone and called up the college. It happened that she caught Howard just as he was going down to dinner. She told him they were homesick for him and there was roast lamb and green peas and strawberry shortcake for dinner, wouldn't he come? He came. Who could refuse Julia Cloud?

But the face of Clive Terrence was a study when, unannounced, Howard entered the living-room. Julia Cloud had seen him coming and quietly opened the door. Such a storm of delighted welcome as met him warmed his heart and dispelled the evil spirits that had haunted him during the week.

In the chatter of talk while they were being seated at the dinner table the visitor was almost forgotten, and he sat watching them glumly while Allison and Leslie eagerly discussed plans for some society in which they seemed to be interested. At last he grew weary of being ignored and in the first pause he languidly drawled:

"Leslie, I think you and I'll take the cah and go in town to a show this evening. I'm bored to death."

Leslie looked at him with flashing eyes and then extinguished him with her cool tone:

"Do you? Well, think again! I'm having a lovely time" —and went on talking to Howard about the senior play that was to come off the next week. It did not suit Clive in the least to be ignored, so he started in to tell about other senior plays in other colleges where he had been and quite made himself the centre of the stage, laughing at his own jokes and addressing all his remarks to Leslie until her cheeks grew hot with annoyance. She wanted so to hear what Howard and Allison were talking about in low, grave tones. She watched the strong, fine face of Howard Letchworth, and it suddenly came over her that he seemed very far away from her, like a friend who used to be, but had moved away. Something in her throat hurt, and a sinking feeling came in her heart. Like a flash it came to her that Howard Letchworth would be graduated in three more weeks, and perhaps would go away then and they would see him no more. She caught a word or two now and then as he talked to Allison that indicated that he was seriously contemplating such a possibility. Yet he had not said a word to her about it! And they had been such good friends! A grieved look began to grow around her expressive little cupid's bow of a mouth, and her big eyes grew sorrowful as she watched the two. She was not listening to Clive, who drawled on unaware of her inattention.

Suddenly Leslie became aware that Clive had risen and was standing over her with something in his hand which he had taken from his vest, something small and shining, and he was saying:

"Want to wear it, Les? Here, I'll put in on you, then everybody will think we are engaged—!"

It was his fraternity pin he was holding out with smiling assurance and the significance of his words came over her as a sentence read without comprehension will suddenly recall itself and pierce into the realization. With a stifled cry she sprang away from him.

"Mercy, no, Clive! I didn't know you were so silly. I never wear boys' fraternity pins. I think such things are too sacred to be trifled with!"

This was what she said, but she was miserably aware that Howard had turned away and picked up his hat just as Clive had leaned over her with the pin, and almost immediately he left. He had been so engrossed with his talk with Allison that he had not seemed to see her repulsion of Clive, and his manner toward her as he bade her

good-night was cool and distant. All the pleasant intimacy of all the months together seemed suddenly wiped
out, and Howard a grown-up stranger. She felt herself a
miserably unhappy little girl.

Julia Cloud, from the advantage of the dining-room
where she was doing little things, for the next day,
watched the drama with a heavy heart. What had come
between her children, and what could she do about it?
The only comforting thing about it seemed to be that
each was as unhappy as the other. Could it be that Howard Letchworth was jealous of this small-souled, spoiled
son of fortune who was visiting them? Surely not. Yet
what made him act in this ridiculous fashion? She felt
like shaking him even while she pitied him. She half-
meditated calling him back and trying to find out what
was the matter, but gave it up. After all, what could she
do?

Leslie, as the door closed behind Howard, turned
with one dagger look at Clive, and dashed up-stairs to
her room, where she locked herself in and cried till her
eyes were too swollen for study; but she only told Julia
Cloud, when she came up gently to inquire, that she had
a bad headache and wanted to go to bed.

Julia Cloud, kneeling beside her gray couch a little
later, laying all her troubles on the One who was her
strength, found it hard not to emphasize her dislike even
in prayer toward the useless little excuse for a young
man who was lolling down-stairs reading a novel and
smoking innumerable cigarettes in spite of her expressed
wish to the contrary.

The first Sunday after young Terrence's arrival it
rained and was very dismal and cold for spring. Howard
had been asked to go to a nearby Reform School for the
afternoon and speak to the boys, and Jane was caring for
a little child whose mother was ill in the hospital. Leslie

was unhappy and restless, wandering from window to window looking out. Their guest had chosen to remain in bed that morning, so relieving them from the necessity of trying to get him to go to church, but he was on hand for lunch in immaculate attire, apparently ready for a holiday. There was a cozy fire on the hearth, and he lolled luxuriously in an arm-chair seemingly well pleased with himself and all the world. Julia Cloud wondered just what she would better do about the afternoon hour with this uncongenial guest on hand, but Leslie and Allison, after a hasty whispered consultation in the dining-room with numerous dubious glances toward the guest, ending in wry faces, came and settled down with their Bibles as usual. There was a loyalty in the quiet act that almost brought the tears to Julia Cloud's eyes, and she rewarded them with a loving, understanding smile.

But when the guest was asked to join the little circle he only stared in amazement. He had no idea of trying to conform to their habits.

"Thanks! No! I hate reading aloud. Books always bore me anyway. The *Bible!* Oh *Heck!* NO! Count me out!" And he swung one leg over the arm of his chair, and picked up the Sunday illustrated supplement which he had gone out and purchased, and which was now strewn all about the floor. He continued for some time to rattle the paper and whistle in a low tone rudely while the reading went on, then he threw down his paper and lighted a cigarette. But that did not seem to soothe his nerves sufficiently, so he strolled over to the piano and began to drum bits of popular airs and sing in a high nasal tone that he was pleased to call "whiskey tenor." Julia Cloud, with a despairing glance at him, finally closed her book and suggested that they had read enough for that day, and the little audience drifted away unhappily to their rooms. Leslie did not come down again all the afternoon until just time for Christian Endeavor. Young Terrence by this time was reduced to almost affability, and looked up hopefully. He was about to propose a game of cards, but when he saw Leslie attired in raincoat and hat he stared:

"Great Scott! You don't have to go up to college tonight, do you? It's raining cats and dogs!"

"Allison and I are going to Christian Endeavor," answered Leslie quietly. "Would you like to go?" She had been trying to school herself to give this invitation because she thought she ought to, but she hoped sincerely it would not be accepted. It seemed as if she could not bear to have the whole day spoiled.

For answer young Terrence laughed extravagantly:

"Christian Endeavor! What's the little old idea?"

"Better come and find out," said Allison, coming down-stairs just then. "Ready, Leslie? We'll have to hustle. It's getting late."

In alarm at the idea of spending any more time alone the young man arose most unexpectedly.

"Oh, sure! I'll go! Anything for a little fun!" and he joined them in a moment more, clad in rubber coat and storm hat.

Leslie could scarcely keep back the tears as she walked beside him through the dark street, not listening to his boasting about riding the waves in Hawaii. Suppose Howard was at meeting! He would think—what would he think?

And of course Howard was at the meeting that night, for he happened to be the leader. Leslie's cheeks burned as she sat down and saw that Clive had manoeuvred to sit beside her. She tried to catch Howard's eyes and fling a greeting to him, but he seemed not to see his old friends and to be utterly absorbed in hunting up hymns.

The first song had scarcely died away before Clive

began a conversation with a low growl, making remarks of what he apparently considered a comic nature about everything and everybody in the room, with a distinctness that made them entirely audible to those seated around them. Leslie's cheeks flamed and her eyes flashed angrily, but he only seemed to enjoy it the more, and kept on with his running commentary.

"For pity's sake, Clive, keep still, can't you?" whispered Leslie anxiously. "They will think you never had any bringing up!"

"I should worry!" shrugged the amiable Clive comically with a motion of his handsome shoulders that sent two susceptible young things near him into a series of poorly suppressed giggles. Clive looked up and gravely winked at them, and the two bent down their heads in sudden hopeless mirth. Clive was delighted. He was having a grand time. He could see that the leader was annoyed and disgusted. This was balm to his bored soul. He made more remarks under cover of a bowed head during the prayer, and stole glances at the two giggling neighbors. Then he nudged Leslie and endeavored to get her to join in the mirth. Poor Leslie with her burning cheeks, her brimming eyes, and her angry heart! Her last vision of the leader as she bowed her head had been a haughty, annoyed glance in their direction as he said: "Let us pray." She felt that she could not stand another minute of this torture. Almost she felt she must get up and go out, and she made a hasty little movement to carry out the impulse, and then suddenly it came to her that if she went Clive would follow her, and it would look to Howard as if she had created the disturbance and they had gone off together to have a good time. So she settled down to endure the rest of the meeting, lifting miserable eyes of appeal to Allison as soon as the prayer was ended. If only there had been a seat vacant up front somewhere, a single seat with no other

near it, where her tormentor could not follow, she
would have gone to it swiftly, but the seats were all
filled and there was nothing to do but sit still and frown
her disapproval. Perhaps Allison might have done something to quiet the guest if he had noticed, but Allison
was, at the moment of Leslie's appeal, deeply wrapped
in setting down a few items which must be announced,
and he almost immediately arose and went forward with
his slip of paper and held a whispered converse with
Howard Letchworth during the hymn that followed, afterwards taking a chair down from the platform and
placing it beside the chairman of an important committee that he might consult with him about something.
During this sudden move on the part of Allison, Clive
Terrence did have his attention turned aside somewhat
from his mischief-making, for he was watching Allison
with an amazed expression. Not anything that he had
seen since coming to the town had so astonished him as
to see this young man of wealth and position and un-
doubted strength of will and purpose, get up in a church
and go forward as if he had some business in the affair.
He sat up, with his loose handsome under lip half-
dropped in surprise and watched Allison, with a curious
startled expression, and when a moment later the leader
said quietly: "Our president has a message for us" and
Allison arose and faced the crowded room with an
eager, spirited, interested look on his face, and began to
talk earnestly, outlining a plan for a deeper spiritual life
among the members, his expression was one of utter be-
wilderment, as if he suddenly saw trees walking about
the streets or inanimate objects beginning to show signs
of intellect. He was thinking that Allison Cloud certainly had changed, and was wondering what on earth
had brought it about. It couldn't be any line that his
guardian had on him, for he was a thousand miles away.
Was it that little, quiet, insipid mouse of an aunt that had

done it? She must be rich or something, the way the brother and sister seemed to be tied to her apron-string. Where did Al Cloud get that line of talk he was handing out, anyway? Why, he talked about God as if He were an intimate friend of his, and spoke of prayer and Bible reading in the way common, ordinary people talked of going to breakfast or eating candy, as if they were necessary and pleasurable acts. Why, it was inconceivable! What was he doing it for? There must be a reason.

For fully five minutes he sat quiet in puzzled thought, watching this strange gathering, gradually taking it in that they were all taking part in the proceedings and that they seemed interested and eager. Why, even those two giggling girls who had "fallen" so readily for his nonsense had sobered down and one read a verse from the Bible while the other repeated a verse of poetry! He turned and blinked at them in wonder. What had so influenced them that they all fell in line and performed their part as if it were being rehearsed for his benefit? What was the motive power? The query interested him to the point of good behavior all through the remainder of the meeting, and while he was standing waiting for Allison and Leslie at the close. It seemed that somehow there was a real interest, for they lingered as if there were vital matters to discuss, and Leslie was the centre of a group of quiet common-looking girls. It must be some sort of social settlement work or other connected with the church and someone had induced these two who were to his thinking of a higher order of being by right of wealth and social position, to take an interest and "run" this society or whatever it was. He could not make it out at all. He was much disgusted that the young people insisted on staying to church and had a bad hour living through it, although he was surprised to find it as interesting as it was. The minister seemed quite human and they had a great deal of singing. Still it was all a bore, of course. He found a great many things in life to bore him.

As soon as he and Allison were out on the street he broached the subject:

"What's the little old idea, old man? Are you a sort of grand mogul or high priest or something to this mob? And what do you get out of it?"

Allison turned and looked solemnly at him through the dark, and answered with a kind of glow in his voice that seemed to lighten his face and puzzled the questioner more than all that had gone before:

"I'm just one of them, son, and it happens to be my turn just now to be presiding officer; but I get out of it more than I ever got out of anything in life before."

"Oh!" said Clive inanely, quite at a loss to know what he meant.

"I never knew before that people could know God personally, be His pal sort of, you know, and work with Him, and it's been GREAT!" added Allison.

"Oh!" said Clive once more, quite weakly, not knowing what else to say, and they walked on for almost a block without speaking another word. Clive was thinking that certainly Allison had changed, as that unmannerly chump on the train had said. Changed most perplexingly and peculiarly. But Allison had forgotten almost that Clive was there. He was thinking over some good news he had to tell Jane about a protégé of hers who had taken a shy part in the meeting, and wondering if he could get away for a few minutes to run up and tell her or if it would be better to call her up on the 'phone.

Howard Letchworth had not come home with them. He had whispered a hurried excuse to Allison about someone he had to see up at college before they left for the city, and hurried away at the close of the meeting, and Leslie with a choking feeling in her throat and burning tears held back from her eyes by mighty effort, announced to Allison that she wasn't coming home just now, she was going to stay for a little after prayer meeting the Lookout Committee were having. She would walk home with the Martins, who went right by their door. For Leslie was done with Clive Terrence and she wanted him to understand it. So Clive was landed at home with Julia Cloud for companion, who had not gone to church on account of staying to nurse Cherry, who had taken a bad cold and needed medicine. Allison hurried away to give Jane her message, and there was nothing for Clive to do but to go to bed and resolve never to spend another Sunday in such boredom. For he "couldn't see" hobnobbing with an "old woman," as he called Julia Cloud, the way the others seemed entirely willing to do. What was she anyway but some poor relation likely who was acting as housekeeper? But at least for once in his life Clive Terrence realized that there was such a thing in the world as a live religion and a few people who held to it and loved it and *enjoyed* it. He couldn't understand it, but he had to admit it, although he was convinced that behind it all there must be some ulterior motive or those people would never bother themselves to that extent.

But Leslie came home from the church with a heavy heart and crept up to her room with bravely cheerful smiles to deceive Julia Cloud; and then cried herself to sleep; while Julia Cloud, wise-eyed, kept her own counsel and carried her perplexities to the throne of God.

28

DURING the next three days there were stirring times, and Leslie, even with a heavy heart, was kept busy. Clive Terrence was ignored as utterly as if he had been a fly on the ceiling, and Leslie managed to keep every minute full. Moreover, her mind was so much occupied with other things that she had not time to realize how fully she was cutting their guest out of sight of her, nor how utterly amazed it made him. He was not accustomed to being ignored by young ladies, even though they were both beautiful and rich. He felt that he was quite ornamental himself, and had plenty of money, too, and he could not brook any such treatment. So he set himself to procure revenge by going hot-foot after the Freshman "vamp"—who, to tell the truth, was much more in his style than Leslie and quite, *quite* willing—though Leslie, dear child, was too absorbed to know it.

She came home at lunchtime a bit late and called Allison from the table to give him an excited account in a low tone of something that had happened that morning. Julia Cloud, from her vantage point at the head of the table, could see the flash in her eye and the brilliant flush of the soft cheeks as she talked and wondered what new trouble had come to the dear child. Then she noted the sudden stern set of Allison's jaw and the squaring of shoulder as he listened and questioned. Meanwhile she passed Clive Terrence the muffins and jam, and urged more iced-tea and a hot, stuffed potato, and kept up a pleasant hum of talk so that the excited words should not be heard in the dining-room.

"Jane's had a perfectly terrible time!" had been Leslie's opening sentence, "and we've got to do something about it! Those little cats in the AOU have done the meanest thing you can think of. Jane looked just *crushed!* They've hauled up that old stuff about her father being a forger and urged it as a reason that she shouldn't be made treasurer in place of Anne Dallas—who is leaving on account of the death of her father and she has to go home and take care of her little sisters—and JANE HEARD THEM!"

A low growl of indignation reached Julia Cloud's ears from Allison, who squared his shoulders into position for immediate action.

"They said—" went on Leslie in excited whisper. "They said that since we had such a large sum to look out for now that the subscriptions for the sorority house were coming in, we should put in a treasurer of tried and true integrity. Yes, they used just those words, *tried and true integrity!* Think of it! And OUR JANE! The idea! The catty little snobs! The jealous little—*cats!* No, it wasn't Eugenia Frazer who *said* it, it was Eunice Brice— but I'm certain she was at the bottom of it, for she sat with her nice smug little painted face as sweet and complacent as an angel, all the time it was going on, and she *seconded the motion!* Just like that! With a SMILE, too! She said she fully agreed with what Miss Brice had said. *Agreed!* H'm! As if every one didn't know she had started it, and got it all fixed up with enough girls to carry the motion before the rest of us got down from an exam. Yes, they had it thought out as carefully as that! They knew all the sophomore girls would be up in that exam, till almost twelve o'clock, for it's always as long as the moral law, anything with Professor Crabbs—and they counted up and had just enough to a name to carry their motion. They even got Marian Hobbs to cut a class to get there. They hadn't counted on my getting in in time to hear, I guess, or else they didn't care. Perhaps they wanted me to hear it all; I'm sure I don't know. I suppose that must have been it. They thought perhaps I'd tell you and that would stop you from going with Jane. You know Eugenia and Eunice are both crazy about you, especially Eugenia—!"

An impatient exclamation from Allison reached the dining-room thunderously:

"Where was Jane?" Julia Cloud caught that anxious question, and then Clive, who had evidently heard also, roused himself to ask a question:

"Who is this *Jane* person they talk so much about? I don't seem to have seen her! Where is she?"

"She is Miss Bristol," said Julia Cloud, stiffening just a little at the young fellow's tone of insolence. "She is in college and very busy, but has been unusually busy since you have been here because she is caring for a little child whose mother has been very ill."

"Oh!—You mean she's a sort of sehvant?"—He drawled the question most offensively, and Julia Cloud had a sudden ridiculous impulse to seize his sleek shoulder and shake him. Instead she only smiled and quoted a Bible verse: "I have seen servants upon horses, and princes walking as servants upon the earth."

Clive eyed her with a puzzled expression:

"I don't getcha!" he answered finally, but Julia Cloud made no further comment than to pass him a second cup of coffee. She could hear the soft excited whispers still going on in the living-room and she longed to fly in there and leave this ill-bred guest to his own devices, for she knew something must have happened to trouble her children, and that if this intruder were not present she would be at once taken into their confidence. Still she had to sit and smile and keep him from hearing them.

Leslie was talking more softly now, with cautious looks toward the dining-room.

"Jane had finished her exam and hurried down because she thought there would be a lot of business and she wanted Emily Reeder to be put in treasurer and was trying to work it, and hadn't an idea Alice and I were working it to put *her* in. We didn't think she would get there and meant to have it all finished before she came, but someone turned around and gave a queer little cough just as Eunice finished her nasty speech, and we all turned quickly and there in the open door stood Jane, as white as a sheet, with her great, big blue eyes looking black as coals and such suffering I never saw in a human face—and she just stood and looked at them all, a hurt, loving, searching look, as if she was reading their souls, and no one spoke nor moved, only Eunice, who got very red, and Eugenia, who straightened up and got haughty and hateful, looking as if she was glad Jane heard it all. She had a kind of glitter in her eyes, like triumph—and it was very still for a whole minute, and then Jane put out her hands in a little, quick, pleading motion and turned away quickly and was gone—"

"And what did you do?" Allison's tone had hope, threat, condemnation and praise all held in abeyance on her answer.

Leslie drew herself up eagerly, her eyes shining.

"I—? Oh—I wanted to run after her and comfort her, but I had something else to do. I jumped up and offered my resignation to the AOU, and said I wished to withdraw my subscription to the Sorority House, that I couldn't have anything to do with a bunch of girls that would stand for a thing as contemptible and mean as that."

"Of course!" said Allison with a proud look at his sister.

"And Phoebe Kemp jumped up and withdrew hers until they all apologized to Jane, and then Alice Lowe said she'd have to withdraw hers, too—she's given the highest amount subscribed, you know; she has slews of money all in her own right, because she's of age, you know—and then the girls began to get scared and Elsie Dare got right up and said she thought there had been some kind of a mistake—a blunder—they mustn't get excited—they must begin all over, and somebody must go after Jane and bring her back and explain—as if there was any way to explain a bold, bare insult like that!—and they sent a committee after her. They wanted me to go, but I declined to go in their name. I said I had handed in my resignation and I wasn't one of them any more, and they might send somebody who would better represent them, and they said they hadn't accepted my resignation and a lot of stuff, but they sent off a committee to find Jane, and they tried to think up something quickly to say to her, and they got Eunice Brice to crying and made Eugenia real mad so the powder came off her nose from rubbing it so much, and I came away. I've been hunting for Jane for half an hour, but I can't find her in any of the places she always is, and I thought I better come and tell you—"

"That's right. I'll find her—" Allison made one step to the hat-rack and took his hat, then raising his voice: "Cloudy, I've been called away on business suddenly. Don't bother keeping anything for me, I've had all I want—" and he was gone.

Julia Cloud gave a glance at Allison's plate and saw

that he had scarcely touched his lunch, and she sighed as she heard Leslie run quickly up the stairs and shut the door of her own room. Was Leslie going to spend the afternoon in weeping?

But Leslie was down again in a moment and standing in the doorway, her curls tumbled, her eyes bright and anxious, an indignant little set of lips and chin giving her a worried expression.

"Jewel, dear, I've got to go; there's something important on—I'll tell you about it all when I get back. No, please, I couldn't eat now. You get Cherry to save me some strawberry shortcake." And she was off like a breeze and out of sight.

"Wait a minute, Leslie, I'll go up with you," called Clive with his mouth full of shortcake and cream, but Leslie was already whirling down the street like the wind. Allison had taken the car, so there was nothing left for Clive to do but finish his shortcake and think up some form of amusement with the Freshman vamp for the afternoon.

Allison, meantime, had made a straight dash for the college and sent a message up to Jane that he must see her at once on very important business. After what seemed to him an endless wait, word came down that Jane was not in her room and her roommate knew nothing of her whereabouts. Allison made a wild dive for his car and drove to every one of the places where Jane sometimes went to help out with the children when their mothers were particularly busy, but no Jane materialized. He drove madly back to the college, forgetting his usual cool philosophy of life and fancying all sorts of terrible things that might have happened to Jane. He swept past Eugenia Frazer without even seeing her and brought up in front of the office once more, intending to send up and see if Jane had yet returned, but on the steps stood Leslie waiting for him.

"She's gone to the woods up above the old quarry!" she said anxiously. "I've just found out. Benny, the kitchen boy, told me. He says he saw her go out between Chemistry Hall and the Boys' Gym about an hour ago. She must have gone right after she left the meeting. Nobody seems to have seen her since. Nobody but Benny knows anything about her going to the woods and I gave him some money and told him not to say anything about it if anyone asked. I was just going to hunt her—"

"That's all right, kid! You take the car and follow up the road. I'll go through the woods and look for her—!" said Allison, springing out.

"You will be careful, won't you! You know that quarry is terribly deep—"

"I *know!*" said Allison, his tone showing his own anxiety. "And Jane hasn't scrambled around here as much as we have; she hasn't had the time. And there is so much undergrowth close up to the edge, one could come on it unaware—especially if one was excited, and not paying attention—! I better beat it! Jump in and drive me around college and I'll get off at the gym."

Leslie sprang in and Allison stood on the running-board. His sister cast a wistful glance at him as she started the car.

"Allison—I think maybe you needn't worry—" she said softly. "You know Jane is—REAL! She isn't weak like some people. She won't go all to pieces like—well, like I would. God means something to her, you know."

"I know!" said Allison gravely, gently. "Thank you, kid! Well, I get off here. Meet me at the top of the second hill in half an hour, and hang around there for a bit. I may whistle, see? So long."

He dashed off between the buildings and disappeared between the trees in the edge of the woods. Leslie whirled off down the drive to the street. As she passed the big stone gateway, ivy garlanded and sweet with climbing roses, three seniors turned into the drive, and the foremost of the three was Howard Letchworth. Her heart leaped up with joy that here was someone who would understand and sympathize, and she put her foot to the brake to slow down with a light of welcome in her eyes, but before she could stop he had lifted his hat and passed on with the others as if he were just anyone. Of course he had not seen her intention, did not realize that she wanted to speak with him, yet it hurt her. A week or two before she would have called after him, or even backed the car to catch him, but now something froze within her and with her heart beating wildly, and tears scorching her eyes, she put on speed and whirled away up the hill. It seemed to her that all her lovely world was breaking into pieces under her feet. If it had not been that she was worried about Jane, she would have been tempted to abandon everything and rush off in some wild way by herself, anywhere to be alone and face the ache in her heart. It was such a torrent of deep-mingled feelings, hurt pride and anger, humiliation, and pain—all these words rushed through her mind, but there was something else besides, something that ought to have been beautiful and wonderful, and was only shame and pain, and she had not yet come to the point where she was willing to call that something by name. She knew that soon she must face the truth and have it out with herself, and so her cheeks flamed and paled, and the tears scorched and hurt in her eyes and throat, and she tried to put it all away and think about Jane, poor hurt Jane. Jane gone into the woods to have it out with herself. But Jane was strong and Jane trusted in God. Her God was strong, too! Jane would come through only the sweeter. But what would become of her—little, fiery, tempestuous Leslie, who always did the wrong thing first and was sorry afterwards, and who forgot God when she needed Him most? These thoughts flitted like visions through her brain while she put on all speed and tore away up the hill at a much faster rate than she had any business to do. But the road was clear ahead of her and there was some relief in flying along through space this way. It seemed to clear the mists from her brain, and cool down her throbbing pulses. Yet just when she would think she had control of her thoughts, that stern, distant expression on Howard's face would come between her and the afternoon brightness, and back would roll the trouble with renewed vigor. What a world this was anyway and why did people have to live? Just trouble, trouble, trouble, everywhere! And who would have thought there would come trouble between her and Howard, such good friends as they had been now almost two years—two wonderful years! And again her weary brain would beat over the question, what had been the matter? What made Howard act that way? Surely nothing she could have done.

29

MEANTIME Allison was dashing over fallen trees, climbing rocks, and pushing his way between tangled vines and close-grown laurel, up and up through the college woods, and across country in the direction of the quarry, a still, wonderful place like a cathedral, with a deep, dark pool at the bottom of the massive stone walls. There were overarching pines, hemlocks, and oaks for vaulted roof with the fresco of sky and flying cloud between. It was a wonderful place. Once when they had climbed there together and stood for a long time in silence watching the shadows on the deep pool below, looking up to the arching green, and listening to the praisings of a song sparrow up above in some hidden choir, Jane had said that this was a place to come and worship—or to come when one was in trouble! A place where one might meet God! He had looked down at her sweet face upturned searching for the little thrilling singer, and had thought how sweet and wonderful she was, and how he wanted to tell her so, and would some day, but must not just yet. He hadn't thought much about what she was saying—but now it came back—and he knew that she must have gone here with her trouble.

He need not have worried about the quarry and the deep, dark pool. He kept telling himself all the way up that he need not, but when he reached the top and came in sight of her he knew it. Knew also that he had been *sure* of it all along.

She was sitting on a great fallen log, quietly, calmly, with her back against an old gnarled branch that rose in a convenient way, and her head was thrown back and up as if she were seeing wonderful visions somewhere among the green, and the blue and white above. It was as if she had reached a higher plane where earthly annoyances do not come, and felt it good to be there. There was almost a smile on her beautiful lips, a strong, sweet, wistful smile. She had not been looking down at the deep, treacherous pool at all. She had been looking *up* and her strength had come upon her so. For one long instant the young man paused and lifted his hat, watching her in a kind of awe. Her face almost seemed to shine as if she had been talking with God. He remembered dimly the story of Moses on the Mount talking with God. He hesitated almost to intrude upon a solitude so fine and wonderful. Then in relief and eagerness he spoke her name:

"Jane!"

She turned and looked at him and her face lit up with joy: "Oh! It is you! Why—how did you happen—?"

"I came to find you, Jane. Leslie told me everything and I have hunted everywhere. But when you were not at college I somehow knew you would be here. I wanted to find you—and—enfold you, Jane—wrap you around somehow with my love and care if you will let me, so that nothing like that can ever hurt you again. I love you, Jane. I suppose I'm a little previous and all that, being only a kid, as it were, and neither of us out of college yet, but I shan't change, and I'll be hanged if I see why it isn't all right for me to have the right to protect you against such annoyances as this—"

He was beside her on the log now, his face burning eagerly with deep feeling, one arm protectingly behind her, the other hand laid strongly, possessively over the small folded hands in her lap.

"Perhaps I'm taking a whole lot for granted," he said humbly. "Perhaps you don't love me—can't even like me the way I hoped you do. Oh, Jane, speak quick, and tell me! Darling, can you ever love me enough? You haven't drawn your hands away! Look up and let me read your eyes, please—"

No, she had not drawn her hands away, and she did not shrink from his supporting arm—and she was the kind of girl who would not have allowed such familiarities *unless—Ah!* She had lifted her eyes and there was something blindingly beautiful in them, and tears— great wonderful tears, so sweet and misty that they made him glad with a thrill of beautiful pain! Her lips were trembling. He longed to kiss her, yet knew he must wait until he had her permission—

"Allison! Listen! You are dear—*wonderful*—but you don't know a thing about me!"

"I know all I want to know, and that is a great deal, you darling, you!" And now he did kiss her, and drew her close into his arms and would not let her go even when she struggled gently.

"Allison, listen. *Listen*—please! I must tell you! *Wait*—!

She put her hands against his breast and pushed herself back away from him where she could look in his face.

"Please, you *must* let me go and listen to what I have to say!"

"I'll let you go when you tell me yes or no, Jane. Do you, can you love me? I must know that first. Then you shall have your way."

Jane's eyes did not falter. She looked at him. "You promised, you know—!"

"Yes, Allison—I love you—but—*NO!* You must not kiss me again. You must let me go, and listen—you promised, you know—!"

Allison's arms dropped away from her, but his eyes held her in a long look of joy.

"All right, darling, go to it"—he said with a joyous sound in his voice—"I can stand anything now, I know. It seems too good to be true and it's enough for me. But hurry! A fellow can't wait forever."

"No, Allison, you must sit back and be serious. It isn't really *happy*, you know—what I have to tell you—!"

Allison became grave at once.

"All right, Jane, only I can't imagine anything terrible enough to stop this happiness of mine unless you're already married—and have been concealing it from us all this time—!"

In spite of herself Jane laughed at that, and Allison breathed more freely now the tenseness was gone out of her voice. His hands went out and grasped hers.

"At least I can do this," he pleaded, and Jane lifted her eyes, now serious again, and smiled tenderly, letting her hands stay in his passively.

"Listen, Allison—my father!"

"I know, Jane, dear—I heard it long ago. Your father was a forger! What do you suppose I care? He probably had some overpowering temptation and yielded, never dreaming but he would be able to make it right. You can't make me believe that any parent of *yours* was actually bad! And besides, if he was, it wouldn't be *you*—"

"Allison! Listen!" broke in Jane gravely, stopping the torrent of words with which he was attempting to silence her. "It isn't what you think at all. My father *wasn't* a forger! He was a good man!"

"He wasn't!" exclaimed Allison joyously. "Then what in thunder? Why didn't you tell 'em so, Jane?" He tried to draw her to him, but she still resisted.

"That's just it, Allison, I can't. I *never* can—"

"Well, then *I* will! You shan't have a thing like that hanging over you—!"

"But that is just what you *must not do*. And you *can't* do it, either, if I don't tell you about it, for you wouldn't have a thing to say, nor any way to prove it. And I won't tell you, Allison, ever, unless you will promise—!"

Allison was sobered in an instant.

"Jane, don't you know me well enough to be sure I would not betray any confidence you put in me?"

"I thought so—" said Jane, smiling through her tears.

"Dear!" said Allison in a tone that was a caress, full of longing and sympathy.

Jane sat up bravely and began her story.

"When I was twelve years old my mother died. That left father and me alone, and we became very close comrades indeed. He was a wonderful father!"

Allison's fingers answered with a warm pressure of sympathy and interest.

"He was father and mother both to me. And more and more we grew to confide in one another. I was interested in all his business, and used to amuse myself asking him about things at the office when he came home, the way mother used to do when she was with us. He used to talk over all my school friends and interests and we had beautiful times together. My father had a friend—a man who had grown up with him, lived next door and went to school with him when he was a boy. He was younger than father, and—well, not so serious. Father didn't always approve of what he did and used to urge him to do differently. He lived in the same suburb with us, and his wife had been a friend of mother's. She was a sweet little childlike woman, very pretty, and an invalid. They had one daughter, a girl about my age, and when we were children we used to play together, but as we grew older mother didn't care for us to be together much. She thought—it was better for us not to—and as the years went by we didn't have much to do with one another. Her father was the only one who kept up the acquaintance, and sometimes I used to think he worried my father every time he came to the house. One day when I was about fourteen he came in the afternoon just after I got home from school and said he wanted to see father as soon as he came home. Couldn't I telephone father and ask him to come home at once, that there was someone there wanting to see him on important business? He finally called him up himself and when father got there they went into a room by themselves and talked until late into the night. When at last Mr.—that is—the *man*, went away, father did not go to bed but walked up and down the floor in his study all night long. Toward morning I could not stand it any longer. I knew my father was in trouble. So I went down to him, and when I saw him I was terribly frightened. His face was white and drawn and his eyes burned like coals of fire. He looked at me with a look that I never shall forget. He took me in his arms and lifted up my face, a way he often had when he was in earnest, and he seemed to be looking down into my very soul. 'Little girl,' he said, 'we're in deep trouble. I don't know whether I've done right or not.' There was something in his voice that made me tremble all over, and he saw I was frightened and tried to be calm himself. 'Janie,' he said—he always called me Janie when he was deeply moved—'Janie, it may hit hardest on you, and oh, I meant your life to be so safe and happy!'

"I tried to tell him it didn't matter about me, and for

him not to be troubled, but he went on telling about it. It seems the father of this man had once done a great deal for my father when he was in a very trying situation, and father always felt an obligation to look after the son. Indeed, he had promised when the old man was dying that he would be a brother to him no matter what happened. And now the son had been speculating and got deep into debt. He had formed some kind of stock company, something to do with Western land and mines. I never fully understood it all, but there had been a lot of fraudulent dealing, although father only suspected that at the time, but anyway, everything was going to fall through and the man was going to be brought up in disgrace before the world if somebody didn't help him out. And father felt obliged to stand by him. Of course, he did not know how bad it was, because the man had not told him all the truth, but father had taken over the obligations of the whole thing. He thought he might be able to pull the thing out of trouble by putting a good deal of his own money into it, and make it a fair and square proposition for all the stockholders without their ever finding out that everything had been on the verge of going to pieces. You see the man had put it up to father very eloquently that his wife was very ill in the hospital and, if anything should happen to him and he were arrested it could not be kept from her and she would die. It's true she was very critically ill, had just been through a severe operation, and was very frail indeed. Father felt it was up to him to shoulder the whole responsibility, although, of course, he felt that the man richly deserved the law to the full. Nevertheless, because of his promise he stood by him.

"That night the man was killed in an automobile accident soon after leaving our house, and when it developed that the business was built on a rotten foundation, and that father was in partnership—you see the man had been very wily and had his papers all fixed up so that it looked as if father had been a silent partner from the beginning—everything came back on father, and he found there were overwhelming debts that he had not been told about, although he supposed he had sifted the business to the foundation and understood it all before he made the agreement to help him. Perhaps if the man had lived he would have been able to carry his crooked dealings through and save the whole thing, with what help father had given him, and neither father nor the world ever have found out—I don't know.—But anyway, his dying just then made the whole thing fall in ruins, and right on top of father. But even that we could have stood. We didn't care so much about money. Father was well off, and he found that if he put in everything, he could satisfy the creditors, and pay off everything, and he had courage enough to be planning to start all over again. But suddenly it turned out that there had been a check forged for a large amount and it all looked as if father had done it. I can't go into the details now, but we were suddenly face to face with the fact that there was no evidence to prove that he had not been a hypocrite all these years except his own life. We thought for a few days that of course that would put him beyond suspicion—but do you know, the world is very hard. One of father's best friends—one he thought was a friend—came to him and offered to go bail for him for my sake if he would just tell him the whole truth and own up. There was only one way and that was to go to the man's wife and try to get certain papers which father knew were in existence because he had seen them, and which he had supposed were left in his own safe the night the man talked with him, but which could not be found. As the wife had just been brought back from the hospital and was still in a very critical condition, father would not do more than ask if he might go through the house and search. And that woman sent back a very indignant refusal, charging father with having been at the bottom of her husband's failure, and even the cause of his death, and telling him he had pauperized her and her little helpless daughter. And the daughter began treating me as a stranger whenever we chanced to meet—"

Allison's face darkened and his eyes looked stern and hard. He said something under his breath angrily, Jane couldn't catch the words, but he drew her close in his arms and held her tenderly:

"And were those papers never found, dear?" he asked after a moment:

"Yes," said Jane wearily, resting her head back against his shoulder, "I found them, after father died."

"You found them?"

"Yes, I found them slipped down behind the chest in the hall. It was a heavy old chest, a great carved affair that had belonged in the family a long time, and it was seldom moved. It stood below the hat-rack in the alcove in the hall, and I figured it out that the man must have meant to keep those papers himself, so there would be no incriminating evidence in father's hands, and that he must have picked them up without father's noticing and started to carry them home; but that when he was going away, putting on his overcoat, he had somehow dropped some of them behind that chest without knowing it. Because they were not all there—two of them were missing. Father had described them to me, and three— the most important ones with the empty envelope— were found. The other two were probably larger, and looked like the whole bundle, which explains how he came to think he had them all. But the two he had and must have had about him when he was killed would not in themselves have been any evidence against him. So, my father was arrested—!"

The tears choked Jane's voice and suddenly rained into her sweet eyes as she struggled to recall the whole sorrowful experience.

"Oh, my darling!" cried Allison, tenderly holding her close.

"Father was very brave. He said it was sure to come out all right, but he wouldn't accept bail, though it was offered him by several loyal friends. He saw that they suspected him, and the papers all came out with big headlines, 'CHURCH ELDER ARRESTED.'"

Allison's voice was deep with loving sympathy as his lips swept her forehead softly and he murmured, "My poor little girl!" but Jane went bravely on.

"That was a hard time," she said with trembling lips, "but God was good; he didn't let it last long. There came an old friend back from abroad who had known father ever since he was a boy, and who happened to have been associated with him in business long enough to give certain proofs that cleared the whole thing up. In a week the case was dismissed so far as father was concerned, and he was back at home again, and restored to the full confidence of his business associates—that is those who knew intimately about the matter. If father had lived I have no doubt everything would have been all right, and he would have been able to live down the whole thing, but the trouble had struck him hard, he was so terribly worried for my sake, you know. Then he took a little cold which we didn't think anything about, and suddenly, before we realized it, he was down with double pneumonia from which he never rallied. His vitality seemed to be gone. After he died, the papers said beautiful things about his bravery and courage and Christianity, and people tried to be nice, but when it was all over there were still people who looked at me curiously when I passed, and whispered noticeably together; and that man's wife and daughter openly called me a forger's daughter and said that my father had stolen their income, when all the time they were living on what he had given up to save them from disgrace. The daughter made it so unpleasant for me that I decided to go away where I was not known, although I had several dear beautiful homes opened to me if I had chosen to stay, where I might have been a daughter and treated as one of the other children. But I thought it was better to go away and make my own life—"

"But you had evidence. Did you never go and tell those two how wrong they were and how it was their father, not yours, who was the forger?"

"No, not exactly," said Jane, lifting clear untroubled eyes to his face. "You see that was part of father's obligation; it was a point of honor not to give that man's shame away to his wife—he had promised—and then, the man was dead—he could not be brought to justice; what good would it do?"

"It would have done the good that those two women wouldn't have gone around snubbing you and telling lies about you—"

"Oh, well, after all, that didn't really hurt me—"

"And that brazen girl wouldn't have dared come here to the same college and make it hot for you—!"

"Allison! How did you *know?*" Jane sat up and looked into his eyes, startled.

"I knew from the first mention that it must have been Eugenia Frazer. No girl in her senses would have taken the trouble to do what she did to-day without some grievance—! Oh, that girl! She is beyond words! Think of anybody ever falling in love with her! I'd like the pleasure of informing her what her father was. Of course, though, it wasn't her fault. She couldn't help her father being what he was, but she could help what she is herself. I should certainly like to see her get what's coming to her—!"

"Don't Allison—please! It isn't the right spirit for us to have. Perhaps I'd be just like her if I were in her place—"

"I can't see you being like her—you angel!" And Allison leaned over again to look into the eyes of his beloved.

"Well, dear, we'll get the right spirit about it somehow, and forget her, but I mean she shall understand right where she gets off before this thing goes any farther. No, you needn't protest. I'm not going to give away your confidence. But I'm going to settle that girl where she won't dare to make any more trouble for you ever again. And the first thing we're going to do is to announce our engagement. I feel like going up to the college bulletin board right this minute and writing it out in great big letters!"

"Allison!" Jane sat up with shining eyes and her cheeks very red. Then they both broke down and laughed, Jane's merriment ending in a serious look.

"Allison, you really *want me*, now you know what people may think about my father?"

"Jane, I've known all that since I first saw you. Our beloved pastor kindly informed me of it the night he introduced us, so you see how little weight it had with any of us. I had no knowledge but that it was all true, although I couldn't for the life of me see how a man who was unworthy of you could have possibly been your father; but it was you, and not your father, I fell in love with the first night I saw you. I'm mighty glad for your sake that he wasn't that kind of man, because I know how you would feel about it, but as for what other people think about it, *I should worry!* And Jane, make up your mind right here and now that we're going to be married the day we both graduate, see? I won't wait a day longer to have the right to protect you—"

The tall trees whispered above their heads, and the birds looked down and dropped wonderful melodies about them, and Leslie stormily drove her car back and forth on the pike and sounded her klaxon loud and long, but it was almost an hour later that it suddenly occurred to Allison that Leslie was waiting for them, and still later before the two with blissful lingering finally wended their way out to the road and were taken up by the subdued and weary Leslie, who greeted them with relief and fell upon her new sister with eager enthusiasm and genuine delight.

An hour later Allison, after committing his future bride to the tender ministries of Julia Cloud, who had received her as a daughter, took his way collegeward. He sent up his card to Miss Frazer and Miss Brice and requested that he might see them both as soon as possible, and in a flutter of expectancy the two presently entered the reception-room. They were hoping he had come to take them out in his car, although each was disappointed to find that she was not the only one summoned.

Allison in that few minutes of waiting for them, seemed to have lost his care-free boyish air and have grown to man's estate. He greeted the two young women with utmost courtesy and gravity and proceeded at once to business:

"I have come to inform you," he said with a bow that might almost be called stately, so much had the tall, slender figure lost its boyishness, "that Miss Bristol is my fiancée, and as such it is my business to protect her. I must ask you both to publicly apologize before your sorority for what happened this morning."

Eunice Brice grew white and frightened, but Eugenia Frazer's face flamed angrily.

"Indeed, Allison Cloud, I'll do nothing of the kind. What in the would did you suppose I had to do with what happened this morning?"

"You had all to do with it. Miss Frazer, I happen to know all about the matter."

"Well, you certainly don't," flamed Eugenia, "or you wouldn't be engaged to that little Bristol hypocrite. Her father was a common—"

Allison took a step toward her, his face stern but controlled.

"Her father was *not a forger,* Miss Frazer, and I have reason to believe that you know that the report you are spreading about college is not true. But however that may be, Miss Frazer, if I should say that your father was a forger would that change *you* any? I have asked Miss Bristol to marry me because of what *she is herself,* and not because of what her father was. But there is ample evidence that her father was a noble and upright man and so recognized by the law and by his fellow-townsmen, and I demand that you take back your words publicly, both of you, and that you, Miss Frazer, take upon yourself publicly the responsibility for starting this whole trouble. I fancy it may be rather unpleasant for you to remain in this college longer unless this matter is adjusted satisfactorily."

"Well, I certainly do not intend to be bullied into any such thing!" said Eugenia angrily. "I'll leave college first!"

Eunice Brice began to cry. She was the protégé of a rich woman and could not afford to be disgraced.

"I shall tell them all that you asked me to make that motion for you and promised to give me your pink evening dress if I did," reproached Eunice tearfully.

"Tell what you like," returned Eugenia grandly, "it will only prove you what you are, a little fool! I'm going up to pack. You needn't think you can hush me up, Allison Cloud, if you *are* rich. Money won't cover up the truth—"

"No," said Allison looking at her steadily, controlledly, with a memory of his promise to Jane. "No, but *Christianity* will—sometimes."

"Oh, yes, everybody knows you're a fanatic!" sneered Eugenia, and swept herself out of the room with high head, knowing that the wisest thing she could do was to depart while the going was good.

When Allison reached home a few minutes later Julia Cloud put into his hand a letter which his guardian had written her soon after his first visit, in which he stated that he had made it a point to look up both the young people with whom his wards were intimate, and he found their records and their family irreproachable. He especially went into details concerning Jane's father and the noble way in which he had acted, and the completeness with which his name had been cleared. He uncovered one or two facts which Jane apparently did not know, and which proved that time had revealed the true criminal to those most concerned and that only pity for his family, and the expressed wish of the man who had borne for a time his shame, had caused the matter to be hushed up.

Allison, after he had read it, went to find Jane and drew her into the little sun-parlor to read it with him, and together they rejoiced quietly.

Jane lifted a shining face to Allison after the reading.

"Then I'm glad we never said anything to Eugenia! Poor Eugenia! She is greatly to be pitied!"

Allison, a little shamefacedly, agreed, and then owned up that he had "fired" Eugenia, as he expressed it, from the college.

"O, Allison!" said Jane, half troubled, though laughing in spite of herself at the vision of Eugenia trying to be lofty in the face of the facts. "You ought not to have done it, dear. I have stood it so long, it didn't matter! Only for your sake—and Leslie's—!"

"For our sakes, nothing!" said Allison. "That girl needed somebody to tell her where to get off, and only a man could do it. She'll be more polite to people hereafter, I'm thinking. It won't do her any harm. Now, Jane darling, forget it, and let's be happy!"

"Be careful, Allison, some one is coming. I think it's that Mr. Terrence."

"Dog-gone his fool hide!" muttered Allison. "I wish he'd take himself home! I certainly would like to tell *him* where to get off. Leslie's as sick of him as I am, and as for Cloudy, she's about reached the limit."

"Why, Allison, isn't Leslie interested in him? He told Howard that they were as good as engaged."

"Leslie interested in that little cad? I should say not. If she was I'd disown her. You say he told Howard they were engaged! What a lie! So that's what's the matter with the old boy, is it? I thought something must be the matter that he got so busy all of a sudden. Well, I'll soon fix that! Come on up to Cloudy's porch, quick, while he's in his room. Cloudy won't mind. We'll be by ourselves there till dinner is ready!"

BUT matters came to a climax with Howard Letch-worth before Allison had any opportunity to do any "fixing."

The next afternoon was Class Day and there were big doings at the college. Howard kept out of the way, for it was a day on which he had counted much, and during the winter once or twice he and Leslie had talked of it as a matter of course that they would be around together. His Class Day had seemed then to be of so much impor-tance to her—and now—now she was going to attend it in Clive Terrence's company! Terrence had told him so, and there seemed no reason to doubt his word. She went everywhere with him, and he was their guest; why shouldn't she? So Howard went glumly about his duties, keeping as much as possible out of everyone's way. If he had not been a part of the order of exercises, and a moving spirit of the day, as it were, he would cer-tainly have made up an excuse to absent himself. As it was, he meditated trying to get some one else to take his place, and was on his way to arrange it, just before the hour for the afternoon exercises to begin, when suddenly he saw, coming up the wide asphalt walk of the campus, young Terrence, and the girl who had come to be known among them as the "Freshman Vamp." His eyes hastily scanned the groups about, and searched the walk as far as he could see it, but nowhere could he discover Leslie.

With a sudden impulse he dashed over to Julia Cloud, and forgetful of his late estrangement spoke with much of his old eagerness; albeit trying his best to appear careless and matter-of-fact:

"Isn't Leslie hereabouts somewhere, Miss Cloud? I believe I promised to show her the ivy that our class is to plant."

It was the first excuse he could think of. But Julia Cloud was full of sympathy and understanding, and only too glad to hear the old ring of friendliness in his voice. She lowered her tone and spoke confidentially:

"She wouldn't come, Howard: I don't just know what has taken her. She said she would rather stay at home—"

"Is she down there now?"

Julia Cloud nodded.

"Perhaps you—"

"I *will!*" he said, and was off like a flash. On his way down the campus he thrust some papers into a classmate's hands.

"If I don't get back in time, give those to Halsted and tell him to look out for things. I'm called away."

Never in all his running days had he run as he did that day. He made the station in four minutes where it usually took him six, and was at the Cloudy Villa in two more, all out of breath but radiant. Something jubilant had been let loose in his heart by the smile in Julia Cloud's eyes, utterly unreasonable, of course, but still it had come, and he was entertaining it royally. It was rather disheartening to find the front door locked and only Cherry to respond to his knock.

"Isn't Miss Leslie here?" he asked, a blank look coming into his eyes as Cherry appeared.

"Miss Leslie done jes' skittered acrost de back yahd wid a paddle in her han'. I reckum she's gone to de crick. Miss Jewel, she'll be powerful upset ef she comes back an' finds out. She don't like Miss Leslie go down to them canoes all by her lonesome."

"That's all right, Cherry," said Howard, cheering up; "I'll go down and find her. Got an extra paddle anywhere, or did she take them both?"

"No, sir, she only took de one. Here's t'other. I reckum she'll be right glad to see yeh, Mas'r Howard. We-all hes missed you mighty powerful lot. That there little fish-eyed lady-man wot is visitin' us ain't no kind of substoote 'tall fer you—"

Howard beamed on her silently and was off like a shot, forgetful of the chimes on the clock of the college, which were now striking the hour at which he was to have led the procession down the ivy walk to the scene of festivities.

Over two fences, across lots, down a steep, rocky hill, and he was at the little landing where the Cloud canoe usually anchored. But Leslie and her boat were gone. No glimpse of bright hair either up or down stream gave hint of which she had taken, no ripple in the water even to show where she had passed. But he knew pretty well her favorite haunts up-stream where the hemlocks posed and bent to the water, and made dark shadows under which to slip. The silence and the beauty called her as they had always called him. He was sure he would find her there rather than down-stream where the crowds of inn people played around, and the tennis courts overflowed into canoes and dawdled about with ukeleles and cameras. He looked about for a means of transport. There was only one canoe, well-chained to its rest. He examined the padlock for a moment, then put forth his strong young arm and jerked up the rest from its firm setting in the earth. It was the work of a second to shoot the boat into the water, fling the chains, boat-rest and all into the bow, and spring after. Long, strong, steady strokes, and he shot out into the stream and away up beyond the willows; around the turn where the chestnut grove bloomed in good promise for the autumn; beyond the railroad bridge and the rocks; past the first dipping hemlocks; around the curve; below the old camp where they had had so many delightful picnics and watched the sunset from the rocks; and on, up above the rapids. The current was swift to-day. He wondered if Leslie had been able to pass them all alone, yet somehow he felt she had and he would find her up in the quiet haven where few ever came and where she would be undisturbed. Paddling "Indian" he came around the curve silently and was almost upon her, but was unprepared for the little huddled figure down in the bottom of the boat, one hand grasping the paddle which was wedged between some stones in the shallow stream bed to anchor the frail bark, the other arm curved about as a pillow for the face which was hidden, with only the bright hair gleaming in the stray rays of sunshine that crept through the young leaves overhead.

"Leslie, little girl—my darling—what is the matter?"

He scarcely knew what he was saying, so anxiously he watched her. Was she hurt or in trouble and if so, what was the trouble? Did the vapid little guest and the Freshman Vamp have anything to do with it? Somehow he forgot all about himself now and his own grievance—he only wanted to comfort her whom he loved, and it never entered his head that just at that moment the anxious Halsted was inquiring of everyone: "Haven't you seen Letchworth? Class Day'll be a mess without him! Something must have happened to him!"

Leslie lifted a tear-stained face in startled amazement. His voice! Those precious words! Leslie heard them even if *he* took no cognizance of them himself.

"I—you—WELL YOU ought to know—!" burst forth Leslie and then down went the bright head once more and the slender shoulders shook with long-suppressed sobs.

It certainly was a good thing that the creek was shallow at that point and the canoes quite used to all sorts of conditions. Howard Letchworth waited for no invitation. He arose and stepped into Leslie's boat, pinioned his own with a dextrous paddle, and gave attention to comforting the princess. It somehow needed no words for awhile, until at last Leslie lifted a woebegone face that already looked half-appeased and inquired sobbily:

"What made you act so perfectly horrid all this time?"

"Why—I—" began Howard lamely, wondering now just why he *had*—! "Why, you see, Leslie, you had company and—"

"Company! *That!* Now, Howard, you weren't jealous of that little excuse for a man, were you?"

Howard colored guiltily:

"Why, you see, Leslie, you are so far above me—"

"Oh, I was, was I? Well, if I was above *you*, where did you think that other ridiculous little simp belonged, I should like to know? *Not* with *me*, I hope?"

"But you see, Leslie—" somehow the great question that had loomed between them these weeks dwarfed and shrivelled when he tried to explain it to Leslie—

"Well—?"

"Well, I've just found out you are very rich—"

"Well?"

"Well, *I'm* POOR."

"But I thought you just said you *loved* me!" flashed Leslie indignantly. "If you do, I don't see what rich and poor matter. It'll all belong to us both, won't it?"

"I should *hope* not," said the young man, drawing himself up as much as was consistent with life in a canoe. "I would *never* let my wife support me."

"Well, perhaps you might be able to make enough to *support yourself,*" twinkled Leslie with mischief in a dimple near her mouth.

"Leslie, now you're making fun! I mean this!"

"Well, what do you want me to do about it, give away my money?"

"Of course not. I was a cad and all that, but somehow it seemed as though I hadn't any business to be coming around you when you were so young and with plenty of chances of men worth more than I—"

"More what? More money?"

"Leslie, this is a serious matter with me—"

"Well, it is with me, too," said Leslie, suddenly grave. "You certainly have made me most unhappy for about three weeks. But I'm beginning to think you don't love me after all. What is money between people who love each other? Only something that they can have a good time spending for others, isn't it? And suppose *I* should say I wouldn't let *you support me?* I guess after all if you think so much of money you don't really care!"

"Leslie!" Their eyes met and his suddenly fell before her steady, beautiful gaze:

"Well, then, Howard Letchworth, if you are so awfully proud that you have to be the richest, I'll throw away or give away all my money and be a pauper, *so there!* Then will you be satisfied? What's money without the one you love, anyway?"

"I see, Leslie! I was a fool. You darling, wonderful

princess. No, keep your money and I'll try to make some more and we'll have a wonderful time helping others with it. I suppose I knew I was a fool all the time, only I wanted to be told so, because you see that fellow told me you and he had been set apart for each other by your parents—!"

A sudden lurch of the canoe roused him to look at Leslie's face:

"Oh, that little—liar! Yes, he is! He is the meanest, conceitedest, most disagreeable little snob—!"

"There, there! We'll spare him—" laughed Howard. "I see I was wrong again, only, Leslie, little princess, there's one thing you must own is true, you're very young yet and you may change—"

"Now, *I like that!*" cried Leslie. "You don't even think I have the stability to be true to you. Well, if I'm as weak-looking as that you better go and find someone else—"

But he stopped her words with his face against her lips, and his arms about her, and at last she nestled against his shoulder and was at peace.

Chiming out above the notes of the wood-robin and the thrush there came the faint and distant notes of the quarter hour striking on the college library. It was Leslie who heard it. Howard was still too far upon the heights to think of earthly duties yet awhile.

"Howard! Isn't this your Class Day? And haven't you a part in the exercises? Why aren't you there?"

He turned with startled eyes, and rising color.

"I couldn't stay, Leslie. I was too miserable! I had to come after you. You promised to be with me to-day, you know—"

"But your Class Poem, Howard! Quick! It must be almost time to read it—!"

He took out his watch.

"Great Scott! I didn't know the time had gone like that!"

Leslie's fingers were already at work with the other canoe, tying its chain to the seat of her own.

"Now!" she turned and picked up her paddle swiftly, handing Howard the other one. "Go! For all your worth! You mustn't fail on this day anyway! Beat it with all your might!"

"It's too late!" said the man reluctantly, taking the paddle and moving to his right position.

"It's not too late. It *shan't* be too late! *Paddle,* I say, *now,* ONE—and—TWO—and—!"

And they settled to a rhythmic stroke.

"It was so wonderful back there, Leslie," said Howard wistfully. "We oughtn't to let anything interfere with this first hour together."

"This isn't interfering," said Leslie practically, "it's just duty, and that never interferes. Here, we'll land over there and you beat it up the hill! I'll padlock the boats by that old tree and follow, but *don't you dare* wait for me! I'll be there to hear the first word and they'll have waited for you, I know. A little to the right, there— *now*—step out and *beat it!*"

He obeyed her, and presently came panting to the audience room, with a fine color, and a great light in his eyes, just as Halsted was slipping down to inquire of Allison:

"Where in thunder is Letchworth? Seen him anywhere?"

"Heavens, man! Hasn't he showed up yet?" cried Allison startled. "Where could he be?"

Julia Cloud beside him leaned over and quietly drew their attention to the figure hastening up the aisle. Halsted hurried back to the platform, and Allison, relieved, settled once more in his seat. But Julia Cloud rested not in satisfaction until another figure breathlessly slipped in with eyes for none but the speaker.

Then into the eyes of Julia Cloud there came a vision

as comes to one who watching the glorious setting of the sun sees not the regrettable close of the day that is past, but the golden promise of the day that is to come.

About the Author

Grace Livingston Hill is well known as one of the most prolific writers of romantic fiction. Her personal life was fraught with joys and sorrows not unlike those experienced by many of her fictional heroines.

Born in Wellsville, New York, Grace nearly died during the first hours of life. But her loving parents and friends turned to God in prayer. She survived miraculously, thus her thankful father named her Grace.

Grace was always close to her father, a Presbyterian minister, and her mother, a published writer. It was from them that she learned the art of storytelling. When Grace was twelve, a close aunt surprised her with a hardbound, illustrated copy of one of Grace's stories. This was the beginning of Grace's journey into being a published author.

In 1892 Grace married Fred Hill, a young minister, and they soon had two lovely young daughters. Then came 1901, a difficult year for Grace—the year when, within months of each other, both her father and husband died. Suddenly Grace had to find a new place to live (her home was owned by the church where her husband had been pastor). It was a struggle for Grace to raise her young daughters alone, but through everything she kept writing. In 1902 she produced *The Angel of His Presence, The Story of a Whim,* and *An Unwilling Guest.* In 1903 her two books *According to the Pattern* and *Because of Stephen* were published.

It wasn't long before Grace was a well-known author, but she wanted to go beyond just entertaining her readers. She soon included the message of God's salvation through Jesus Christ in each of her books. For Grace, the most important thing she did was not write books but share the message of salvation, a message she felt God wanted her to share through the abilities he had given her.

In all, Grace Livingston Hill wrote more than one hundred books, all of which have sold thousands of copies and have touched the lives of readers around the world with their message of "enduring love" and the true way to lasting happiness: a relationship with God through his Son, Jesus Christ.

In an interview shortly before her death, Grace's devotion to her Lord still shone clear. She commented that whatever she had accomplished had been God's doing. She was only his servant, one who had tried to follow his teaching in all her thoughts and writing.

*You'll be thrilled with
the romance and adventure of
America's best-loved author!*

———

*Don't miss all the
Grace Livingston Hill
romance novels!*

———

Tyndale House Publishers, Inc.